RISING FROM THE ASHES

RISING FROM THE ASHES

Marchela Wells

Rev. date: 04/30/2016

To order additional copies of this book, contact:
Xlibris
1-888-795-4274
www.Xlibris.com
Orders@Xlibris.com
727305

<u>Rising from the Ashes</u> is a love story between two consenting adults, and thus, there are situations which contain explicit sexual references and descriptions. Also, there is a scene of teen rape described. This scene is meant to convey, to the reader, the attitude of the heroine toward men throughout the first several chapters of the novel. As her view softens over the years, she longs for normality. One day the key to that normality arrives in the form of a man who falls in love with her at first sight.

I have had a lifelong love of reading. One day I sat down at my computer and started to type. I don't know where the words originated. The words flowed from my fingertips like magic. Before I knew it, a story began to develop. Characters sprang forth from the screen as if they were real. I fell in love with them, feared for them when they experienced criminal attacks, and rejoiced with them in their love.

I hope that you, too, will take my cherished friends Christina and Cliff into your heart.

Marchela Wells

Thanks and much gratitude to the following who have helped immensely with this effort. The book could not have been completed without their help.

From Ladies Who Critique: Monica Moore; Rosalyn Baker.

For Xlibris: Alex Stein; Travis Black.

PROLOGUE

I was born Christina Laura McIntyre, but that was a name that belonged to another person in another time. Now, it's Tina, because Tina would never allow those boys or even men to violate her that way again. Christina did fight back but lost the struggle that terrible night seventeen years ago. Tina was born when Christina died. You ask: Do I remember that night? There is not even one second of that terrible night that I can ever forget.

****

It was a cold December night at one of the away games that it happened. Our football team was playing one of the school's toughest opponents, McAllister High. I was supporting them as a member of the cheerleading squad. It was during the third quarter; the crowd was cheering wildly. The band was playing our school fight song when my bladder sent out an emergency call. I suddenly regretted having had those three cokes and a large glass of tea before the squad boarded the bus. My bladder was on serious overload.

After telling the squad leader of my problem, I hurried back to the away team's locker area where there was a separate area for the girls' restroom. I passed by three boys standing at the back of the crowd. While the crowd was cheering, shouting, and encouraging their respective teams, these guys did not seem much interested in the game. They were each smoking a joint, and leering at the nearby girls. They gave me a wolf-whistle when I passed them by, but my bladder was screaming for relief, so I paid them little attention.

I got lost for a few minutes and went down a wrong hallway which led into the main school. When I ran into the locked entrance, I realized my error and retraced my steps. I finally spotted the arrow which pointed to the away team's restrooms. As I approached I noticed that two overhead lights near the restrooms were busted, their glass on the concrete below. The entrance was dark. As I looked around, all seemed normal; I did not see anything out of place. All was quiet and deserted. I entered the restroom without any concern.

Just as I was about to enter a stall with an open door, three dark figures jumped from inside the surrounding stalls where they had been hiding. My neck was grabbed from behind by a pair of strong hands. A left hand choked my throat while a right hand clamped tightly over my mouth. I could not scream. I fought and kicked, scratching the boy behind me seriously across his face. He cried out in pain then kicked me hard in the middle of my back. The other two boys held my arms and legs, forcing me down onto the floor.

One boy pushed up my skirt, pulled my shorts down around my knees; then he ripped my panties apart. I kicked fiercely at him, but missed my target and only hit the inside of his leg. He grabbed a towel from the counter behind him and jammed it into my mouth as a gag. He then gave me a hard punch in my nose for my efforts. All the while the second boy ripped and jerked at my V shell top, tearing it in half, exposing my bra which he sliced in half with a pocket knife. The third boy took the shreds of my cut bra and bound my hands tightly together behind my back while I jerked and tried to free them. The three combined were just too strong for me to break free.

I struggled to turn my body, but the boy choking my throat now grabbed my hair. He twisted his other fist tightly into it and jerked my head back. I tried to move my head and kick my feet again, only succeeding in making the situation more violent. Suddenly I felt the jarring blow of a fist to my face, and I tasted blood inside my mouth. Hands slapped my face repeatedly over and over. My cheeks were burning, then I gasped as a fist slammed into my stomach.

"Stop struggling, bitch. Just lay back and relax. You're going to have a good time. You'll like it," the boy holding onto my hair whispered in my ear.

Freeing one leg momentarily from his grip, I finally was successful in landing a glancing kick right where I aimed, he groaned in agony. Unfortunately, he was able to straighten quickly again. Evidently I had missed my target slightly, only succeeding in making him even angrier. He grabbed and wrenched my loose leg, twisting it violently, sending a searing pain up my back.

I screamed through the gag as best that I could. "**umm mmm mmmm mmmm unnnn**" repeatedly, for which my reward was another punch to the face. More blood gurgled from my mouth and nose.

"Hear that, Jack? She loves it."

"**Spread your legs, bitch,**" one boy shouted over and over while alternately slapping my face and then my inner thighs, demanding that I spread my knees. I kept them locked together. The other two boys now grabbed my knees and pulled on them, all the while I tried to hold them closed together. After they had been able to pry them open slightly, all three began slapping on the inside of my thighs much harder. The stinging blows against my skin became agonizing.

"Open your legs, **OPEN THEM WIDE!**" All three shouted at me.

Slowly they succeeded in forcing my knees further apart. One boy now wrapped his legs around my right knee, pinning it in place while the other wrapped his arm around the left knee and pulled. All the while both boys slapped my inner thighs harder and harder, demanding I relax and spread myself open.

"Open them wider, **OPEN YOUR LEGS, BITCH!**" The boy behind me shouted over and over into my ear. "**Or else I'm going to punch you in the face again.!**" he threatened.

More repeated slaps against my inner thighs and face rained down on me. Finally, as the space between my knees allowed access they now began striking directly across my crotch, sharp stinging blows.

"LET US IN, BITCH, OPEN YOUR LEGS, STOP KICKING, OPEN UP, OPEN YOUR DAMN LEGS!" they all growled angrily at me.

Finally, when I could stand the pain of the repeated blows to my face and crotch no longer, I relaxed my legs slightly and let my knees spread even more. I prayed that would satisfy them. How could I have been more stupid?

"**Wider, bitch, wider,**" they demanded as they continued to slap at my crotch until I finally gave up and let them lift my legs up and bend them back until my knees were beside my head. To further my humiliation my bladder released when the boys bent my legs up. I squirted urine over the two boys in front and continued, leaving a pool on the floor.

"Damn it, she pissed all over me," one boy cried.

He then slapped my face hard, several stinging blows that caused stars to float in my eyes. The other boy punched me with his fist. I struggled and twisted to escape, his next blow sent me into a pit of blackness.

I don't know how much later I struggled back to consciousness, but when I did, I could feel one of the boys ramming his penis in and out of me. I bucked my buttocks, wiggling my butt back and forth, but the position of my knees next to my head only seemed to make it seem like I was trying to help him violate my exposed bottom.

"That's it, girlie. Keep that up. It feels so good," he smiled down at me.

From my position beneath him, I was locked in place by the other two boys holding my ankles. My knees bent in half near my head; my arms tied together underneath my back gave the boys easy access to whatever they wanted to do to me. Forced to watch as they continued their assault, their vile organs constantly pushing in and out of me one after another, I begged to be released. In response, the third boy jammed his huge penis into my rectum.

When he had finished, he called out to the boy holding my left ankle, "Payne, your turn again," as they swapped places. Ultimately each took his turn violating my body.

"**Payne**," I locked that name in my brain. These boys will pay for what they are doing to me. Later another boy referred to that same boy as James. I put the two names together. **James Payne,** I will remember that name until the day I die. I repeated it over and over in my mind.

The boy, I now knew as James Payne, was especially brutal, raping me three times and then expelling his juices over my face and hair.

He constantly taunted me "Tell me you like it, bitch. C'mon, you know you do!"

When the three had finally finished with me, they tossed the remains of my torn cheerleader uniform on top of me. After carefully checking that there was no one in the hall to see them, they slipped out the door leaving me naked, bleeding, raped and ashamed, weeping uncontrollably. After some time had passed, one of the teachers finally came looking and discovered me. The boys had left me lying in that pool of my urine.

An ambulance took me to the hospital where I was humiliated even more as the police lady took samples for the rape kit. I provided the police with the one name that I had: James Payne. I repeated his name over and over as I wailed loudly, amid my embarrassment and shame. Unknown male doctors examined my privates and humiliated me even more. I vowed never to let another man see me naked again.

They are ALL evil. Every one of them. I hate them.

My parents finally arrived hours later, having driven much of the night to get to the town where the team had played football. They saw my shame, my broken and bruised body. I think, at one point the sheet covering my naked body slipped down and even my father saw my exposed breasts. It was so embarrassing, humiliating and degrading.

I wanted to die. "Please, GOD, let me die," I cried silently, over and over. Eventually, I realized there was no God. A caring God would never have let this happen. I swore an oath against Payne and the other two boys. Someday, I would kill them all.

While Dad held and tried to console both of us, my mother wept uncontrollably. Dad swore to find the boys who had done this to me and bring them to justice.

For weeks after that, I would shower for extended periods, scrubbing between my legs trying to wipe away the evidence of my humiliation. I had trouble going to the bathroom, the rawness of it caused me great pain. I often thought of ending it all. I could not sleep, waking night after night screaming, until mother came and sat beside me on my bed. She rubbed my head, calming me until I would drift off. Very often I would awaken again a short time later with the same nightmares. The boys are holding me down, punching me until I surrendered to their desires.

What purpose could life hold for me now? No man would want someone like me, violated and degraded in an unforgivable manner. My parents tried to get me involved in church again; I refused to go with them. What was the point? Religion no longer meant anything to me. God had abandoned me in my hour of need. I now abandoned him completely. I would find my own means of protecting my body and soul.

Even more terrifying was having to testify against the three boys in court a year later. As I sat on the witness stand, I was afraid, sitting so close to them, as they glowered at me from beside their attorneys. They snickered and made rude finger gestures at me, as I related the things they had done. Memories of that night swept through me again. I could still feel the bra straps binding my arms and their fists striking my face and stomach. My knees locked beside my head, my entire bottom and privates exposed, naked and ready for whatever they wanted to do. All of the terrible memories were brought to life again as they threw fake kisses my way.

Then the humiliation of the questions from their lawyers, accusing me of being a willing participant, of inviting the boys to come to the restroom with me, of being a tease and exposing myself to them, Tempting them with sexy smiles and come-hither motions.

I felt that they were raping me all over again. I vomited on the floor of the witness stand. The bailiff supported me as he escorted me out of the room, sobs racking my body as I passed by their chairs. Thankfully, the jury did not believe their lies and returned a verdict of Guilty for each one after only fifteen minutes of deliberations.

The three boys shouted and screamed at me. The judge threatened to restrain them if they did not act civilly. The judge pronounced each boy a sentence of fifteen years in the state penitentiary, their looks of hatred struck fear in me.

James Payne cried out to the courtroom when the judge had finished.

"Bitch, I'm going to find you when I get out. No matter how long it takes. You just wait. You hear me? Especially, if you get married by then, I'm going to enjoy having your husband watch while we have sex, and you suck me off. Don't forget, bitch. Don't ever forget…"

Two bailiffs were finally able to jam a gag into his mouth and stop his shouts.

I wept in terror, struck hard in the gut by the force of his threats.

The judge banged his gavel over and over again trying to establish order. When Payne had finished shouting, the judge added another two years to his sentence for his threats.

To everyone's shock and disgust the boys were later discovered to have raped several other girls. Their parents had conspired with each other to cover up the crimes. Buying the silence of the girls and their parents with large cash bribes. As a result, my parents sued the school and the boys' families and won a twenty-million-dollar civil judgment, five-million dollars from the school for failing to provide adequate security for the girls' restroom and five-million from each of the boys' parents.

All of the money was designated to be held solely for my medical costs, education or whatever use that I wished when I reached age twenty-one. The money meant nothing to me. I wanted none of it and refused to spend it. I was always afraid somehow it would happen again.

I held my head in shame at school, afraid that other girls were laughing at me behind my back, calling me a slut or whore as my belly expanded. I held my bladder daily until I was ready to explode, afraid to enter the school bathrooms. Always terrified that there were boys hiding inside, waiting for me, ready to use my body for their evil purposes. Closed stall doors sent my brain into wild anxiety.

But the growing life inside me was a constant reminder. I changed to a new high school after that life became real in my arms. I held that life in my hands only briefly. Her skin was perfect, except for a tiny birthmark on her left buttocks just below the level of where a girls' shorts would fall. I noted the unusual shape, kind of like the state of Florida. But then the nurse came and told me that the adoption agency had found new parents for the child. I was never to see her again. Grief tore me apart, but I knew there was no way that I could keep her. I held her only briefly, then had to kiss her goodbye forever. She was to be my hidden secret.

I was ashamed to face the questions from my former school friends and changed high schools again. The shame of my past forced me to attend college in a different city. I never again went to the Ladies' room alone, always taking care to have at least two girlfriends come with me. For years after, the assault was never far from my mind, and I endured endless counseling sessions. My parents supported me through it all, including the many, many times nightmares awakened me screaming. The counseling sessions helped me maintain my sanity; I struggled to have a semblance of growing up normally.

During my junior year at college, I finally settled on a major in business administration and graduated second in my class. I dated on occasion and only after my closest girlfriend got on her knees and begged, but never as a single, choosing only to double date and always going to very public places. I never allowed myself to be alone with any of the boys. After a few dates, they lost interest, always wanting to get me alone for making out, petting and perhaps even more. I was too afraid, memories of the pain too raw, and would have none of it. The boys eventually drifted away and no longer bothered me. I was happy. The boys were evil monsters. I wouldn't allow them to touch me or even hold my hand. Disgusting, evil, horrible creatures.

My emotional scars ran so deep that I always kept my secret, even from my closest friends, ashamed of what had happened. I was afraid that someone would find out, so I buried my secret in the past. Smiling and laughing away the pain in my heart, especially when I listened as other girls told of their love affairs and trysts.

Some bragged with tales of making love with their boyfriends, how much they had enjoyed their first sexual experiences. Others spoke of the kindness and gentleness in the way the boys had treated and loved them. I inwardly wept as I listened; remembering the violence and hate that I had experienced. I knew that I would probably never have that loving, gentle relationship with a man. I came to believe that all men were evil. They just wanted to hurt me, to take what they wanted and leave me in pain.

My childhood dreams of happiness and love lay at my feet in ashes.

CHAPTER 1

After graduation from City College I interviewed and was hired on as an assistant to a VP at a real estate firm. From there I slowly progressed through three other jobs until, at age twenty-nine, I landed a coveted position supporting a senior VP, Larry Bertram, with Tilden Industries. Even though I had the twenty-million in the bank, more than enough to live comfortably without working, I wanted to be involved in life. I wanted to earn my money; I refused to spend a dime of the money from the rape. The money stayed in a trust account earning money from investments. I believed that spending the money would be like a whore taking money for turning a trick.

I longed to have a normal life, career and maybe… someday… in the future I could only see in a daydream, find someone who could restore a sense of peace to my life. As the years passed my views of men changed somewhat over time. Perhaps they even softened as I met and interacted with men in daily life who were kind and caring. Sometimes I even dreamed again that just maybe I might find my own Prince Charming. A man who could help me overcome the secrets hidden in my past. On occasion, I dated several men who turned out to be exceedingly boring and dull. Usually after the first date they seemed to expect me to let them paw at my breasts or feel up my legs. Why did men always believe that one date gives them full access to all parts of my body? I swore off men completely after that incident.

But there was a new man in my life who began to alter all my dark thoughts about men once more. Larry, my boss, and I hit it off right from the start. Larry was brilliant, where I still lacked the experience. I was more insightful and often was able to offer suggestions that fit in perfectly, whenever he had missed the finer points of his current projects. He was extremely good looking, fun loving, something of what I was looking for in a man. I could joke and poke fun at him; he did the same with me.

Larry was married with two children and loved his wife dearly. I never had any issues with flirtation from him, for which I was extremely grateful. The thing that I admired most about him was his total support for me and my work. I prayed that I might find another like him for myself. Yes, if there were only such a man. Perhaps I could learn to love, just as so many others had; but where could I find that person? I was getting older, my chances of finding someone seemed to have slipped into the past. After a time, I completely gave up the search.

Four years ago, shortly after I started at Tilden, Larry brought two representatives from Vacation Airlines to my office. I could tell from the expression on all of their faces that it was bad news. But the news was far worse than I could have ever believed. Both my parents had died in a plane crash. They had been on their way to the South Sea Islands to celebrate their fortieth wedding anniversary.

I had seen them off at the airport. At first, I refused to believe them. It was all a terrible mistake. It was not possible that was the last time I would ever see them.

"**NO**!" I screamed and collapsed back into my chair. These were the only two people in the world gave me love. Now, they were gone. I was now truly alone. An orphan amid a sea of millions of humans, none of whom cared for me.

I stayed in a state of shock for months. During the slow times in the office, I found myself sometimes picking up the phone to dial mom. To tell her of some exciting thing happening in my life. Then, breaking down in tears when I realized that she would never be there for me again. Once, I even found myself driving over to their old house to stop and leave something for Dad. It wasn't until I turned up their old street that I realized what I was doing. I stopped my car and cried for thirty minutes, alone and broken.

Larry was very understanding and gave me that extra time to grieve. He covered my phone when I needed time alone. Let me have an office to myself, keeping my constant tears hidden from the other ladies in the office. Very often when I was in the dumps, he would assign me extra work to take my mind off of my troubles. My current project, working with every single detail of a new contract with T & J Industries, was just such an example. He had given me tremendous access and responsibility to dig into and formulate nearly every aspect of this multi-million-dollar effort, offering me a few ideas here and there. But, for the most part, it was all my baby.

Contract details; staffing levels; I had even worked directly with his counterpart at T & J. It was thrilling and very rewarding and took my mind completely off of the last guy I had dated who had unexpectedly shoved his hand down my blouse and felt my breasts.

GOD! Men, that's ALL they want from me.

Luckily, Charlotte, my bodyguard, had been there to assist and had surprised the hell out of him when she opened the car door and pointed a gun at his sorry ass.

The airplane crash was found to be caused by a faulty airplane part not discovered during routine manufacturing review or maintenance. I was awarded another seven-and-a-half million dollars each from the Manufacturer and also the Maintenance Companies for the loss of each of my parents. A total of thirty million dollars. I was now beyond wealthy but had lost all that had meant the most to me: my parents, the ownership of my body, and my peace of mind. Again, the money went into my bank accounts. I couldn't spend it. It was blood money; I refused to touch it. The bank convinced me to invest it in stocks and bonds. The money accumulated over time. I refused to give more than an occasional look at my bank balances; the money represented too much pain in my life and only brought painful memories.

I would have given my entire fortune to have my parents back or not have been raped. I felt degraded, worthless, abandoned. Through it all, Larry was very understanding and gave me that extra time to grieve, which I so desperately needed. He was truly the best boss ever. Focusing my energies on work allowed me to keep my sanity, and my pride intact.

In my private life, I surrounded myself with things to protect myself. I found a great apartment in one of the most exclusive locations near downtown, The Grecian Condominium, where I lived with my housekeeper/cook, Marianne Williams, and my bodyguard/driver, Charlotte Parker. Both women kept my residence clean, my clothes looking sharp and ready each day, my car well maintained, and delicious, refreshing meals at breakfast and dinner.

Charlotte is a striking blond haired ex-marine. She was everything that a guy might desire, except she was no push-over. Charlotte wouldn't put up with crap from anyone. She could handle just about any size or shape man, and that is why I needed someone like her to shadow me whenever I dated. I didn't want men using my body as their personal property. That had already happened once, and I had vowed never to let it happen again.

Even if I had to die an old maid, **NEVER AGAIN** would men force me to do things that I did not want to do. Especially when it came to my body. Anyone who tried, I vowed, would **NOT** live to regret it.

My staff was always supportive when I needed to unwind from a hard day at work. They provided an ear to listen to my woes, or a shoulder to cry on when I felt depressed. They made me feel safe and protected, yet alone and unloved, missing out on what I could see in so many women where I worked: a family life, children, friends and close relatives.

Marianne, on the other hand, was the kind of lady who I could get close to emotionally. She was of Mexican descent having been born in the U.S. after her parents immigrated. She was gregarious and chatty and often made me see how ridiculous several of my ideas about men had been.

'Miss Tina,' she would scold. 'You should not define all men as evil just because you had a couple of bad experiences. Some men are very nice; you just need to find the right one. Someday, you will see. A man will come along and sweep you off your feet. You just wait. You are so pretty and have a great job. That man is out there, and he is just waiting for you to appear.'

'You take my dad, for example,' ...... And then she would excite me with so many funny stories about her father and the good times she had growing up.

But I always came back to her, "Yes, but that was years ago. Times have changed, there aren't any more Romeo's out there. Nowadays, there are just Don Juan's who want to get into my underwear."

"You just wait. You'll see! One day it will happen, and you will see! You need to let go of all of the negatives in your life. Be happy," she would say, and that was the end of that. Once she had said that part, it was pointless to argue further, so we always just laughed and changed the subject.

Sometimes at work, thinking of what Marianne had told me, I dreamed that perhaps a promotion at work might mix me in with new people. Perhaps my future was there; I knew that several of the executives were single men, but in my current job I didn't exactly move in their circles. Perhaps one of them might make me whole again. If that failed, I would at least gain some happiness from being more valuable to the company. I was restless. I needed something new in my life. I desperately wanted to find that mystical man that Marianne always told me was waiting for me to find him.

I tried to bury my loneliness in activities such as visiting the workout fitness center together with my staff. It featured state-of-the-art exercise equipment, including E-Zone entertainment system consoles on cardiovascular machines for watching cable TV, DVDs or listening to music, while we ran on the treadmills. There were lots of toys to distract my mind.

We three stretched our bodies with yoga exercises or lifted small weights. It is so nice to have my staff keeping me company while we broke out in a sweat together. As an ex-Marine, Charlotte was a little more into the physical aspect of the training equipment. She had the muscles and rock-hard body to show for it, and she was an expert marksman. We established a regular pattern of running and exercise routines to keep all three of us fit and ready for whatever life might throw at us.

The camaraderie I shared with them helped fill part of that void. But alone in my bed during the darkest part of the nights, I always sensed that there was still something missing that I desperately wanted. I could not put my finger on it. Sometimes when I watched certain men at the office, I'd be lost in a daydream. I wished that my Prince Charming would arrive on his white horse to carry me away. Hell, I could even settle for a hunk in a nice BMW. See? I'm not really that picky, am I? Sadly, at the end of the day, it was always back to my apartment and a movie I had seen many times before or old TV rerun. My dreams full of vague shapes, my heart searching for something.

Charlotte and I often went to a local shooting range to practice. Her weapon of choice was the Glock 42 which held six rounds in the magazine and one in the chamber. I preferred the M & P Bodyguard .38 Special, which featured a Crimson Trace laser sight for targeting in low light conditions, which was an excellent option because my aim was not nearly as good as Charlotte's. She was so good that she could even shoot holes in the paper targets that left a smiley face. My targets often just looked like a piece of shredded confetti, bullet holes everywhere.

We both possessed concealed weapons permits, so whenever I left the apartment, my pistol was always inside my purse. Charlotte preferred to carry her automatic in a holster behind her back. The holster had her cell phone, a switchblade, a small can of mace and several other items she had yet to explain to me. Charlotte and I also had attended self-defense classes to develop skills to fend off attackers and protect ourselves from unwanted male advances. All in all, I felt very safe, well protected, and able to defend myself if an occasion arose. I was happy that I had never had to use those skills but wanted to be ready if something were to happen to me again.

As Charlotte drove me to work one Tuesday, there was a hint of rain in the air. Dark clouds were roiling in from the Gulf of Mexico, beautiful, but dark and heavy with rain.

"I sure hope that it doesn't rain," I said with a touch of melancholy." I was so looking forward to lunch with Larry. I hate to get out in the rain and get my hair wet. It takes me the rest of the day to get it untangled."

"Yes, ma'am. I know exactly how you feel. But I checked the weather report before we left, it said the clouds would pass over; we are going to have a bright sunny day today," Charlotte said cheerily.

"Oh…, Charlotte, I forgot to mention, I will be going out with Larry for a business lunch today. I don't have the restaurant location yet, but I'll call you with the details."

"By the way, Marianne said that she needs to go out grocery shopping this morning. Could you ask her to pick up some of those ripe Ruston Louisiana Peaches? They grow the most delicious peaches; I'm pretty sure they are in season just now. I have a taste bud that is begging for one. Perhaps she could make us a nice peach cobbler."

"That sounds yummy," Charlotte replied. "I'll be sure and have her get some. I'll see you at the restaurant for lunch, but as usual, you won't see me."

"I just don't know how you do it, Charlotte. I can be in the most open places, and I know that you are around somewhere if I need you, but I was only able to spot you one time. How are you able to become so inconspicuous like that?"

"Practice, ma'am! Just lots of practice. It is what you pay me to be --invisible, even so, there are many times that I wished that I had one of those invisibility cloaks on which scientists are working."

We both had a good laugh over that as she pulled up to my office building. I hopped out and waved good-bye. Charlotte watched me until I disappeared into the building before she pulled away.

****

Neither of us noticed the man standing on the corner take down her license plate number. Crushing a cigarette under his heel, he turned and got into a dark sedan with a broken front headlight.

****

CHAPTER 2

The office staff had been buzzing with stories about the beauty of our new headquarters building for several weeks. I had seen the original plans before the start of construction. Other than listening to some of the ladies emote at length about the size of their new offices or the beauty of the conference room under construction, I had paid little attention, being overburdened with the details and research required for the new contract.

Larry had me deeply involved in a new business project the company was hoping to land with T & J Industries. The details had taken up nearly every minute of my day for weeks. If our bid was successful, it was going to be our biggest ever contract. It would mean millions of dollars to the company's bottom line. The new building under construction would allow the company to move all of the scattered staff from around the city to one central location. Additionally, there was to be an entirely new division created to oversee that contract. There was to be a new VP over that group. I wanted to be that person, but how could I get the who-ha's to notice me?

Yesterday Larry received instructions from upper management to make some changes to the floor seating in the tower to accommodate staff to support that contract. He scheduled a working business lunch with the construction supervisor, a gentleman by the name of Clifford Stinson. He invited me along to help fill in any missing points during the meeting, since

I had handled most of the paperwork, and had worked extensively on both the contract and staffing. Several new staff were to be added, as well as reallocating some existing staff from around town to fill open positions. This was my first time meeting Mr. Stinson. Larry had worked with him in the past.

We were walking back to Larry's office when I asked him for some background on the supervisor.

Larry, being the typical 'guy' personality gave me a fairly blank stare and replied,

"Oh, you know, he might ask: what the measurements of the new office cubicles should be, or whether they should have a window view, or if private offices were needed for new managers."

'*Men!*' I thought walking back to my office. '*Some help that was!*'

Measuring floor layouts were not my forte. What I had wanted was more detail on this construction manager. I wanted to prepare some notes to impress my boss with my insights. I wanted that promotion; it offered me an opportunity to meet and mingle with new people. Having an intelligent conversation with this construction guy just might be the key to that job.

After looking around my office in frustration, I decided to go to central office files and obtain a copy of the current floor plans for each of the twenty-four floors in the tower being built. Perhaps I could find something that Larry had missed. There would be about one-hundred new employees to need seating. That sounded very much like we would need at least two entire floors of space. Somewhere in the back of my mind, I had a vague memory about open floors. Perhaps the blueprints would jog my memory.

On returning to my office, I laid the plans out on my desk. I struggled to understand some of the most cryptic notes scribbled here and there on each floor. I then noticed that floors eight and fourteen appeared to be offer just the opportunity for changes I was looking. Those two floors had originally been extra space; the initial thought was to lease those out to long term clients.

'*Eureka!*' Just what I need. I took my ruler and traced in the restroom areas from other floors. I added in a medium sized conference room, and two large offices on opposite ends for managers. Next, I penciled in several larger squares to house some half-height cubicle areas for remaining staff, a small room for a photocopy and large printer machines. Lastly, I added a larger break room for staff.

'*That looks great if I don't say so myself,*' I congratulated myself.

On floor fourteen I moved one managers' office to the center, leaving the other in place on the outside wall. This office was to be the new VP office and needed to be larger than any of the manager's offices. I added a smaller office outside that for the VP's assistant. The conference room I placed at the far end. Each area would be open to the glass exterior of the building providing the new employees exciting views of the city. I finished off with a similar space for the break room and copy room areas.

Floor eight would provide space for the temporary staff assisting with the move, and then floor fourteen would house the new staff, hired if we won the contract bid with T & J.

I mentally patted myself on the back.

'*I'm pretty sure that Larry has forgotten all about those two floors. I'm going to look brilliant.*' I congratulated myself, '*that promotion is in the bag.*'

I crossed my fingers in hope that neither Larry nor this guy Cliff Stinson would have noticed these two areas before now. I folded my copies over twice and stuffed them into a large manila envelope just as Larry poked his head into my cube, and gave me a big smile.

"Time to go, Tina. We have about twenty minutes to make it to the tower. I checked the radio for traffic conditions, and there don't appear to be any major wrecks or traffic backups, so we should be right on time." Houston traffic was always a bitch. The slightest thing seemed to cause traffic tie-ups, often causing people to take hours to go a few miles, rather than a few minutes.

I made a quick stop at the Ladies room to check my hair and performed a quick survey of my outfit, a purple and green striped button down blouse, blazer, and slacks. All seemed to be in good order; my hair was pulled back in a simple bun. I tucked a stray hair and put on a fresh coat of lipstick.

There, I smiled – I looked like the perfect VP Assistant. Overall, a nice business office appearance I thought to myself. I was ready to meet this guy, what was his name? Oh yeah. Clifford Stinson. I was going to bowl Mr. Stinson over with my expertise about construction. By the time this lunch was over, both Larry and this construction guy would be eating out of my hands.

After one last glance at the mirror I turned and hurried out to the elevator where Larry stood tapping his foot.

"Sorry, Larry. You know we girls need to have a last minute checkup, sort of like you do with your truck. You know, checking the fuel gauge, oil pressure, air in the tires."

"Oh? So how is your tire pressure today?" Larry laughed.

"Ha, Ha. You're very funny today! Didn't you say we needed to get going, or we would be late?" I tried to change the subject. Larry was always pulling my leg. I think he did that on purpose to keep me in a good mood. Well, he certainly was good at it. I needed to thank him for that someday. I wonder if he has an unmarried brother?

The elevator bell rang, and the down arrow flashed signaling our ride down. We stepped in and were quickly on our way to the parking level two. The elevator, packed with staff going to lunch, we ended up on opposite sides. As we each squeezed out, Larry's truck was easy to find being parked close by the elevator door.

Larry drove a large, custom pickup. The extreme height of the suspension was useful in high water but made my access to the truck in my heels difficult. Larry had to give me an assist to reach the side step and steadied my arm as I climbed aboard. He usually parked in the off-site lot but, because he knew we were going out to lunch, he had parked it in a reserved space next to the elevator for my convenience.

"Larry, have you picked out a restaurant yet?"

"Not yet, I was going to let Cliff offer his ideas, and if I'm right, he'll know just the place. He's always great about knowing good places to chow down."

Putting my cell phone to my ear, "Charlotte, Tina here. We still haven't decided on a restaurant yet. Can you meet us over at the new tower? I'm in Larry's truck. You know, the one with the orange and red vinyl flames on the front fenders. …Yeah, that one. I just don't know what it is about guys and their' tricked up rides. Okay, sure thing. See you there."

I was always a little hesitant to travel around in Larry's big rig since his mufflers were loud and tended to give me a headache. It was undisputedly a 'guys' truck, tricked out with all sorts of flashy dials and knobs. As it turned out, the traffic was very light, and we made it to the site with five minutes to spare.

"Say, Larry, not to change the subject, but do you happen to have a brother?"

"Sorry, No. I have three sisters, though. Why do you ask?"

"Oh, no reason. I was just wondering."

I lived on the opposite side of town and had never actually seen the new tower until Larry pulled up in the front parking area. The building was impressive, and now I fully understood why everyone was excited. It stretched upward majestically toward the white clouds and blue sky. Brilliant rays of sunlight reflected off the glass skin. Areas of the interior, exposed at different levels, one could see workers climbing about attaching things. There were men welding giant steel beams together, sparks flying out into the air like a river of fire. Other workers were pouring concrete support stanchions everywhere I could see. It was an incredibly impressive sight. Two huge cranes were lifting giant steel girders skyward as we pulled up and parked.

It was beautiful, especially since several of the lower floors already had the glass skin installed.

"Wow!" I exclaimed as Larry pulled in and parked next to a row of workers trucks. The parking lot had not yet been swept clean of construction debris, so there were piles of used and unused materials scattered here and there. Larry gave a short blast on his air horn, which was hidden under the hood, the blast startled off a flock of birds roosting in a nearby tree, and scaring the hell out of me at the same time.

'Gosh, Larry. Did you have to have a horn that's so loud?"

"You never know when it will come in handy," he laughed. "What with all of the low hanging fog out where I live; I use it kind of like a ship foghorn when the fog is thick."

Shortly after that I noticed a man, six-foot-one or two, about thirty-four or thirty-five walking through the rubble toward us. He had a warm smile on his face as he approached. He clearly admired Larry's fancy rig. He waved at Larry, and then his eyes caught sight of me.

'Wow! He certainly is handsome.' I sat up straighter on the seat. Something stirred deep within me, below my stomach.

He was wearing a light brown Sharkskin suit. Over that he wore a gray and yellow construction safety vest, and a yellow hard hat. He had the most piercing brown eyes. His face had the appearance of a man in charge of things. His face was serious and his eyes remained concentrated on me. I felt something strange sweep through my body.

I could not help myself as my lips split into a smile. My heart skipped a beat as the man's smile broadened. When he reached the passenger side door, he grabbed the handle, climbed in and slid in next to me.

'Ohhhhhh.' A shiver ran through my entire body.

The cab of the truck immediately filled with a strong woody, herbal smell. Probably a pine scented bath soap, but underneath it was a hint of something strong, very masculine. My senses were overwhelmed by the delicious scent; my nose could not drink in enough. It was like an elixir. I felt light headed. I looked over at Larry to judge his reaction, but it did not seem that he had noticed the wonderful smell of our passenger.

The touch of the supervisor's arm and leg against my body brought my attention back to the man. At the same time, it ignited a fire in my stomach as bright as the cast vinyl flames on the side of the truck. My breath caught in my chest; my mind began processing strange thoughts that I couldn't understand.

The supervisor was carrying two telescoping tubes which, I assumed, contained the building blueprints. His other hand held his cell phone. He seemed to be speaking to his assistant telling him that he was out for a business lunch with the client, and would be back in a few hours.

"*Ohhhhh!* The gentle, sweet sound of his voice next to my ear sent thrills up and down my spine.

As he pushed the end button on the phone, he reached around, his arm brushing my shoulder sent a thrill directly to my heart. He then passed the tubes to his other hand and lay them on the back seat next to the brown envelope that I had brought. He quickly grabbed his hard hat with his other hand and tossed it carelessly onto the back seat. A few seconds later he unsnapped his vest, folded it, and set it beside his hat. As he reached across to shake Larry's hand, he brushed my wrist softly, and I felt something like an electric surge sweep through my arm.

I had the oddest sensation sweep through my legs. A strange thought crossed my mind about his lips. I immediately rejected it.

'*What the hell?*

"Hi, Larry. Who's the beautiful young lady we have trapped between us?" he asked.

Larry glanced sideways at him and smiled, "Hi, Cliff, I would like you to meet my assistant, Tina McIntyre. She's most of the reason that I have still got a job at Tilden. Tina always seems to fill in the blanks for me when I forget to include something in my reports to upper management."

Cliff turned his dark brown eyes in my direction and extended his hand in greeting. As I took hold I immediately felt a second spark of tension jolt my nerve endings to life; my breath, still held in my chest. His hand was large but surprisingly soft in contrast to the rough callouses I had felt with other construction workers I had known. My stomach was queasy.

"Hi, Tina. ...Clifford Stinson but most people just call me Cliff. ...You do breathe, don't you, Tina?"

My face turned red as I finally exhaled. I had not breathed since he had gotten in beside me. For some reason, I had wanted to treasure his wonderful scent as long as I could.

'*Had he noticed that?*' My heart was pounding as if I had just run a marathon.

"Hello, Cliff. I am very pleased to meet you." My voice sounded strange and breathy.

Somehow I managed to get the words out, though my throat was tight and my legs felt like Jell-O at the point where we were touching the leather truck bench. His hand wrapped around mine like a vice. Holding on gently, but firmly, as if he did not want to release my hand. I glanced down and noted there was no wedding ring, then I felt the soft touch of his other hand brush against my arm, then slide up and, as if by accident, brush my chin.

I lifted my eyes to his. '*Ummmmm*,' I sighed under my breath. I felt that I could drown in those beautiful soft pools of coffee-colored intensity. My breathing increased, my chest felt constricted; I felt a knot in the pit of my stomach.

'*Heart attack. I must be having a heart attack. Should I tell Larry to call an ambulance?*'

"Tina, your skin is so soft,..." he said, then blushed, realizing the impropriety of his words, breaking my train of thought. With that, he released his grip on my hand and turned to face forward. His face becoming a mask as he gazed out the windshield. The blood vessels on his hand seemed to be throbbing, his fingers twitched.

'*Could he possibly be affected as I was? Oh, my God! What is happening to me?*'

I wanted his hand around mine again desperately. I wrung my hands together and squirmed to keep myself from reaching over to grab his hand again.

"Hey, Larry," he said as he looked around me at Larry, "do you have reservations somewhere? If not, then let's head over to the Houston ship channel and check out *Brady's Landing*. It is a hit and miss place sometimes, but when it's on the hit side, the food is extremely fresh and delicious."

"Isn't that the restaurant that used to be Shang-Hi Reds?" Larry replied.

"Yep, the very same. They changed owners a few years back and tore down the old place, and remodeled a couple of years back. The view of the ship channel is exceptional. Big old ships slipping lazily by, very cool to watch while you munch on some tasty seafood. They serve mainly buffet style and have a wonderful spread. They also offer a lunch menu with several imported beers and wines for those who want something special."

"I know where that is, let's do it," Larry smiled and turned left to take the ramp onto the South Loop freeway to get us there quickly. As we exited on Broadway Street, Cliff seemed to squirm a bit in his seat because the torque from the left turn pulled him even closer to my side.

The warmth of his body, the strength of his arms and legs caused me to want to push back against him harder. To let him know -- *'No, I can't go there.'*

Suddenly a car that had been behind us made a swerving right turn in front of us against traffic forcing Larry to compensate. I reacted by grabbing hold of Cliff's thigh to steady myself.

Cliff swung his left arm around my shoulder and held me tight. With his right hand, he reached over and swallowed mine inside his palm.

'Ah! I was in heaven; somehow my brain told me that it wanted to be in more car crashes, as long as Cliff was there to hold me.'

Larry struggled to keep the truck from skidding off the side of the road onto the sidewalk or into other cars. Cliff and I bounced wildly around in the truck cabin. The car that had cut us off swerved and then made a hard right at the next intersection and sped away.

"Shit! Excuse my French" Larry cried out as he fought to regain control of the truck. "What an idiot! Probably an illegal alien who has no idea of traffic laws in the U.S."

As the truck steadied and continued down Broadway, Cliff loosened his hold on my shoulder. He left his arm in place and continued holding my hand.

I was unsure of what he was doing. *'Was he doing that on purpose?'*

I tried to study his face, but it was still a mask, looking absently forward out the windshield. Only a slight tick in his cheek reflected anything unusual.

I curled my fingers inside his palm and made no effort to release my hand from his grip. My fingers felt so natural and protected inside his palm. My entire body relaxed, the knot in my stomach disappeared.

I looked up at his face, but he did not turn his head again. He continued to stare forward as if he was unaware that his arm was around my shoulder. Or that my hand was still inside the soft grip that he had, imprisoning my fingers inside.

Watching him, I noticed there was a vein in his throat which throbbed in time with the gentle squeezes of his hand on mine.

I was confused, '*was he doing this on purpose?*' I could not make it out. He had only known me for a few minutes, '*why would he do this?*'

"Thanks," I whispered in his ear, "I would have hit the dashboard without your hand on my shoulder."

I was very grateful for his help and somehow wished we could stay in the truck all afternoon with his arm around my shoulder. Maybe even his lips on mine!

'*GOD! Where had that thought come from? I must be losing it... or something...*

'*I shut the last thought down. It was totally ridiculous.*'

His hand tightened around mine momentarily and then relaxed, still holding mine firmly. My fingers, curled up inside his palm, felt like they had found a home. I felt drawn to him, somehow sensing I would be safe held in his arms. Cliff made no motion to remove his arm until we had reached the restaurant.

I felt treasured and safe held like this. I became more and more convinced that his actions were deliberate.

'*Did I want this?*' I was confused. Something told me that I did. Still, he made no other gesture or move.

'*Perhaps I was mistaken; I'm probably misreading all of this. Surely he is just polite. Probably just good manners*' I thought.

Whatever it was, I wanted it to continue, and from somewhere a second thought broke through.

'*I never want it to stop.*'

CHAPTER 3

Larry drove into the parking lot only to find it was full of cars and trucks. It seemed to be a very popular lunch location. We drove around for several minutes before Larry was able to find a space large enough for our oversize ride.

Cliff released my hand as it were an afterthought as he opened the passenger side door. Then he reached behind the seat to retrieve his cardboard tubes.

'Yes,' I thought, "*he must have simply forgotten about my hand inside his own.*' Suddenly I missed the feel of his hand around mine, keeping it warm and safe, kind of like it belonged there.

"Can you also grab my manila folder, Cliff? I have some notes I might need." I asked with a nervous smile. I would need that folder just in case Larry would ask for my help.

"Sure thing," he replied as he climbed down while holding the tubes and envelope in one hand, he turned to offer his other hand to assist me out of the truck.

'*Most guys just stand there and laugh at me while I struggle to climb down. Why is he treating me like this?*'

"Thanks, Cliff. This truck suspension is just so high. I can hardly get in or out without someone to help."

I slid forward and dropped into Cliff's arms knowing that was the safest way for me to exit.

The smile that split his face was a thing to behold as his arms enfolded me.

I felt a sudden rush of hormones sweep through me as our bodies crushed against each other. I could feel the strength and warmth of his chest against mine. I struggled to maintain my composure. He looked down into my eyes for just a moment, and I thought that I saw something. Something that I wanted desperately. I felt a thrill throughout my whole body. But just as quickly he looked away with a slight blush on his cheek.

'*What was that about?*' I wondered. My heart sank in disappointment. I had seen something in his eyes, if only for a moment. God, I wanted that moment to last forever.

"Thanks again, Cliff. You sure know how to make a girl feel safe."

I wanted to stay there, held safe in his arms.

Cliff looked down at me and smiled. "Not a problem, I just didn't want you to muss up that beautiful outfit you are wearing. Besides, I am famished. If you broke your leg or something, I might miss out on that big Steak and Lobster lunch I am going to have your boss pay for," he said teasingly.

The expression on his face said something else, something hidden. His cheeks seemed a tinge too red, and his lips seemed to quiver when he looked at me. It was as if he wanted to say something more.

'*But what? Was it just because he thought I might break my leg and he would miss his lunch? That cannot be all there is, can it?*'

'*What is he trying to tell me? One second he is ignoring me, staring out the window. The next he is all perfection, holding my hand to help me from the truck, offering compliments about my clothing.*

Perhaps it's his upbringing. His parents must have taught him good manners, and I have been reading too much into all of this.'

By this time Larry had made his way around to the passenger side, I had unwillingly untangled myself from Cliff's arms.

"All right then, let's head in," Larry said, as he nudged me with his finger making me aware that I was still staring up at Cliff.

'Gah! Get a grip, girl.' I forced my legs to move, one leg in front of the other, now the left, now the right, I began to think I might need a wheelchair at this rate.

'What was happening to me? Was it Cliff or something else? Maybe I'm coming down with something. Maybe it's...'

"Stop it, Tina. You're our of your mind,' I shouted my idiotic thought down before it had time to finish.

'Love?'

'Dammit, keep your thoughts to yourself?'

I felt tempted to reach out and grab his hand as we walked.

'What the hell is wrong with me? It's just not possible. Things like this don't happen to people like me. Besides, I HATE ALL MEN!

...Well, maybe not ALL of them... I could think of at least one exception, and he was only a few inches away.

I took a quick step forward so that I was leading our group and wouldn't be tempted to take any rash actions. Then I regretted that choice because I could feel his eyes looking me over, Appraising every inch of me.

'GAH! I should have paid more attention to my clothes and what they looked like from behind. Can this get any worse? What does he think of me? I've been acting like an idiot since the very moment that he saw me. I'll never live this down. When we're old and gray, he'll still be making jokes about this.'

'What the hell, Tina? Who said anything about getting old? What are you talking about? This is the absolute last time you're ever going to see this guy. You're a fool to think otherwise.'

We strolled over to the main entrance and followed the crowd of happy lunch-goers in front of us. I led while Cliff and Larry trudged behind. This lunch was my first visit here since the old restaurants' exterior skin had been removed and refurbished. But I immediately recognized the interior motif as having very much of the old restaurant's charm. At the moment, the restaurant held little that I was interested in, my thoughts and feelings were laser focused. Not on food, the business contract or even how

I dressed. My mind could only see the man walking not two feet behind me. I was strongly tempted to turn around and...

'*STOP IT TINA.*' I screamed at myself.

"Larry, I love it," I said approvingly. "Mom and Dad brought me here years ago. Back then it used to have an exterior covering of rusted sheet metal planks, kind of like you might see in Shang-Hi or the Orient."

Yeah, that's it Tina. Talk about the building and the food. No issues there.'

I turned and looked up at Cliff. I bit my lip hard to keep from saying what was on the tip of my tongue. Instead, I took a deep breath and said:

"Thank you so much for suggesting it, Cliff, I love this old place."

I struggled to sound more intelligent than I felt at the moment. At this rate, I was acting like a star struck school girl. '*What I had wanted to ask was would he kiss me.*'

'*Snap out of it, Tina.*'

While we waited for an escort to a table, I kept watching at Cliff like I was in a trance. Cliff kept staring blankly ahead, as if unaware of my gaze, but it seemed to me that his cheeks blushed a light pink every few moments. It was as if he could sense my eyes as they searched every inch of his face. I memorized every curve, every line around his mouth, the line around his face where he shaved, the curve of his eyebrows.

'*What a hunk,*' I thought to myself.

Larry's voice, advising the waitress that we wanted a table by the window, brought me back to the present. She had asked us to wait nearby on a bench until they called Larry's name. After about ten minutes our table was ready, and a waiter led us over to a table by the window just as tug pushing an old barge, filled with shipping containers, slipped past outside our window.

After sitting for a few minutes a second waitress brought a delectable sparkling white wine and some buttered rolls for starters. Cliff sat beside Larry, directly across the table from me, providing an excellent opportunity for me to study his every feature.

I let my mind wander from the table to the charming view of the waterway. My thoughts became confused by the nearness of Cliff's leg to my own as they brushed against each other under the table.

'WHAT WAS WRONG WITH ME? I DON'T LIKE MEN.'

"Ma'am?"

It took a few seconds for me to realize that the waitress was trying to hand me the menu. My mind was so entangled with the person sitting across the table from me that I was unable to concentrate. I flushed again, took the menu and stared at it blankly. There did not seem to be anything printed on it at first. My eyes could only focus on the strong, gentle hands holding the menu across the table, hiding his face from my view.

I shook my head to try to clear my thoughts.

'What is wrong with me? 'What is wrong with me?' I repeated over and over.

I tried to focus my mind on the thing in my hands. It had all kinds of print and pictures. My eyes could only see Cliff's fingers as they drummed on the outside of his menu. None of this made any sense to my overloaded brain.

I looked around and could see people eating and talking happily among themselves, and then tried to slow my thoughts.

'TINA, We are at a restaurant, you need to make a meal choice. You're just embarrassing yourself.'

I realized that I had to get away, to have a minute to clear my head of the wild thoughts of climbing over the table and kissing this total stranger.

'Get a grip, you idiot.'

When I looked back again, I soon realized that my tablemates had already made their selections; a sharply dressed waiter had replaced the waitress; he was slowly tapping his pencil on his notepad, waiting for me to respond.

'What was wrong with my brain?'

In a panic, I finally forced my tongue to work.

"I believe that I would just like to have the buffet today."

I could hear my voice saying the words, but there was something wrong with my brain, it kept feeding me irrational thoughts and desires. If I wasn't very careful, I'm afraid that I'm going to say one of those things out loud.

'I've got to get away.'

Yes, choosing that would give me a few minutes of peace away from this table. Right now I could not for the life of me make any choice of something to eat.

"Ma'am," The waiter smiled at me. "You may proceed to the buffet bar whenever you are ready," and with that, he pivoted on his heel, returned to place the men's orders.

"If you will excuse me, I am going to browse the buffet."

I breathed a sigh of relief. *'Yes, a quick look at the buffet would wipe away all trace of this thing that was happening to me.'*

I rose from my chair.

Surprisingly, Cliff stood at the same time.

I smiled up at him and almost became lost again in those mesmerizing brown eyes and hypnotic smile. I forced myself to look away, then searched around the room trying to find the serving area for the buffet. Seeing a line of people toward the side, I slowly made my way there, praying that I wouldn't collapse or knock over someone's lunch on the way.

I stood in line and grabbed a tray, and then walked slowly down the line of the buffet, the last thing on my mind was the mountains of steaming hot seafood trays, vegetables, and desserts. Instead, all that I could feel were a pair of brown eyes staring at me from across the room. My mind was racing, swirling with illicit thoughts.

For some unknown reason, I had a flashback of Cliff holding me as I slid out of the truck. I desperately wanted to feel Cliff's body against mine again. I glanced over to the table where Larry and Cliff were and noted they seemed to be in animated conversation while both looked in my direction.

I tried to analyze my feelings. Normally I accepted men for what they were. Either the hard working married type, struggling to keep their family fed. Or office climbers, eager to stab others in the back to climb the office totem pole. This man Cliff seemed so different than that.

'Why then was I not afraid of him? Any other man would have sent me running for the hills. For some reason, I felt uncomfortable in his presence. And yet, I wanted to be near him, to listen to his soft voice. That usual tension in my gut was missing. I was almost certain that if he asked me, I would walk out with him without an escort.'

This feeling that I was having, it had never happened to me before.

'But why, oh why, was I so nervous?'

My legs went wobbly on me as Cliff met my gaze again and that beautiful smile broke across his face again.

'Ohhhh!'

My stomach flipped over, and I knew that I wouldn't be able to hold anything down. I felt a thrill way down, at my innermost core.

Finally, I found the selections of salads and decided that this would be my safest choice. I put some lettuce on a cold plate, a few sliced tomatoes wedges; a smattering of black and green olives; three slices of cucumber, and then added a glob of ranch dressing on the side. The plate rattled on the tray as I turned and walked back over to our table. I struggled to keep it level and not spill.

I hoped the salad would keep my stomach from growling. I prayed that I would be able to eat it and hold it in my stomach.

As I approached the table, I could hear a few snatches of their conversation and my name whispered several times. Cliff stood up from his seat again, walked around and adjusted my chair for me as I sat down.

I looked up at him, "Thank you." I groaned, my was voice, husky. His eyes spoke silently to something inside of me.

'God, he was even more handsome this close to me.'

"And what were you two gentlemen chatting so happily about while I was away?" I asked. I was curious as to why Cliff appeared to have been asking my boss about me.

All the while my brain ran wild like a runaway circus parade. I couldn't stop the wild thoughts forming in my brain. Thoughts of going places, doing things, having time alone to share my life with this man.

'He must have some ulterior motive. Perhaps he and Larry were preparing some practical joke on me Yes, that's it. The jokes on me and I'm falling for it, head over heels.'

"Oh, nothing of importance," Larry offered.

"Just taking some notes about a certain pretty lady who is gracing our table today," Cliff teased, looking me straight in the eyes and nearly causing me to swoon.

I wanted to reach over and dab that crumb of buttered bread on his lips with my finger. I shook my head as if trying to get a stray hair out of my eyes, but in reality trying to force my eyes somewhere other than those tempting lips.

"Oh? And what lady might that be? And just exactly what were these notes? May I see your notepad, please?"

I chewed on my lip, wishing desperately to know what Larry had told him. *'Does he know? Can he read my thoughts?'*

Cliff tapped his head with his finger, "All up here, Tina, safely locked away from prying eyes."

"That is not fair," I pouted.

Larry saved me from further embarrassing myself by poking Cliff in the side,

"That's enough flirting with my assistant, Cliff. How's the tower coming? I can see a lot of the exterior glass attached. Can I get a quick tour when we drop you off?"

'Flirting? Is that what Cliff is doing? GAH! My heart leaped in my chest.*'Surely not. Why would he 'flirt' with me? I'm a nobody, just an unneeded lunch guest. ...But then, if that's true...'*

"Only on the condition that you allow Tina to accompany us," Cliff looked over at me and smiled. "That is... if she would like to tag along."

'Tag along?' I was not about to let this hunk out of my sight.

"I wouldn't dream of letting Larry venture in without me. He would probably miss out on something important -- like we had wanted a twenty-four story building and the one there has only twenty-three," I laughed.

"Ouch, that hurt," Larry grimaced. "You have such little faith in my abilities," he joked, and then gave me a strange wink of his eye as if he was in on some great secret.

My cheeks flushed again. '*Larry, I need help here, not all my secrets told behind my back.*'

"Not to fear, Tina. I counted the floors just before I came down to meet you guys and I can assure you that there are a full twenty-four floors under construction." Cliff smiled.

His eyes met mine again and that smile. I felt like melting into the floor.

The waitress brought out the men's lunch and set it before them. Cliff had ordered, as promised, a mouth-watering lobster tail and ribeye steak with a side order of baked potato and Brussel-sprouts.

It looked so delicious that I wished that my appetite had not taken a wrong exit somewhere on the south loop. I had no idea what Larry had ordered. My mind and eyes could only fixate on the man sitting directly across from me, causing my mind to spin in circles; my stomach to fill with butterflies, and strange thoughts nearly escaping from my mouth.

Just at that moment a large tugboat chugged by close to our window and gave a long blast on its fog horn, distracting nearly all of the diners. Several of the younger children rushed over and put their faces against the window glass to get a closer look.

I stirred my salad around randomly trying to focus my attention somewhere other than three feet across from me. Finally, I stabbed one of the tomato wedges with my fork, lifted it to my lips and looked across at Cliff. He was chewing away on a delicious looking chunk of lobster.

'*God, I'm so jealous. Lobster is one of my favorite treats.*'

Sadly, I looked down at my salad and lifted a leaf of lettuce, twirled it into the ranch dressing. Pushing the lettuce between my lips I relished the smooth taste of the dressing. I desperately tried to distract my thoughts to food rather than those lips tasting that tempting lobster tail. But I didn't have much success.

'Perhaps a cucumber might do the trick,' I mused, stabbing it with my fork.

'Focus, Tina. Don't make a fool out of yourself. He's just a good-looking guy who has no interest in you.'

I tried to distract my eyes from Cliff by staring out at the ship channel. I watched the boats passing by lazily. My mind was in overdrive trying to understand why my body was being affected so strongly by the attraction of our lunch guest.

I was like a goofy teenager, my breath panting over a good looking high school football quarterback. My palms were sweating, and I could feel the pounding of my heart. I knew that I would have to make a trip to the Ladies room to fix my makeup before I could escape from the restaurant at this rate. I had nearly finished my plate of salad and was trying to distract myself by watching a fishing vessel slip by when my irrational thoughts were interrupted by a query from Cliff.

"So, Tina, did you have any specific ideas for the changes Larry has been telling me about?" Cliff smiled again.

'Oh what exquisite white teeth.'

'What?'

I was taken off guard when I finally realized they wanted me to say something.

'Had they been talking? I hadn't caught a word, so wrapped up in other things, like the lock of hair falling over his forehead, the way he swirled his small slice of steak in the sauce.'

"Excuse me; I was distracted by the boats passing," *I mumbled out loud, at the same time my cheeks took on the same tint as the tomato on my fork.*

"Larry was saying," Cliff replied, "that he thinks we should rework the layout on floor eleven and seventeen. Move some of the staff into smaller cubicles so that we can fit all of the new people into the existing space. I wasn't sure, and Larry says you're usually pretty good with suggestions and are more familiar with this project,"

He stroked his chin as he brought me up to date on the discussion.

'*Ummm. Please --let me do that for you.*'

'*Get it together, Tina,*' I screamed at myself.

"Oh! …yes! I did come up with a thought. But let's wait until the waiter clears the dishes so I can show you my ideas."

I could not believe it. I had been able to form a complete thought in the middle of my confusion. I was excited,

'*Cliff wants my opinion. Wow!*'

Larry motioned for one of the wait staff to come over,

"Hi… We need to use the table for some office talk. Can you have the dishes cleared away to give us some room?"

"Yes, sir. With pleasure." The waiter motioned for one of the bus boys to come over with his cart and quickly cleared the table of our plates and silverware.

"Will there be anything else, sir?"

"Yes, could we each have a glass of cold water?"

I wish that he had ordered a double Bourbon on the rocks. I desperately needed some liquid reinforcement.

"Yes. Coming right up, would you like any dessert?" the waiter asked hopefully.

"No, that will be it for now." Larry waved the waiter off.

I gave thanks to heaven. I could not have even swallowed a raisin at this point.

As the waiter left, I reached down beside me and lifted my manila folder and then asked Larry if it would be okay to show my suggestions.

My hands were trembling; my heart was pounding, beating nearly out of my chest.

'*Don't blow it, Tina. Keep calm. Just go over the plans slowly. You'll be all right.*' My subconscious seemed to be totally confident in my abilities.

Me -- not so much.

"Sure thing, I am kind of anxious to see them myself," Larry said. "I hadn't thought to dig out the actual plans. I was just working from memory. Your idea to review the plans is so much better."

A waitress arrived with our water. Larry motioned to put all three glasses close to the window so that we could work on the plans.

That was a good thing. My hands were shaking so much I surely would have spilled the water all over myself, or worse, perhaps even on our lunch guest.

'*Crap, Crap, Crap.*'

I dug a fingernail into my palm trying to see if some pain would clear my mind. And, wouldn't you know, just at that moment Cliff reached up and ran his hand through his loose hair again, my focus lost, my brain nearly misfired.

'*Please, Cliff, let me do that for you,*' I begged.

I flushed. I prayed that I had not said that out loud.

Cliff looked at me quizzically, a small smile parting his lips. His tongue gently stroked across those luscious looking lips.

'*Ahh!*' I dug even deeper with my fingernails. Finally, my mind began to clear away some of the fog. The rush of pheromones had totally destroyed my train of thought. I could barely remember my name.

'*I wonder is this what taking heroin did to druggies. If so, I desperately need a fix.*'

'*GOD, have mercy on me,*' I begged.

He didn't.

Cliff flashed his billboard quality smile; his teeth perfect in every way, "Are you okay?"

'*Okay? Okay? How can you ask that when all that I want to do is rush over there and...? And What...? Exactly What Did I Want?*' I wondered.

'*The answer crossed my brain in a flash. ...NO! -- That. Could. Not. Be. So.*"

I immediately dismissed the pornographic video from my mind.

'*That was insane. But...*'

"Sure, I am fine. It must have been that cucumber. It had too much oil on it." I mumbled.

I realized that I needed to call Dr. Stanton, my old psychiatrist. I was desperately in need of treatment.

'I wonder, does he makes restaurant calls?' I almost reached in my purse for my cell to call him.

I squeezed my toes inside my shoes. I leaned on the sides of the shoes, desperate for something, anything to distract my errant thoughts and bring them into focus.

This is my big opportunity to shine.

'Don't blow it, Tina, Don't blow it, Tina.'

I repeated that over and over to myself.

These feelings and thoughts that I'm having – where the hell were they coming from? This guy, ohhhhhhh! This guy is so wonderfully handsome and nice. What the hell is going on with me? I must be going insane. And that last thought -- about what I wanted. God! If he had any idea of my true thoughts, I would have to jump in the ship channel and drown. This was so embarrassing. I had pictured the two of us, together, in my apartment. I was stepping into the shower behind him. We were both naked............ **OHHHHHHHHHHHHHHH!** *I saw myself taking a sponge and helping him wash his body. Our lips pressed together in a passionate kiss. My hand stroking his stomach, reaching down.........*

I kicked myself under the table, HARD.

"OWWW! That hurt!"

"Excuse me?" Cliff questioned. "What's wrong? Did I step on your toe?"

'God, could this be ANY more embarrassing?'

"No, I'm sorry. My shoe pinched me; it's a bit tight today."

'Please, dear Lord, just let me get through this. I'll do anything you want. Just let me get through this.'

CHAPTER 4

I braced myself, took a deep breath, slowly pulled the string tab on the envelope and lifted the flap. I reached in and retrieved the blueprints that I had drawn on earlier. Spreading them out on the table, I thumbed through them until I located the one for floor eight.

Or it seemed to be floor eight. I couldn't be sure. Nothing on the page made much sense to my eyes. They could only focus on Cliff's strong right hand as it reached across to assist me in spreading the papers, his fingers gently brushing against mine.

'*Ummmmmm.*' I sighed.

I turned and addressed Larry. I did not want to give the impression that I was the one going to lead the meeting or embarrass my boss. Nor did I want to make it any more obvious, than I had already, that I was enamored of our guest.

I mumbled a silent prayer to the god of VP assistants.

'*Please -- help me. Please!*'

"Larry, I was looking at the blueprints, and I saw two floors that are currently unassigned. If I remember correctly, these were the ones that we had originally planned to lease out to a client. Especially since we did not need the floor space at the time the plans were being formed."

"Wow!" Larry responded. "I had totally forgotten about those, Tina. Great catch! Please continue. Let's have a look at what you have."

He turned to Cliff, "Like I said, she's the best. Always coming to my rescue just when it is needed." Larry emphasized my skills to Cliff.

I was totally flattered; Larry was impressed, I felt a thrill that my boss had given me such a sincere compliment in front of Cliff. Gaining strength from Larry's praise, I further calmed my nervous voice, my fingers stopped trembling.

"All right gentlemen. I brought these blueprints for reference. My notes are pretty crude, and I am sure that you both can do better than I, but this might give you some ideas."

'I suddenly felt stronger. I'm going to get throught this after all. Thank you, Lord.'

With that, I pushed my finger along a crease in the paper to help it lay flat.

At the same time, Cliff reached over and did the same; our fingers met in the middle. The touch of his skin on mine was electric.

"...Oh," Realizing that I had said that out loud, I blushed.

'I mumbled, drawing my hand back and desperately fighting the urge to have Cliff hold it again. Evidently there was no 'god of VP assistants,' I was all alone in this, there was no one going to save me.'

I stood and walked to their side of the table so that I could more easily highlight my changes. Cliff stood as well, moving next to me as I leaned over the plans. My hip brushed against his.

'Ummm.' I no longer cared if Cliff heard me or not.

I stepped an inch further away and tried not to stand too close. Even so his hand settled on the table beside my own and brushed against mine as I gestured here and there at my scribbles. I tried to focus my mind on the blueprint.

'Gah! I don't think I can take much more of this.'

I felt like melting into Cliff's arms and letting him kiss me passionately. I dug the toe of my shoe into my left heel.

'I hope that Larry is not seeing this. I'll never live this down if he tells anyone back at the office.' I thought desperately.

"Let me see now; this is the eighth floor, all that I did was trace in the restroom facilities from some of the other floors. Then I thought it might be a nice touch to add in two larger offices on each end for managers with a conference room beside the main elevator.

"For the regular staff, I was wondering if we could do something like half-height cubicles on the outside areas and this whole area surrounded by half-glass partitions. The entire staff, as well as visitors, could then enjoy some spectacular views of the surrounding city and towers.

"There are also areas for a copy and printer room and a break area for staff. We should be able to locate about fifty people on each floor this way. What do you men think?"

I felt reinvigorated as I finished my little speech and looked over at Cliff only to be lost again in those deep pools of brown copper. My hand had come to rest against Cliff's as I spoke my last thought.

I refused to move it again. It just felt so nice where it was.

He smiled at me and then turned back to study the plans for a moment. Then he turned to Larry,

His thumb reached up and slid across my knuckles.

'**Mmmmm**." I purred. His touch was like a burning match to an old piece of paper. My entire body was on fire, desperate for him to hold me.

'If he keeps doing that I'm going to need an ambulance.'

"I see what you mean. She has some great ideas here. We can probably toy around a bit with them, but from my initial review, I don't see any major changes that would be better than this. What do you think, Larry?"

Larry shrugged and pointed to Cliff's tubes.

"Looks like the ones that you brought along won't be necessary. We can work directly from this copy."

Cliff turned back to me, his eyes meeting mine again,

"I assume that the ones you have for floor fourteen will be similar?"

My knees were weak; I nearly sank into his chair. My tongue was twisted into a knot and was dry as a bone. I pinched my arm hard and finally got my tongue working again. Cliff had said that my ideas were great.

"I liked more than his ideas. That was for sure. I was desperate to say something intelligent, but it seemed that everything coming out of my mouth was just blabber. I bit my lip to help steady my nerves.

"Yes," My voice came out sounding like a frog.

GAH! I struggled to clear my throat.

"but they don't have to be," my voice cleared again.

I flipped through the papers and put the one for fourteen over floor eight pointing to the changes that were different from the other floor plan.

"I thought we might make this one the Division Head suite and private exit on this side; with an entry office here for their assistant. The other managers' office would be at the opposite end of the floor, the conference room located just here in the center, opposite the staff cubicles as I have drawn there."

'DAMN, DAMN, DAMN,' he brushed my palm again with his own.

I bit my lip -- hard.

'I wish that I had something stronger to drink than water. I wonder if they serve Scotch? Or maybe Hemlock? It would be a faster death, or so I have heard. 'Sigh... That hair hanging down over his forehead was out of place again. Surely he wouldn't mind if I just reached up and....'

Larry looked over at me and smiled, saving me from myself again.

"Great work, Tina."

Then he turned to Cliff,

"Like I always say 'Tina has saved my rear on more than one occasion.' It looks like I owe her big time on this."

Cliff dragged the plans over close to Larry and pointed out my pencil sketches. "What do you think, Larry?"

"What I think is that we need you," Larry said, winking at me for some strange reason, "who know a lot more about floor plans than either of us, to take these back to your office. Go over them carefully with the drafting team to see what can be added or changed, or whatever it is that you guys do to make the magic happen."

"Great, I can get started on that first thing tomorrow," Cliff smiled again. "This afternoon we have an issue on floor nine that I need to deal with first. If it is okay with you guys it has been a while since I have been to this restaurant; I would like to take a stroll around the walkway and koi ponds, unless, that is, you guys are in a hurry to get back to your office."

"That would be great. Why don't you take Tina on ahead while I pay the check?" Larry offered.

"I thought that you would never ask," Cliff flashed that billboard smile and reached for my hand. "Shall we go?" he whispered to me.

'I would go just about anywhere with you right now.'

My hand automatically reached out to claim his without my mind even thinking. I curled my fingers inside his palm; I knew. deep down inside me, that I had found something wonderful. I took a deep breath and let it out slowly. I felt exhilarated as we turned and walked to the exit. I looked back and saw Larry's eyes were following us with a smug smile on his face. I stuck my tongue out at him as he smiled back.

(*Traitor!*)

Something told me Larry had noticed my attraction to Cliff and was just playing along, to give us some private time. I could only pray that I lived long enough to reach the truck in the parking lot.

'*Oh, if only Larry could stay in the restaurant for another twenty minutes, maybe I could get Cliff to let me taste those luscious lips!*' My cheeks blushed a bright red at the sinful thought.

"Are you all right?" Cliff looked at me strangely.

"Sure, just got a little overheated, the humidity is very high today." I lied.

Walking out of the restaurant and down the wooden walkway, we strolled beside the charming Koi stream surrounding the restaurant. After a few minutes Cliff paused and turned to me, looking me directly in my eyes he asked:

"Tina, is there any chance that we might meet again, say for a dinner? I would suggest a movie, but that would put us in a crowd of other people and a movie blasting in our ears, and we wouldn't have a chance to talk and learn more about each other. I feel certain that you have felt something happening between us. We need to explore that before we miss our chance."

Our hands, bound together by his firm grip, had a calming effect on my nerves. I drew strength from him like a magnet drawing an iron nail to itself. My breathing began to steady, my heart slowed. I suddenly realized he felt the same nervousness as I. We were both struggling to find ways to break down the barriers between us. He was truly interested in knowing me.

"Yes, Cliff, I would love that as long as I get to pick the restaurant." Letting go of one hand, I reached into my purse and pulled out one of my business cards and offered it to him. He captured my hand again unexpectedly and took the card and brushed my knuckles with his thumb again.

'*The sensations went straight to my inner core.* **Ummmmmmmm.**'

I knew that I wanted to see him again. In fact, I wanted to stay with him longer today. The old fear of being with a man alone rose like a chill up my spine; I willed it away. I wanted to know Cliff better and resolved to do whatever it might take.

We were interrupted by a shout from Larry as he exited the restaurant,

"Hey, wait up you guys. You forgot the blueprints," he shouted, waving them above his head with a ridiculous smile on his face. "Let's head on back to the tower; I'm anxious to see all of the work you and your crew have done."

He winked rather mischievously at me.

I blushed, certain that Larry had noticed the fact that Cliff was now holding both of my hands. This time, when we reached Larry's truck, I had the thrill of having Cliff assist me in climbing into my seat. His hands around my waist were firm and gentle as he lifted me. He squeezed in beside me and again took my hand. My fingers curled up naturally offering no resistance. I let them rest there, inside his, on his thigh.

'*Oh, happy days.*' I thought to myself.

My fear of being alone with Cliff was like a dark shadow in the corner. No matter how much that I might be attracted to him I was still hesitant to put myself in a position where Larry or someone else was not close.

I wondered if it might somehow be possible; could I ever overcome that fear of being alone with a man? Especially this man whose simple touch seemed to set my nerve endings on fire. I knew that at some point, if I kept sending out romantic signals, Cliff would be looking for more than a dinner date and then what would I do? But I could not seem to control my emotions when I was around him. I almost felt like giggling, I was so happy.

As long as it was going out to a movie or restaurant where there would be lots of other people around, and I could meet him there, and then leave on my own, I was okay. Inevitably guys always wanted to hook up and get me alone in a car, in a house, or worse, their apartment. For seventeen years I had been able to fend off that kind of attachment.

'Did I want that to happen with Cliff? He seemed like a very caring person, well-mannered, clean, polite and attentive. I was attracted to him, and he seemed to reciprocate the feeling.'

'He's the one,' my subconscious whispered to my heart.

I could no longer argue the point.

'Perhaps,'

I let the thought trail off as a warm feeling of happiness swept through my body.

CHAPTER 5

The drive back to the tower was less eventful. No cars cut us off, and the traffic was light with only the typical Houston freeway backup.

My hand remained inside Cliff's and my nerve endings tingled, but the confusing rush of thoughts had disappeared. His touch had a calming effect on me; my body settled, my mind focused. I was happy and at peace. I wanted to be here with him more than anything in the world.

This time, when Larry pulled into the tower parking lot he was able to find an area near the door that was cleared of debris. Cliff opened the passenger door, grabbed his hat and vest and hopped down just before Larry had come to a complete stop. He was sure-footed and quickly turned and extended his hand to assist my descent.

I grabbed my purse and then gripped the handle beside the door frame and slid down, eager to feel Cliff's touch again.

His arm encircled my waist as he let me down gently. I could feel the strength of his arm supporting me. I remained in his hold slightly longer than was needed to lower me from the truck. After a long moment, he took my hand again and we turned toward the open doorway. It was if there had been some secret, unspoken agreement between us.

Larry had to do a quick step trying to catch up to us.

"You guys have somewhere to be right now? You don't seem to be interested in these things any longer!" He teased, holding up the blueprints again as he winked at me.

I flushed again,

"Come on, Larry. Don't be such a slow-poke." I joked. "There are twenty-four floors in this building, and I might want to tour each and every one. We might never have such an excellent tour guide again."

I had never felt this happy before. I couldn't point to anything that had happened between us since that first moment we had seen each other that made any sense. I just knew that the man holding my hand was the 'more' that I had been searching for these many years.

Cliff and I wandered around the first floor with Larry tagging behind as Cliff pointed out various rooms that were nearing completion, and explained some of the special features. Cliff stopped at his temporary office on floor two and picked up two hard hats for us. He explained that the building was under construction and that safety regulations required all workers and visitors wear hard hats at all times.

Cliff smiled and helped me adjust the straps on my helmet so that it did not bounce around on my head. Clifff had released my hand for the first time since we had left the restaurant. My mind began racing again, questioning, searching. I felt alone for the first time in over an hour. I didn't like the feeling.

Larry hung back just far enough from us that I still felt comfortable but also gave us several feet of space to ourselves.

"A penny for your thoughts, Tina." Cliff ventured, capturing my hand in his again.

The moment that we touched the troubled thoughts in my head vanished.

"Oh, sorry. I was just admiring the work that your crew has done. Do you have any idea of a projected completion date yet?" I questioned, trying to focus his thoughts back to the building.

It was too soon to reveal what I wanted to say to him.

"We hadn't put a firm date to it yet, Tina, but at least another six to eight months before the building is completely ready. Several of the lower floors should be ready in a few more weeks. Depending on how many changes we have to make to the floors we discussed today. Those might be ready within a month or so since they are currently completely vacant, and won't require us to dismantle stuff we already have in place.

Several floors are ready now for the Plexiglas skins, but deliveries were delayed due to confusion at the manufacturer. We should have the upper floors framed and ready for their exterior skins in about another two months. The interior work will continue, probably beyond the eight months. We will need to make changes that your company will want as we get nearer to the completion date. Some of the areas will require a specialist, such as the new data center where they will be installing heavy duty air handlers ---"

I suddenly became aware that his thumb was sliding back and forth across my knuckles sending waves of pleasure up my arm. I lost track of his words. My focus switched to his calm breathing, the gentle way that he squeezed my hand, and the line of his chin as he spoke. Oh, and that delicious smell, a mixture of pine scented bath soap and something distinctly male.

"...and join crews working on the upper ones."

He turned and looked at me again. I looked around, pretending as if I had been paying close attention.

I had only been hearing the gentle kindness in his voice. I loved the pride that he took in his work, the way his eyes lit up with excitement over this or that detail. And something else that I couldn't quite identify in the way he looked at me.

"Is there a different floor that you wish to see next, Tina?" Cliff questioned.

"Whoa, Cliff," I replied. "You lost me back there when you talked about air handlers. It is a good thing that we have got you running this show because it would be totally over my head."

I smiled and lost myself again in those bright brown eyes as he returned my gaze. I chewed on my lip, the pain keeping my errant thoughts at bay. His lips were moist and inviting; I desperately wanted to feel them pressed against mine.

"Sorry, Tina, I just enjoy the excitement of a large project like this and get carried away when people want to know more," Cliff said while looking over toward where Larry was standing.

"Hey, Larry, do you want to see your new office? I believe the area is framed in, so you should be able to get a pretty good idea of your new digs."

"You bet I would," Larry brightened up at that thought. "Lead on!"

Cliff soon ushered us into a freight elevator and we made our way to the sixteenth floor. The elevator doors opened up on an area strewn with stacks of ceiling tiles, drywall, and other construction materials. The smell was clean but had a strong odor of fresh paint. Cliff led us down the hallway and to the right where he pointed to an area which was framed with drywall. The ceiling tiles were installed, and the entry door was leaning against one of the walls. The lighting fixtures hung loosely just below the ceiling tiles, not yet fully attached in place.

Larry was very happy with his office size and wandered from side to side, seemingly trying to place his new desk and cabinets in their places in his mind's eye.

"Hey, Tina. Look at the view from here. It's simply spectacular." Larry cried as he strolled over to his window. "Just look at those office towers stretching from there all the way to the other side of downtown."

I watched as Larry took in all of the details of his new office to be and smiled. I knew how much pride that he took in having a clean, tidy office with everything in its place.

The view from my vantage point was pretty good too. Cliff was a very handsome man. Muscular arms, taught body, strong chin, tempting lips, I could go on forever.

He released my hand to move Larry's door away from the entrance to my office. I suddenly felt alone again.

"Hey, Tina," Cliff warm voice interrupted my thoughts. "Your office is just over here. Come, let's take a look."

I took one step and my fear instinct erupted out of nowhere.

'You cannot go with Cliff alone,' it warned.

I felt the comfort of my pistol in my purse but knew there was no way that I could ever pull that on Cliff.

'Still, who knew if there might be someone behind a wall waiting to grab me, able to knock out Cliff before he could respond?'

"Larry," I called out, "can you come along? Cliff wants to show me my office."

"Why don't you two go along? I will be right there." Larry suggested.

I froze. *'No way could I follow Cliff without Larry.'*

"Larry, come on, don't be a drag. Let's go." I begged firmly.

"Okay, I am right behind you." Larry finally relented and stepped in line behind me.

'I felt safe again as Cliff captured my hand in his, Larry was my rock; I had known Cliff for less than two hours. Perhaps my imagination had blown things out of proportion. Maybe I just had a bad case of wishful thinking. Oh! How would I ever know? How could I be certain? I could be misreading all of his signals. Damn! How had I gotten into this mess? And more specifically, did I want to get myself out of it? It was decision time! I had to stop playing this game of cat and mouse. Should I go left or right? I couldn't find an answer anywhere.'

I looked around at Larry, but he simply looked back at me, confused and unable to understand what I was trying to ask of him. He shrugged his shoulders.

'Oh! Men! They are just no help when you need them.'

The state of my new office was not as complete as Larry's, but there were enough drywall, ceiling tiles and a couple of loose hanging light fixtures already in place that it provided a good understanding. It was much larger than my existing one, and I was happy to see my window view was almost as impressive as Larry's.

"Anything special you would like us to do for your office, Tina?" Cliff asked.

'It would be perfect if you could stay in here with me every day so that I could kiss you whenever I wanted,' I thought to myself.

Looking up at his face and speaking aloud I said, "Perhaps, you could put the electrical outlets on the floor. I just hate having all those long electrical cords stretching everywhere to the walls looking messy and hazardous if you trip over one."

"Sure thing, Tina. Once I have your desk and credenza sizes, and you provide a schematic of where you want them that should be fairly easy. Anytime you think of something else; please give me a call."

'I could use an hour or two in your arms right now,' I thought. *'And I definitely could think of several things to occupy our time.'*

"I will check the order forms for my furniture and fax it over to you. Is your fax number on our company employee-index?"

"Sure thing. Just check under Clifford Stinson. My cell and fax number are both listed."

I wondered if he wouldn't mind if I called him tonight. We could chat over the phone, and I could get a better understanding of how he feels about me. I knew for sure that I was desperate to learn more about him.

Cliff continued our tour, including one of the floors without its external Plexiglas skin. When the elevator door opened, the wind was biting and whipped through my pants legs and blouse giving me a chill. I stepped closer to Cliff to have his body block the wind.

"It is very chilly up here," I said. "and scary too. I feel like I might trip over something and fall all the way back down to the ground."

What I wanted was to trip and have Cliff fall on top of me and kiss me passionately. The longer I was this close to him the wilder my thoughts became. I knew that I had to get away. Have some time to catch my breath. To organize my thoughts, to make up my mind about the things that I was feeling.

"Tina, I would never let that happen to you," Cliff responded as he took hold of my hand again.

I felt safer and warmer almost immediately. I inched even closer and could feel his warmth through my clothing. I desperately wanted his hands on me, touching me, caressing me, warming my body.

"You are so warm," I cried over the howling wind, "how can you be so warm with the wind like this?"

'*Was this the sign that I was so desperate to find? My hand in his, my nerves calming every time we touch?*'

"You get used to it. I have been doing this kind of work for many years, and my body has learned to adjust." He replied. "Come, we need to get you back inside the building, I see that you are too chilly out here."

"Larry, have you seen enough or is there something else you would like to look over?" Cliff inquired.

'*Oh no. Cliff, I don't want to leave just yet.*' I tried to think of something that would keep me here, close to him.

"No, I think we have taken up more than enough of your time," Larry responded.

My heart sank in disappointment.

"We'll let you go back to your job now, Cliff, and I'll take Tina back to our office. Give me a call when you and your team have the revised plans for the floors we discussed. I'll drop by and pick them up so that upper management can give their final approval."

"*Or, I could come by myself, say tomorrow? We could sit and talk, you could show me more of the building, and perhaps I can steal a kiss or two.*'

"That would be great," Larry agreed.

'*What would be great? Had I said something out loud? GAH! I'm going to die right here.*'

"OK, let's head on back," Cliff said, his voice a whisper above the sound of the wind in my ears. "I'll escort you two back to your ride. I'll see you, then tomorrow."

'*What a relief! Cliff must have offered to come by on Wednesday, and I had missed it., Thank God! I'm going to need a tranquilizer the next time we meet. My thoughts are going to get me into serious trouble.*'

I held on to Cliffs' hand until he assisted me back into the truck. As we drove away, I looked back and waved. He stood there, watching me, until Larry finally turned a corner and we could no longer see each other.

I missed the feel of his hand already. My hands were cold. I rubbed them together to get the circulation running. It didn't seem to work as well as Cliff's palms enclosing them within his own.

Larry looked over at me after we had gone a few blocks.

"You two certainly seemed to be a hit with each other. You were like two love birds, walking here and there, and never letting go of each other's hands."

My cheeks turned a bright red, I looked out the passenger window.

"Oh, did we? I didn't even notice."

Larry gave a loud snort.

I blushed even brighter. "Say, isn't that the new Neiman-Marcus store over there," I desperately needed to change the subject.

"I don't know about that, but I think your mind is still back there in the tower from the look of your cheeks," he teased.

"Hush, I don't know what you're talking about." I turned completely to the side and was quiet the rest of the trip.

Larry whistled a little tune that I didn't appreciate. I think it was a recent hit by Lady Gaga titled *Poker Face*.

I squirmed the entire time. He was doing this deliberately.

"Shame on you, Larry," I shrugged.

He ignored me and kept whistling.

The further away the truck traveled from the tower, the more my thoughts became disturbed.

'Who was this Cliff guy anyway? How did he get me so upset? Just another guy who would break my heart when I chased him away with my fears. He was probably just playing along with Larry, teasing me, making me feel foolish, and then revealing that it was all some silly practical joke.'

'But those eyes, those lips. I wanted to see them again, to taste them against my own. His touch ignited a spark in my body that drove me wild. I wanted to twist my fingers in his luscious hair, to kiss his lips until he swallowed me whole. I wanted him to sit beside me in the truck again, our legs touching, my hand swallowed up inside his.'

"We're almost there, Tina," Larry interrupted my daydream again. "You might want to stop by the Ladies room again and check the air in those tires!"

"Larry, I don't know what you are talking about, and besides, I don't have any tires, silly."

I only wished that it were as simple as that. I would have an air pump installed in the powder room by tomorrow. My mind ran the entire lunch episode over again like a TV rerun. *'What had just happened to me? Exactly what was it about this man that got me so upset? He was super handsome, sure, but was that all? Had I been fooled by a good looking face and a bunch of muscles?'*

'What had this man done to me in the space of a few minutes that had upset my entire world? Changed my feelings about being alone with a man. How was that possible? Could this possibly be what I had read about in books? I had no personal knowledge of love other than that which I had for my parents. But this was different than that. Much stronger, I felt drawn to this man like a magnet. I wanted to be with him, to learn more about him. For the first time in my life, I wanted to kiss a man on his lips. I wanted to kiss Clifford Stinson on his lips.'

I tried stretching my arms and legs when I got back to my office. I had to get rid of this tightness in my body. I twisted my arms behind my back and pulled my shoulders tight. Oh, that felt so good. But when I sat down in my chair, I felt a shiver run throughout my entire body.

'God! That man was driving me wild, and he isn't even here.'

I picked up my desk phone receiver and looked up his name on the office on-line employee list. Yes, there it was, Clifford Stinson. I dialed the first six digits and stopped. I couldn't think of what I might say. I hung up the phone and felt confused. I desperately wanted to speak with him again but was unable to come up with an excuse for the call.

'Damn. Why hadn't I left my purse there or maybe one of my shoes? That would have given me the perfect excuse. Let's see, did he say anything that I might call and inquire about saying that I was confused or forgotten to ask?

'Oh, yes. He hadn't shown us the heliPad site. I started to dial again but stopped at the third number. Why would I call about that? I don't fly helicopters myself, and couldn't think of a reason why the company would have me flying around in one of theirs.'

My stomach had an ache in it as if I hadn't had anything to eat since breakfast. Come to think of it; I had only that small salad. I usually only ate a salad along with a large lunch, and my stomach was rather angry at me today.

My stomach rumbled several times when Larry had called me to his office. It was very embarrassing. Especially when Larry asked me if I was hungry.

'GAH! He was really enjoying torturing me. -- Awrgg!'

'Ohhhhhhh! Men! They get you all excited and leave you hanging. Oh, well. I probably would have to let him go after the dinner on Friday. As soon as I gave him my ground rules, he would probably want to dump me as soon as he could.'

I moped around my office for the rest of the afternoon, fiddling with papers that were completed already. Finally, at 4:30 p.m. I gave up, told Larry I was heading out early and left for the day. I hoped that tomorrow would be better.

'Perhaps I can convince Larry to take us to lunch again.'

'Shoot. Then I would have to go without food again. No, that won't do.'

CHAPTER 6

That evening Marianne had the most wonderful pot roast prepared with all the trimmings. Baked potatoes, green beans, carrots, purple hull peas and a sumptuous brown gravy. I was starved, this Cliff guy had upset my equilibrium, I'd only eaten a small salad for lunch and had paid the price the entire afternoon. I ate two full helpings of the pot roast and three helpings of the cobbler. Both Charlotte and Marianne watched in amazement. I had never done anything like that before in my life.

As we were sitting around after dinner, Charlotte brought me up to date on a disturbing bit of information. Totally oblivious to my surroundings I had not noticed Charlotte following not far behind Larry's truck. She had observed the black sedan which had cut our truck off on Broadway Street. She was able to take down the license plate number of the car.

"I found the license plate information using one of my contacts in the police department," Charlotte reported. "The plate was stolen. The plate on the sedan did not match the car which had cut you off short. There was no information about the sedan as it was a common model in town. However, from my vantage point traveling behind both vehicles it had seemed that the incident seemed to have been deliberate, rather than a random action.

"I'm currently following up with any other information on either the car, plate or three occupants that I saw inside the car. I was tempted to follow the car after it fled the scene. Then I decided it was better to follow Larry's truck in case that the car tried to intercept you guys at some other location. I'm also waiting to obtain a possible photo of the occupants from my police contact, just in case they had run a red-light camera in the area."

"I'm very concerned," Marianne added. "Please be careful, there are just so many bad people in the world."

We discussed the unusual event for another fifteen minutes, but could arrive at no firm conclusion as it still might have been just an accident.

"Don't you recall anything about the car or occupants?" Charlotte asked.

"No, my thoughts had been so wrapped up in the new office plans. I had no time to focus on the car," I replied, not wanting to give her too many details.

My stomach, now full and happy, allowed my mind to drift as I mused over my lunch escort. The touch of his hand when it held mine. The electric tingle when our fingers or legs touched. The deep brown of his eyes. The lock of his hair, hanging down nearly to his eyes. I could almost feel my hand reaching up and smoothing it back again.

'Oh! I had that same tingle in my stomach again.'

Charlotte broke through my spell. "All right, Tina, out with it. You have been dragging around the apartment like a lost duck for the past hour. What is up with you? And that dinner, you ate enough to satisfy a horse."

"To tell the truth, I met someone today." I wanted to sigh but held back mightily against the temptation.

"By 'someone' I surmise that you are speaking of 'someone of the opposite sex?" Marianne teased.

"Okay, give it up, girl," Charlotte demanded. "I had my eye on you at lunch, and you did seem a bit distracted. I thought that was just you being excited to be showing those guys those plans you had brought along. I did notice that you hardly ate anything except a small salad, which is not like you at all. Now out with it. We want to hear all of the juicy details."

"I... I... It was all so sudden" I flushed. "Cliff walked out of this door, and I just went haywire. I could not think straight. Every time my hand brushed against his I felt an electric tingle. When our legs brushed against each other in Larry's truck *oooh!* My heart beat nearly out of my chest. And his smell was so overwhelming, I just couldn't get enough.

"My mind went crazy when he got into the truck and sat beside me. I thought that I could sense some of the same reaction in his breathing. It seemed to catch whenever our fingers touched. He held my hand, and I felt as if I had found a new home. I felt safe and protected when I looked into his eyes."

"You've got it bad, girl. Go on, tell us more. What was, ...you say his name is Cliff? What was this guy Cliff like? Did you kiss, or possibly from the sound of it, go straight to home base," Charlotte teased.

I turned completely red. "Charlotte, how shocking! How could you even think that? No, certainly not, all that we did was hold hands. Nearly the entire afternoon he held my hand. His hand was just so-- nice to feel the strength his hand on mine. It made me feel so safe."

My thoughts drifted back again as I looked down at my hand, wishing that Cliff were here to let me place it inside his again.

I wish that he was here now and that I could feel him next to me again. I wanted to kiss him so badly. I had never really kissed a man in my entire life. I only knew that this man was the only one in the entire world that I wanted to experience that thrill.

"I know, I watched you two out by the Koi ponds," Charlotte said with a smile. "You two looked so sweet together. I did notice that you hardly ever let go of his hand."

I flushed.

Marianne broke into my thoughts "I remember once in High School; Ted Houston was my boyfriend at the time. Every time he kissed me I thought I would faint straight away." Suddenly she woke from her daydream and looked at us. "Why don't we catch a good TV show or something?"

While Charlotte fiddled with the remote control, Marianne smiled at me.

"You see. I told you so. I told you that someday someone was going to come and wake up your heart. He's going to be the one. I told you, didn't I?" Marianne giggled.

"Yes, Marianne. You did tell me. But I just never expected it to happen really. At least not like this. It was so sudden, I don't know what it was, his smile, his touch.'

'*OHHH!*" My entire body shivered in excitement.

Charlotte interrupted our discussion: "C'mon you guys. Enough of that mushy stuff. I found another show with McConaughey. He's my dreamboat. Pay attention. Let's watch the show and forget all about tall, dark and handsome construction supervisors for the evening."

I totally agreed and tried to redirect the embarrassing conversation away from my lunch date to see a re-run of an episode of *Magic Mike*, gushing every time Matthew McConaughey appeared. We all three swooned over the good looks of McConaughey, wishing that we could be kissed by him until our toes curled.

For myself, however, it was not McConaughey that I was seeing. It was a certain construction manager reaching out to take my hand in his.

Sigh......

CHAPTER 7

Early the next morning, the downstairs receptionist rang my extension. "Miss McIntyre, there are two large boxes for you that came by special messenger. They're here at my desk, I think that one of them is filled with flowers," she laughed, "but the other is rather heavy and looks very impressive. Do you have someone that you could send down, or should I have Joe from the mail room bring them up to your desk?"

"Do you know who sent them?" I asked.

"No, there's no name on the outside, but I'll bet there's a card on the inside. Tell you what; Joe's here at my desk. I'll just have him bring them up along with the morning mail."

A short time later, Joe dropped off the two boxes. I opened the lighter box first. Sure enough, enclosed were two dozen beautiful long stem white roses, with a hand written card from Cliff.

Tina,

Sometimes things happen in life that are unexpected. The challenge is always to recognize the ones that matter. I built this last night for you as a reminder of yesterday. I hope that our meeting meant as much to you as it did to me.

Cliff

The second box contained a scale model of the new tower. It had the general appearance of many floors with their glass exteriors complete, while other parts were completely bare to the steel girders. The overall effect was unique, it had been created as a vase to hold the flowers.

I went to the area fridge to pick up several bottles of water. I used those to fill up the office tower vase about two-thirds full. I clipped a half inch from the bottom stems of the flowers and dropped them into the vase. Then tossed the small cut ends into my trash. I placed the vase on the back corner of my desk next to the treasured picture of my parents. I sat and admired it for several moments trying to formulate a thank you for Cliff's gifts. In the back of my mind, I wondered if someday soon I might also have a photo of Cliff and myself to share that same space. I checked the office online telephone guide and found Cliff's number again and dialed.

He answered on the second ring.

"Hello. Tilden Tower. Cliff Stinson, how may I help you?"

"Hi, Cliff, it's Tina. I just received your two wonderful gifts of flowers and an office tower. Did you do that yourself? I've never seen anything like it before. They look great together; I'll take a photo with my cell and send it over to you."

"It was a rush job. I did it at my home workshop last night. I wanted you to have it while I was still fresh in your memory. I also hoped that you might call, so we could firm up that dinner engagement you promised. Would you be free, say this Friday evening around seven?"

"Cliff, I would love that. But I'm not sure that it would be a good idea for us to become involved. Let me pick a nice public place where we can just eat and talk if that would be all right with you?"

Like so many men away in my past; I was afraid of destroying the man's hopes before he was too much involved. He seemed such a nice man.

I dreaded hurting his feelings -- and my own. I realized then that it was the 'my own' that would hurt the worst.

"Sure, Tina. I will be happy no matter where you choose," he replied. "But I have high hopes that when we talk, I can change your mind."

It sounded to me that he was going to be very insistent.

'*Oh. I hope so. Please don't run away at the sound of my problems,*' My subconscious begged.

"I thought that you might relish a great steak since you seemed to enjoy the one on Tuesday? If it would be okay with you, then let's meet at B & B Steakhouse on Washington Street downtown. Can you meet me there, say around seven p.m. Friday?"

What I was thinking was remembering how fun it was seeing him twirl his cuts of steak in the sauce. Then watching his beautiful lips as he smiled and licked the small bits of butter away.

"Sure, but why don't I come by and pick you up? We could ride over together," Cliff asked hopefully.

My subconscious begged me on bended knee to say yes, but I had to push her aside.

"I am not sure that would be a good idea at this point, Cliff. That is one of the things I want to discuss with you. And one thing further, since the restaurant was my choice, I would like for it to be my treat. I don't want any argument about that."

B & B's was an upscale restaurant with upscale prices; I didn't want to take advantage of his pocketbook. Especially since he was bound to leave completely disappointed in me.

For some reason, my subconscious got up off the floor and hollered at me that this was a bad idea.

'*He's a guy, Tina. Guys like to be in charge, pick up the tab, and take you out in their fancy rides. Oh! I just don't even know why I am even sticking around with you. You never pay attention to me!*'

"I am not too sure that I am happy with that," Cliff replied sounding disappointed. "I'm not used to having someone pay for my meals, but …. Okay, if you insist, your treat! But, next time it will be on me. I will insist on that. I will see you at B & B Steakhouse Friday at seven p.m."

CHAPTER 8

On Friday, I took off from work at noon so that I could get my hair done and allow myself time to get dolled up for the date. Normally I wore slacks and a blouse to work, but this was a special occasion. I had gone to Neiman Marcus to select something that would be more appropriate than the floaty type dresses I usually wore when going out. I spent quite a bit of time fussing with the clothing assistant. After going back and forth with the assistant, I decided on a knockout little black dress with a pair of Christian Louboutin black pumps. I wanted something that featured my silhouette, which I had worked pretty darn hard to keep. I didn't want to flaunt my money because that had brought out the gold digger in so many men.

I stopped by the Grecian Condominium Spa, opting for a massage, facial and body wrap. I wanted to look my best, but I didn't want to appear rich, just smart and businesslike.

Time seemed to fly by as I dressed and put the finishing touch on my hair. I fished around in my jewelry case trying to decide whether I should wear a necklace, earrings, or possibly my ruby and diamond ring. I tried on one and then another, I just could not find the right combination. Finally, deciding that perhaps a lot of fancy jewelry might scare him off, I left off any extras for the evening except for a simple pearl necklace.

I gave a final fluff of my hair, looked around to see if I was forgetting anything and grabbed my clutch, then added my .38. I sat, waiting impatiently, on my couch and nervously chatting with Marianne. I watched the clock minute hand move ever so slowly. I was like a schoolgirl waiting on her prom date. When the clock finally signaled that it was time, I nearly jumped up and ran to the elevator.

"You look very nice this evening, Ms. Tina. I know that Mr. Cliff will like you. Just act yourself and don't fidget so much," Marianne called out after me. "And remember what I told you. He's probably a very nice man, give him a chance. You'll be surprised what might happen if you just play nice."

'Oh, why was I so nervous?' I wanted at the very least to have Cliff as a friend, and in the past, my money had either frightened off many of the men I had dated or caused them to care more about my money than for me. I wanted something so much more to happen with Cliff, so I knew that I had to take it slow.

My current apartment at Grecian Condominium was a short drive from the restaurant, but I had wanted to be a few minutes late so that Cliff would be sure to be there before me. I waited until five minutes to seven. Instead of having Charlotte drive me, I had decided on taking a cab. The driver was waiting for me when the elevator door opened. I gave him the address, and after just a few minutes the cab pulled up in front of the restaurant, at five minutes past seven.

I opened the passenger door and stepped out onto the sidewalk. Turning round, I handed the fare to the driver. When I turned around, there he was, standing outside, waiting, dressed in a sharp blue cotton suit and tie. He looked yummy enough to eat. I could feel my heart beat even faster. My cheeks flushed, and my breath caught in my chest when he caught sight of me and smiled that cheerful smile. Butterflies flittered around inside me and a knot formed in my stomach.

"Good evening, Tina, you look stunning tonight. I like your hair, that dress, and those shoes. Wow, You're a knockout!"

"Thank you, Cliff. You look charming yourself." I returned the compliment. The tension between us was electric. I tucked my clutch under my arm and twisted my hands together, desperately wanting to reach out and grab hold of one of his.

As if he could read my mind, he reached out his hand for mine. I smiled and grabbed hold as if my life depended on it.

"Thanks," I whispered.

My heartbeat slowed, and my breath became normal as we touched. I looked into his eyes and smiled back at him. Cliff turned and held the door for me to enter, never releasing my hand. I gave him another warm smile, all the while thinking what good manners he had. He was totally unlike other men I had dated.

I was in a state of torture. My mind was swimming with warnings.

'How far did I want this to go? What if he was not interested in me? What if he was just polite? Why was my hand trembling so?'

I did notice that the knot in my stomach had dissolved almost from the moment our hands clasped together.

The waiter escorted us to my usual table which I had on permanent reservation.

Cliff pulled out my chair, I eased onto it, "Thank you, sir."

'Oh, so nice. He is always the perfect gentleman,' I thought.

He released my hand after I sat down, walked around the table and slipped into the seat directly opposite me while the waiter removed the extra glasses and silverware. A second waiter appeared momentarily, "will you have something to drink, Ms. McIntyre?"

Cliff looked at him curiously, evidently surprised that the wait staff seemed to know my name.

"Yes, please. I would like a frozen strawberry Daiquiri. Cliff, do you have a preference before we order?"

Cliff studied me for a moment and then answered, "Yes, I'll have a cosmopolitan, straight up, without ice, please. Thank you." He looked over at me and winked.

The waiter left the menus for us to peruse, pivoted on his heel to leave for our drink orders.

"Cliff, I was not sure whether you had been to this restaurant before. Because this evening is my treat, I am hoping that you will let me make the selections for our dinner and then we can talk? Or if you prefer, I will defer to you and let you choose."

"It is a bit of a surprise, but you are correct. I have not been here before. Since you are more familiar with the menu, I will be happy to follow your suggestions."

His smile was so disarming, the curve of his lips was tantalizing, and his teeth looked perfect. For a moment, I considered the rest of his body and then stopped.

'What am I thinking? I'm not measuring him for a suit. Just be nice and polite. That's what Marianne has said, go slow. Don't run him off.'

The waiter returned with our drinks and set them down, and turned to Cliff.

"Sir, are you ready to order at this time?"

I took a sip of my Daiquiri and winked at him.

"We have agreed that since Ms. McIntyre is more familiar with your menu, she will order for the both of us." Cliff took a sip of his Cosmo.

The waiter turned to me "Ms. McIntyre?"

"We would like to order the Chateaubriand Wellington for two, with wild rice and glazed carrots on the side. Please add a Pinot Noir for both of us along with the meal."

That lock of hair fell over his forehead again; my fingers twitched with a desperate desire to reach over and comb it back in its place.

"Yes, ma'am" the waiter smiled as he left.

'I am sure that he was hoping for a large tip. We will have to see how the evening goes,' I thought to myself.

Cliff shifted a bit in his chair; he seemed a bit nervous as he toyed with a fingernail. He lifted his eyes to me and spoke softly.

"Tina, I was so happy that you agreed to spend some time with me away from work. I don't often get a lot of time on my own, what with the responsibilities of getting this building completed. There seem to be things to do nearly around the clock. I am pushed and pulled every which way, with deliveries being late, and wrong supplies delivered. Too many of some things and not enough of another, and then the usual squabbles among the crew. Thank you for inviting me."

I screwed up my courage as I looked at the tables around us to make sure there was no one listening. I did notice two gentlemen who looked out of place and scraggly, sitting a few tables away drinking beer.

'*That's very odd.*' I thought.

But they seemed to be chatting with each other, so I forgot about them and looked back at Cliff.

"Cliff, I felt an attraction to you on Tuesday when we had lunch. There are things from my past that usually get in my way in my daily life. One of those is a dreaded fear of being alone with a man at any time.

"That's why I chose this setting for our dinner. I am familiar with this restaurant and have eaten here many times. I feel safe here and always sit at this table, close to the bar and front window. It is a very public place and the manager is aware of my particular needs."

I neglected to add that Charlotte was lurking somewhere nearby, just in case I needed rescue. I wanted to get the bad part over as soon as possible, so I ended with my normal 'get out of jail free' card,

"Cliff, I cannot go into a lot of detail of what my issues are right now, I simply ask that you accept them and perhaps we can move on from there, or not. I leave it up to you. If you can accept those conditions for any future relationship that we might have. If not, we can have a pleasant dinner this evening and remain friends in the future."

"Sure, Tina. I don't have any problem with that and will respect your request. Do you have any other issues that I need to know?"

The lock of his hair on his forehead was driving me wild. I decided to sit on my hand to prevent it from escaping and doing what I dared not do.

"No, that one is critical to me. I am pretty sure that I don't have any others that would involve you at this point."

"By the way, is Tina a shortened name for Christina?" he asked, changing the subject.

His hand reached up and pushed the errant hairs back into place, only to have them fall out of place again.

My hand ached to run my hand through his hair and to feel his face against my palm.

"Yes," I said, surprised by the question.

"What a beautiful name. If you wouldn't mind, I would rather address you as such. I think that it suits you much better than the nickname. I like the way it rolls on my tongue. Besides, I want to be different than any other man in your life. Everyone calls you Tina. I don't want to be another 'everyone' in your life. I want to be special."

I was taken aback somewhat by his request; no one else had ever thought to know my true first name and the rest ...My, my! Besides, Christina had died seventeen years ago. But the way that he said my name sent chills down my back. I hadn't used my full name in so many years; it sounded so pretty the way he pronounced Christina. He already was someone special to me. Oh, if I could just tell him. I needed to know if he has the same feelings as I did. It's probably just this one night. I'll probably never see him again.'

"Yes, Cliff, Christina would be fine. Would you rather I address you as Clifford?"

"Cliff is just fine. It is just that I love the name Christina, how it sounds and the beautiful lady to whom it belongs."

"Why, thank you, Cliff." I squirmed in my seat.

'Yes, Cliff, the way that it sounds on your tongue, I wish that I could hear you say my name every day.' A flutter rippled through my stomach.

"So, not to change the subject again, but you were speaking of issues that you have had with the materials shipment? It sounds like you need an order coordinator to make sure that you get the right stuff delivered at the right times."

"Yes, I did have one, but he left us two weeks ago because his mother fell ill in Canada, and I have not had time to replace him yet."

"I might help you with that. I know of a young man who just graduated college and is looking for a job. I think that he would be a great fit for this kind of job. He interviewed with me last week, but we did not have an opening at the time. I checked his background and all his college professors rate him highly, noting that he is quite meticulous and well organized. If you are interested, I will fax you his resume and my notes; you can follow up with him if you wish."

"That would be great, right now everything is so disorganized. I would love the help and will speak with him."

We were interrupted by the waitress bringing our dinner. After the waitress had completed setting our food and drinks, she asked, "Will there be anything else?"

"Not at this time," I replied.

Cliff echoed my response.

As she walked away to handle the next order I looked over at Cliff. He had extended both of his hands to me across the table. His eyes were serious and hopeful.

"Do you mind if I say a blessing for this meal?" his eyes met mine, I felt that strong pull again.

"Yes, please."

I was shocked; no man has ever done this. I reached across and let him take my hands. I curled my fingers inside his palms, letting my hands absorb the pleasure of his touch. His voice was calm and soft as he spoke.

Come, Lord Jesus, your presence be here with us,
Bless this food bestowed by Thee to nourish our bodies.
Bless our loved ones everywhere, keep them in Thy loving care.
Amen."

My heart melted. Such a tender and heartfelt expression.

"That was beautiful. Thank you, Cliff."

I knew instantly that this man was different.

'Is he the one?' My heart said yes, my mind said nothing, it was too busy fighting other battles.

"So, do you say that prayer for all of your dates?" I smiled at him as we both cut into our Beef Wellington and took a small bite. My eyes focused on his lips as he spoke. They were so firm and moist. I daydreamed of how they would taste on mine.

Looking me straight in the eye he began to speak; I was mesmerized by his words. Every word pierced my heart. My ears could not believe their meaning. A feeling of peace and joy filled my soul. His words were magical.

"No, Christina. In fact, you are my first date in about five years. …And I know that it is far too soon. However, before any more time passes, I want to let you know that I fell in love with you the moment that I saw you sitting with Larry in his truck. And when you stepped out of that cab a few minutes ago, my heart nearly burst, and I knew that I loved you. I realize that we have only known each other for three days, but I am certain of my feelings for you.

"I want you in my life forever. Christina, will you marry me?"

My subconscious fainted, my face turned bright red. I was in the middle of chewing on a particularly delicious piece of meat. I suddenly choked as it attempted to go down my windpipe instead of traveling merrily to my stomach.

Cliff jumped to his feet and around the table, slapping my back as I continued to cough.

A waiter rushed over with a glass of water which I downed in one long gulp.

Cliff repeatedly asked, "Christina, are you okay?" as he slapped my back again several times. The guests at the other tables were all staring at us.

Oh! I wanted to melt into the floor. When I was finally able to catch my breath again, I waved him off,

"I am fine now. Thanks."

'What had just happened? My 'go slow plan' had flown out the window.'

I searched his face to see if he had been joking, what I found was pure unbounded love. I recognized it immediately as the same thing I had seen in his eyes when I had slid out of Larry's truck and into Cliff's arms.

'Yes. This man is in love with me.'

"Did you just say that you loved me? And that you want me to marry you? I am so sorry; it was just such a surprise. Please forgive my reaction."

I looked him directly in the eyes. Surely, he must be joking? Was this what he and Larry had been discussing? His eyes were so bright and sparkling, seeking, desperately begging for my answer. I found the answer there, in those magical soft orbs of brown. He was serious. He did love me.

'I wanted to fall into his arms, to kiss him fervently, to have him hold me. My entire body awoke with a desperate need which I knew immediately was desire. I wanted this man in my life.'

My subconscious was just coming around again and shaking her head, *'Yes, yes, you dummy. Say Yes!'*

But I had to ignore my subconscious again. It was too soon. My mind raced, struggling for something to say.

"Cliff, I don't know what to say. You have caught me totally off guard. I was not prepared for that… for you. What a wonderful proposal. *I could barely catch my breath.*

"But Cliff, we have only known each other for three days. How can you be sure? How can I be sure? Please, let me have some time to consider. I am shocked… pleasantly shocked, and I am not saying 'no' to you. It is just that it is all so sudden. Let me say it again, Wow. You are a treasure! You sure know how to sweep a girl off her feet."

My subconscious immediately stood up and left the restaurant in a huff.

'I'm not coming back! You are just too much for me.' She shouted back at me as she faded out the door.

"Then it is not a 'no.' I was so afraid that it might be." Cliff seemed to breathe a sigh of relief. "At least it might be a "maybe." I can live with that, but not for too long. I wanted you to know from the very beginning you have won my heart if you will have it.

———

"I could not conceal my true feelings from you for one second longer. I understand that it is a shock to you, and I did not expect an answer tonight. My heart wishes for one, but my head tells me to be patient. When we met Tuesday, I am certain that you felt something. I could tell from the way that you acted, almost from the moment I sat beside you in Larry's truck. And I repeat, whatever it takes, I want you to be mine."

I looked around at the other tables. It seemed that the guests seated at the tables, close to us, were all waiting expectantly for the answer to Cliff's question. That is, except for those two bums about three tables away. They seemed to be laughing at the two of us. I ignored them. Turning back to Cliff, I blushed again and struggled for a response. Perhaps a kiss might satisfy them. Yes, Cliff deserved a kiss for that charming speech. I rose and stepped to his side. He looked up at me puzzled.

I leaned over and planted a tender kiss on his mouth. Boy... did his lips taste yummy, a delicious combination of meat sauce, melted butter and most of all, Cliff. The whole restaurant erupted in applause.

I held the kiss, probably much longer than I should have. My knees felt weak, I opened my eyes and looked into his, 'Ummm! I moaned into his mouth. I could feel his body tense, his hand reached up and stroked my face, his touch soft, tender, loving.

I lifted my hand and touched his cheek and slowly, carefully brushed his errant lock of hair upward. I smoothed it gently down, then ran my fingers through his hair to comb it in place.

'His hair felt like velvet between my fingers. His lips. GOD! His lips tasted every bit as wonderful as I had dreamed. I moaned into his mouth, my body wanton for the need of him.'

Reluctantly, I broke our lips apart and realized that everyone in the restaurant was watching. Both Cliff and I were now totally embarrassed as several of the guests tipped their wine glasses at us in salute. I felt so warm and happy inside as I returned to my seat. The two men close by both had smirks on their faces. Somehow they looked familiar, but then they raised the beer bottles they were drinking from and tipped them in our direction, spilling a few drops of beer on their table.

'Oh well. Guys will be Guys. And some guys are jerks.

"I have wanted to do that all evening," I spoke softly. "Let's make that a down payment of the reward that I owe you for making me feel so good tonight."

"Which, the kiss or straightening my hair?" he asked.

"To tell you the absolute truth, both."

I flushed again, my cheeks, sore from the repeated rush of blood, ached terribly.

'Will I suffer a lifetime of blushing when I marry this man?

Had I expressed that thought? *"When I Marry This Man."* Have I *already decided?...*

'I knew the answer instantly.'

"If we are telling the absolute truth this evening, Christina, I need you to know that I have wanted to tell you that I fell in love with you since that first day. And I will hold you to that reward you promised." Cliff smiled hopefully.

"Now that my cards are on the table, and you know what I want, tell me something about yourself that no one else knows. Perhaps a story from your childhood. Something that I can treasure in my heart until you say you will be mine."

Whoa, change of subject. From marriage to a history lesson. This guy is like greased lightning. If he keeps this up, I am going to have a very tough time staying up with him. My heart is still pounding from his proposal, and that wonderful, marvelous kiss, my mind was in a whirl.

I thought for a few moments, considering his request, trying to remember something that would serve the dual purpose of slowing my erratic heartbeat, but give him an insight into my crazy life.

"When I was a child," I began, "I was playing with my older brother while my mother taught a piano lesson. My brother and I decided to decorate the house with flowers. Mother had several azalea bushes in full bloom outside. We spent the afternoon breaking all of the limbs with flowers off the bushes and bringing them inside. The problem was that we had a big old screen door on the house and every time we would come in or go out; the screen door would slam loudly.

"Mother was so mad when her lesson completed. She scolded us very hard for making so much noise; her young student had trouble keeping her attention focused. But then mother saw all of the pretty flowers scattered everywhere in the house. She felt bad about having hollered at us about the door slams and apologized.

"How's that for my first challenge?"

"You get an A for that," Cliff grinned. "But, gosh, I kind of feel sorry for that poor piano student."

I tossed my cloth napkin at him striking him on his shoulder. His laugh was gentle and playful.

"Oh, I see how it is. If I say teasing things to you, then you are going to throw things at me. Christina, two can play that game…" as he tossed the napkin towards me.

I caught it in my hands with a giggle.

"You have no idea. I was a holy terror. I was a tomboy early in life. I climbed trees and chased after rabbits. My family lived in a rural area and dad owned a farm."

I was totally amazed. It had been years since I had thought of those pleasant early years. But they came before my secret. If Cliff learned of it, he would probably want to leave right away.

"Okay. Your turn. Come on, fess up to something bad you did before today, big fella," I teased.

"Let me see. Since we're talking 'way back there': When I was age ten, I poured one of those Kool-aide packets down the back of a girl's dress in fourth grade. I was sent to the Principals' office and had to stay after school and write on the blackboard twenty times that I would never do that again. Does that count as my confession of bad deeds?" he smiled.

I laughed. "Cliff, you and I might just get along just fine. Let's finish our meal before you make me choke again."

"If that meant that I could earn another kiss….."

"I think that I might already owe you one. Let's not go down that path or they might arrest us for disturbing the peace."

"If we could share the same jail cell, I'd be okay with that" he laughed.

Oh, I loved this playfulness. I had never experienced that with a man before. Marianne was right. If I just gave a guy a chance.

I *was* surprised by what would happen. Not only that, I loved the result. But was what I was feeling actually love? I truly didn't know. I had never experienced love with a man before. I was afraid to make a mistake. How would I know? Was there some mystical signboard that would light up and tell me?

"Shush now. You're getting me tickled. I have not had such a good time at dinner in I don't remember."

"So tell me a more about yourself, Christina," Cliff begged.

"There is not a lot to tell. I was born in Corpus Christi, but my parents moved around the country a lot, so I have been in a lot of places. But I think that Texas is my favorite place in the world, not that I have seen a lot of Texas, though. When I was young, my father was in the U.S. Navy, and he was always changing duty stations. After he had retired, dad owned a small farm up in Washington State. I have a lot of fond memories of the farm.

"I moved to Houston about ten years ago and worked in several different companies, before arriving here at Tilden Industries. It is a great place to work, and I just love working alongside Larry. He's a kind and considerate boss and has taught me a lot.

"My brother died in a car accident when he was eight years old, my parents were killed in an airplane crash four years ago, and I had a hard time recovering.

"After my brother died, my mother withdrew into herself. She seemed to have always favored him, and I felt unloved in her treatment of me. She was always talking about the loss of her little boy. I was just an unfortunate mistake. I am not so sure that she wouldn't have preferred that it had been me instead of him. She always longed to have him back."

"Christina, I am so sorry for your loss. I know just how hard that can be. I had only one great-grandparent that I knew, my great grandfather,

Henry Stinson. The other three died long before I was born. When I was growing up Grandpa Stinson, as we called him, did many favors for me, took me fishing, built a playhouse for me, and many other things.

"When he died, I was visiting a friend in Colorado and failed to attend his funeral. I have regretted that to this day. He did so much for me, and I had failed to visit or call him during his final illness. I have an ache in my heart to this day that I was so young and foolish to treat him in that manner. I am truly ashamed of how I acted toward him."

"Please tell me some about your past," I asked, "if you don't mind, especially since I have now revealed nearly all of my deepest darkest secrets."

But I had held back the darkest one. Perhaps he will like me and stay if he does not know.

"As for myself, until this last Tuesday, my life was dull. I graduated from Williams High School in Sugarland. My dad was a carpenter working in home construction, so I guess that I followed in his footsteps. After working for some local high rise apartment contractors I was lucky to get on with Russell & Son Contractors, they specialize in Office Towers. The work is demanding, the people that I work with are highly skilled and know what to do without being micro-managed.

"I was living day to day just waiting for my life to happen when you appeared with Larry. I suddenly knew what I wanted in life, and it was you. I don't mean to embarrass or scare you away, but that is just the way it is. I have dated several women from time to time, but none of them meant anything to me, the last one was about five years ago and since then I have been focused on work. That has helped me advance to my current position as Construction Manager.

"Then when I saw you, sitting there in Larry's truck. You took my breath away; I knew at that very moment that you were what was missing in my life. That only you could fill the empty place in my life. There was something in the way your pretty blue eyes looked at me that turned on a light bulb in my head. I admit, you were not what I had expected.

"I had always envisioned the girl of my dreams as, blond, buxom, sexy, and vivacious. You know the pretty girl in the movies type. And there you were, the complete fulfillment of the picture I had created inside my mind, except for the hair, of course. I love your dark brunette even more. That girl vanished the very moment I saw your face. Your eyes and smile, the curve of your face, everything about you captured my heart.

"I wanted to get to know you better, and I wanted you to know me. I will be happy to follow whatever rules you have to make that happen. I looked carefully at your hand when I got into the truck and saw there was no wedding ring, and my heart leaped for joy. Are you involved with anyone? Please say no, or my heart will break."

"I will confess, Cliff that I, too, was affected by you. And, no, I am not involved with anyone at present. When I saw you walking toward the truck my stomach got queasy; my nerves ran away with me. My appetite vanished, and all that I could think of was your beautiful brown eyes. When you held my hand with your arm around my shoulder in the truck, I wanted to turn and kiss you. I could barely tie two words together during that whole lunch.

"My heart tells me to run away with you right now. But… I just don't know; please let me have some time. I am afraid of making a mistake. My entire being wants to say yes to you. But let's let things come about naturally. When I look at you, my heart beats faster, but I am afraid to act on that. I have to know you better before I can decide."

"Christina, I am more than willing to wait. I am not going to rush you into something before you are ready. What do you say that we simply enjoy each other's company for a time? There are lots of things we might do together that would allow us to get to know each other better. Like, go to a movie, dancing, tour a museum, take in a baseball game and so much more. What do you say? And next time, remember, it will be my treat. I insist."

I reached over and touched his hand. "Yes, Cliff. Those all sound exciting and things that I would like to do with you."

My heart raced faster as his hand grasped mine, wrapping around mine tenderly. The whole world seemed as if it had settled into place around me. We continued to talk and laugh together until the meal was over.

"Would you like for me to give you a ride home?" Cliff offered.

I wanted to give in, just this once, but an ancient alarm bell went off in my head, there is that trick to get me alone with him in a car where I could not escape.

"No, not yet. I still have issues, but someday soon that may change." My heart sank, and I wanted to argue with myself, tell myself how foolish that I was. I was on the verge of changing my answer when he spoke again.

"All right, at least let me call you a cab?"

"To tell the truth, my friend Charlotte promised to pick me up here at nine p.m., so she should be along shortly. I have enjoyed this evening. More than you know." I signaled for the check. Upon receiving it I browsed it for a second, staring at the line for a tip. This has been a stellar night, I thought, so I signed for a fifty-dollar tip. I was quite happy with myself, and the waiter. In fact, I was quite happy with the whole world.

Cliff escorted me to the front of the restaurant, and sure enough, Charlotte pulled up as we exited. We stood, bathed in the lights of the restaurant and overhead street lamps. Cliff held my hand gently and rubbed his thumb over my knuckles. After a minute Cliff opened the passenger side door for me and then, on a whim, I reached up and pulled his lips to mine, and we kissed a long sweet kiss. If he had asked me again at that moment, I would have gone home with him.

I was in love, and I had finally realized it. Yes, Love. I was head over heels in LOVE. Bells, whistles, and fireworks were exploding inside my head. I wanted to stand in the middle of the street and scream it out loud.

"TINA MCINTYRE IS IN LOVE WITH CLIFFORD STINSON."

"A'hem," Charlotte **went** into her protective mode and interrupted our parting kiss.

"Until next time, Christina," he whispered in my ear, sending a chill down my spine.

I smiled up at him; my heart overjoyed that at last I had found the man of my dreams. I turned in my seat and waved goodbye as the car pulled away.

"Until next time, Cliff, and I hope that it is soon."

Next time I will say yes, a million times yes, I whispered to myself.

He raised his hand to his mouth and blew me a kiss.

Oh! I wanted so badly to tell Charlotte to turn the car around so I could throw myself into his arms and get another real kiss. My toes turned up at the thought.

***

Neither of the two lovers noticed the two men who rose from the table close by where Tina and Cliff had sat. The two men stepped outside the steakhouse just as Charlotte pulled away. Another man emerged from the shadows across the street and crushed a cigarette underneath his shoe. He was somewhat taller, and his face, ruined by the aged scars of a young girls' deep fingernail scratches across his face. He gestured at one of the two coming out of the restaurant to follow after Cliff. The other man came over and seemed to have a discussion about what had transpired between the two lovers earlier.

Upon hearing the details of that lover's transaction, he laughed cruelly. After a moment, the two men climbed into a dark sedan with a busted out headlight. The third man returned and joined them a few moments later and soon the trio had disappeared into the darkening night.

CHAPTER 9

Arriving back at my apartment, I did a little happy dance as I removed my dress and slipped into my nightgown and robe. When I returned to the den where Marianne and Charlotte were waiting, I was so thrilled. Perhaps there are happy days ahead for me. My life had always been a struggle to stay hidden, not get involved with men, shy away from romantic entanglements. Maybe that was all about to end. Had I found my Prince Charming?

'Oh, I hope so! I hope so!'

Charlotte brought me back to earth with a sudden crash.

"Tina, I am a bit concerned. As we were leaving the restaurant, I saw a man in the rear view mirror come out from behind a building across the street. When he stepped into the glow of a streetlight; I am certain that I have seen his face before. I had noticed him earlier; he appeared to be watching you. He was too far away from me to get a good look. I am going to go through my files and see if I can find him.

"Now, I do admit that there were a few other men hanging around there in the area. I think that the restaurant hands out their leftovers to the homeless after they close. He might have been with them, but there was something about him that seemed different. I just couldn't put my finger on it. I think that you should be a bit more careful in the future.

"In the meantime what do you say to take different cars to allow me to have an opportunity to tail anyone who might be suspicious? You drive your Audi to the office, and I will tag along in my car staying as far back as possible. It may have been nothing; I just want to play it safe."

"Oh, Charlotte," I scolded. "Sometimes I think your imagination runs away from you. Why would anyone be stalking around in the middle of the night at a public restaurant? I agree with your first thought. It was probably just some homeless bum looking for a handout."

"You should listen to Charlotte, Miss Tina," Marianne added. "She looks after you really good."

"Okay. But I still worry," she observed. "That's what you pay me to do."

Charlotte then changed her tone. "Now, tell us about your date. I nearly fell over when I saw you walk to his side of the table and give him a kiss. We are not going to bed until you provide all the details. Now, fess up girl. What happened in there?"

"Ladies, you are not going to believe this. Cliff told me that he loved me. He wants me to marry him!"

I wanted to tell them that I had almost given in to the emotions of the moment. That I had felt like running away with him to paradise that very evening, but I held back. The looks on the faces of my two employees were priceless. Both of their mouths dropped open and for once in their lives they seemed to be at a loss for words. Marianne was the first to gain use of her tongue again.

"Ms. Tina ...Did I hear you right? Did you just say that he said that he loves you? How is that possible? Was he serious? What exactly did he say? Are you sure that you heard him correctly? You only met on Tuesday."

"Whoa! Marian, go slower. One question at a time, please. He was serious and I did hear him correctly. Let me start over again. We were just beginning our dinner when it just popped out of his mouth. He said that he could not hold back any longer and told me that he had fallen in love with me at first sight when he was approaching Larry's truck. You remember that I may have had similar feelings when I saw him walking toward us. I was not sure what it meant, but my whole body seemed to light on fire.

"I liked him instantly. I wanted to have him hold me forever in the truck and missed his touch when we had arrived and went inside the restaurant. All during our meal I could not think straight, my heart was pounding and everywhere that we touched was magical.

When our legs brushed under the table, or when our fingers met each other on the building schematic. I could not seem to get enough of him; I wanted to touch his face with my hand, run my fingers through his hair. I was totally mad with a desire to be held by him."

I neglected to add that when I kissed him, I had surrendered to my desire. Held the kiss longer that I should have. Brushed his cheek with the back of my palm and then tucked in a loose strand of his hair. Then actually stroked his hair and ran my fingers through it for just a second.

'Oh! – to do that again,' I remembered the feel his hair between my fingers, the taste of his lips on mine, and the soft touch of his fingers on my cheek.

"But how, why?" Charlotte questioned. "I have heard of such things, but never really believed they happened except in fairy tales. And? So what did you say to him? You have us on pins and needles here."

"Out with it, girl," Marianne begged.

"I told him that it was too soon. That I needed some time to consider, that I thought that he was wonderful and asked for some time to think. He agreed and said that he had not expected an answer immediately, and then I gave him that kiss. The entire restaurant applauded, and we had a pleasant dinner. What else did you think happened?"

They both looked at me rather disappointedly.

"Ms. McIntyre, that was so romantic. I hope that you two get together. You deserve to have some happiness in your life,"

Finally, I bucked up my courage and said it. "Ladies. I'm in love. Yes! You heard me right. I love this man. I don't know how or when it happened, but I'm positive. I love him. I'm going to marry him. The next time he asks I'm going to say yes."

Marianne smiled and then jumped up and gave me a hug. Charlotte quickly joined in the hug, and soon we were dancing around the den in a little jig.

Later as I slipped into bed, my mind went racing back over the evening, replaying in my mind every second. From the time that the cab dropped me off, until my final goodbye wave.

Surely, it cannot be true. I had always thought that I would end up an old maid. But that kiss by the car—yum, his lips were so enchanting. I was tortured by his body pressing against mine. His arms around me, holding me tight. I wanted badly to hold him against me again. To feel safe in his arms, protected from the bad things in the world. Yes, I did love him.

It was insane but true. Considering that I had known him for such a short time, it made no sense. And yet I knew that I would never be complete without him in my life. The next time he asked, I would give him the answer he wanted. It was the answer that I wanted as well. I would be his, and he would be mine. No more loneliness, only happiness and the joy of having someone of my own to treasure. At last, I had found happiness, and name of that happiness was Clifford Stinson.

That night my dreams were about the man in the shadows, watching me and of being captured by a sex maniac and tortured in his underground dungeon. At breakfast, I make a mental note to take a sleeping pill to keep away dreams of being tied up in a dungeon. That kind of stuff kept me awake all night. Just to be safe, I checked my gun again to make sure it was loaded.

Sigh… But Cliff, I missed him already and wished he was here so that we could talk some more. I had a lot more to learn about him; I was anxious to get started.

CHAPTER 10

The weekend dragged by slowly. Then Cliff had to work late every night the following week, so we did not get a chance to see each other at all. That caused me to fall into a major funk. My only relief being, we spoke on the phone every moment possible each day. He would call whenever he had time during the day and tell me about his day. He would ask me how Larry was coming along getting final approvals for my changes for the building. I always sensed there was an ulterior motive behind those questions. I could never exactly pin him down on it, though. I felt that he was hiding something, but had no idea what or why.

Every night he would call and we would talk until the wee hours of the morning. He would ask me to tell all about my early life, tales of my childhood, things that I enjoyed in school. He was especially interested in subjects that I had taken in college.

I probed into his school years. What subjects he had enjoyed. How many girls he had dated. His favorite teachers, why he had liked them. Somehow I forgot to ask him about his family. I made a note to bring that up each time, but whenever we spoke it always slipped my mind.

I missed his soft voice and sweet words when we weren't on the phone. I missed the touch of his hand holding mine. In short, I missed him terribly. I needed to give him my answer, to feel his lips on mine again, to have his arms around me.

I drove to work in my Audi A5 Cabriolet every day and parked in the underground parking area. Charlotte shadowed behind me each day but had nothing further to report, and I began to feel safe again.

Charlotte's mystery man must have been nothing. Just a bum, walking down the street or looking for a handout, just exactly as I had told her. She worried too much, but then, that's what I had hired her for, so she had a right.

On Wednesday evening, Cliff called around nine p.m., and we spent the next several hours reminiscing.

"Christina, you know, it's just so hard for me to believe," Cliff stated after we had been talking for three hours. "You are such a pretty and dynamic woman. I don't understand how you could have made it through that denizen of woman-hungry wolves either in school or where you work with only a few dates. Surely there was a least one Lothario that revved up your engine a bit."

"Cliff, there may have been one or even two, for that matter. But as I explained last Friday, I have an issue. Guys were just not on my radar. I focused on classes and making good grades. In fact, I graduated second in my class. I was quite proud of my achievements. I have been out since then on a few dates, but no one ever clicked with me before. No one that I wanted to be a part of my life."

'I couldn't tell him the truth -- that I had avoided boys like the plague. That I had driven them off whenever one had expressed even the mildest interest. I didn't want to lose Cliff with the truth about my phobia's.'

"How about yourself? You said you hadn't dated in five years? That must be a record."

"You may be right. But the last girl that I dated was someone who came on so strong that her actions repulsed me. We went to a movie and all throughout the show she kept putting her hands on my leg, she reached into my shirt, wanted me to touch her. I felt sickened that she was so brazen. Gosh, there were people on both sides of us that I knew personally.

"I was so embarrassed; I didn't want that kind of thing in my life at all. I swore that very night that the next girl I dated would be the woman whom I would marry. And so, here we are today. I am so excited that it has worked out like this."

"Cliff, you are one of a kind. You don't know how safe that makes me feel. Perhaps we can go somewhere this weekend. I yawned…. It's nearly 2:30 a.m. and I have to be in the office early tomorrow. Larry told me that he had some revisions to make on the RFP on which we've been working. I'll talk to you when you get a chance in the morning. Good night, sweetheart."

"Okay, Christina. As I have said before. I love you. Sleep tight. Good night."

The following morning the phone was ringing on my desk when I returned from giving Larry an updated packet on the T & J contract. My heart beat faster as I lifted the receiver when I saw Cliff's caller ID flashing.

"Hi, sweetheart," Cliff's voice rang like a wonderful melody in my ear. "Do you like Salsa? Even if you don't, I have reserved us a table at *Gloria's* on Saturday. So dust off your dancing shoes and be prepared to party hearty. We're going to get 'down and dirty' pretty lady."

"Oh! My feet are already skipping under the desk. It has been so long since I have had a chance to go dancing. How did you know? I would love to go. Especially with you. I guess that means I have to go shopping again to find something nice to wear."

I was too afraid and embarrassed to explain the details and reason that I didn't know how to dance. *'Perhaps, he can teach me. I would love to learn, especially while being held close in his arms.'*

"Christina, anything you wear would look great to me, even an old potato sack. Just make sure you have some comfy footwear. We may dance the night away."

After we had hung up, I was happy as a lark. My head was spinning with visions of his arms around me, holding me tightly as we danced and swayed to the beat of a wild Latin rhythm.

"Hey, Tina. You in there?" Larry's voice interrupted my daydream as he knocked on my office door.

"Sorry, Larry, my mind was a million miles away." I flushed.

"I have noticed. It seems like it has been that way since last Tuesday's lunch. Anything special I need to know?"

"Larry, you will be the first, no -- sorry, you will be the second to know when I am ready to tell."

"You've hurt my feelings, Tina. I thought that I was right up there at the top of your list to tell things. How the mighty have fallen!" he pouted rather unseriously.

"Shush!" I giggled.

"What was it that you needed?" I asked after a moment when he had stood there, looking at me rather strangely.

"Oh, yeah, I almost forgot. I have the final revisions here. They've just been approved upstairs by the CEO. I need to get the changes into the document and get it faxed over to them by 1 p.m. Can you handle that? The changes are all here marked in red."

I reviewed the papers that Larry handed to me and after a few minutes' study was able to give him a positive response. "Sure, I should be able to get this done with plenty of time to spare. Oh, by the way, Cliff said to tell you hello and that work on your office suite is finished. You can drop by anytime that you want to get a second look."

"So, how are you and Cliff getting along these days?" Larry asked.

"Do you really need to ask? I am floating on air over here if you hadn't noticed."

The rest of the day seemed to be going by routinely. I hummed a little tune to myself, *Let me Love You,* as I keyed the update into my computer. I was able to complete the revisions, except for one area where Larry had forgotten to add an important clause, it had been missed by the management team as well. After Larry apologized for missing that and had it approved again, I quickly printed out the corrected copy. Larry gave it one final read through for typos. Then I faxed the document over to T & J's executive offices with twenty minutes to spare.

I looked lovingly at the beautiful flowers and vase on the corner of my desk and dreamed of my tall, dark and handsome prince charming.

CHAPTER 11

It was 1:42 p.m. when I heard a buzz of activity and voices outside my cubicle. I was in the middle of typing up a financial report for Larry when he stuck his head in and told me that there was an emergency meeting.

It was due to start in five minutes in the main conference room on the eighth floor of our building. This area was the only one that was large enough to contain most of the entire staff. I grabbed my purse and slung the strap over my shoulder, joined Larry as we strode down the hall to the stairway.

"What's going on?" I asked.

"I have no idea, maybe it's about the new contract," he replied

When he opened the stairway door, we quickly learned that there were already many others having the same thought. There was a mad crush of employees going up, both in front and behind us, so we melded in and slowly took each step due to the crowd ahead of us. We finally reached the eighth-floor exit and stepped out into a huge gaggle of staff. The floor was emptied of material already having been shipped to the new tower leaving only some free standing walls which formed a large open room with no tables or chairs. There was already a crowd of staff milling around, and the area was filling up fast.

Larry and I were able to find an area to squeeze into about half-way from the front, and we stood, waiting for the meeting to start. I could hear some mumbling from behind me about some disaster that was on the TV and radio news reports, but there was not enough for me to form a clear picture of what they were talking about.

Due to such a large number of staff attending, and others still struggling to get in from the hallway, the meeting did not get started until ten minutes later. Eric Johnson, our company president, finally entered and walked to the front of the room and held up his hands asking for quiet. It was another two or three minutes before the last voice had died away. Mr. Johnson looked over out the left side window and shook his head. I glanced that way but could only see some smoke in the far distance, probably a house fire or something.

"May I have your attention, please? I have an announcement. I don't have any answers yet, so there will not be a question/answer time after I finish. Please bear with me until I can get more up-to-date information.

"There has been an explosion at our new headquarters site," he said.

There were gasps and shouts of disbelief from many around the room.

"It appears to have been a car bomb," he continued. "There may have been some injuries among the construction crew because some of the structure may have collapsed. I don't have anything else at this time. I will let you know more as soon as the police can give me some updates."

Larry immediately grabbed my hand, knowing that I would need some support.

My head was spinning, fear gripped my stomach tightly.

"Cliff! Oh my God! Cliff!' I screamed and collapsed in a pile on the floor.

I didn't remember anything after that until I looked up and Larry was kneeling beside me, Eric Johnson was standing on top of me with a very concerned look on his face. There was also a crowd of other employees standing around behind them. I could hear several of them talking among themselves.

"Cliff? Who's Cliff? Is that Clifford Johnson she's asking about?" One employee asked.

"No, I don't think so. He's standing over there by the window," another replied.

"Tina, are you all right? Can I get you a glass of water or something?" Larry's voice was shaking with concern. It probably was not very often that he had to deal with an office assistant unconscious and splayed out on the floor.

"Ms. McIntyre! Is there anything you need? Larry, perhaps you should carry her down to the nurse's station on level two?" Mr. Johnson suggested.

I regained my senses somewhat, "No, No, I will be fine, just give me a minute. You say that there was a car bomb?"

Then I remembered the smoke that I had seen in the distance and struggled to gain my feet again. I forced my feet to propel me toward the one thing that I most dreaded. I pushed through the crowd at the window. I now could clearly see a huge plume of black smoke rising in the distance, most likely our new office tower. A feeling of terror grabbed my heart like a vice.

'Oh, please dear God! Let Cliff be okay.'

I cried inwardly, tears welled in my eyes, my head was spinning. My knees gave way. I sank to the floor, not wanting to see the horror of the black smoke and what that might mean.

Larry was beside me again, this time holding a glass of water,

"Here, drink this, Tina. It is going to be okay; there is no word yet. I'm sure Cliff is fine. Let's not make things worse than they might be."

His hand supported my back while I swallowed a sip of water.

My mind was racing like a freight train.

'Who had done this? Why attack our new building? Perhaps there was someone with a grudge against our company. If so, maybe there might be a similar bomb at our current location.'

Suddenly the fire alarm rang out loudly.

CLANG! CLANG! CLANG! CLANG! CLANG!

There were screams and shouts from employees from all directions.

I struggled to my feet as Larry supported my arm and shoulder. I could hear him mutter something, probably a curse word, and then he grabbed my arm and dragged me along to the exit. The stairway was crammed with crowds of people fighting to descend. We were pushed and pulled in all directions, and I had trouble keeping my feet underneath me. I probably would have tripped, and stumbled had it not been for Larry's strong arm supporting me through all of the pushing and shoving and sheer confusion.

After what seemed like ages, we finally reached the street exit and poured out of the building behind several hundred fellow employees. Everyone scattered to their assigned fire drill designated locations as quickly as they could. The building was surrounded by fire engines, police cars, and ambulances. All of their emergency lights were blinking.

A couple of the fire trucks, which had just arrived, still had their warning sirens blaring away at full volume. It was mass confusion and terror. I looked up at our building to check for smoke, but there was none. And then I remembered that during the entire descent, I had not smelled any smoke. Perhaps there was no fire, and it was just a false alarm.

I had just begun to calm down a bit when suddenly there was a tremendous explosion near the middle of the building and glass and concrete chips began raining on the street.

There were more screams and warning cries "WATCH OUT!" "LOOK OUT" from all sides as everyone ran back to get out of the way. Many people tripped and fell over each other in terror.

Fortunately, our drill locations were far enough away from the sides of the building that no one was hurt. The firefighters and police began running into the building. Other officers pulled police barricades from their car trunks as they established a cordoned area, pushing us further back away from the building. More police and fire engines began to pour into the area. Behind them appeared the first TV news trucks with reporters jumping out and pointing their microphones at anyone who would talk to them.

It was chaos.

I pulled out my cell phone and dialed Cliff's number, my fingers fumbled with the buttons. The tiny beeps sounded, and I waited for the ring. Shortly a terrifying message spoke from my cell:

"We're sorry. The number you have dialed is not in service at this time. Please hang up and try your call again later."

Thinking that there was some terrible mistake, I hit the speed dial for Cliff's number. This time, it rolled over to voicemail. My heartbeat slowed. I must have misdialed the first time. But this was still unusual, why would his number go to voicemail?

"Larry," my voice now shaking with terror. "What in the hell do you think is going on? First our new tower, and now our current building. Who could be doing this? Are we at war or something? And now Cliff's cell is not working."

Suddenly, I realized, there was no point in remaining here. We could do nothing to aid in the situation. Where I desperately needed to be was in the new tower. Only there could I find the answer to the ache in my heart.

"Larry, we need to go to the tower. I must find out what has happened to Cliff. We can't do anything here, at least there we might get more news about what is happening. My car is in the underground parking which is blocked off with fire engines. Can you take me in your truck?"

Larry looked at me, saw the pain in my eyes and agreed. "You're right. Let's find out if we can get to my truck and head over there. Luckily I parked in the remote lot today so we should be able to leave from there quickly."

We pushed through the crowd of staff and police until we were able to reach the employee parking lot a block away. At the entrance, two policemen were blocking cars from entering. At the exit police were slowly allowing people with their cars there to leave. Clearing out people and vehicles from the area, thus making the emergency services work easier. However, they were closely verifying all those wishing to leave, taking names and checking company ID badges.

Larry and I climbed into his truck and exited the area, only to discover that the police had already set up a second perimeter blockade. Evidently they were trying to isolate and possibly capture the person who had caused this terrifying incident. At the outer location, the police stopped each vehicle and used bomb detection equipment and dogs. We finally made it past that checkpoint and skirted around the huge police command vehicle which was buzzing with activity.

The drive to the tower this day was not nearly as pleasant as my first one. There were huge traffic tie-ups all along the way due to cars stopping on the freeway and gawking at either the smoke from the tower or the fire at our old building. Later it became even thicker as we slowly crept closer to the new tower. My nerves were totally frayed, and tears streamed freely down my cheeks.

Over and over I tried to rationalize what could cause someone to take this kind of action against our company. We weren't involved in overseas work in the middle-east. I could not imagine what else might be the cause of someone causing this kind of hateful action.

Larry looked over at me from time to time and offered words of encouragement. The problem was that neither he nor I had any idea of what had happened. Still, I certainly did appreciate his comforting words.

"Cliff's fine. He's smart," Larry smiled. "He knows the building better than anyone and unless he was at the direct center of the blast from the car bomb, he would have known what to do and where to go. Perhaps his cell phone was damaged or maybe he just turned it off."

Oh, this was so frustrating, not being able to speak to Cliff, not being able to see if he was still alive, or badly injured. We inched slowly along the freeway. We could now see the top of the tower in the distance. That provided some comfort at least, to know that the entire building had not collapsed as we had feared. We slowly edged closer to the tower. The traffic was almost dead stopped in many places.

Some people had even left their cars in the roadway, gotten out to watch from the side of the freeway. Many had their cell phones out taking video to post on the Internet news sites. Cars and trucks were honking continuously, trying to get people to move along. It was a nightmare.

Police sirens screamed behind us as they tried to reach closer to the front of the jam. To force people to move their cars from the area. After an hour, we reached an exit that would allow us to take a side street parallel to the tower; it offered us a way to get a bit closer because it had less traffic.

Larry swerved in and out of traffic as openings occurred. As we edged closer to the tower, I noticed someone that I thought that I recognized. He was walking away from the direction we were traveling. I could not quite place him in my memory. He might have been an employee from the past, or from one of the other companies where I had worked. He had several small scratches on his face.

I knew that face, and it haunted me as Larry continued driving. I was too distraught and frightened to focus my mind on anything other than getting to the tower; holding Cliff close in my arms. Finally, we were within two blocks of the tower. Larry pulled over and parked, and I forgot about the man.

"Let's hoof it from here. I don't think we will be able to get any closer driving." Larry climbed down and walked around to the passenger side to help me descend. As I slid into his arms, I broke out in tears again. Huge sobs racked my body as I remembered that the last time that I had gotten out of Larry's truck like this was into the arms of Cliff.

"I'm sorry Larry, there have just been too many things happening today, my nerves are nearly totally gone."

"Cheer up, Tina. I'm sure that when we get there, you will have tears of joy finding Cliff waiting for you. Let's make it these last two blocks and see what we can find."

We struggled on, each step bringing me closer to either heartache and loss, or unending happiness with Cliff in my arms.

'Why had I not told Cliff yes when I had the chance? He deserved a better answer than I had given him. I should not have hesitated, but followed my heart. When I found him, I would tell him yes, I would marry him. I wanted him, to see him, to be held in his arms. To have him comfort me and tell me that everything would be all right. I could not live if I were to lose him now. It would

be too painful to endure. First, my brother, then my parents. I could barely force myself forward. I was fearful of what I might find.'

Just at that moment we came around a corner from which we caught a good view of the lower tower. There did not seem to be as much damage, at least from this vantage point, as we had feared. There were the ruins of what was probably the vehicle which had exploded, large sections of the ground floor windows had been blown out. It did not look, at least from our position across from the vehicle, that there were actual floor collapses as had been described.

Of course, we could only see the exterior area from here. My heart felt relieved. The horror that had been in my mind was now somewhat diminished. But there was no sign of Cliff yet. I began to pray quietly under my breath,

'Oh, God! Please let him be okay. Please let me see him again and let him be well and whole.'

A policeman approached us shortly after that and inquired who we were and why we were there. Larry explained that he was a VP with the company, and I was his assistant. We displayed our company badges and after a few more questions the officer waved us on.

"Please do not attempt entry anywhere inside yet. The building hasn't been assessed for safety yet," the office advised us.

"Officer, do you have any information about the construction workers who were inside at the time of the explosion?" Larry asked.

"No sir. I believe they are gathering that information now. I think that there is an aid station on the opposite side where several of the injured were taken. Cuts and bruises are being addressed there. The more seriously injured workers have been taken to local hospitals. They might have a list and would be able to direct you further."

"Thank you, officer," I said.

"Larry, let's walk around that side over there. It looks like it has fewer obstacles on the sidewalk. We should be able to get to the opposite side of the structure in that direction."

We walked carefully, struggling to climb over or around large chunks of debris scattered everywhere. I tried to peer into the ruins of the first floor but could not see anything. Once, I thought that I had seen a lady stumbling over a cement block. But then I realized it was simply my reflection in a broken window pane.

There were more police and fire personnel as we approached the last corner of the building. We flashed our badges again, and they waved us past. Rounding the last corner, we saw a small group of what appeared to be injured workers with several nurses and a doctor treating them on the ellipse of a nearby building.

We increased our steps trying to get there as quickly as possible.

'Where is he? God, where is Cliff? Please, God, let him be alive,' I worried.

"Is that him, Larry?" when I saw a worker stumbling around a corner of the building.

"...No, it was just another worker," Larry answered.

'Cliff... Please be here, please be well. Cliff...'

I had known grief in my life, but nothing like this. The pain was overpowering. I could feel my heart on the verge of tearing itself in half. I knew that if Cliff had been killed my life would be over. There was no one else in the world who could take his place in my life. He had awakened love within me beyond my wildest dreams. I could no longer think of my life before he had appeared. I only knew that I could not live without him.

CHAPTER 12

As it turned out, there was not an official triage station. Just an area where a few nurses and a doctor had gathered on a nearby buildings' front lawn and treated those people who were only slightly wounded with small cuts and abrasions. There were some people there ranging from those who had been walking past the building when the explosion occurred to a few workers from inside with minor scrapes and cuts. There was no list of the injured or worse who might have already been taken to local hospitals.

Larry approached one of the workers as soon as the nurse had applied a bandage to a cut over his eye. "Have you seen Cliff Stinson?"

"Yes, Sir. The last that I saw Cliff he was helping to carry one of the guys down from near the worst of the explosion. He was hobbling around on one leg helping other badly injured workers. I don't know where he might be right now. He was heading toward a stairway leading down to near where the explosion took place to see what help he could be there. I haven't seen him since then. Wish I could be of more assistance."

"Thank you so much, Sir!" I interjected.

The message of hope that he had given took a great burden from my heart. Cliff was alive, and at least healthy enough to be helping others. We decided to wait around near the aid station in the hope that he might show up with another patient.

Shortly afterward several more injured were brought to the area. These appeared more serious, with broken bones and deep cuts that were still bleeding.

More ambulances and medical staff arrived with desperately needed supplies. Those workers suffering the worst injuries were immediately placed in an ambulance and taken away to hospitals. Other ambulances arrived and took their place and soon there was a long, orderly row of ambulances waiting their turn for patients.

There was still no sign of Cliff. I looked desperately into each face searching for him.

Larry asked among the wounded after him, but most had not seen him. Others had seen him, but he had moved away from their areas after ascertaining that the most seriously injured had already been removed. Those remaining were ambulatory and would be moving toward the triage area as soon as they gathered what belongings they could find.

'Where was he?' The minutes ticked away mercilessly, ten, twenty, still no sign. Still no positive word.

'Where could he be? Cliff, I need you. I need to see you. I need to touch you, to know that you are okay. Please, Please Lord. Let him be well.'

Then, suddenly, I saw what looked to be Cliff stumbling out of one of the wrecked sides of the tower. He was limping terribly, his face covered with soot. His left arm hung limply by his side. There was a cut on his cheek with dried blood where it had run down his neck. His shirt was torn nearly in half. One leg of his pants was ripped all the way from his knee to his waist, held up only by his belt.

A thrill ran through my entire body as I was running as fast as I could to get to him. All that I knew or cared about was that he was alive.

"Cliff! You're alive" I screamed as I ran. When I reached him, I stopped and stared. I was afraid to touch him; he looked so badly torn up everywhere.

"Hi, sweetheart! What's up?" He broke into his trademark billboard smile, and then he leaned down and gave me a tender kiss. "Don't worry about me, precious. I'll be fine."

"Where does it hurt, big fella? I want to find a place that I can grab onto, but you look bad all over."

"It hurts pretty much all over, but if you don't mind, let me grab onto you first. That will be much safer," he said, wrapping his uninjured right arm around my shoulder for support.

"Christina, I was so afraid for you. They told me that there was an explosion at your building as well as this one. I was half out of my mind with worry. But there were so many of my workers and friends injured here that I felt that I owed it to them to do what I could to assist, no matter my injuries."

"I could just slap your face for causing me so much worry. What were you thinking? Instead of slapping you I am going to give you another big kiss," I said while dragging his head down to my level and tasting his sweet lips on mine.

"I am so mad at you, look at you! Your clothes are all torn; your arm hurt, and I see a big cut on your face where you've been bleeding. But rather than fuss at you, I will tell you what I am going to do with you, you precious idiot. I am going to marry you. I've wanted to tell you all week, but you kept getting tied up at work."

"What did you just say?" He looked at me incredulously.

"You heard me the first time. I should have told you last week, but I was a fool. I love you, and I am going to marry you. It looks like you need someone to take care of you because you don't seem to do much of that for yourself. Now, let's get you over to the doctor before something else happens."

"Christina, you have made my dreams come true," tears formed in his eyes.

"Look, you wonderful, big idiot. Let's get your cute behind into that ambulance over there and get you healed and well again before you get yourself into worse trouble."

"Okay, okay. Wow! Talk about throwing a guy for a loop. I never figured when I woke up this morning that I would end up with a fiancée before I went back to bed. You've made me the happiest man in the world."

Larry came running up to us at that point.

"Larry, I would like you to meet my fiancé, Clifford Stinson."

Larry's mouth dropped open, his eyes grew round with astonishment and then he broke into the biggest smile that I had ever seen him have. "How? What? When? Oh, holy bejeezus! Congratulations you two. That is the most wonderful news that I think that I have heard today. So …When's the big wedding?" he asked as he grabbed Cliff's uninjured hand and shook it heartily.

"Hey. Give a guy a chance. She only said yes less than a minute ago."

Larry helped me get Cliff over to the ambulance where the EMT's assessed his injuries. They placed him on a gurney and soon had him in trussed up and ready to go.

"Can my fiancée join me," he asked as they lifted him up and slid the gurney into place and locked it. "I don't want to let her get out of my sight now that she has said the magic word."

"Sure. Hop in Miss! There is a pull-down seat over here. Let me help you up and get you buckled safely. Ambulances can be a bumpy ride, and we don't want you bouncing around in here," the EMT said. He smiled as he reached down to help me climb aboard.

I happily joined Cliff in the ambulance and took the proffered seat and smiled at Cliff while the EMT adjusted my seat belt. I looked back at Larry.

"Larry, I am so happy right now. But it looks like you'll be riding back to the office alone. I hope that you don't mind."

"I don't mind at all. And, Tina, I'm very happy for you. After everything that has happened to you over the years. I couldn't wish a happier thing than for you to find someone like Cliff to share your life. I've known Cliff for a very long time; he's a swell guy. He attends the same church as my family and I. You deserved to find someone like him.

"I've often worried about you, knowing what a sensitive and kind lady that you are and the tragedies you've endured in the past. Now, I won't have to any longer. I'm so happy for the both of you. You go along with your new fiancé. I'll meet up with you there if you need a ride home after that.

I'll give you a call when and if our building is ready to be occupied again. I am sure that it is a real mess right now, and the police and fire departments will not want us back into the building for several days."

So take whatever time you need to get Cliff well again. Who knows, we may even work from home for a time. We both have lots to sort out before we can get back to work. Don't worry about that for the time being. I'll be in touch."

"We'll be okay, Larry. Charlotte will be along for us when we're ready, thanks for all of your help, and everything that you've done for me in the past. You are a dear friend, besides being the best boss ever. Now you run along home; I'm sure that your wife and children are worried about your safety. I'm going to be fine, Bye for now, and take care of yourself." I waved as the ambulance pulled away with its siren screeching. Larry had been my dearest friend.

As I watched, the EMT took good care of Cliff. He dressed the cut on his cheek with some antiseptic wipes and assessed the condition of his arm.

"What happened to your arm, sir?" he asked.

"There was a large piece of concrete from the blast that struck me below my shoulder. I don't remember a lot about it, but my arm went numb after that. I focused mainly on getting those more seriously injured out to safety."

"We can't do a complete exam here in the ambulance, but as soon as we get you to the medical center, they will take some X-rays and will get you fixed up and back out on the street again good as new. Now, let me see that leg."

He carefully pulled apart the torn edges of Cliff's trousers and found a long cut stretching up from above the knee. It did not appear to be bleeding.

"Yeah," Cliff said as the EMT gave a long whistle. "There was a jagged piece of rebar that I was thrown against. Luckily, I don't think that it's deep, just a long scratch."

"I could add some dressing to this, but I would like to have the hospital doctor perform a more thorough exam. Since the hospital is right on the edge of downtown, we should be there in about two minutes."

I was eager to speak more with Cliff with a thousand questions swirling through my thoughts. But while the EMT was checking him out from head to toe for other injuries, I did not want to interrupt or distract them from his most important duty. That was to get my fiancé, *(Oh, I loved the sound of that)*, well and healthy again.

I mouthed "I love you," over and over, my heart running over with love for this brave, courageous man.

CHAPTER 13

Upon arrival at the medical center, Cliff was immediately taken to the ER. The doctors did a complete workup while I waited just outside leaning against the nurse's station. I could hear everything happening in the area, as it was shielded only by a thin curtain.

"Sir, we need to cut away this torn clothing to inspect your injuries," I could hear the ER doctor speaking. "I need to cut this entire pants leg off so that I can get a better look. Your arm, sir, it's not broken; however it looks like a nerve in your back was struck by the concrete block and some damage had been incurred.

"This is normal for this type of injury. The nerve will be fine in a few days, and your arm will function again just as before. The other injuries are superficial and after reviewing the X-Ray and other tests, I'm going to release you to the custody of the young lady who brought you here."

"You mean, my fiancée," Cliff corrected.

"Yes, sir. Your fiancée. And a very pretty one at that, sir."

I smiled to myself.' *I'm sure that the doctor had said that simply to cheer Cliff up.'*

"Since your clothes are torn and ripped, we have a set of hospital scrubs that you can wear."

"Nurse, please hand Mr. Stinson a pair of scrubs from that locker," the doctor ordered.

After the nurse had found the appropriate size hospital scrubs, the doctor and nurse quickly left the exam area to check on the next arriving patient. I could hear Cliff stumbling around trying to get the scrubs on.

"Cliff, do you need any help?" I asked.

"Not yet. I had some trouble with the shirt, but I finally got it on. The pants were a bit harder since my arm is still numb right now. But maybe, yes, can you help me with my shoes? There's no way that I can get those back on."

"Yes. Are you decent now?"

"Yes, sweetheart. You may come in."

I stepped behind the curtain and found him sitting on the hospital bed. Before I did anything else, I walked up to him and kissed him on his lips.

(*Oh, I could get used to this. His lips tasted just as yummy just as they had at the restaurant, just without the butter.*)

"I love you, Cliff. Now where are those shoes?"

"My shoes are in that sack under the bed. Thank you so much for helping, by the way, I love you as well."

I helped him get the shoes on and laced them up. They were very dirty, covered with soot and grit.

"Lean on my shoulder, Cliff, and let's go to the discharge area," I asked as I put my arm around his waist, helping him down off the bed.

We passed by the doctor working on a man in the next exam area.

"Thank you, doctor. Am I free to go now?'

"Yes, just stop by the lady in admissions," the doctor replied without even looking up from the broken arm that he was trying to set. "She will handle your payment. Your discharge papers are on top of that clipboard. Good luck to you, sir. You were very lucky to escape with such minor injuries."

Cliff grabbed a sheet from the clipboard, and we proceeded to the admitting area and located the discharge person. After Cliff has settled up his bill, I supported him as we walked toward the ER exit.

"All right big boy. You belong to me now, and I have got some stuff to share with you, but I don't want to do it here. Give me a minute and I am going to give Charlotte a ring. She should be here in about ten minutes, and we will take a ride over to my place where we can talk in peace. Are you hungry?"

"Come to think of it, I haven't had much time to consider food over the past several hours," he replied rubbing his stomach. "But I do believe that the grumbling in my stomach is signaling that it needs some grub. Why? Do you want to stop somewhere and pick up something for dinner?" he asked.

"Not exactly," I said with a smile. "Let me give Marianne a buzz and tell her that there will be a guest for dinner today."

"All right, Christina, Out with it. Who exactly are this Charlotte and Marianne that you keep mentioning? More secrets from your past?"

"Cliff, like I said, let me take you to my place where we can sit and discuss stuff like this in a more relaxed atmosphere. I have got a million questions for you, and I know that you will have two or three for me. As for Charlotte, you'll be meeting her in just a few minutes."

My cell phone buzzed just then. It turned out to be Charlotte to advise me that she was waiting for us just outside the ER Entrance area. Cliff and I walked out together with me supporting. He was still limping a bit from the injury to his leg. His arm was now in a sling, and he had a large bandage covering the cut on his cheek.

Charlotte gave me a strange look as we approached, but she quickly stepped out and helped me to get Cliff seated. After Charlotte and I had Cliff situated in the back seat so that he could stretch out his leg more comfortably I phoned Marianne and told her that we were having a male guest for dinner today and to have an extra place setting. Having done that, I took the time to introduce Cliff.

"Charlotte, this is Clifford Stinson, my fiancé, the man we spoke about the other night. Cliff, this is Charlotte Parker, she is my personal bodyguard and driver."

"Hello, Cliff," Charlotte beamed. "You probably did not see me the other night, but you sure gave me a shock when Tina jumped up and gave you that kiss. Yes, I was there, but I am paid to be invisible so don't be too surprised, in future, you happen to catch a glimpse of me from time to time. I try always to stay in the background, but sometimes that is just not humanly possible."

"Hello, Charlotte. I am very pleased to meet you. And especially so if you are there to protect my fiancée."

He turned his face to me, "A bodyguard?" he mouthed quietly, questioning why I would need a bodyguard.

"I'll explain when we get to my apartment," I replied.

"Fiancé? Wow," Charlotte cried. "Something going on that I don't know about Tina? I don't remember you mentioning that you were engaged when you left for work this morning."

"It was a sudden thing. You know, like bombs going off and cars blowing up. I decided to take the plunge before things happened that would rob me of the opportunity of marrying the man of my dreams."

Cliff's face broke out into a huge smile when he heard that statement.

"Man of your dreams, huh? Well, you are certainly the woman of my dreams, that's for sure."

"Welcome again, Cliff," Charlotte turned in her seat. "It's a real pleasure to meet you. I've already heard a lot about you from my boss. Now, just to keep things straight between us, you'd better take good care of my boss, or I'll be looking for you."

"Charlotte," I replied roughly. "There will be none of that. Cliff has had a pretty rough day today, and I think that he requires some TLC. And that is why I am here."

"Yes, ma'am." Charlotte returned to her driving duties and did not say anything else the rest of the way back to the Grecian Condominium. However, her sly smiles, as she looked into the rearview mirror, told me everything I needed to know.

I sat in the front passenger seat; my body twisted around so that I could keep my eyes on Cliff. He returned my gaze with a questioning eyebrow raised at me. I was bursting to tell him all, but I wanted him to be on my couch and comfortable before the inquisition began.

CHAPTER 14

When we finally made it up to my apartment, Marianne greeted us with a warm smile. Then she saw Cliff and became a burst of energy, wanting to know all of what had happened. She had been watching the news as it slowly dribbled out, but much of it inaccurate and was confusing.

Eventually, it had been announced that no one had been killed but there were many walking wounded and a lot of damage to both buildings. The fire department and building inspectors were working overtime to get a better understanding of the two blasts and whether either building could be occupied anytime soon.

"But you, Mr. Cliff. What happened to you? Did Charlotte do that to you because you were going to kiss Ms. Tina again, or were you in the explosion?" Marianne teased.

"Oh, shush, Marianne. First, I need to formally introduce Cliff to you properly. His name is Clifford Stinson and he is my fiancé. Cliff, this is Marianne Williams, my housekeeper."

I could have knocked Marianne over with a feather. Her jaw nearly dropped to the floor, and then she screamed a happy sound and ran over and hugged and kissed Cliff's cheeks several times.

"Oh, Mr. Cliff, that is so exciting. I have been so worried about my Tina. She really needs someone in her life and ever since I heard that you proposed the other night I have been praying very hard that you would be the one. Thank you, thank you, thank you."

"You are welcome, Marianne. But I only regret that we had to meet like this. I look a wreck, my clothes are all torn, so all I have is these hospital scrubs. I am certainly not looking my best."

"From the news that I just heard, I think Tina would love you no matter what you had on," Marianne replied.

Marianne then focused our attention on the dining area where she had set out four bowls of hot vegetable soup with oyster crackers.

"I know you must be hungry, and I fixed a special meal, just for you. Please, come over to the table and I will get the silverware."

"I'm famished," Cliff said as we sat at the table. "Please, I need to say grace before we eat."

We all paused and bowed our heads.

"Lord God,

Forgive us our sins and those who sin against us.
We thank you for this food and ask that you bless and sanctify it to the nourishment of our bodies. Bless the hands that prepared it; replenish the source where it came from, in Jesus name.

Amen."

Cliff then wolfed down his soup down eagerly, which made Marianne extremely happy that he enjoyed the dish so much. The three of us watched and chatted and tried, mostly without success, to keep from staring at our handsome dinner guest. I was again impressed with his strength of faith and took consolation in his expression of gratitude.

For the main dish, Marianne had prepared one of her specialties, beef, and lamb dinner.

After we had all chatted and completed our meal I had an idea.

"Charlotte, let's get Cliff's clothes sizes. If you wouldn't mind, would you and Marianne run down to Neiman Marcus and pick up some things for him to wear. I don't want him to feel uncomfortable sitting around with three ladies, half-dressed."

My real motive was to give Cliff and myself some alone time where we could talk freely.

Cliff begged to let him pay for everything, but I wouldn't hear of it. I stepped into the foyer and told the two ladies that money was no object; they were to pick out the best of everything. I explained that he liked to wear nice dress suits, as well as some slacks and dress shirts. They were to buy some underwear and pajamas and a robe plus a full set of toiletries.

"Marianne, Cliff will be staying the night. Can you tidy up the guest bedroom?

"Yes, ma'am. I had guessed as much when you called. I straightened the room; it's ready now."

"Charlotte, here's my credit card. You and Marianne can go together. Cliff and I have some things to discuss. Please take your time. I'll handle things here."

Both ladies gave me a knowing smile and were quickly out the door and disappeared behind the elevator doors, Marianne giving me a wink just before the doors closed.

Returning to sit beside Cliff, I realized that somehow I did not feel that fear of being alone with him as I had other men. Cliff was now the man in my life. He was gentle, kind and best of all; he was in love with me, and I was head over heels in love with him. I belonged to him, and there was nothing to fear. I felt easy and relaxed in his presence. I felt happy. But there were things that needed to be spoken and heard. Secrets of my past and present that I needed to share with him.

I sat down beside him on the couch, screwed up my courage and began.

"Cliff, I have a few confessions to make before we go any further. I told you earlier that I love you. I want you to know that is true; I don't know how or when maybe it was from that first moment. I also want you to know that since I was age sixteen I have had a terror of being alone in a room with a man. I don't feel that way with you. You make me feel safe and protected when I am with you.

"I am nearly totally inexperienced with men. When I was age seven, I met a boy my age on the playground and begged him to kiss me. At first, he was reluctant. I was overweight, wore frumpy clothing and considered myself ugly. I was desperate to experiment and to be like the other girls in my class who told me they were doing. You know, kissing boys and that sort of thing.

"Finally, the boy agreed to one kiss. It was short and sweet. When his lips touched mine, I thought it was divine. He, on the other hand, was totally disgusted. He hollered out "Yuck" and ran away. I was so embarrassed, totally humiliated as the other girls stood around laughing at me. I never tried that again, and it was not until I was a senior in high school that I began to notice boys again and would have been willing to go on dates.

"I was a high school cheerleader and one Friday night we were at an away game and during the third quarter, I left the group and went by myself to the girl's restroom. While there I was brutally assaulted by three teenage boys. Ever since that night, I have had night terrors and a dreadful fear being alone with a man.

"I refused offers from other boys for dates, and I did not attend the school prom because I had heard that that is where so many girls went out with boys afterward and lost their virginity. I could not bear the thought of another boy having sex with me, fearing that it would be the same painful experience as my assault.

"In the past week you seem to have removed that fear from my heart, at least where you are concerned. Tonight is the very first time in those seventeen years that I have ever been alone with any man, other than my father and a psychiatrist, who I had to visit regularly for over four years. I feel liberated around you. Your presence and your touch give me a peace of my mind. I want to thank you from the bottom of my heart for that."

Cliff thought for a time and then looked me in the eyes.

"I was afraid that it was something like that making you so afraid. But, Christina, that is all in the past. I want to help you build a life with me. Let's build that life together. What happened then is now history. You mustn't let it rule your life forever. Neither of us can change what happened. Please, let me hold you. I have been dying to do that since that day in the truck when I held you around your shoulders. Let's build new memories together.

"Last Tuesday, I wanted to stay there with you all day, it felt so right, so natural. Your body seemed to respond to my touch. The look you had in your eyes when our eyes first met melted my heart. And even more exciting was that you let me hold your precious hand all the way to the restaurant. At the time, my heart was pounding so loudly in my chest that I thought Larry could hear it on the other side of the truck."

"Than, all the time that we were eating, the way that you acted told me that you were as affected as I. You were so precious and charming in your nervousness. Several times I wanted to laugh for the joy of watching you. But I realized that it might hurt your feelings since you would have never understood that I felt exactly the same as you."

Cliff leaned in and took possession of my lips. Our tongues explored each other's mouths. His strong arm wrapped around my shoulder. There was no other place in the world where I wished to be than here, beside him, treasuring and loving him. No danger could touch me here. I was safe in his arms. Had he asked again, I would have probably run away and eloped with Cliff that very evening, I just did not want him to leave. I wanted him by my side, tonight, tomorrow, and all the days in the future.

This! -- This is what I had always wanted and never fully understood. From time to time I had daydreamed of finding someone but never believed that would truly happen. I was already long past the age at which most women had already married, borne children and set up their homes and families.'

'My life had become boring. Rising from my bed at the same time every day. Eating with my staff, dressing, and going to the same old job. I had buried myself in my work, but lately, it had become less interesting.

Returning to my same apartment, eating, showering and getting ready for bed. Day in, day out, a routine that was unsatisfying and left me feeling empty and alone.

'I wanted more, so much more and now I knew that more in the person of Cliff. He would be my life and future. I no longer could imagine my life without him in it. In fact, I wanted him being the center of my life, making decisions together, going places together. I wanted to know everything about him. Where he was born; his childhood; his high school years. Had he dated other girls or possibly women? I was jealous of every kiss that he might have given before the ones he had given me.'

As we finished our kiss, Cliff began looking around the room. I watched as he began to take in his surroundings, studying the apartment, taking in the luxurious furniture, exquisite paintings, and sumptuous furnishings. I began to detect a hint of amazement, or was it astonishment, or even fear. I sensed his realization that very expensive things surrounded him. I began to be afraid.

"Please say something, Cliff," I begged.

He spoke, hesitantly, "Is all of this yours? …How? …Where? I don't understand. I am almost embarrassed to ask this, but -- are you wealthy? Everything that I see here looks so very expensive."

"Yes, Cliff, I am not only wealthy but very wealthy. But please don't let these things change how you feel about me. It certainly does not change how I feel about you. I want us to work. I want us to be one person more than anything that I have ever wanted in my life."

"I'm speechless. How could I ever hold onto you? What could I possibly provide that would make you want to stay with me? I am just an ordinary working person. I would be so afraid that one day you would look at me and see how little that I can provide that you don't already have, and you would no longer want me."

"Cliff, you have everything that I want. You have a love for me that is genuine. I recognized it the first day although, at the time, I did not understand what it was until later that day. I see it in your eyes now. I feel it in my heart. It is I who would be devastated should you ever look at me and decide that you wanted something, or someone else.

"Money means little to me. Yes, it does provide this place where I live. It gives me the ability to have people around me who keep me safe and protected. But I would give it all up in a heartbeat if it meant keeping you by my side.

"I pretty sure that I had the same experience that you did when you came out of the tower and came toward me in the truck. My heart beat faster; my emotions nearly ran away with me. At the time, I was totally confused and unsure of myself. I just did not understand what my body was telling me.

"When you got in and sat beside me, everywhere that we touched was like a hot flame. I wanted to stay in the truck with your arm around me and my hand inside yours. My appetite was thrown for a loop. All that I could hear was the blood rushing in my ears. You turned my entire world upside down and ever since that moment I have not been able to get you out of my mind."

I waited expectantly for his answer, my heart pounding so hard that I was sure that he could hear it. My entire future might turn on his answer. I desperately hoped that he would give the right one.

'Oh! Please, Cliff, don't turn away from me.'

"Christina. I do love you. As I told you, I have loved you since the first minute. I don't know how or why it happened to me, but it is true. I want you by my side. You are all that matters to me, not your money, not the things you have. I need only you. If you can accept me as I am, then I will truly be the luckiest man in the world."

I sank into his arms, and he kissed me tenderly. We held each other for a long time, relishing in each other's taste and feel. His tongue explored the depths of my mouth while I fisted my fingers in his hair. He was injured in so many places that I was afraid that I would cause him pain in some way by touching him anywhere else. I kissed his uninjured hand while he trailed a row of kisses from below my ear and down my neck.

We remained there, holding each other, talking, and joining our lives together for several hours until Charlotte and Marianne and the hotel concierge returned with a cart full of new men's clothing.

"Oh, ladies, no!" Cliff objected "You should not have gotten so much. Please let me pay you back, Christina. It's too much. I can hardly accept this much from you."

"Cliff, do you love me?"

"You know that I do."

"This is my first gift of love to you. Please don't refuse it."

"Christina, it seems that you have given me no choice. I feel like I have just received a stack of early Christmas presents, and I want to open all of them at once."

"One other thing," I said, looking hopefully into his eyes. "And I don't want any argument about it. You are going to stay with us tonight. I have a guest room, and it has been made ready for you."

"Is this how it is going to be? You buying things for me and me having to accept them without question?"

"I am afraid so, Cliff. That is what happens when people love each other. They share their lives and all that they have. Get used to it. I want to share my world with you."

"And I with you, but, at the moment, I have a bit of a problem, and I am not sure how to solve it." Cliff looked at me confused and embarrassed.

"Can I help?" I asked, uncertain of what the problem was.

"I am not sure. You have done so much already, and I am a bit embarrassed to say this, but perhaps you can offer a suggestion. As you might remember my left arm is numb and useless at present and I would like a shower to get some more of the soot off of my body. I feel so grimy from the dust and trash. I would like to change into the wonderful pajamas and robe you have provided."

'Damn! Somehow this had completely slipped my mind. How was he going to clean himself? The room was ready; the clothes were available, there was a private shower and spa tub in his room.'

I appraised myself. I am a thirty-three-year-old healthy American female. I have never been with a man other than those terribly nasty, evil boys who had ruined my life.

I struggled with my fears and finally made up my mind. I was going to have to take the plunge. It was now or never for me, here was my prince charming. Everything that I had ever dreamed of in a husband. I was going to have to do something that was totally foreign to me. I silently prayed that he would not turn me away. If he did, I was not sure if I could survive that kind of rejection.

My heart was beating wildly; anticipation and fear surged through my thoughts. I thanked Charlotte and Marianne for their help and explained that Cliff was tired and injured and needed to take a shower.

"Why don't you ladies go on about your work? I will help Cliff get ready for his shower."

They looked at each other, smiled and left for other parts of the apartment.

Meanwhile, I directed Cliff to his room and turned on the shower, and lay out his night clothes on the bed. Then I helped him set out the shower gel, toiletries, and towels. I was nervous; my hand was trembling.

'Can I do it? Can I be that brave?' I felt weak, and my knees almost buckled at the thought of what I was about to do. I made up my mind. Nothing was going to keep us apart, even my ancient fears. I must show him how completely that I trust and love him.

CHAPTER 15

"Okay, Christina. I think that should do it. I think that I can handle the rest," Cliff insisted. "My arm isn't broken, so I should be able to wash and dry myself using my other arm. If you could help me with this top, I can try to do the rest myself."

"Lift your good arm then and I can pull this off over your head and then slip it off your left arm," I said as I helped him with the hospital scrub, then tossed it into the trash. He would no longer be needing that, and for what I wanted, he would need even less.

His chest was strong and rippled with muscles.

'God, I wanted to run my hand over it, feel the hair on his chest between my fingers.'

As I started to pull down the scrub bottom, he grabbed my hand gently.

"Christina..." he cautioned.

I released my grip on the scrub bottom and smiled up at him. I realized then that I was going to have to attack this from a different direction. I kissed his lips and then turned and left him standing beside the shower. As I walked out, I closed the door quietly behind me. My lips curled up in a secret smile at the surprise that I was going to give.

I went to my room and slipped out of my dress, my fingers fumbling nervously with the zipper. I reached behind my back and released my bra, freeing my breasts from their prison. Nervously I slid my panties down and stepped out of them. Upon catching sight of myself in my dresser mirror, I struggled to send strength to the eyes of the woman that I beheld. I retrieved a robe from my closet, wrapped it around myself, and then returned to his room.

My fingers were trembling as they touched the door handle.

'This is it, no turning back. If I open this door, I will have chosen my future.'

But then a small doubt crossed my mind: *'What if he refuses me? How will I ever live down the shame of that rejection?'*

Then I remembered the look of love that I had seen in his eyes and all doubt disappeared.

I slowly turned the knob and opened the door to the shower room quietly and stood, watching for a few seconds, as Cliff struggled to try to wash. Blood pounded in my ears, and my legs felt weak. I closed and locked the door behind me, my eyes never leaving his back.

He back was facing me, and he did not hear the door open or close over the noise of the shower. I watched as he tried to get the shower gel out of the bottle, onto his mostly lifeless left hand and then back onto his good hand to rub his chest. My heart pounded as I stood quietly, naked beneath my robe, behind him, admiring his firm muscles and toned body. It was very clear that he worked out routinely, his body reflected it. I let my robe pool quietly at my feet and stepped into the shower behind him.

Suddenly I had a memory of that day at lunch. I had already seen myself in this exact scene. I could feel my face blush from my nakedness. I desperately wanted to crush my body against his. I felt like a little child who was doing something my parents had forbidden me over and over not to do. On the other hand, I suddenly felt liberated.

All of my years of terror and fear of men had vanished. I knew that this was right, this is what two people do who are deeply in love with each other. They surrender themselves completely to one another. There is no shame or embarrassment, only love. I was more certain than ever; I love this man completely, I am his.

He must have sensed my entry behind him because he quickly turned to face me. There was a brief look of shock on his face at first, his eyes taking in the fact that I was now completely nude. His eyes then lifted to mine; his thoughts were hidden from me. At first, he seemed to hesitate. Then his eyes softened, became gentle and more loving. I think that he was more afraid for me than himself. His eyes looked deeply into mine, asking the question before speaking.

"Christina, are you sure?"

My hand reached up and stroked his cheek gently; I nodded my head.

"Yes, Cliff, I'm sure. More sure of this than anything in my life. I belong to you and hold nothing back."

I answered his unspoken thoughts with my eyes, surrendering myself to him. He lowered his lips to mine and kissed me tenderly. I took the shower gel from his good hand and began to wash his chest and stomach. The touch of his skin against my palm burned my hand. My mind was on fire with desire for him.

I felt his strong muscles ripple beneath my fingers; then I wiped the last traces of soot from his face and neck. I took great care not to wet or damage the large bandage on his cheek as I washed his face. His eyes became large and round as I stroked his chest and stomach muscles.

Slowly I washed his good arm and then held myself against him, relishing the feel of our bodies as they were melded together, my breasts against his warm stomach and my arm circling his waist. His penis was hardened and now firmly pressed against my leg. His body felt so wonderful and natural against mine, and I was not ashamed or embarrassed. I only felt love.

He stroked my face with his good hand, his fingers touching my lips, and then combing through my hair as the water soaked my head. I rubbed his weak arm, soaking it with the gel, and then I washed his bruised shoulder and back as I trailed kisses from his neck down to his shoulder. We kissed again and again, my mouth welcoming his eager tongue inside.

His good arm surrounded my body and his hand rubbing up and down my back and across my bottom.

I knelt down in the shower to allow myself leverage to wash the dirt and grime from his powerful legs, taking great care to avoid scraping the long scratch above his left knee. I kissed it tenderly, wishing that my kisses might be a magic balm to bring healing to his body. My eyes sought out and found his. Seeking and finding there the love that my soul so desperately needed.

After taking the bath cloth, I soaked it with the fresh smelling gel and washed him around his manhood. I felt his erection swelling inside my palm. I looked up into his eyes, begging him to love me for myself and not my money. To let me be all that he wanted me to be. To be his, and his alone.

"Mine," I whispered, a pleading cry from the depths of my soul, "please love me."

Using my hand, I soaked his swollen organ with suds and slid my finger underneath, stroking between his legs and buttocks. His eyes became erotic as I held him gently, lovingly.

"Please, Cliff. Please hold me to you, I want to be yours. I need you inside of me."

"Yes," he replied, kissing my hair.

He took the cloth from my hand and washed under my arms, then my breasts, and over my stomach. We kissed again in a whirl of passion as he pulled the cloth softly between my legs across my womanhood.

"Mine," he whispered back.

His palm massaged my mons and then his fingers slipped slowly between my folds, gently stroking and teasing the entrance to my vagina. He then reached further between my legs and buttocks. My body electrified, my senses longed for more. My body yearned for his touch, his kisses, the feel of his chest against my breasts, his breath, hot in my ear, sent me over the top.

"Yes, only yours."

I was lost in my passion, I wanted him desperately. I turned the shower off and lifted his towel. I dried him slowly, his arms, his chest, his torso, his legs and then his back. He then turned as he used his good hand to perform the same duty for me.

"Please make love to me, Cliff" I begged. "I need you; I want to surrender myself to you."

I helped him to the bed where I lay beneath him. He was incredibly strong, tender and loving. I whispered in his ear how very much that I loved and needed him.

"Please be gentle with me. I am ashamed that, since I know so little about this, I will disappoint you and my body will not be what you had imagined. I will fail to please you in some way. My only experience with this was painful as the boys cared very little how badly they injured me."

"Christina, there is nothing to fear. I am just as inexperienced as you. I have heard and read about performing intercourse, but until this moment, I have never actually been with a woman like this. I know that probably is hard to believe, but I am serious when I say that I am a virgin. I have always believed in waiting until I found the right woman. I know that you are that woman. We are going to have to help each other learn the steps. I don't want to hurt you in any way."

I felt a sudden joy in his confession. I was to be his first love. He was to be mine.

I felt the stiffness of his erection pressing between my legs seeking guidance. I grabbed his cock and rubbed it up and down across my folds, lubricating it with the juices of my arousal until I felt that it was in position over my folds to enter.

"I'm so wet." I whispered, "Yes, just there, Cliff, you need to push inside me now. Can you feel the entrance?"

He answered, not by a verbal statement, but rather the forceful entry as he pushed his rock hard organ inside of me. My entire sex filled by his throbbing organ.

"Oh, Cliff. That feels so much different than I remember. It does not hurt like it did when those boys violated me. You feel wonderful inside me.

It almost feels as if we were made for each other. Yes, just that way. Please, Cliff. Yes. Ohhhhh!"

I moaned as he began a gentle in and out motion that excited my senses as his hand rubbed across my clitoris while he pushed himself in and out of me. Since neither of us was an expert at this, he kept hitting my clitoris about every other attempt.

Each time that he hit my most sensitive part, my senses exploded, my breath tensed, my body seemed to be on fire. I did not remember anything like this from my rape. This sensation was entirely different; the feeling was an extreme pleasure to my entire body. Not the pain of the boys ramming into to my openings, caring little if they hurt me or not, most likely taking pleasure in the injuries they had inflicted on my body.

This feeling was something that I knew that I would get used to and probably enjoy with the right partner. I was now more certain than ever that Cliff was that partner. Everything about Cliff excited me, his tender face, his loving arms, his sweet voice, the smell of his bath oils, the stubble of his beard, the words he used to tell me of how much he loved me. The wonderful feeling of our bodies joining as one. We were one. We are one. I am his. He is mine.

As we continued, lost in each other, Cliff became more experienced and controlled in the use his muscles to bring us mutual enjoyment. We kissed deeply, our tongues exploring each other. He nibbled at my earlobe with his tongue inside my ear. He whispered words of love amid his excitement and desire. His hot breath, inside my ear and against my neck, sent shivers down my spine and raised my level of arousal to a fever pitch.

He gently massaged my breasts with his good hand and then ran his hand through my hair, twisting it between his fingers. Occasionally he fisted my hair tightly and pulled gently on a clump of hair, mussing the crown of my head with his palm. As his body slowly began to reach a climax, his thrusts inside me became more forceful. His knees pushed my legs further apart until his penis had pushed into the far reaches of my vagina. I could feel his juices as they throbbed upward inside his skin and were released deep inside my womb.

His touch was loving, his kisses were overpowering, and our bodies joined in a dance of love until we exploded in fits of passion, my senses shattered as he came inside me. He pushed even more restlessly until I felt him release again, his breathing paused, his seminal fluid buried deep within my body. My insides responded by squeezing his organ in a fit of orgasmic splendor which caused my climax to split me into a thousand pieces.

We were all sensation as I relished in his touch. His skin on my skin, his penis deep inside of me until at last Cliff collapsed on top of me, his energy spent, his lust satiated. His weight pressed me down into the mattress. I felt short of breath but totally satisfied. After a few minutes, I whispered in his ear,

"Cliff, you are quite heavy like this. Please roll over onto the bed and let's rest for a time."

"Oh, …sorry. I should have known better," he said shyly, as he rolled off of me, and lay spent, his head resting on the pillow next to my head.

"Wow. That was something else. I have never felt anything like that before." He said, his voice full of wonder, his smile was breathtaking.

"I am certainly glad of that, Cliff. I don't think I would enjoy listening to tales of other womanly conquests from your past and how I did not measure up to your expectations. I don't want to share you with any other woman, not in the past or present."

"As far as I am concerned I think you did better than any woman in history. Wow! That was incredible."

"Oh, shush! I can't believe for one second that I was better than, say, Cleopatra, or Helen of Troy" I teased.

"Well," he teased, "I sure don't know about those two ladies, but I am positive that they couldn't hold a candle to you. You are beautiful in every way, and all that I could ever desire."

Cliff awakened me three more times that night to join us together in passionate embraces and each time we exploded together in bursts of love and powerful orgasms, each more enjoyable than the previous. As we joined our bodies together, our passions seem to fuse our bodies into one.

Our movements became more practiced; our bodies seemed to anticipate each other, rising and falling in unison. We could not seem to get enough of each other. Our very souls seemed to cry out for the joining of our bodies into one.

"Cliff?"

"Yes, Christina?"

"I love you more than life itself."

"I love you beyond words, Christina."

Finally, we drifted off to sleep in each other's arms.

Chapter 16

I was awakened to the sound of breathing and for a moment, I was totally disoriented. The room looked strange. '*This was not my bedroom.*' For a second I was afraid, but then I realized that my arms were wrapped around Cliff like a vine. Our legs were intertwined and I could smell the delicious smell of Cliff and sex all over his hair. I relaxed and sank back onto my pillow. I stretched my arms as a feeling of joy and happiness took control of my mind.

Memories of my past faded from my thoughts. It was as if they had been washed away by our lovemaking. Cliff's eyes were still closed in sleep. He looked so peaceful and happy. I continued to watch him sleep. His breathing was soft and rhythmic. He slept for another ten minutes before he opened his eyes. I was so happy as I dreamed of waking up this way every day for the rest of my life. Nothing in the world could make me happier than that.

"Good morning, Christina. Did you sleep well last night?" he asked, with a yawn, as his eyes opened and his lips formed that wonderful smile.

"To tell the truth, I had the most magical night of my life. I was just lying here, watching you, thinking of how much my life has changed since you appeared last week. Oh, my -- has it only been a week? It has been the most wonderful and revealing week of my life. I have already given it a name. I can now split my life into two chapters. The first one being MLBC and the second is MLAC. I am very excited and anxious to learn more about the second chapter as the first one has closed for good."

"Hmm? I am trying to think here, MLBC and MLAC? Gosh, Christina, you've got me stumped. I don't have a clue what they mean. Give me a hint, please."

"Sweetheart, isn't it obvious? ML means 'My Life' BC means 'Before Cliff' AC means 'After Cliff.' From now on you will write all of the chapters of my story. I am so anxious to see what each new chapter holds for me -- correction, I mean for us."

"I could lie here all day being held by you," Cliff teased, "but I hear a growling in my stomach that tells me that the next chapter must have something to do with food, and I need to take a minute in the restroom."

"Cliff," I giggled. "I just realized that I am in your bedroom, and all that I have with me is my robe and no underwear. I am going to have to sneak out and hope that neither Charlotte nor Marianne is up yet. What time is it? There isn't a clock in here. Do you have your watch?"

"Hold on one second, I think that it is lying on the floor over here on the other side of the bed. If I could have my leg back, sweet lady, perhaps I can find out!"

"You may, but only on a temporary basis. I am trying to get it healed over here with my magic balm." I winked at him and gently lifted my leg to allow him to turn over and reach his watch.

"It is nine-thirty. --Man! I don't think that I've slept this late since I was a teenager," he cried.

"There is no way that my staff can still be sleeping," I moaned. "But perhaps they are out running an errand; maybe I can make it to my room without being seen. Why don't you take care of your needs while I go and find some clothes to wear."

I hopped out of the bed, grabbed my robe and tried to slink quietly through the den area. I paused when I caught sight of myself in the dresser mirror. My hair had that just fucked look, tousled and swirled into a jumble of disorder. I ran my fingers through the disaster, to little avail.

Then, screwing up my courage, I opened the door knowing that if either of my staff spotted me like this, they would know what we had been doing all night -- as if they had not already figured it out for themselves.

I was stopped almost immediately when I saw two place settings on the dining room table. Bacon, eggs, toast, orange juice and a steaming cup of coffee for each of us. I looked around, but there was no one there. Then I noticed a note leaning against one of the coffee cups.

'Ow!' As I walked to the table my crotch was very sensitive from all of the unexpected exercise that it had experienced the prior evening. I struggled to walk naturally because my legs wanted to do the cowboy polka, bow-legged and all.

Tina,

We did not want to disturb you guys, so just to let you know, Marianne and I will be gone all day today. We had some shopping to do and may take in a movie this afternoon. Your breakfast is here on the table, and Marianne fixed some sandwiches for lunch for you guys, they are in the fridge. You two have a good time and don't worry about us. We will give you a ring later to see if you want to dine in or go out for an engagement celebration.

Love,

Charlotte, Marian

I could not have been happier. I was definitely going to have to give those two ladies a raise in pay. I returned to Cliff's room and advised him that our secret was out, no use to hide any longer.

"So, how about another shower? I am not sure that I got all of that soot off of you last night, and I want to have a second chance," I said with a pout.

Cliff smacked my butt playfully, "sounds like a winner to me. My arm feels a little bit better this morning, but I still might need some assistance with the soap. Are you up for that?"

"You bet, big boy. Let's get you cleaned up and ready for action. I might want to revisit some of those things you did to me last night after we have breakfast. Are you up for that?" I teased playfully.

"You are one naughty girl, Christina, and yes, I will most definitely be up for that. But first things first, let's get cleaned up, have some breakfast and then let's see where this day will take us. Oh, by the way, I love your hair like that!"

I flushed a bright pink. 'Shame on you, Cliff."

After showering, kissing, showering and more kissing, my legs began to relax somewhat, and we finally made it to the breakfast table. I clasped my thighs together, not wanting to give a burlesque show underneath the glass surface of the table.

'Oh! How embarrassing.'

Cliff reached across the table for my hands. I slipped my hands into his and then curled my fingers into his palm while he gave grace for our meal.

"Sweet Lord Jesus,

We take this time to thank you for this meal and for bringing the two of us together.

As we begin this life together, I ask your particular blessing that I can be the man who will provide Christina the protection and love that she deserves. Show me the way to be that strong anchor in her life and let her know how much that she means to me.

Amen."

'Oh! I am going to love this chapter of MLAC. He is everything that I had ever dreamed... Everything that I could want.'

Cliff grabbed the remote from an end table and turned the TV on to see whether we could get the latest news about the bombings at our buildings. It was all over the local news stations and had even made the national news channels. There were lots of scenes of the destruction of the tower.

It did not appear to be as bad as they'd first feared -- just a lot of broken glass and blown out drywall and doors on the first three floors. Tilden was very lucky because several pieces of expensive equipment had not yet been installed and were in large cargo containers, safe outside in the parking lot. The exploded car had crashed short of the side of the building when it hit a fire hydrant. Police reports said that it had been stolen from a store parking lot a few days earlier. As for my building, that had extensive damage as well from a fire that had started after the explosion. The fire department, having been already on scene, was able to douse the flames before more than one area was damaged.

There was speculation that it might have been a terrorist attack since they seemed to use simultaneous bombings at different sites as a trademark. However, there did not appear to be any other similarities, and our company was not involved in any activities in the Middle East.

It was all still a big mystery, but the talking heads on the TV argued back and forth that the bombings were the result of this or that reason. Bottom line: they had no idea what they were talking about and we finally just turned the TV off and began our own speculations. Neither of us could come up with anything better than the TV, so we ending up laughing at ourselves.

Cliff then phoned the owner of the company that he worked for, explained that he was all right, but had suffered several injuries. He had seen most of the workers in the building, and none appeared to be seriously injured other than a few broken bones.

The owner informed Cliff that further work on the tower would be stopped temporarily until the police and building inspectors had cleared the building for work to resume. The company would assume responsibility for all medical bills for the injured employees. Since Cliff had already paid for his hospital bill, all that he needed to do was submit a copy of the receipt, to be reimbursed.

The owner had not received any updates as to when people could return to work. He advised Cliff to call into the main office and announcements would be made through the central switchboard operators. The owner further advised Cliff that they did not want to lose any of their valuable employees and salaries would continue for everyone in the interim.

Cliff then said he had a better idea about how to occupy our time, and shortly we were back in bed utilizing some of his suggestions. I thought they were rather nice suggestions. He had me mewling like a kitten, begging him to satisfy my animal needs. I had suppressed my sexual needs for so long and erected so many barriers that I was astonished that my body could respond so naturally to his.

I had been afraid that I would never be able to satisfy a man because of my trauma, but all of that had been washed away by the intuitive tenderness of the man in my bed. Oh, how strange and wonderful that sounded. I lazed in his arms for hours until I became anxious to do a little shopping myself. I only regretted a few times that I heard him wince when I accidently would touch one of his bruises.

"Cliff, what do you say we get out of this apartment, get some fresh air and go someplace?"

"Fine. Do you have somewhere particular in mind?" he asked.

"Not really, I just want to get out and show the world what a great guy that I have found for myself."

"Come to think of it; there is a place that I would like to take you," Cliff stated excitedly.

"Oh yeah? Where's that, big boy?" I begged, giving him my best pouty face.

"I'd like for it to be a surprise. Let's get dressed and be on our way," Cliff teased mysteriously.

"Great. Let's do it. I think that there should be plenty of things for you to wear on that cart the ladies brought up last night. I'll go to my room and get dressed. I love how you look in a suit, so see what they picked out for you. I will be back to help you with your belt, buttons, tie, and shoes."

While Cliff was getting dressed, I went to my bedroom and found that Marianne had already picked up the clothes that I had been wearing yesterday. I blushed at the thought of her seeing them scattered around on the floor. Not like me at all. Oh, well. Life goes on, I thought.

Then I struggled with the tangled mess of my hair until it looked reasonably under control and less like it had just been through a tornado. I hummed a little tune to myself while I dug through my dresses trying to find just the right one.

Finally, I chose a scuba-knit sheath dress with floral print with an elongated popover which I thought would reflect my happy mood and go with either of the suits that the ladies had selected for Cliff. I phoned down to the front desk and told them to have my car ready in ten minutes because we were on our way. After I had the great pleasure of helping to get Cliff all buttoned, zipped, and dressed, I grabbed Cliff's hand, and we headed down to the main foyer. The valet was pulling my car just outside the main entrance as we arrived and when Cliff saw my Audi he was surprised.

"Wow! Nice ride you have there. What kind is it?" he asked.

"That is an Audi A-5 Premium Plus Cabriolet. I loved the color and had it custom painted, moonlight blue metallic with black roof. It has an HD DVD/CD player with a Bang & Olufsen sound system. I love the ventilated sports seats and headroom heater. If you want more details, we will have to drop by the dealership. It is just so fancy that I cannot remember everything. I just know it has lots of power and takes me wherever I want to go like I am riding in a fancy carriage from the past."

Then, inspiration struck me, "Would you like to drive?" I smiled.

"Are you sure that it is okay? I might put a dent in it or something." He asked.

"If you do, I will just get another one. Like I told you, I am not short of a dime or two. So, let's head on out," I laughed as I handed the advanced key bud to Cliff and he opened the passenger door for me. He leaned in gave me a kiss and then quickly went around and got in behind the steering wheel. It took him several minutes to become familiar with the dials and operation of the car. When he was ready, he pushed the Start button and the engine purred awake. With a gentle push on the accelerator, we were on our way out to discover the world together.

CHAPTER 17

Cliff drove out of the hotel and took the entrance to Highway 59 then took the 610 loop around downtown. He eventually transferred over to I-45 North.

I looked over at him. "Where are we going?" I asked.

"It is a surprise. I will explain when we get closer," he demurred.

As we talked about our plans for the future, the freeway was packed at several points with thousands of cars and eighteen wheelers. After about twenty miles the traffic cleared and the Audi quietly cruised north. After about forty-five minutes we exited at the Woodlands Parkway and headed west. He made several turns and was soon on a residential street named Majesty Row directly beside a sparkling lake.

"Are we closer now?" I asked again.

"Yes, we are very close now. You may check your hair and makeup because we will be arriving in less than five minutes," he said, looking at me with a huge smile.

"Arriving? Arriving where? Cliff, where are you taking me?" I begged.

"Sweetheart. In about four minutes from now, you will be meeting my parents. I could not face them if I did not bring you to their home. They would be devastated and hurt to find that I had become engaged to the prettiest lady in Houston and didn't bring you by the first chance that I had. But don't worry about your appearance. You look simply gorgeous."

"Why Cliff, you say the sweetest things. I am shocked, pleasantly shocked and happy that you have brought me here. Yes, I would love to meet your parents, especially because they will now be my parents as well."

He leaned over and stole another kiss from my lips, as he turned the Audi into the driveway of a beautiful two story cape style home.

Cliff got out and came around and opened my door and took my hand. I had butterflies in my stomach as we walked up the front walkway and Cliff rang the doorbell. After a minute, a pleasant-looking middle-aged man with salt-and-pepper gray hair came to the door. Upon seeing Cliff, he reached out and grabbed him in a bear hug.

"Cliff, we were worried. We heard about the bomb going off in the tower you were building but didn't hear how you were. Your mother has been worried out of her mind." He turned and called back into the house.

"Ruth… Ruth…, Cliff's home! Come on up here." A few seconds later Cliff's mother came running up to the door. She was a beautiful middle aged lady, her hair was a mix of dark brown and streaks of gray, the relief of seeing her son evident in her radiant smile I immediately recognized it as having been passed down to her son.

"Cliff, why didn't you call? We were so worried. We never heard your name on the TV news, we were beginning to think the worst. I was just about to have George call all of the hospitals to locate you. Now, let me look at you. -- Your face, that bandage, oh -- your arm doesn't look right. Are you okay?" She fussed but was obviously delighted to have her son safe and home.

"Dad, Mom, I'm so sorry. After the bombing I was just so busy and then something else came up. I simply forgot. But first things first. I need to introduce you to my fiancée, Christina McIntyre."

"Christina, this is my mother and father, Ruth and George Stinson."

Their mouths dropped open, it took a few seconds for them to recover.

"Cliff, Christina, oh my goodness! Engaged! First a bombing, and now engaged. George, did we skip a day or two or something?" Ruth cried as she rushed to embrace first her son and then me."

"Congratulations! Why you could push me over with a feather." Mr. Stinson said as he grabbed Cliff's hand to shake it and then drew me in for a big bear hug.

"Hello. I am so pleased to meet the both of you," I replied between hugs. "You have the greatest son ever, and I want you to know that I love him dearly. Believe it or not, we have only known each other for about one week now, but already he is the center of my world."

"I'm sorry, Mom and Dad. So many things have happened to me -- to us, in the last twenty-four hours that I just have not had a minute to myself. But first, may we come in? We'll be happy to tell you everything."

"Oh, son, Ms. McIntyre," she gushed, "where have my manners gone? Sure. Please come in. Come in you two, please. Would either of you like something to drink or eat?" Ruth asked as she led the way through the foyer and into the living room.

"You may call me Tina, Mr. and Mrs. Stinson. Clifford seems to like my birth name better, but most people just call me Tina. And no, we just had breakfast a short time ago."

"Please call me Ruth …and George, you can just call him George. Kind of fits him like a glove." She smiled and squeezed his hand.

"What a beautiful home you have here, It's so warm and inviting. Very much like your son," I said while looking around at the comfortable and pleasant rooms."

"Yes," Ruth replied. "Cliff has that effect on everyone. We are so proud of him and his work, but now, please, you must tell us everything. What has been going on with you two? Where did you meet? How long have you known each other, what about the bombings yesterday? Were you in the building when it happened, Cliff? I see the bandage on your cheek. Where are you hurt?"

"Mom, Dad that is a long list of questions. How about letting Christina and I tell it more or less from the beginning and then you can tell us of any other things you might have heard on today's news? We have been rather busy and have not had too much time for TV."

"Sure, son. Let's all have a seat here in the den, you two can share the couch and Ruth, and I will sit over here in the den chairs." Mr. Stinson replied.

Cliff and I settled onto the brown faux leather Futon sofa. Cliff related the events of the last week. How we had met, how he had fallen in love with me at first sight, I interjected that I had done the same. I told them how he had declared his love and asked me to marry him on our first date.

Cliff explained that I had been so shocked and surprised that I had almost choked to death at the restaurant. We both told them about our activities during the previous days' bombings and subsequent trip to the hospital. I explained that I was very worried about Cliff's health and took him back to my apartment to let him sleep in my spare bedroom.

Neither of us shared our nocturnal activities. I blushed when I realized that they may have guessed as much from the way we were looked at each other and kissed each other every few minutes, and the tender way he held my hand with my fingers curled up inside. Or perhaps the fact that I constantly studied his face as he talked. How often I lifted his hand to my lips, or the puppy love look that I had on my face as I watched him tell our love story. But, no matter, I was not ashamed or embarrassed. This is the man who I love. I love him with all of my heart and body. I was proud to claim him as my own and show the world that we are one.

"Wow! You two have had an eventful week. Let us be the first to congratulate the both of you and wish you only happy things in the future. We had begun to despair that Cliff would ever find anyone," Mrs. Stinson said, smiling brightly.

Both Ruth and George rose and hugged us again, squeezing me tight as each gave me a kiss on the cheek, I felt so excited. Cliff's parents were exceptionally gracious and had welcomed me into their family with open arms. How could they be otherwise with a son like Cliff?

"Now, Cliff, when are you going to introduce your pretty fiancée to your two brothers and three sisters?" Mr. Stinson said rather coyly.

"Holy Mackerel!" I cried. "Do you mean there are five more like Cliff? Cliff, it sure sounds like I have a lot more to learn about you than I thought. Five siblings! And yes, Cliff, when am I going to meet them? And just when were you going to mention this to me? Perhaps I chose the wrong son?" I teased.

I suddenly remembered all of the times I had meant to ask him this very question.

"Christina, as you are well aware, we have been engaged less than twenty-four hours. One must have time to tell everything" Cliff smiled and kissed me again.

"Oh, sorry, that's right. I guess that we both have a lot of secrets still to be shared," I hugged him again tightly.

"Hey, son," George interjected, "I have an idea. Why don't we have a big backyard Bar-B-Que this weekend and you and Tina can come? We can get all of the family together. Bring your swim suits and it will be a great party. Tina," he continued, "Cliff not only has five siblings, but each of them is married and has children. So, the answer is no, you did not choose the wrong son, everyone else has already claimed. Cliff was our only hold-out. We can make it into an engagement celebration. What do you say?"

"Oh, yes, Cliff. Please, Please, Please! I would love to come. It has been so long since I have had a real family. And siblings with kids, that sounds so nice. It would make me feel like I belonged."

"Now Christina, if you are really into self-flagellation," Cliff smiled, "Then my brothers, sisters and their families are a great way to do that. When we all get together it can be one big party, lots of teasing, laughing and just good old having fun. And when they find out that I am engaged...."

"Wow! I believe that they were beginning to think that I was gay or something. Especially because I have not had a date in five years. Boy, it has been no end to the teasing. Every one of them has been giving me phone numbers of women they wanted me to date. Even some of the kids slipped me their teachers' telephone numbers. They are going to be shocked."

"You belong to me now, big boy. It sounds like we will have to put an ad in the *Houston Chronicle* letting everyone know that you are off the market."

"Then it's settled," Ruth laughed. "And Tina, if you have anyone that you would like to invite we would be happy to welcome them as well."

"Thank you, Ruth. I do have two staff members who have been with me a long time. I know they would love to get out and be around a family for a change. Are you sure that it would be okay? And this sounds like it might be quite an event. If you need some help to cover the costs, I do have a rather large expense account. I would love to help."

"I am sure that will not be necessary. We can make out just fine." Ruth smiled.

"I know that it is not necessary, Ruth, but I really would like to help. I can hire a catering firm to supply the food. It would make me feel more like a real part of the family, and take a lot of the burden off of you two regarding getting you home ready and preparing food for so many. I have not had a family event in so long. I will just need to know if there are any food allergies or other issues that I could advise the catering firm. I was an only child after my brother died young, and my parents and grandparents are no longer alive. I can afford the expense, and you have been so gracious in welcoming me. I really want to help."

George and Ruth looked to their son for guidance.

"Mom, Dad, I think that it might be a great idea. And I think that if it helped Christina feel more like a part of our family, I would be happy for her," as he squeezed my hand. -- And it just so happens that my company is having some unexpected downtime at the moment, and I would like to help plan the event as I seem to have some time on my hands as well."

George then led Cliff and myself out to the patio where there was a beautiful in-ground pool with a side area with a large Bar-B-Que grill and tables underneath a beautiful wooden and canvas canopy. There were lots of lounge chairs for enjoying the sun.

Cliff looked around, "Dad, I just had an idea. What with the bombing and all, my workers are not going to be allowed back on site until the building inspectors have surveyed for structural damage; they need to make sure that the work areas are safe. That means that I have several experienced carpenters and staff temporally out of work and free to do other things. I could call a few of them and get them over to help you build out a playground for the kids while the rest of us adults mingle. I would be happy to pay for the supplies. What do you say?"

"Son that's a great idea. I will start drawing up some ideas for the playground and try to see what supplies we might need."

"Mom, Dad, I need to make another stop in town before it gets too late. So, please forgive us, we are going to have to get back to town."

I watched as Cliff leaned over and whispered something in his dad's ear.

"Oh, sure thing, son. You and Tina run along now. I will start on the plans right away. I will give you a call later this evening and let you know."

As we waved good-bye to his parents, I was desperate to know where we were going.

"Now, Cliff, we have to get one thing straight early. I don't like all of these surprises, come to think of it, that is not exactly true. I sure did like that you surprised me with meeting your parents. Also, I liked that you surprised me with your marriage proposal. But now my curiosity is burning a hole in my head. What's going on, to where are we rushing off?"

I tried my second best pouty face since the first one had not worked that well.

"Sorry, pretty lady. Another secret yet to be revealed."

"Aw! You are frustrating at times! But I still love you with all my heart."

'I am going to have to work on some new pouty faces. Nothing seems to work with this guy. Then I remembered one from my childhood. It worked magic on my parents. My face was all red and twisted up, my mouth wide open, a loud scream emanating from it, fake tears streaming down my cheeks and my feet kicking the floor, my arms flailing. Yes, that's it. I will try that one next. I'm sure that one will work.

'On second thought, I think that I just may have to let it all go. I love whatever this man surprises me with, and I don't want to change him one iota.

Ah, Cliff. I love you to pieces.'

"Cliff, have I told you that I love you, today?"

"Yes, but I love nothing more than to hear you say it again. I love you, as well."

CHAPTER 18

I don't know why, perhaps it was my 'spidey' sense, as I called my ability to sense danger to myself. But as we pulled out of the driveway I noticed a dark sedan with a broken left headlight as it pulled out and began following my car. It looked vaguely familiar. I had seen the car parked across the road by Lake Woodlands which his parents' house was facing. At first, I did not think much about it. As I watched my outside car door mirror, I began to notice that the car was making all of the same turns that Cliff was taking. I pulled my purse closer, feeling the hidden protection inside.

"Cliff, sweetheart, can you take a turn that you might not normally take on the way back to the freeway. I want to check something out."

"Oh? Okay. What's up?" He looked over at me quizzically, as he made an immediate turn onto Lake Front Circle Drive.

"Okay, Tina. This street will take us down to the Woodlands Parkway. It's going to take a bit longer than going straight on *Timberloch Place* to *Grogan's Mill*, what gives?" he asked.

"Cliff, check your rear view mirror. Don't make a big production, but I think there is someone following us. Watch and see if the black sedan with a broken headlight turns down this same street. If it does, is there another street that cuts over that we can make a quick exit to the freeway?"

"Now you have got me concerned, yes, I see the car now. The car has turned and is now behind us. Hold on tight, sweetheart, I am going to wait until the last second and then cut over on East Shore Drive ahead. It will take us directly to *Grogan's Mill*. From there it is an easy on-ramp to *Woodlands Parkway* and *I-45* is not far beyond that."

I pulled my seatbelt tighter around my waist and grabbed hold of the door armrest. Just as we had nearly completely crossed the East Shore intersection, Cliff turned the wheels sharply and accelerated into the turn sending us flying forward down the residential street. A few seconds later the Audi was merging into the traffic on Grogan's Mill. I turned in my seat and could see the sedan struggling to keep up with us.

My Audi built for performance, there was no way that car could catch up to us unless we got caught in a traffic jam. I prayed silently that for once in my life Houston traffic would give us a break, and we could escape. My prayers were answered, we sped away rapidly, weaving in and out of traffic until I could no longer see the car in the distance. Cliff continued at an accelerated rate, speeding all the way to Houston, where he took a random exit and then made several turns to throw off any pursuit that might be behind us.

"Gosh, that was scary, Cliff. But you certainly drive quite well. There were several times back there where I was sure we were going to crash. I felt like I was riding with James Bond in a movie. You were just superb, especially since you were able to maneuver the wheel with just your one arm. I don't know who that was, but they scared me out of my wits. I think that I could see that there were two men in the car, but I could not make out their faces."

"You know, I only just caught a brief look at that car, but it looked very similar to the one that cut Larry off in traffic when we were going to lunch the other day," Cliff noted.

Cliff continued to make a roundabout route through downtown, going this way and that to throw off any possible tracking of our route. Then he took the on-ramp to the freeway and soon we were back on the West Loop.

I don't know who was in that car, or why they had wanted to follow after us, but being with Cliff soon caused me to forget my worries. I was safe as long as I was with him. Probably a carjacker, or someone wanting to rob us. No matter. No one could touch me here. I was safe with Cliff by my side. But I was still mystified as to where we were going. I reached over and tried to tickle the information out of him.

"Are we there yet? Are we there yet?" I laughed.

"Oh no, you don't. I know what you are trying to do. Please be patient with me. It's not very far now. Okay, I see the exit just ahead."

We exited on San Felipe and very quickly pulled up in the parking lot in front of Jones Brothers Jewelry. All memory of the car chase slipped from my mind as I realized what Cliff had up his sleeve. I was too focused on my love for Cliff, to have any thoughts about men following in strange cars to raise it to the level of attention which it deserved.

"I am beginning to get the picture now. Oh, Cliff, I am so excited." I grabbed him around the waist and squeezed.

"**Ouch**! Not so tight, sweetheart. I still have some bruises here and there. But my most tender spot is in my heart for you. You can squeeze all that you want there, and I won't complain."

"You say the sweetest things. God, how I love you." I leaned into his uninjured shoulder and nuzzled his neck.

Cliff got out and quickly came around to my side to open my door. He took my hand in his and escorted me into the store, where we were greeted by the saleslady, Julia Winters, as shown on her badge.

"How may I help you two lovebirds today?" she cooed, knowing a sale when she saw one.

"I am in the market for a nice engagement ring. Do you have any special rings for us to look at today?" Cliff asked.

"Do you have a price range in mind, sir?" Ms. Winters questioned.

"Yes, please. I was thinking in the range of say ten to twenty thousand dollars or possibly higher. If you could show my fiancée some of those for her to select."

"Certainly, sir. Please step this way. And your names are…?"

"This is my fiancée, Christina McIntyre, and my name is Clifford Stinson."

"Very good, Ms. McIntyre and Mr. Stinson, just over here we have a nice selection of Radiant Cut Yellow Diamond Engagement rings. But I have one that arrived only this morning that I think that you may like, Ms. McIntyre," she purred as she reached in the jewelry display case and pulled out the most exquisite ring. The ring was a double band of white diamonds wrapped around a center ring of exquisite yellow diamonds, all of which sparkled and twinkled from every facet.

Oh, Cliff, It's very pretty. I don't think that I have seen another like it. May I try it on?"

"Yes, certainly," Ms. Winters bubbled.

I surmised that she must be tabulating the commission in her mind from the way she was chewing on her lip.

"Look, Cliff, -- the ring fits perfectly on my finger as if it had been made just for me. I don't believe that we will need to look any further, Ms. Winters. This one is so beautiful, and its already sized for my finger. Cliff, I love the ring, I love you. I don't know how much happier a girl could be than I am at this moment."

"Are you sure, Christina? We could look at some other rings or even a different store. I want you to have a ring that you will treasure."

Ms. Winters developed a small pout, probably her dreams of a big commission evaporating.

"Cliff, this is the ring that I want. The ring and setting are so unique. The ring says everything to me. The white diamonds surrounding the gold diamonds show me that you treasure me. Your love is represented by the white diamonds; That love is like your arms, surrounding and holding me; I'm the golden diamonds in the center, within your embrace. It demonstrates that you are thinking of me always and will be there to protect me and hold me forever."

Ms. Winters pout disappeared and was replaced by a wide smile.

"I guess that's it then. How much will that be? Cliff asked, turning to a happily beaming Ms. Winters.

"That particular ring normally goes for twenty-five-thousand-five-hundred dollars, Mr. Stinson, however if you let me check with my manager, I think that I can get you a discount."

While Ms. Winters went to the back to verify a price, Cliff and I exchanged a rather sloppy kiss.

"You are so wonderful to me, Mr. Stinson."

"You deserve it, the future Mrs. Stinson."

"Mrs. Stinson" …Oh, I love the sound of that!"

Ms. Winters returned and said, "The price will be Eighteen-thousand-seven-hundred-dollars."

"Can I take it with me today?" Cliff asked.

"Yes, sir!" Mrs. Winters replied. "Let me fill out the paperwork and get it processed. Will that be cash, check or charge, Mr. Stinson?"

"That will be a check," Cliff said with a wink at me.

I raised my eyebrow at him.

"Sweetheart, I have been saving up for years for just such a day as this. Yes, there is plenty in my checking to cover this and a lot more if needed."

I grabbed hold of his good arm and curled my fingers inside his palm while we waited for Ms. Winters to complete all of the paperwork. When she was done, Cliff motioned that he needed his hand back to write the check. I reluctantly released it with a pout. But then he had trouble keeping the checkbook steady on the countertop, being able to write only with one hand. I reached over and held it steady while he filled in the check information. He took great care with his pen, and the result was almost a work of art.

After the check had cleared through the National Check Clearing machine next to the register, Ms. Winters was about to place the ring in its jewelry box when I reached over and extended my left hand.

"Will you allow Cliff to place it on my finger, please?" I begged

"Oh, yes, sorry. Here you go, Mr. Stinson," as she handed off the ring to Cliff.

Cliff then dropped to his good knee "I didn't do a good job of this the first time. So let me make it official now. Christina McIntyre, you would make me the happiest man in the world if you would say yes. -- Will you marry me?"

"Yes, Cliff, Yes, a thousand times yes. I love you with all my heart and soul. I will marry you."

Cliff took the ring out the of the small box and slid it gently onto my ring finger.

Ms. Winters and the manager, who had now come to the front of the store, applauded. I leaned over and gave Cliff a kiss which deepened further and became more involved until we heard an 'Ahem,' from the store manager.

"Sorry, love is just so new to both of us," I blushed. "We got lost in the moment and forgot where we were. Come on Cliff; we had better leave before we do something that makes them call the cops."

Both the manager and Ms. Winters wished us well and waved happily as we pulled away.

I was so thrilled. *'What had I ever done to deserve such a wonderful man as Cliff?'* I kept staring at the engagement ring on my finger, turning it this way and that. Finally, I grabbed hold of Cliff's thigh and gave it a little squeeze. I needed to do something special for him.

"Christina. May I ask a favor of you?"

"You don't need to ask, Cliff. I will do anything, go anywhere that you want. You should already know that."

"I would like to go to church in the morning. I know that you said that it had been a while since you last attended, but it would mean a great deal to me. I would like to share that special time with you. My faith has meant a lot to me, I want us to start out on the right foot together. I know that you will enjoy your time there, perhaps it will reawaken your faith."

"Cliff, you are the one who has reawakened my faith. I give thanks every day for you and that you have come into my life. Someday, should we have children, you will be the head of our family and lead us in the paths that you will lead all of our family."

My love and admiration grew each moment that I was in his presence. Cliff was everything that I had ever dreamed that I could want in a husband and lover. I surrendered myself to him body and soul.

Chapter 19

As Cliff pulled into the church parking lot the next morning, I was surprised to see that the 'church' was not in a regular church structure, but it was held in a college athletic complex. There was a huge football stadium on one side, and the side we pulled next to seemed to be more like an office complex for the athletic department. I could see many other churchgoers and their children arriving as well.

"Oh, I forgot to mention. We're meeting here on a temporary basis. We have a new church building under construction just down the freeway from here. So the church decided to lease out this large building for our Sunday services until our new building is completed. The college does not have any activities here on Sundays', so we got a very good price on the temporary lease."

Cliff got out of the Audi and came to my side and opened the passenger door for me. He took my hand in his and escorted me toward the entrance. Along the way, there were several couples who waved at us, and several of them came over and shook Cliffs hand in welcome. Cliff introduced me as his fiancée which raised a spark of happiness in my chest each time that he said the word. All of them gave us their congratulations, and the women, in turn, gave me a hug and welcomed me to the service.

After passing through the main entrance, Cliff led me over to the information kiosk. Cliff has been attending the men's single Bible study, but he felt that I would feel uncomfortable as the only female in a large group of men. Instead, he inquired if there was a mixed singles group for our age. The lady at the kiosk directed us to a room on the second floor where we found a mix of people standing around chatting. A few of the men recognized Cliff and came over to greet him.

Several of the women gathered around me and peppered me with questions as to how I have been able to ensnare the most eligible bachelor in the church. I could tell they were teasing me because of their shy smiles and giggles.

"It took a car-bomb to bring me to my senses," I responded. "He proposed to me on our first date. But it was not until the moment that I thought that I had lost him that I realized how very much that I truly loved him and needed him in my life."

One lady responded, "That sounds like the most un-romantic story that I have heard. Car-bomb? I would have said yes to him if he had just looked at me. You are one very lucky lady. I tried to get him interested in me five years ago, but nothing came of it."

I thought to myself. *'So you are the mystery woman from five years ago. I am happy to report that you are the one who convinced him to wait for me. Thank you so very much.'*

Another chimed in, "don't be concerned, Christina. That is just Lilly's jealousy shining through. She had a huge crush on Cliff for nearly a year, but he totally ignored her. Now, she's with Charles Sanchez over there, but she seems happy enough. I guess that she just never completely got over that crush on Cliff. But forget all that, we all want to offer you our congratulations and best wishes for a long and happy life together. And from the look of that huge ring on your finger, I would say you are certainly off to a great start."

We were interrupted about that time as the class director went to the front of the room and called for our attention. After a few minutes, everyone had taken their seats and listened as he welcomed visitors including Cliff and myself as well as two other young couples. After that, he announced the list of members whose birthdays were this month and we all sang the "Happy Birthday" in unison. I was never a great singer, so I let Cliff take the lead for that, but I did join in with everyone. After all, it was just happy birthday and not the Hallelujah Chorus. I squeezed Cliff's hand when we were done. I loved the fellowship and friendship of these people. I knew that I would fit into the group and felt that I was finally finding a place in life with other people, especially so after my nearly two-decade-long hiatus from the world. My spirits lifted and I looked up at the man standing next to me. *God, I love this man so very much.* I felt as if a great burden was being lifted off of my back and replaced by the tender shackles of love and extreme happiness.

Then the class leader gave the announcements for a weekly Bible Study at a local restaurant. After that, a clipboard was passed around containing blank forms for people to submit prayer requests. Then a second list for people wishing to bring refreshments for the class each week. This all seemed normal and awakened distant memories of my teenage years when my parents had taken me to Sunday School.

When he had completed all of those tasks he introduced our class speaker for today, a nice young man named Lawton Page. The director then spoke a short prayer asking that the speaker be granted the wisdom to impart a message to those in the audience who needed to hear this message and take it to heart.

Mr. Page began the lesson by reading from the Bible his chosen lesson verse for the day.

> *For I know the plans I have for you," declares the LORD,*
> *"plans to prosper you and not to harm you, plans to give you*
> *hope and a future.*
> *Jeremiah 29:11 New International Version[11]*

For some reason, those very words struck a chord inside my soul. He spoke of the dangers existing in the world -- People who wished to cause us harm, and block us from happiness. His emphasis was on how Jeremiah was speaking to us today that Jesus has plans for each of us. He wished to protect us from harm that others wish to inflict on us, and that there was a future for us. He wanted to give us happiness and fulfillment in life and a future in which we could rejoice.

Everything that he said seemed to be directly speaking to me. I thought about how my life had been nearly destroyed seventeen years ago by a group of boys out for their thrills. I had let that incident take control of my life and ruin my happiness. I wanted desperately for that part of my life to be behind me, and then came the bombings.

But then, by some miracle neither Cliff nor I had been harmed in the incident. Sure, Cliff had suffered a few cuts and bruises, but all in all, we were alive and now we were together. I did have hope for the future.

After the class, I went up and thanked Mr. Page and told him that I believed his message was directed at Cliff and myself, and that he had offered me comfort, and I was very grateful. After shaking hands with the director and other class members, we proceeded into the main sanctuary.

The sanctuary was different from the churches that I had attended when I was small. Instead of long rows of wooden pews, there were rows of cushioned metal straight back chairs. Cliff and I walked down toward the front section and settled in about five rows from the front. When the service began, it was not the sound of an organ and the old standard hymns, but three guitars, a snare drum, and a small electric piano.

The song leader was a rather tall, hefty looking gentleman who sang in a beautiful tenor voice. Behind him was a small choir of about twenty people, men, and women. The songs were upbeat, praising God and encouraging all to have faith and trust in the Lord. After the collection plate was passed, the minister approached the pulpit, offered a prayer that his message would be God's message and gestured that all be seated.

Opening his Bible, he led the church congregation in reading the word from the Bible:

"Be strong and courageous; don't be frightened or dismayed, for the Lord your God is with you wherever you go." Joshua 1:9

I instantly knew that this message was another one directly specifically at me. I felt that God had known that I would be attending the church this date and had placed these messages on the hearts of the minister and Sunday school speaker. Tears welled in my eyes. I squeezed Cliff's hand. I felt that these messages were designed to give me the strength to face my future. I took comfort that there was hope for me. All would be well. It may not be exactly as I would wish, but Cliff and I would both survive, no matter what, and happiness would be our reward in the end. I treasured that promise and locked it away within my heart.

CHAPTER 20

I awoke in the middle of the night by a terrible scream. My head was groggy from missed sleep over the past few days, and it took a few minutes to realize that the scream had come from my mouth. Suddenly there was a pounding on my door.

"Tina, are you all right?" I could hear Charlotte shouting from the other side.

I quickly ran to the door to let her inside. My mind began to clear. Cliff had returned to his apartment yesterday for some of his personal belongings and was now working with the police, fire department and building inspectors to assess the damage to the tower. As a result, he had not been staying with me this last evening, and my nightmares had returned. In my dream, there was a man walking down the street away from the tower, someone from my past, someone from long ago. I could not place him.

Charlotte looked at me as if I had seen a ghost. "Tina, what's wrong? Your face. It's twisted and frightened as if you had seen a ghost or something."

"Yes, Charlotte. That's it exactly. The other day when the bomb went off in the tower, and Larry was driving me to get closer, we passed by a man walking away from the tower. At the time, I thought that I recognized him as being someone familiar. Someone that I had known in the past, but I could not place his face until I saw him again in my dream. It was him, the guy who raped me when I was sixteen and then threatened to find and kill me during his trial. I am sure that was him. I could clearly see my fingernail scratches were still on his face, even after all these years. When he was holding my throat, I had nearly ruined his face when I dug in deep with my long fingernails. His name was James Payne."

"All right. Give me a few minutes. I have his folder in my file cabinet. Let me check." She turned and returned to her room. A few minutes later she returned with a folder in her hand. She had a very serious look on his face which sent a chill up my spine.

"Tina, this is the same guy that I saw watching you outside B &B's restaurant the other night. I did not get a really good look at the time, but I am positive that this is the same man. And there, all across his cheek and nose, those must be your fingernail tracks. You did well, marking him like that, I'm sure that other girls would have avoided him. Anyone looking at him would have known that those were the result of a girls' fingernails, and that girl would have been desperately trying to defend herself. We need to notify the police right away."

Even though it was two fifteen in the morning, Charlotte was able to get the police on the phone and demanded that they come to our apartment immediately. When she explained that we had a possible lead on the people responsible for the recent bombings that got their attention. She was advised that detectives would arrive at the apartment shortly. The complex where we lived had very tight security and so we needed to notify them to provide access and directions to our apartment. Charlotte called on-site security, explained the situation to them and requested they direct the detectives to our apartment as soon as they arrived.

****

"Ms. McIntrye? I am detective Sandra Connor with the HPD arson and bomb division, and this is my partner, Detective Frank Kelly. Do you have some time to answer some routine questions about the bombings?

Detective Connor was a middling attractive brunette in a plain business suit while Detective Kelly was a rough looking man with a no-nonsense attitude and ruffled suit to match.

"Yes, detectives, will you please come in? Would you like something to drink? Tea, coffee, I can have my housekeeper prepare something for you."

"No, thank you," they both replied in unison.

"Please, won't you have a seat here in the den." They both settled onto my leather couch, and I sat across from them in one of the easy chairs. Charlotte and Marianne looked on from the kitchen table.

Detective Connor got right to the heart of the matter. "Ms. McIntyre, I understand that you called in information that might lead us to some suspects in the case of the bombings at Tilden Tower and the later one at your company's current offices. Please provide us any information that you can and start at the beginning please."

I then related the story of my rape, the trial, and the final threat of James Payne to come after me when he got out of prison. The detectives listened patiently and then their ears perked up when Charlotte spoke.

"Detectives," Charlotte explained. "On the Friday night that Tina was at the B & B restaurant, I did see a man who might have been watching Tina. He was too far away from me and in a dark alley. I noticed him at the time, but there were several other bums hanging around in hopes of getting scraps from the restaurant after it closed.

"I didn't put too much weight on it at the time. On the prior Tuesday of that same week, I was following behind Tina when the truck she was riding in was cut off. I didn't get a good look at the two men in that car, but it seemed deliberate to me, rather than random. At the time, I thought it might have been just a case of road-rage."

"One more thing, detectives," I continued. "When Cliff, my fiancé, and I were visiting his parents and got ready to leave there was an old car that followed us when we left. I have already discussed this with Charlotte.

We had thought that it might have been just some carjackers or men trying to rob us. But now, as I look back on these events and remember that James Payne was the person I had seen on my way to the tower the day. And knowing it was he who threatened to find me after he was released from prison. I am more than certain that he must be behind all of these actions."

Charlotte brought out her files on the three men, especially the picture of James Payne. The detectives took notes all during our talk and expressed great interest in following up on what might give them a break in the case.

"Here is a recent prison photo of James Payne," Charlotte said, handing the photo to Detective Connor.

"May we keep this copy?" Detective Connor asked.

"Yes, I can get more." Charlotte agreed.

Detective Connor discussed my information with her partner for a few minutes.

"Ms. McIntrye, I believe that we will need to place you under police protection. From the sounds of it, this guy may have a serious grudge against you, and it's possible that he is trying to act on it. We don't yet have any proof of his involvement yet. But we will get with the head of the bomb squad unit and see if they have found out anything yet.

"Also, we are going to check with the prison where he was confined and see if he talked about finding you to his other cellmates. In the meantime, I will be stationing a uniformed officer outside your apartment. I will also have the bomb squad go over your car to make sure there are no devices hidden explosives inside. Please notify us when you plan to go out and we can have additional protection assigned as needed.

"Now, you mentioned that your fiancé was in the car when you were followed. I will need all of his information, and I may need to assign some officers to protect him as well. You never know with these criminals today. Especially hard-time prisoners. He could have picked up knowledge of bombs and many other things from his cell mates. We will also try to find out his known associates. You mentioned that both times you observed him he seemed to have a partner."

By the time the two detectives left, my nerves were on edge. Bombs, and being stalked by a hardened prison rapist, how was I ever going to get any sleep again? I needed to alert Cliff. Dialing his cell number, it rolled to voice mail. Turning my mind back to my present situation I had to take into account the possibility that Charlotte and Marianne might also be in danger. We had to make plans that would include protection for them as well.

After an extended discussion with Charlotte and Marianne, we made plans for how to carry on the simpler parts of our lives, grocery shopping, clothes shopping, exercising. The harder parts would have be worked out later.

I tried Cliff's number again, another voice mail message. I began to get worried. Where was he? Why was his phone going to voice at this time of the morning? Perhaps he had turned it off. All kinds of dread scenarios began to play out in my mind. Perhaps he had been taken hostage by the men trying to get to me.

Or perhaps, no, I did not want to go there. Not yet, I could not allow myself to think those thoughts. Be patient, Cliff's fine. He will call, he has my cell number, so I comforted myself that when he was able, he would call.

Just at that moment my cell rang. Cliff's caller ID showed on the phone.

"Cliff, thank God. Where have you been? I have been trying to reach you. Are you all right?"

"Whoa, Christina. Slow down a bit. What is going on? I'm fine. I've been on the phone for hours trying to get my workers lined up for building the playground. Dad called me last night and faxed over some exciting plans the kids will love. I know that it is early, but since the time is so short we have been in a rush to gather materials and supplies, and I've made sure my guys have all the right equipment. Now, what's up on your end?"

"Oh, the party. I had completely forgotten. I was going to call my friend who is in the catering business this morning. Thanks for reminding me. Now back to the other matter. The police just left here a little while ago –

"Police? Why were they there? Are you in some trouble?"

"Yes, Cliff. Just listen for a minute. The day of the bomb blast at the tower, Larry was bringing me over to find you. When we got near the tower, I saw a man walking away from the area. Tonight I finally realized who he was. His name is James Payne. He was one of the boys who assaulted me when I was sixteen."

"I testified against him at trial, and he threatened to find me when his term was completed. I had not remembered, but he was sentenced to seventeen years behind bars. That was exactly seventeen years ago. He has been released, and I am pretty sure that he is behind all of this: the bombing at the tower, the bombing at my office building, the car that cut us off at lunch, and then the same car chasing us from your parents' home.

"The police are placing me under a 24/7 watch, and I asked them to include you as well. These S.O.B.'s obviously know that we are together and are trying to hurt the both of us. We need to work out plans so that we can go about our normal lives as well as take precautions regarding these criminals. The police suspect that he may have other accomplices, so I am afraid for you as well."

"That is scary, Christina. Not so much for myself. I'm really worried for you. I'm coming over to the Grecian to get you. I think that the safest place for you right now is with me. If you will contact the police and tell them that I'm on my way to get you and that we are going to be going out to my parents' home to work on the playground.

"Perhaps they can provide us an escort, or at least a squad car or two at Dad's home that might scare these guys off. I don't want anything to happen to my parents, and obviously, they now know where they live. I'll contact Dad and make him aware of what happening. It's 5:30 a.m. now. I should be at the hotel in about twenty minutes. I love you. Please don't take any chances. I have waited so long to find you; I don't want to lose you now."

CHAPTER 21

It was 8:30 a.m. when Cliff and I arrived at his parents' home as we had stopped off at a local IHOP and had an uneventful but satisfying breakfast. There were already a large number of cars, pickups and two delivery trucks full of various materials being unloaded and carried around to the back of the home. Cliff led me around the side of his parents' home, where there was a flurry of activity by workers laughing and joking with each other as they put together all kinds of weird looking materials.

"Hey, Cliff!" several of them called out when they saw us. "Thanks for calling us. This stuff is fun. Not like the usual boring drywall and ceiling tiles you have us working on," they joked.

Cliff noticed his Dad standing and directing the construction of one unusual object, which I thought looked rather like a mushroom stalk.

"Hey, Dad. This one looks great. Where do you need me to help?"

"Oh, good that you are here, son. Over there. See that strange looking tangle of feet and stuff. Have a look at this drawing and see if you can get those guys over there to make it come out looking somewhat like this."

"Boy, that looks like a challenge. But the kids will love it. All right, I think we can manage, though. Sweetheart, see if you can find mom and you two work on getting the food arrangements completed."

I wandered around through the maze of materials and workers and finally spotted Ruth sitting by the pool.

"Hey, Ruth. Let's see if we can figure out what we need the caterer to have on hand for everyone on Saturday. Have you decided what kind of food that you want? Bar-B-Que, Mexican, or something else?"

"I know that everyone loves Bar-B-Que, so let's stick with that. Now let me see if we can calculate how much we will need. There will be so many people."

"Ruth, I am so new to the family that I don't have any idea since I have not met them yet. Just how many will there be?"

"Oh, silly me. I forgot. Now let me see. First, there is Cliff's oldest sister Mary. She and her husband Tom Rogers will be driving in from Beaumont with their three children. Then his next oldest sister Cynthia and her husband Mike Anderson with their two children are coming from Dallas His older brother Al and wife Carol and three children live here in the Houston area. His younger brother Michael and wife Kristen live in the next subdivision over with their three young children. And finally, his youngest sister Gail and her husband Lee Mashburn live down in Sugarland with their two children.

Let's see now; that is twenty-three so far, and then there are you and Cliff, George and myself, your two staff, also I called George's mom and dad, and they will come as well. They are getting a bit older now, so I believe that Cliff is making arrangements for someone to bring them. They live down in the Tomball area."

"Ruth, this is wonderful. I have not had a family in several years, now suddenly I'm gifted with so many."

"Tina, just a word of caution. Since you said that you haven't been around family, especially one as large as ours I need to tell you. Family is comprised of many different types of people. Some get along great, and others, well, different politics, different attitudes, can cause some embarrassing things to happen when they all gather together. So be prepared for anything. My group can be a rowdy bunch at times. But in the end, we all love each other very much."

"And another thing that I have not mentioned yet." I struggled to find the words. "I had some trouble in my past which seems to be tumbling back into my present. There will probably be a couple of HPD squad cars in the area during the party. They will be here to help keep us all safe."

"I'll let George know. We have a pretty good neighborhood watch program here, so they can also be on the lookout for any strangers as well."

"Christina," Cliff cried as he approached. "I think that I have got my project pretty much under control over here. Why don't we walk over by the lake? There is a bench over there; we can discuss a rather important matter we need to clarify."

"What's that?" I asked.

"You know I like surprises," he winked, "so let's walk over and sit by the gazebo and discuss."

"Aw! You and your surprises."

"Ruth," I asked, turning to his mother, "has he always been this way? But, I must say, so far they have been the best surprises of my life, so I am not complaining too loudly."

"Yes. Cliff likes to keep his thunder hidden until the last second, and then surprise you in a unique way."

"All right, but this had better be good. Because your mother was just about to tell me some juicy things about when you were little," I winked at Ruth.

"Now, mom, you are *not* going to tell her about that time that I--"

"I wasn't, but now that you bring it to mind. Tina, why don't you come back when you guys are finished. You are going to have to hear this story!"

"Mom, that is so embarrassing. Please, pretty please? Can I offer you a bribe or something to not tell?"

"Perhaps, if you give me a sweet kiss, I could forget all about it again."

Cliff gave his mother a kiss right on her lips. "Was that sweet enough, mom?" he blushed.

"Oh, tush. You two run along now. I am sure that you have more important things to do than tease an old lady." She giggled and walked away to find her husband.

Cliff then took my hand and led me around the house and across the street to the edge of the lake where there was a small sitting area with a bench and an umbrella to shade the sun.

"All right, spill it, big guy. What's so important that I had to miss out on this juicy bit gossip about your past?"

"I was thinking that we have not had a second to discuss a certain event that will be happening sometime soon." Cliff teased.

"And exactly what event might that be?"

"I have heard, from fairly reliable sources that there is supposed to be a wedding taking place, --very soon I hope."

"Oh, *that* event, yes, I guess that we do need to think about that. Will you want a long engagement, say -- a week or two," I teased, "or do you want just to hop on a plane for Las Vegas and get it done this afternoon?"

"If it were just up to me, I would choose the plane tickets, but there is my family to consider, and I gather that Mom has been filling you in on the logistics of that."

"Yes, it sounds like you have a large and wonderful family. I haven't had much time to think about our wedding either, what with the bombing, and now a crazy rapist stalking me. All right Cliff, let's talk about it here."

I looked around at the lake and the quiet street. There were no strange cars with broken headlights watching us. Only a few neighbors out mowing their front lawns and a few ladies working in their flower beds.

"We have a few minutes of peace and quiet here so let's see whether we can figure out what we want to do."

The more that we talked, the more that I realized that there are a lot of things that go into making up a wedding. The wedding itself, preacher, location, my dress, who will be attending, food, the cake, and much more. My head was spinning after only a short time.

"You know, Cliff," I said, "I think that we need to hire a wedding planner. We both have many things going on right now; we will probably not think of everything. I want it to be perfect for the both of us, a memory that you and I will treasure for the rest of our lives."

After a time, I remembered that I also needed to contact my friend in the catering business and give them a heads up for the order. After phoning with the details of time, place, the number of people, I asked them also to see whether they could send a few workers earlier to help Ruth get the home straightened up and hang party banners. They gave me some choices on extras, and I made my selections. I then provided my credit card information and told them not to be stingy on anything. I wanted the party to be a big success, and money was not a problem.

Chapter 22

It had been a very long day, what with the meeting with the police, the drive out to Cliff's parents' house, and construction of the playground, the wedding discussion, and then the drive back. I was very tired, but my body ached with a desire that only Cliff could fill. I wanted him with me, in my bed, inside me. It was an overwhelming and powerful demand that seized control of my thoughts. From somewhere deep within me, a primal urge seemed to take over my being. It was as if I could never get enough of his body.

When we arrived back at my apartment, I told the officer sitting outside my apartment door, that we would be remaining there for the rest of the evening. Even though I had eaten very little during the day, I needed Cliff's body more than food. I begged him to join me in my bedroom suite, as soon as I could get the door closed, I asked him to shower with me. I wanted both of us to be clean, and I had learned that bathing with Cliff was the most arousing way to accomplish that.

With our clothes removed, standing naked together, in the shower, we scrubbed and cleaned each other. We used sponges on our bodies to scrub our backs, and he wiped and rubbed my back, under my arms, my neck, and my breasts. He lathered my legs and in between my toes.

I had never felt as clean as when Cliff completed the task with his good hand. Filling his palm with sweet smelling shower gels, then using his fingers to massage and clean between my legs. Then inside my crotch, his other hand sliding underneath and between my buttocks. His fingers, joining at my vagina entrance and pushing. It was tremendously erotic and loving at the same time.

When he had finished, I performed the same for him. I took a razor and smoothed out the skin around his lips and chin. I soaked and lathered his cock with soap, which swelled inside my hands as I lathered it profusely. Then wiping between his legs, as he had done for me, his mouth captured mine occasionally in a deep and loving kiss.

This time, I felt a desperate need that I had suppressed for seventeen years bursting like a dam. I needed to show Cliff how very much I loved and wanted him. I was swept away by my desire for him and sat on the edge of the tub, taking his cock into my mouth, loving and pleasuring him as the water from the showerhead washed away the soap. I rubbed his chest with my hands, then took hold of his balls and gently squeezed as my tongue worshiped his most treasured part.

I was desperate to satisfy an overpowering need surging through my loins. Cliff turned off the shower and lifted me and lay me on the bathroom rug. The floor was soaked with the water from our bodies, but I didn't care. He knelt down between my legs as I gently held his cock and guided it to my vagina. I was soaked, not only from the shower but my arousal so that his entry into me was gentle and loving. His huge organ filled up every need that I could imagine as it slid smoothly inside and then withdrew, only to plunge, seemingly even deeper with each motion.

"Oh, Cliff. What you do to me! God that feels so very good."

His erection was hard and tight, swelling and filling me completely. He pounded into me over and over, filling my mouth with his tongue, drinking up all of the juices inside. I pushed my tongue into him desperately trying to taste all of him. He massaged my breasts and nipples with his fingers until I thought that I would go mad from the pleasure. My breathing was hard and labored as I struggled to take all of him inside of me. Then suddenly I exploded in a frenzied orgasm that shook the both of us. I moaned his name over and over into his mouth.

When he finally erupted inside me, I came again and again with each of his releases. We fell apart on the floor, and I lay sated from the joy of our lovemaking. We had laid that way for many minutes before I sensed that his erection was beginning to become firm and hard again.

Cliff stirred from his position, turned and then lifted me up as he stood. He carried me into the bedroom and lay me out on the bed.

I grabbed his erection in my hand and squeezed it hard. There was a small bit of pre-cum on the tip. I lowered myself and licked it clean. Immediately I looked up into his eyes and before he could object I sank my mouth completely down to his root. I could feel the bulbous tip straining in the back of my throat, and It only excited him more. I kept my eyes locked on his; it was so erotic for both of us. It was a testimony of just how much I loved him.

"God, Christina, your mouth is like a blazing fire on me."

I felt like a wanton woman as I lathered up his magical organ inside my mouth and began to suck on it, pulling my mouth up and down, licking the shaft with swirls of my tongue. Cliff moaned and sank back on the bed, his hands fisting the sheets. He cried out my name over and over as I teased and pleasured him. I continued to suck on him, to stroke and to rub his balls gently in my hand. He writhed on the bed beneath me; his eyes hooded with desire, my mouth owning his body, bring him ever closer to release. I could hardly believe that it was those horrible boys cocks, shaped just as this one had given me so much pain, and yet Cliff's implement could generate such overpowering sensations of joy and happiness inside my sex.

I teased his cock with my teeth several times, then swallowing down to the base I unsheathed my teeth and dragged them with a firm pressure all the way to the top, the sensation of which sent him over the top."

"GOD, Christina, **AHHHHHHHHHHHHH!**" He could hold back no longer.

I tasted the salty flavor of his semen as he released onto my tongue in three huge bursts. The warm liquid saturated and filled my mouth, causing a deep moan to be released from my throat. I rolled the liquid around over my tongue, mixing it with my saliva, opened my mouth to let Cliff see his essence mixed with mine. Then I closed and swallowed the mixture and smiled up at him coyly as it disappeared down my throat.

"Thank you, Cliff, for letting me make love to you," I smiled at him. "I needed to show you how much that I need and love you."

And then in a bit of wanton joy, I stuck out my tongue at him and licked my lips.

He exploded in a burst of laughter and pure love, grabbed my head and kissed me deeply. Then he pulled me upward until I was sitting astride his face, my crotch over his mouth. The things that he did to me next with his tongue can only be described as breathtaking. I had never imagined that I could experience such strong emotions. I felt powerless, my body helpless before the onslaught of his tongue.

My body shook with orgasm after orgasm as he slavered my folds and the entrance to my vagina with his tongue, nibbled on my clitoris. I thought that I would die when he stuck his tongue in my vagina and drank all of my juices as they flowed out of me.

I mewed and cried "oh-Eee Eee" over and over. I could barely move, the sensation of his teeth and tongue as they captured my clitoris and gave me such sweet torture that I thought that I was in heaven.

"Oh GOD! Cliff," I moaned. **"OOO OOO OOO-EEE ee Eee**."

My hips shook and bucked up and down as my orgasms exploded over and over again, I begged him to stop, but he kept on, making me as weak as a kitten. Powerless from his relentless assault on my senses. My legs trembled, I twisted my fingers in his hair, pulling, tugging. This only seemed to make him wilder in his possession of my body.

He called my name over and over, asking me what I wanted, his hot breath streamed into my slit.

I replied weakly, "more, oh God, more. Please, don't stop, God, Cliff, *ahhhhhhhhhhh*!" I was lost to his sweet lips and tongue. **"ooooooooooeeeeeeeeeeeeee."**

I was helpless, trapped in wave after wave of pleasure rocking my body up and down as he fought to control me. I fought to escape from the overpowering release being given by his tongue and teeth. My sex totally captured within his mouth, a prisoner of his wishes. His tongue inside me, teasing my most sensitive parts sent my body into overdrive. His teeth nibbling my folds incessantly. His tongue, teasing the outside of my vagina, drove me wild. His mouth, sucking the juices from my body in an erotic passion of lovemaking, was pure torture that I never wanted to escape.

My torso bucked against his onslaught, struggling to escape the delicious pleasure which overpowered my loins. No matter how my body struggled against him, he kept me pinned in place. I mumbled his name over and over in an incoherent babble of desire and lust. My brain was overcome with the need for him. My thoughts were a jumbled mix of animal desire and pent-up need to be loved and treasured. I existed only to have my body used in sexual abandon.

When he sensed that I was ready. Cliff lowered me onto the bed, climbed on top of me and pushed my legs apart with his knees. He entered me again and again until he had sated himself and could go on no longer. He fell to the side, exhausted, and both of us sank into a peaceful sleep.

The last thing I remember was my arms drifting around his stomach and my hand holding his flaccid cock with my fingers.

I whispered in his ear, "Thank you, Cliff. That was beyond my wildest dream."

After a time, my breathing slowed, my chest relaxed and my arm lay limp against his side. My brain slowly recovered from the rush of pheromones that had overwhelmed me. Deep within my loins, I knew that the need to have him inside me, possessing me would never abate. My crotch ached from the pleasures his body had given me, his feel, his touch, all so much more than I had ever dreamed possible.

He mumbled something incoherently and soon was asleep in my arms.

'*GOD! Cliff, what you do to me.*' I stretched lazily on the sheets, dreaming hazily of the wonderful days ahead. I had never been so high. Experienced such a wonderful feeling of completeness. Life was full of joy, and its name was Cliff. His face spun around and around in my mind.

'Had I been alive before that magical day when he appeared before me and captured my heart with his brilliant smile? I could hardly remember anything before that moment in time. I was not sure that I even existed before then. I wanted only Cliff in my life. I could no longer live without him. I no longer desired to be anywhere except with him by my side.'

My body had experienced an incredible arousal that continued for hours. Even all throughout the next day, my mind was lost in the sensation of his mouth on my genitals. My body flexed and twisted in the bed, yearning, begging to be taken by him again and again.

I often caught myself rubbing my clothes between my legs in a desperate attempt to quell the itch that was throbbing inside between my legs. The taste of him in my mouth, his suckling my breasts, his mouth on my folds and clitoris. *My, Oh, my.* I tossed restlessly in my attempt to gain sleep. Desperately wanting him to take possession of me again. I knew that I would never be sated of this need.

I reached around his waist again, my hand desperately seeking him, desperate to discover if he had that same need. My fingers found their target, and it was hardened and throbbing. I gently tugged on his waist and was rewarded by his lips, turning and capturing mine.

My legs spread open to welcome him inside me again, his voice, soft in my ear, telling of his need and desire for me. This time, he took me gently, slowly, relishing my body, his thrusts inside me at first slow and measured. Then ever more forceful as he pounded into my vagina, filling me, teasing me, filling me, teasing me until we reached union, and our essence mixed in a rush of carnal lust and desire.

"I love you, Cliff."

Then I knew no more and sank into oblivion. My mind in a delicious delirium of desire and fulfillment.

CHAPTER 23

We were awakened the next morning when my cell phone rang.

"Ms. McIntyre, this is Detective Connor. We're in the lobby below and need to come up to meet with you. I have received additional information that I feel is important enough to share."

I phoned down to the front desk and gave clearance for her to come up to the apartment. Cliff and I struggled to find all of our clothes, which were scattered about the room in a wild tangle -- mute evidence of the violence of our lovemaking.

When Detective Connor arrived, she had Detective Kelly in tow. He did not look too happy about being out at such an early hour. I led both to the den and had them sit down on the couch. Then I asked her to fill me in on whatever news that she had.

Cliff was by my side as well, and Charlotte and Marianne looked on from the kitchen. They had evidently been up and about for several hours. What time was it anyway? I could see the den clock just over the detectives' shoulder. 9:45! I hadn't slept this late in years. I blushed as I realized that my staff had most certainly figured out what we had been doing over the previous hours. Mercifully, neither one of them looked at me and focused instead on the two police officers.

"Ms. McIntyre, we just received a report from *Parchman Prison Farm* in Mississippi where Payne was held. The news is not very good, and some of it is rather disturbing. He was released after having served his entire sentence about two months ago. He was a troublemaker during his entire time and is reported to have picked up a lot of nasty skills during his stay there. He bore a particular grudge against you and spoke openly about it to everyone who would listen. Several of the snitches there reported that he has been making plans for the past several years to take actions against you when he was released. I think the reason you were not notified upon his release is that they did not have a current address for you and had received mail return from an old address of yours, and had not followed up."

"In any event, he appears to be a very dangerous character. Most of the plans involve two fellow inmates who were released a couple of years ago. They had been his accomplices when they had assaulted you in high school. Evidently he convinced them to wait for his release before they put their plans into action. Most of the plans involve capturing you and subjecting you to endless rape, and then torturing you to death. After that, they were going to dispose of your body where it could not be found. They were especially mad because of the lawsuit you won in which you were awarded money that would have been their inheritance -- as a result bankrupted their parents."

I was now totally traumatized. "Detective, my God. What can I do? When I was in court that day, and Payne threatened me, I was very afraid. But then, as the years past I figured that he would forget as well. I thought that it was just an idle threat he had spoken in a moment of rage."

"Well, the good news is, that now that we know who they are and that they are here in Houston, we can begin the hunt for them. Especially since they have now committed a major Federal crime in using a car bomb in a public building. We will assign every man possible to this case and should find them soon. We are also going to increase the security around you. We will be placing two uniformed officers on station here, and increase patrols in the area, in case they might try another of those car bombs here."

"We will also have a cruiser in the area of your parents' home, Mr. Stinson. Since they know where that is and have followed you there before. Further, when you leave to go out of your apartment, the officers will escort you in two marked police cruisers. That should be sufficient to scare them off from anything simple they might be planning, like the car chase you experienced a few days ago. Now to help us we need to ask you not to go out in public unless necessary."

"Mr. Stinson, we realize that you are still heavily involved in the investigation to determine the stability of the tower and the damage incurred there. There is already a significant police presence there, and they have all been advised to be on the lookout for these characters. Mrs. Stinson, is there anything else that you can think of that will help us to find and capture these men?"

"Detective, it has been seventeen years since I came in contact with these men. As far as I am concerned, I would have been much happier to have never had that night occur. But that is neither here nor there. Although Ms. Parker is well trained in defense and has a permit to carry a concealed weapon, she cannot be everywhere at once."

"HPD is going to do all that they can to protect you," Detective Kelly replied. "But anything that you can do to help in that effort will be appreciated. All HPD officers have been notified of these men and mugshots have been distributed. Now, you mentioned that you and your family are planning an event for this coming weekend. Can that be canceled or postponed to a later date?"

"Detective, I am not going to let these insane criminals rule our lives," I replied angrily. "This is my first opportunity to meet my fiancé's family, and I am not going to ruin that opportunity on the outside chance that they will try something. Detective Connor said that HPD would have two squad cars in the area. I will be engaging a security firm to provide some additional protection for Cliff's family and my safety. That should be sufficient for this coming weekend."

"I was not trying to offend you, Ms. McIntyre. You and your families' safety is our primary concern. We will do everything possible to see that no harm comes to any of you. We want to capture these men just as much as you. They are a danger to the entire community, as evidenced by their actions so far. They might have killed dozens or even hundreds of people by what they have done. It is only by some miracle that all they have done so far is mostly property damage."

"You are right, detective, I apologize. I shouldn't have gone off like that, but my nerves are on edge right now. Every happiness that I ever wanted is threatened by these men. Please forgive me."

"No apology is needed, Ms. McIntyre. We only want to help. If we are finished here, I think that we need to get back to headquarters and bring them up to date. We will work to make sure that you and your family have a happy and uneventful weekend."

"Thank you, detective. Ms. Parker will see you to the door."

After the detectives had left, I asked Marianne to fix us all some coffee.

"Charlotte, can you check around and find out the best security firm in town and who has the best-trained personnel to offer assistance."

I turned to Cliff, "Cliff, I am sorry to have gotten you and your family involved in this mess. I am embarrassed that my past should cause this kind of problem for anyone, especially since I have just met your wonderful parents. And then to think some of the children coming on Saturday might be involved or get hurt because of me."

"Christina, none of this is your fault. I don't know how you could think such a thing. These are not men. They are animals, wild beasts out to create as much terror and damage as they can for actions that they took which were and are unforgivable. Society has always had such people -- on the fringe, taking what they can get, destroying what they cannot have. They will be captured and brought to justice.

"Please, let's forget about them for this weekend; and only think happy thoughts. Just wait until you meet some of my nieces and nephews. If you think these guys are bad, Just wait until you meet my sister Carol's two sons, Mike, and Sam. Now those two are the ones that you should take precautions. They are holy terrors to the girls, pulling on their pigtails, once they even put frogs down their dresses. You will need to be on your guard at all times."

My fears disappeared and were quickly replaced by giggles as I thought of the two little boys being, well, being little boys.

"You know, Cliff, I think that I am going to love your family. They sound very much like the man with whom I fell in love."

"Oh yeah. And what man was that?" Cliff teased.

"Let me see now; I am having a hard time remembering his name. I only met him a short time back, and his name slips my mind right now." I teased in return.

"Okay, lady, you are going to get it now!"

"Cliff, stop tickling me." I giggled. "Don't do that," I giggled wildly, he continued to tickle me.

"Charlotte, HELP! A fiend is attacking me here."

"Tina, I'm on the phone over here. You guys need to keep the racket down a bit." She laughed and turned back to her phone call.

"I was thinking of giving you a raise, but I just might have to reconsider that. Some help you are when I am in such desperate need," I pouted, but Charlotte knew that I was just teasing when I gave her a huge smile.

"Hahaha! Cliff. Okay, okay. I surrender. Stop tickling me. The man's name was Cliff, although, at present, I cannot remember exactly why I fell for him. It couldn't have been his mustache because he does not have one. Maybe it was those two big brown eyes, or his strong muscular body, or that delicious smell I have named Cliff or some other silly thing like that."

I don't remember much after that point because he began kissing me and we had to retire to my room for a history lesson in why I loved him so much. Ohhh! My favorite classroom subject.

Cliff and I returned to the den about two hours later after having taken a shower and changing into some street clothes. My first need was to quickly firm up the security company. I had asked Charlotte to check out the available firms in town and see which had the best staffing choices and personnel. That was what she was doing on the phone earlier. Her report was positive. She had called some office towers, malls, and other shopping centers and their top recommendation was Metropolitan Security Services.

I placed a call to their main office and asked to meet with one of their head representatives, advising them that I would need extensive security coverage and would like to meet with them in person to go over the details. I spoke briefly with a Mr. Jason Passmore, the head of their entire team and he agreed to meet with me, Cliff and Charlotte at two p.m. in their offices. Cliff and I headed out to the valet area after notifying them that I would need my vehicle right away. We drove to Metropolitan Securities main office on San Jacinto without incident. As promised, there were two police cars that escorted us during our trip.

After arriving there and being escorted into Passmore's office, I went over the entire history of the embarrassing origin of my problem, the recent release of James Payne, the incidents of the car chase, the bombings and also HPD involvement. He agreed that this was potentially one of the most serious cases that his company had been involved. Other than in assisting in the protection of the U.S. President when he was in town. I explained that we were organizing a family get-together for Saturday, and there were many family members traveling from out of town. I wanted them to be safe but did not want any of them to feel like they were in an armed camp.

HPD had agreed to have two cruisers in the area, but there might be other ways for the men to sneak in because it was an open public subdivision. Passmore suggested that he could have several men who could station themselves in the area in plain everyday clothes so that they were not as noticeable. Also, we discussed other options for increased protection for Cliff when he was at the tower. We finalized the terms of the security and price. I was very appreciative of his ideas.

It had been a nerve-wracking day for me, and I was rather hungry. Passmore suggested that he would begin the protection immediately by assigning three bodyguards to us, and they would proceed immediately to any restaurant of our choosing to check it out in advance. Cliff suggested that perhaps we should go someplace that Payne could not possibly guess in advance.

"Do you like Mexican?"

"Sounds great. Do you have someplace special in mind?" I queried.

"Sure do. How would you and Charlotte like to visit one of my favorite eating spots in town? The prices are modest, but the food is great, and the staff is very knowledgeable and polite. It is called *Juanita's*. It is just off Hwy 249 on Louetta Drive. You guys will love it. It's usually packed with people who love good Mexican food. And for once Charlotte will not have to be lurking in the shadows. We can have a pleasant meal in a relaxing atmosphere. What do you say?"

I looked at Charlotte and saw the big smile on her face that she was definitely up for the challenge. A sit-down meal with her boss and her fiancé in an actual restaurant.

"What's not to like. Let's go," she smiled.

I phoned Larry after the meeting and explained that we had probably identified the culprits who had bombed both buildings. He was astounded to learn that it seemed both bombings were caused by people seeking revenge on me. Since the floor that was damaged most in our building was the floor where I worked it was going to be quite some time before that could be completely repaired and ready for workers to return.

He suggested that I had about two months' vacation time on the books. It would probably be a good idea to use it as there was nothing else pressing at the moment. The T & J contract had been secured, the company presidents were meeting for the signing of the contract. There was no other issue in the immediate future I needed to be present to handle. I was overjoyed at the news of the contract as I had worked very hard to help win that bid.

After I had thought for a bit, I realized that this might offer me an excellent opportunity to get to know my future husband much better, and offer me some much-needed relaxation time away from the office. I would be free to give Cliff that TLC for his injuries, and we could also spend some quality time in each other's company.

Cliff had hired the young man, Edward Hale, whom I had suggested. Hale was eagerly going about the process of getting the suppliers back on track. He was focused on getting the correct supplies in the correct amounts shipped to the tower. He had set up a new schedule, which had been adjusted to compensate for the damage done by the bombing.

Cliff was very proud of him because supplies would now actually show up just as he needed them, rather than the disorganized mess from the past. The upper floors of the tower were undamaged, so Hale had arranged those orders to come in priorty, while a damage assessment was completed on the lower floors.

As the work progressed, I was able to go in with Cliff occasionally and observe the progress. It was very exciting, and I thoroughly enjoyed watching, from a safe distance, as men hung some twenty stories in the air, grappling with girders and bringing them into alignment for bolting and welding them in place.

The men affixed the new Plexiglas skin to their brackets, transferring loads of sheetrock, ceiling tiles, electrical conduits, and wiring, and moved a thousand other loads of supplies into the empty floors. From there, other workers eagerly moved them to locations where office rooms were framed. The building was like a giant beehive of activity, with workers scurrying about here and there, offices taking shape in their wake.

Mostly, I just tried to stay out of their way and enjoy all of the exciting activity. It was an exhilarating change of pace. Thoughts of James Payne faded to the background. The closeness of Cliff as I watched him direct all of this was a turn-on for me. My fiancé was an extraordinarily talented leader. Knowledgeable in even the smallest details of the job.

CHAPTER 24

We met with a wedding planner and outlined some basic ideas of what we both wanted to happen with our wedding celebration. When the meeting was over I was certain that the company I had chosen was perfect, and they would be able to carry off just about anything we needed. We provided our contact information, and they began outlining the ceremony and preparing lists of what we would need.

Saturday came around in a hurry. I had taken Marianne over to Cliff's parents on Friday morning to assist Ruth in final preparations and set up of furniture and tables for the party and Marianne had slept over in one of the spare bedrooms. When Cliff and I arrived, the house was decorated out in celebration with streamers and flags. I was tingling with anticipation. I was going to meet an entirely new family, my heart was pounding at the thought. I prayed that they would like me. I knew with a certainty that I would love them.

I had taken some extra time and gone by one of my favorite dress designers and selected a sharply tailored black sequin embroidered bustier dress. It featured a strapless, wrapped bodice and skirt with a front slit, pleat detailed back and hidden zipper. I added a pair of Manolo Okkato low-heel crepe black pumps to my outfit. I wanted to look my best.

After fussing a bit, I decided the only jewelry I would wear was my beautiful new engagement ring. I felt like a queen. I had a bit of a battle but was finally able to get Cliff to allow me to buy him a stunning red sports coat. It had black collars and matching black slacks. He looked divine and sexy.

When we arrived several of the family who lived locally, were already there. I let Cliff do the honors of introducing me to them. There were Al and Carol Stinson and their three children, Gail and husband Lee Mashburn, and children; Michael and Kristen Stinson with their three small children.

About fifteen minutes after we arrived, his older sister Mary and her husband, Tom Rogers, and their children pulled up and piled out of their car. Shortly after that his sister Cynthia with her husband Mike Anderson arrived from Dallas with their two towheads.

I introduced Charlotte and Marianne to all, then we all proceeded to the backyard where the children instantly screamed. They scattered in all directions, ran and jumped and climbed all over the exquisite playground which had been erected. The center of attention for the older ones was a giant spider that had all kinds of hand holds and things to climb on and swing. The smaller ones swarmed around the combination slide, playhouse and swing set built for them.

Charlotte checked out the surrounding grounds and made sure that the security, which we had hired, were all in place. Then we called for a meeting of all of the adults at the head of the pool area. It was far enough so the children wouldn't be upset by our discussion, but close enough that they could still be closely monitored by their parents. Charlotte and Ruth remained near the small children on the swings keeping a close eye on those wandering around the spider and mushrooms.

Cliff led the discussion explaining the reason for the presence of the police cruisers. Also letting them know that there were security personnel in the area, hired for everyone's safety due to the bombings. The family seemed to feel comfortable with the arrangements, and then expressed concern for Cliff and my safety as long as we remained in the Houston area. Cliff brought them up to date on the tower bombing and the status of damage and repairs.

After a time, the families began to break up and mingle with each other. From time to time, each couple would come over, introduce themselves to me and take a seat opposite us. Of course, I related more closely to the women but soon began to realize the value of the men and how well each woman's personality fit in with their husband.

They were all very comfortable with each other, especially with Cliff, having known him much longer. They were warm and friendly, each telling little stories about Cliff or even themselves, opening up to show how much they wanted me to be a part of this wonderful family. We laughed and cried over the silliest things. The men had great laughs, at either Cliff's expense or their own, when discussing the good times, they had all shared while growing up.

After several hours of sharing, joking and having fun, the caterer announced that lunch was served. We all gathered around the tables of steaming barbecue, baked beans, potato salad, green beans with buttered rolls. Cliff's father gave the meal blessing, after which I ate so much that I knew that I would have to spend some extra time in the workout room to pay for my crime, but it was worth every bite.

The parents gathered their children in and helped them fill their plates and then sat with them as we all enjoyed the short respite, away from our daily worries and concerns. Even the children were fairly quiet. But that was normal. We all knew that their screams of pleasure would begin again as soon as their little tummies were full and they could return to their friends for more playing on the swings, slides or splashing in the pool.

George and Ruth joined us in the afternoon. Ruth asked if I had met everyone, and wanted to know whether I was enjoying myself.

"Your family is so marvelous," I replied. "Yes, I believe that I have met everyone, all the ladies have shared their phone numbers with promises of juicy gossip about my fiancé."

"Hey!" Cliff interjected. "Don't believe a word they say, Christina. None of it is true," he said playfully.

"Now, Mom, don't you be putting them up to something. You guys are going to scare away my beautiful fiancée."

"Cliff, if she was not scared off enough by the car bomb and then the bomb at her office, I don't think anything more will do that. Don't you worry, son, this lady loves you with all her heart."

"I know, mom. And I love her more than you could ever believe. She is the most precious thing in the world to me. Oh, Mom, Dad -- Christina and I have been discussing our wedding plans. Nothing is finalized yet, but I was wondering. Would you mind very much if we held the wedding here? Your home would be a great setting; the backyard is plenty large enough. I can hire some of my workers to build an altar and everything. And you might even have Pastor Steven Williams do the honors for us? What do you say?"

"Christina, Clifford, Oh yes!" Ruth broke down in tears of happiness that Cliff had even thought of their home. "Yes, son, George and I would love nothing more than to have the privilege of hosting your wedding at our home. Thank you for thinking of us, and I know that Steve would be honored."

Having met all of the family and letting our lunch settle inside us, Cliff and I joined the children splashing in the pool. It was so relaxing to have some peaceful time together. We raced each other from one side of the pool to the other. Several of my soon to be in-laws joined us for a water volleyball game. I had never felt so loved and were a part of something unique. Family, that was the one thing in my life that I had missed. The friendly banter, the comradery, and fellowship that could be had by the sharing of close relationships and friends. Especially those formed outside of the work environment. These would last a lifetime. I felt that at long last my life had begun to blossom and take root in a world of happiness.

The party was a tremendous success. The kids had a wonderful time, especially when the caterers passed out ice cream treats. I found that Cliff's brothers and sisters were all very nice people. I became fast friends with the ladies, and we gossiped for hours. His two brothers were very intelligent and held important positions with their companies.

All of their kids were well behaved, and the playground went over tremendously with all of them, especially the various shaped structures like the spider and the swinging mushrooms. I even fantasized that Cliff and I might have a few of our own children someday, I just hoped they would be as well-behaved.

Mike and Sam turned out to be just as mischievous as Cliff had promised. Mike had somehow hidden his power squirt gun under the car seat, and the two boys spent a lot of energy in filling it up and soaking all of the girl's dresses. Naturally there was a lot of screaming and running, but in the end, all the young children had their swimsuits on underneath and Ruth saved the day by running their soaked dresses through her clothes dryer while the girls played in the wading end of the pool.

Mike and Sam, however, had to sit on one of the lounge chairs for an hour, forced to watch, all alone, as all of the other children got to play in the swimming pool. In the end, two of the girls came over and took them by their hands and brought them over to the pool where they simply jumped in with all of their clothes. All seemed forgiven, everyone laughed and had a good time.

Everyone promised to do it again as soon as possible. I was kissed and hugged by all as each gathered their family together and took their leave. Cliff and I were among the last to depart. George and Ruth thanked us for giving them the opportunity to have their entire family together in one place for a wonderful family time together. Peoples' lives being so occupied nowadays, we all agreed that there were so few opportunities for such gatherings, but promised to try hard in the future to make it a routine.

CHAPTER 25

It was getting dark, around 7:30 p.m., when we pulled out of the driveway and started back to my apartment. We were just about to turn onto Grogan's Mill when a shot rang out, a bullet struck our front windshield. I screamed and, in a panic, ducked below the dashboard while Cliff whipped the steering wheel wildly and the car spun sideways. A second bullet struck the windshield, and a third bullet crashed into my headrest. I could hear the siren of one of the police cars in the area starting to scream. The squeal of car tires was everywhere, and soon we were involved in a mad crush of cars coming from all directions. It was very confusing. Other than the marked police squad car with flashing lights we were completely confused. Which car might be the bad guys and which were the good guys? I assumed that one of the other cars involved must be from Metropolitan Securities or a curious neighborhood teenager anxious to get involved where he shouldn't, but was uncertain as to which one.

'*Calm down, Tina,*' I forced my mind to go into protective mode. '*It may be up to you to save Cliff's life, think, breathe calmly, get your weapon out, breathe calmly, focus and remember the things Charlotte trained you to do.*' My mind raced, trying to think of what actions I needed to take.

I dug into my purse; my pistol slipped naturally into my hand. "*Breathe, think, focus, calm down,*" over and over my mind fought to gain control of my emotions. I raised myself up from the well below the seat; Cliff was driving erratically, madly swerving here and there, driving into oncoming traffic trying to escape from our tormentors. I reached over and grabbed his thigh after strapping myself back into my seat.

"Cliff, I love you so much, we are going to get through this. Now, can you tell me if you know which car is the one shooting at us?"

"Yes, it's the black sedan. Right now it's just in front of the patrol car that is trying to ram it."

I looked back and could now see the sedan as it ran over a curb and down a stretch of sidewalk, narrowly missing a pedestrian, who had quickly jumped aside to escape being run over. The police car chased after the sedan wildly. But the patrol car could not seem to catch up to it, as the sedan suddenly swerved from one side of the street to the other.

"Cliff, we are going to have to help the police stop these guys."

I looked around desperately for an idea, anything that might help. Then, just ahead, I saw there was a long stretch of empty roadway.

"Gun it, Cliff. Put some distance between us. If you can open up enough space between us, I want you to whip the car around and come back at them."

"Christina – that's madness."

"No Cliff, I want you to open up a space between us. Just do it, please."

Cliff floored the Audi, and it roared away, chewing up the roadway like a hyena from hell. The black car fell further and further back.

"Now, Cliff, Now! Turn us around and come straight back at them. I want you to ram him, ram him hard."

"What? You mean, wreck your car," he glanced over at me with a look of amazement.

"Yes, Cliff, I think that it is the only way out of this."

"HOLD ON TIGHT, THIS IS GOING TO BE ROUGH," Cliff shouted.

I yanked my seat belt on tighter and grabbed the overhead handle as tightly as I could.

"Here we go!" Cliff shouted. **"Hold on tight!"**

Suddenly Cliff whipped the steering wheel hard left, slamming on the brakes. The car groaned in agony as the forces of torque propelling us wildly forward were thrown insanely askance as if a Giants' hand was whipping the car helter-skelter, almost to the point of tipping over. Even though I was held securely in place, I could feel my body swinging wildly, straining against the seat belt. Slowly, surely the car began to settle into place,

Cliff's injured arm had returned to full strength over the last week and now, using both hands he desperately clung to the steering wheel, commanding the car to reverse course. I watched in fascination as the muscles on his arms bulged and strained against the tire's determined need to remain where they had been. Cliff's arms pulled and stretched, his entire face became red from the strain. He was gradually winning the battle between forward motion and our desperate need to swing around in the opposite direction.

My head banged against the passenger side window, stars floated around in my head, I fought to maintain control of the pistol in my hand. With one final angry twist, the car settled into its new trajectory, directly opposite from our previous direction.

"**Way to go, Cliff**," I shouted.

I grabbed the arm rest and pushed down on the automatic window button lowering the side window.

"Drive straight at them, Cliff. I want you to ram them. If you can, see if you can hit them on the driver's side and force them off the road." I cried.

The wind whipped wildly into the open window, tossing my hair back in a long stream.

I think Cliff finally began to understand my plan as he gunned the car again and we flew at the other car at an obscene speed. At the last second, the black sedan tried to twist to the right to avoid the inevitable crash. The Audi slammed into the driver's door of the sedan with a huge

WHAM.

There was a horrible crash and the metal of both cars screamed in agony, as it twisted and tore into new shapes. The hood over my engine crumpled and bent backward. My windshield separated from its' fastenings and flapped upward toward the roof of the car. There was an explosion inside the car as both air bags were released jolting us back against the back of our seats. The other car's driver and passenger doors crumpled inward and their car lifted crazily onto the opposite set of tires before scrunching back down with a loud bang. Twisted and torn the metal fragments of both cars' bonding together as one.

I held my .38 outside the window and emptied the entire chamber into the driver's door. Cliff kept our car jammed and pushing against the side of the sedan. Ramming and pushing it sideways across the street and directly at the approaching police cruiser. It was a wild, unforgettable, terrifying scene. I struggled to get my extra cartridges from my purse.

Suddenly the police cruiser slammed into the back end of the sedan twisting it away, the sedan started to flip over but ended up slamming back down with our car wedged between the two vehicles.

The police car came to a violent stop, and the two policemen inside jumped out with their guns drawn. Suddenly two occupants of the crashed car crawled out the other side and began firing at the policemen. The officers stepped back behind the relative safety of the doors of their car and returned fire. Cliff grabbed hold of my arm as I released my seat belt. He pushed the car driver side door open and pulled me to safety onto the street beside the ruins of my beautiful car.

One of the men shooting at the police suddenly reached into the front seat of the wrecked sedan and pulled out an automatic rifle. He began shooting wildly, the bullets spraying the front of the police car. I finally found my extra cartridges and was able to align them with the opened chamber, jamming the bullets into place inside their slots. Cliff looked at me crazily, I think more frightened for me, than for himself.

"What are you doing, Christina? Where did you get that gun?" he shouted.

"Get down, Cliff, get down, you don't have a weapon. Please, let me handle this for us. I know how to shoot, and this is my favorite weapon."

The adrenaline rush was pushing me to a level of excitement and tension as I had never known. The police were pinned down, and I could see the second police cruiser approaching about a quarter mile away. I had to think fast. The officers nearby were pinned down by the wildly firing fiend with the rifle. I raised my gun and switched on the laser targeting. One or both of the police officers was going to die if I did not take some action. I had a perfect view of the man from my position.

I could see the second occupant fleeing as his legs disappeared over a nearby fence and dropped into someone's back yard. My target laser beam settled on the man's shoulder who was firing. I squeezed the trigger and almost instantly the rifle flew from the man's hands. The bullet had struck him just at the point where the rifle was resting against his shoulder causing him to lose control of the weapon. Instantly the officers were on their feet and rushing toward him. I kept my gun trained on the man, who was now laying on his side in the street, screaming in agony.

The second police car now skidded to a stop only a few feet away. The officers inside jumped out and began screaming at me.

"DROP YOUR WEAPON. DROP THE GUN ON THE GROUND, NOW!"

Both officers pointed their weapons at me. I was terrified but I couldn't. If I did the man might get away.

"Officer," I shouted. "I'm a licensed-concealed-handgun owner. My CHL and Texas Drivers' License are in my purse. I have my gun targeted on the man there who was trying to kill the other officers."

I held my position, never looking back as the officers screamed at me again.

"LADY – DROP THE WEAPON NOW OR WE WILL BE FORCED TO SHOOT."

Just then the first two officers reached the wounded man and took control of him. Rolling him over, twisting his arms behind him and slapping on handcuffs.

I dropped my weapon to the street and raised my arms. One of the officers lowered his weapon and ran toward me, kicking my weapon away.

The second officer kept his gun pointed at me, screaming.

"KEEP YOU HANDS IN THE AIR, DON'T MOVE OR I WILL SHOOT."

Cliff kept screaming at them, **"DON'T SHOOT, DON'T SHOOT. WE ARE THE ONES THEY WERE TRYING TO KILL, PLEASE DON'T SHOOT. OFFICER."**

It went on around me like a slow motion movie reel. The officer finally reached me and grabbed one of my arms from above my head, lowering it behind my back and then he reached and grabbed my other arm, lowering it to join the other. Grabbing me by my wrists, he held them firmly in place.

Cliff had his hands in the air as well, crying, tears streaming down his face. Afraid that somehow one of the officers would make a mistake and injure me.

"Officer, those men were trying to kill us. Please don't hurt my fiancée. Please, don't hurt my fiancée," Cliff pleaded.

"All right, sir, please, just give us a moment to sort out this mess." He loosened his hold on my wrists but did not release them.

"Harry," he shouted at one of the officers in the ditch, "Can you verify if this lady is the one we were protecting?"

"Yes, Jim, you can release her," he shouted. "She just saved our lives. But the other suspect jumped over that fence. Can you call for backup? We need to set a perimeter and see if we can capture him."

The second officer holstered his weapon.

Immediately the officer released my hands and ran back to his vehicle, shouting back over his shoulder – 'Ma'am. Please retrieve your CHL and Driver licenses and be prepared to show it to the officers over there when they are ready. You'll need to remain where you are until everything is sorted out."

I left my gun laying where the officer had kicked it and ran towards Cliff, grabbing him, holding him tightly to my body. Cliff wrapped his arms around me and then began to stroke my hair, trying desperately to calm my jaded nerves.

"That was something I don't get to do every night. Ram myself into another car while my fiancée is firing a gun out the side window!" Cliff whispered in my ear.

I looked up at him weirdly and then began to giggle. Then I broke out into a hysterical laugh unable to control the release of the tension in my body. Cliff joined me as we collapsed down onto the roadway, laughing insanely.

We watched as one officer went about his duty of securing the black sedan to see whether there was anyone else inside. The other officer stood nearby, using his shoulder radio to talk with other unseen police cars. Those circling the neighborhood were searching for the fled suspect. Finally, we focused on the two officers as they struggled to pull the wounded man to the front of their police cruiser.

"You know you're right, Cliff. And I hope that you *never* get to see that again," I finally said after my laughing slowed."

"Ow, my side hurts!" I cried.

Cliff looked at me terrified. "Are you injured? Let me look. Did a bullet hit you? God, please, tell me that you are okay, and where did you learn to fire a weapon like that. I didn't even know that you had a weapon in your purse. Not that I am complaining, you understand, but whooee!! I have never seen anything like that except in a movie."

I looked up at his brown eyes, his iris's grown large from the excitement.

"No, don't be silly, my side hurts because I was laughing so hard. You say the weirdest, oddest things at the most unexpected moments. God, I love you so much.

"Years ago, after I got out on my own," I continued. "I decided that I needed protection and purchased the weapon you see on the ground over there. I would go to the shooting range at least once a week until I learned how to use the gun. I chose a pistol because my fingers just weren't strong enough to load all of those bullets into an automatic magazine.

"That is where I met up with Charlotte, four years ago. We became fast friends, and eventually, she showed me how to do some things that aren't taught in elementary shooting practices. She had been an MP while in the Marines and had gone through advanced weapons school.

"Of course, I am not as good a shot as she. She still has some tricks that she has not shown me yet, but the maneuver that we did when you reversed the car, and then I fired into the drivers' door was one that we have practiced before. Although I never actually got to ram the car, or fire into the door, other than with a paint gun. This was a whole lot more exciting."

Cliff wiped some sweat from his forehead. But from the look on his face, I wasn't too sure that he agreed with me on that last statement.

We settled back and continued to watch the strange movie playing out before us. Other police cars arrived, sirens blasting, until finally Charlottes' car pulled up and she and Marianne jumped out and ran over to us. Both are looking at us rather strangely as we both continued to laugh and hold onto each other. Eventually, an ambulance joined the melee, its siren and flashing lights merrily joining in with the others.

Charlotte looked around at the scene, then down at me.

"Something going on here that I need to know about?"

Cliff and I began howling in laughter all over again. My side was splitting now.

"Charlotte, are you sure that you aren't related to Cliff in some strange way that I don't know? You have the same manner of asking the funniest questions at the most inopportune times. Have a seat and I'll tell you all about it."

It seems Charlotte and Marianne had stayed behind to help take down the banners and straighten up the back yard where the kids had left several pieces of trash. As I was explaining things to Charlotte and Marian, the officer by the wrecked sedan opened the car's driver door, the body of a man slumped downward. It was pretty obvious that he was dead. At that moment, I realized that we would probably be at the scene much of the night answering questions and giving statements.

Charlotte looked over at me and inquired, "Did you do that or one of the policemen?"

"To tell the truth, it's not something that I'm proud of, but yes. I guess that was my shooting. I was about to get to that part of the story…It's the first time that I've ever fired my weapon in a life and death situation, and evidently it was my shots which killed the driver. I'm not sure of how I feel about killing someone. It's left me empty inside. But I know that if I had not taken action, both Cliff and I might be dead."

"I can understand if you are upset about this," Charlotte interrupted. "Tina, you have every right to be proud of what you have done. These men were attacking you. You took control of the situation, just as I have been training you to do. I, for one, am extremely proud. You did what you had to do when the time came.

"It's a terrible thing to have to take someone's life, but when the chips were down, you acted instinctively. You not only saved Cliff and your lives but most likely those two policemen over there. Well done! Well done, Tina."

I slumped against Cliff's shoulder. "Hey, big guy, bet you never thought that when you woke up this morning, that you would end the evening sitting in the street surrounded by a gaggle of police cars did you?"

Cliff began laughing again, which only started me off again.

"Ow! I only wish that when they build these streets, they would plan ahead for things like this and put a nice comfortable bench beside the road on which to sit." I mumbled, my back begging to ache, my buttocks announcing that it did not particularly enjoy sitting on the sharp rock underneath me."

"Officer, may we sit on the sidewalk, please?" Cliff asked. "This roadway is not very comfortable."

"Yes, sir. We are waiting for a supervisor to arrive and then the detectives will have a lot of questions. Please, have a seat over there. There is a nice patch of grass that should be a bit more comfortable. We will get with you as soon as things have settled down a bit.

Turning to me the officer continued, "by the way, that was a great piece of shooting back there, ma'am. I saw you take down that man's rifle down with one shot. Have you ever considered a job in law enforcement?"

Cliff and I collapsed in laughter again as we struggled to reach the sidewalk while Charlotte and Marianne supported us across the street.

The officer shook his head in confusion. "Was it something I said?" he asked as he walked away.

All four of us now laughed even harder.

When I could finally catch my breath, and my nerves had settled, I looked over at the remains of my beautiful Audi. "Cliff, it looks like your greatest fear came true."

He looked over at me, suddenly sobering up and looking around for the source of my statement. "I don't understand. To what are you referring?"

I tried to put on my most serious looking face.

"My car. You were so afraid that you were going to put a small dent in it the other day. Now it looks like your fears came true. I think that you just about totaled it. Can your checking account support replacing it tomorrow? I sure did love that car."

Cliff looked at me, and for a moment, he did not realize that I was kidding.

"You don't carry Collison insurance?"

"Not a dime, just liability."

I held my face taught for only a few seconds longer before I collapsed in laughter again.

"All right, sweetheart," as he finally realized that I was teasing. "That's it; you're going to get it now," as he reached down and began tickling me under my arms and side.

I squealed and twisted away trying to avoid his fingers.

"All right, I surrender. I am sorry, sweetheart, I just could not resist. Now before I let another minute pass I need to tell you something. Do you remember when you asked me if I was wealthy that first night in my apartment?"

"Yes, why?"

"I did not answer you truthfully because we were so new in love. I didn't want to scare you away. --In the past the money that I have has turned men that I have dated into gold diggers, lusting to get my money. I want to tell you now. My parents won a lawsuit against not only the school but also the parents of the three boys. It turned out that they had done this to other girls and the parents were wealthy and had kept it a secret by buying the girls' silence each time."

"The judge awarded me a total of twenty million dollars in damages. Then later when my parents were killed in a plane crash, it turned out to be a defective part inside the planes' engine which should have been discovered in either the manufacturing process or routine maintenance. I was awarded fifteen million dollars for each parent for a total of thirty million."

"I have since invested both of those amounts, and my current worth is around seventy-five million dollars. I don't need to work. I never have. But I didn't want just to sit around in some mansion and live off of that money. I didn't earn it and always felt that I couldn't spend it, knowing where it had originated. I have barely touched it in all of these years. I like to work because it gives me purpose in life.

"When you marry me, I am happy to tell you; you will have an equal share in all that I have. And should I die before you, it will all be yours. It is a gift of my love for you. There will be no prenuptial between us. What is mine is yours. Whatever is yours will be mine unless you have something that you would wish to exclude. There now, I have spoken my piece. Let there be no more secrets between us."

We spent the next several hours giving statements; I showed the Detective my CHL license, and he took my gun as evidence, to be returned to me as soon as everything was documented.

Cliff was silent, and contemplative the entire time. I was unsure of how he had taken this news. Perhaps I should have waited until another time. By the time we finished speaking with the detectives about the happenings of the evening, we were both totally exhausted. We then returned to the apartment via a cab. Cliff said very little to me and seemed a bit distant. I took that to signify that he was still anxious over the car crash and my shooting of the assailant in the other car.

CHAPTER 26

The next morning when my eyes opened, I immediately sensed that Cliff was not in my bed. Ever since the moment I had revealed the extent of my fortune I had sensed a drawing away in Cliff. He seemed changed, but I could not understand why or the extent. The terror of the previous night, the gunfire, the car chase, and wreck. The man who had been killed when I fired into the driver's door turned out to be one of the boys who had raped me. The other man who was captured was the third boy.

The one who escaped by jumping the fence and then the police dragnet had abducted a man from his home and stole his car. He dropped the man dropped off five miles away, alive but shaken. That was James Payne as admitted by the captured man. Thus, two of the men who had ruined my life were now either dead or headed back to prison. The third, the most dangerous of all, was still at large with no clue as to his whereabouts as he had abandoned the stolen car at a grocery store parking lot near the ship channel. They had found blood inside that car so that he may have been wounded by one of my bullets.

And now, Cliff was missing from my room. There was no note on his pillow, no message on my phone. I rose from the bed and searched for him around the apartment. He was nowhere to be found. I asked Marianne and Charlotte, but neither had seen him. I opened the door to the apartment and asked the officer stationed outside He checked the log and advised me that Mr. Stinson had left the apartment around 4:30 a.m. He had called a cab, but the officer had no record of his destination.

My heart began to ache with his absence. 'Where was he? Why had he left with no message? Had I done something to hurt him?' I returned to the apartment and paced back and forth, struggling for insight.

"Ms. Tina," I heard Marianne call from my bedroom. "I was straightening your bed and found this under your pillow," she handed me a small envelope.

My hands trembled as they held the envelope. I could sense its contents without breaking the seal. I slowly slid my finger under the flap, releasing it and revealing a beautifully handwritten note.

Christina,

> *Please forgive me for leaving you like this. This man, Payne, who is pursuing you, needs to be captured. By our being together he seems to be able to locate you more easily. If I can stay away from you, make myself more open to attack, perhaps he will be drawn away from his focus on you. He might come after me in such a way that the police can easily locate and capture him.*

> *Please forgive me. I love you more than life itself. You wound my heart with your love. When I told you that I did not want your money or possessions, I spoke the truth. When you first told me that you were wealthy, I thought that you were saying you had perhaps a hundred thousand dollars or so in the bank. But, seventy-five million, I feel very undeserving. I do have some money that I have been saving over the years, but nothing like what you have described.*

> *I could not bear if one day you looked and me and saw how much less I would bring to our marriage. My feelings for you are so strong. What can I possibly do or give you that would repay you for your trust in me. I despair of the words to write to you that can convey my thoughts.*

I pray that Payne will now focus his energies on me and leave you alone.

I will love you forever.

Cliff.

'Oh! Foolish, foolish man. Does he not see? Does he not understand? Payne will have no interest in him. He only searches for me. I am the cause of Payne's troubles in life. His anger is directed at me alone. Nothing Cliff could do will distract him from that. Cliff is everything to me. He offers me happiness, without him, I will be alone and vulnerable. Only together can we hope to survive this torment.

'I do understand how he might feel that way. The first bomb attack was against the building where he was working. Perhaps he thinks that Payne wants to hurt him more than he wants to strike at me. But my guess is that the bomb in my building was planted long before that car bomb. It was only by some accident in Payne's timing that the car bomb exploded first.

'And the money -- what I revealed was wealth beyond his wildest imagination. How would a man who was like Cliff, a strong leader, used to being in charge, directing others to achieve goals, feel if he were to find suddenly himself subservient to the wealth of a spouse?

'To have that opportunity and basic need in a man's nature ripped away with the sudden gift of wealth beyond his imagination. Somehow I must convince him that what he gives to me is worth more than all of the money in the world. He gives me love, and family, two things which are priceless to me, I have told him this, but he does not understand, he does not believe that is possible since he has had family all of his life.'

'Oh, Cliff, you crazy, foolish man. I love you so much. I must find you and protect you from yourself. Prove your worth to me so that you will understand. Payne will not pursue you; he has probably already forgotten you since his two friends have been ripped away. I must find a way to show you that truth so that you will return and bring the happiness back to my heart, and at the same time do something that will end this threat from a madman.'

I read Cliff's note over and over.

'But How? Why would he believe that I wanted to control his life?'

I thought back over my actions since the first day, trying to identify the cause of Cliff's concern. I took out a notepad and pen from my nightstand and began to write down things that I might have said or done that caused this misunderstanding between us.

When he asked for a date, I told him I would only go to a restaurant of my choosing. And then I did not let him make the choice for his meal; perhaps he hated my selection. The first night in my apartment I had refused to let him pay for the new clothes that I had bought for him. When I had pushed so hard to pay for the catering for the party, it may have seemed like I was taking over.

When the subject of the security firm came up, I had rushed to have Charlotte do the research. Perhaps Cliff knew of a company already, and I had not asked for his input. After our visit to his parents, I had almost raped him in my desire to make love. Aroused him in the shower, pushing him to love me, to take me there on the floor, and then pleasured myself at his moral expense. I am sure that he was torn by this, shaking his core beliefs, I had come to understand that he held deeply religious beliefs, perhaps I had overstepped myself, and his own faith.

This last one was the most troubling of all. I had done to him what those boys had done to me. I had used my repressed sexual desires to awaken his. Done to him what I so despised from my past. I was ashamed and humbled.

Yes, he had become a willing participant in that night, but it has I who had nearly torn the clothes from his body brought him to a state of arousal which I had used to satiate my carnal needs. It was not love that I had gotten from him. It was pure animal lust, and I had used my body as a weapon to subdue and conquer his.

I was appalled. I had been too controlling. Telling him, ordering him, it was my way, or the highway attitude seemed to stare blankly up from my notepad. How could he ever learn to trust me if I hardly ever let him take charge, be himself, 'wear the pants' so to speak?

Why had I not listened to my subconscious that first day? It had warned me that I was wrong. I had pushed my own warnings aside and overridden what I now realized was wrong about my actions.

Obviously, I had much work to do to repair the damage that I had created myself. I prayed that he would give me that chance. I desperately needed to find him and show him how much I needed him, that he would be the head of our family. I needed to make our relationship into more of a partnership. I must also convince him that Payne seeks revenge against me alone.

Realization dawned on me at last that in my life I must surrender everything to him. I must lay myself bare at his feet. My livelihood, my fortune, my possessions. They meant nothing to me. I must give everything up in my present life to salvage my future one. I must depend on him for the food that I eat, the clothes that I wear, my safety and in the end my very life.

Nothing less would be sufficient to demonstrate how deeply that I loved him, trusted him, and wanted and needed to share his life. This would be the price I must pay to redeem myself. Nothing less than total surrender, body, and soul. I would strip myself naked of everything in my life and lay it at his feet.

But could I do that? I had surrounded myself with things to protect myself: my apartment in an impregnable building, my expensive clothes, my staff and friends, my money, my job. Most of all my pride, my hidden secret. Yes, even that had to be given over. There could be nothing of me left hidden to show him how very much I trusted his judgment. If I truly wanted him to know that he ruled my life, even my innermost soul, I had to show him my full and complete trust in him. I would be his and only his. I would bury myself in devotion to Cliff and his needs, not mine. Then and only then could there be the union, the 'us' that I needed so very much.

I was not afraid that Cliff would misuse that trust. He had shown me already in so many ways that he could be trusted. That he was not mean or vengeful, that he truly cared for me. I was the one who had been hesitant. I held things back, not giving him what he needed and deserved from me at nearly every step along our path. From now on, there would be no 'me' in our relationship. There would be only togetherness. We would walk side by side, neither of us leading. Instead, we would have a true partnership.

That would start from today. I would see to it, or die in the effort.

CHAPTER 27

I telephoned Ruth and spoke with her at length. I explained how much that I loved Cliff and felt that somehow my actions toward him may have alienated him, made him feel less needed. How he was mistaken in thinking Payne would come after him instead of me. I desperately needed to see him and try to regain his trust. It did not take long to convince her because she could hear the pain in my voice and the tears springing from my soul.

"I can completely understand your feelings. I have done the same with Cliff's father on occasion. They are both very strong leaders and sometimes the actions or words that we say to them can be taken the wrong way. They are, after all, just men. Men think differently than women. But I'm sure there is no harm done. Cliff loves you very much. He's at our villa that we built on Lake Conroe," she spoke gently in my ear. "Cliff asked me to give you the address when you called. But you are to come alone, and be sure that you are not followed."

My heart blossomed with happiness. Cliff wanted me there. But then a warning caution sprang into my mind. Perhaps he wants to call the whole thing off, to admit it was a mistake, to have a private place to say our goodbyes. I scribbled down the address on my notepad, just below my list of sins.

'Oh, Cliff... please forgive me. Please love me again. Give me a second chance.'

My mind raced with ideas of how to get away. There was a policeman in the hallway. When I would leave there would be a squad car following me. And my car was wrecked and had been towed to a junk yard. We had arrived home in a cab last evening, I would have to rely on Charlotte, but in some way conceal the new life path that I had chosen from her. The other concern was Payne. What if he is hiding somewhere nearby and sees me leave. He will follow after me as well, and I won't be able to hide my actions.

'Damn. There must be a way.'

Suddenly I had an idea. Surely Payne does not know how to fly! And the police, they would be slow to react and since I was not a fugitive from the law, they probably wouldn't put too much effort in tracking me if my plan were to succeed. I smiled to myself and picked up my cell to call an old friend, Joseph Worthington.

He answered on the third ring, "Joe Worthington, Ajax Helicopters, how may I help you?"

"Hi, Joe, this is Tina McIntyre. How are you today?"

"Oh, Hi Tina, it's been a long time since we last spoke."

"Yes, Joe. I am in a desperate situation right now. I am sure that you have heard about the bombings at my company and also at the new tower my company is building. It seems that the person who is behind those terrible acts is a man who was sent to prison for assaulting me seventeen years ago. He has now been released and searched me out. He is trying to kill me. So far with no success, I thank God! I need your help to escape in a manner that he will be unable to follow me."

"Tina, that is shocking. I am so sorry to hear that you suffered through that trauma, and now this. I will do anything that I can to help. What is it that you need me to do?"

I explained the germ of my idea and took his suggestions -- *I was learning, you see, to let men take the lead when needed*, as to how to accomplish my goals. We spoke for about thirty minutes, ironing out the details of his plan. By the time I hung up my heart was beating rapidly, my hopes were soaring, and I felt my soul come alive in anticipation of success. Cliff was worth it —to me, he was worth everything.

My Plan:

Step 1. Leave my building normally. I would ask Charlotte to drop me off at the JP Morgan Chase tower where I maintained all of my large bank accounts. I would tell her that I wanted to rearrange some of my assets, and it might take several hours. I would tell her that when I was done, she should pick me up around noon.

Step 2. Notify the bank that I needed to meet with both the President and CEO of the bank this morning. The tower had an unused HeliPad on its roof. It had rarely been used in the past, but Joseph had a friend in security working at the tower. He could check whether it was still serviceable.

I would meet with the bankers as arranged. Create an account for Charlotte and Marianne and move one-million dollars each to those accounts for their use. Then I'd transfer all of the remainders of my money into Cliff's name, irrevocably. After that, I would proceed to the roof area. It was currently unused, but Joe had arranged for the door to be unlocked when I arrived and locked again as soon as I had passed through by the security guard at the tower who would help.

Step 3. I would prepare two letters. One for Charlotte and one for Marian, explaining a vague outline of what I was doing. I'd have one of the bankers give the letters to Charlotte when she arrived to pick me up.

Step 4. I would meet Joe and his helicopter on the roof at 11:30 a.m. He would fly me to Lake Conroe, where I would meet with one of Joseph's staff, who would drive me to the lakeside Villa. Neither Charlotte nor the police waiting below could know of this or why I never came out of the bank again.

I would simply have vanished without a trace into a future that I so desperately wanted. Once I had ascended to the helicopter pad, I would leave everything that I possessed -- My life, my job, my friends at work, my staff, my money, my clothes, and my jewels. I would retain nothing of myself.

Step 5. I would meet with Cliff and resolve all of our issues. This final step was the perhaps the riskiest of all. -Cliff--. I was uncertain of how he would receive me and the news that I would bring. I had a strong suspicion that he might assume Payne would be following him, and he might have laid a trap. My belief was that he probably did expect me to come so quickly. He must know that my love for him was too strong to leave him alone to face danger by himself for very long.

Step 6. I was placed my fate in Cliffs' hands. I loved and trusted that Cliff would know what to do and would take control of our lives and future with confidence. Separate we were weak, together we would be unstoppable.

I penned the two letters explaining to my staff a vague outline of my plans. I explained that they would receive a checkbook from my bank, each containing one million dollars for them to use as they saw fit. That I was canceling the lease on the apartment, and everything in it should either be donated to Goodwill or the Salvation Army including my clothes and jewels. I was leaving my past behind and taking only what I was wearing.

I wished them well in the future and told each one how much I loved them and thanked them for their service. I folded the notes, stuffed them into envelopes, wrote their names on the outside and stuffed them in my purse. Finally, I phoned Chase Bank and advised them that I needed a 9:00 a.m. meeting with the President and CEO. Then I went into the den.

"Good morning Charlotte. Marianne, what's for breakfast this morning?"

"For you, Ms. Tina," Marianne replied. "I have pancakes, maple syrup, bacon and a nice glass of cold milk. I was not hungry this morning; my stomach was still upset from all of the excitement last night. Charlotte has already eaten."

"That sounds like just the thing my stomach needs right now, Marianne."

"By the way, Charlotte, I have a meeting with my bankers at Chase Tower this morning at 9 a.m. Please have your car ready in about thirty minutes and meet me at the main entrance."

"Yes, ma'am."

"Also, the meeting will probably take several hours, so I need you to meet me back there, say around noon."

"No problem. Anything special you need help with?" Charlotte looked at me suspiciously.

"No, I'm sure that HPD will be sufficient bodyguards for the bank, and besides they do have their internal security staff. I have already alerted them to the problem."

I ate my breakfast and took great care to appear normal, portraying that today was going to be no different than any other day. I returned to my room, rummaged my closet for the last time and chose a simple knee length day dress. I added a simple gold bracelet that had belonged to my mother. I checked my hair, applied my makeup and grabbed my clutch, containing just a simple wallet, my ID and about ten dollars would be all that I possessed.

I looked around the room one last time, and a tear came to my eye, but I quickly wiped it away. I had decided, there was no going back. My future lay ahead of me, all of this belonged to my past. They were just things - things could be replaced; my life would be joined to Cliff, or if he rejected me, I would no longer care and end the pain of my loneliness myself.

When I passed through the den area, Marianne was there straightening up some magazines. I paused a moment, walked over to her and gave her a strong hug, kissed her cheek and wished her a pleasant day.

I probably would never see her again. I secretly wished her well and stepped into the hallway and again paused by the elevator. Looking back, I could see the strange look on her face. I raised my hand and waved cheerfully as the elevator doors closed.

I stopped by the front desk and closed out my lease, made final payment and arranged for my belongings to be donated to either the Goodwill or Salvation Army. Charlotte met me in the valet exit, and we proceeded to Chase Tower. The drive to the bank was pleasant and uneventful. I did not see anyone following me other than the one police cruiser. The sun was out, and it was a very nice day. Charlotte watched me in her rear view mirror several times.

I think that she had guessed that something unusual was happening. I fought back the tears; she had been a dear friend and protector to me.

Charlotte pulled the car up into the valet lane outside the tower and then hopped out to open my door. I gave her a big smile. Then pulled her body to mine.

"I don't think that I have ever told you how much that your help and friendship has meant to me over the past years. You have been my main support; I owe you my life. Please take care of yourself." I struggled to keep the tears away.

Charlotte, sensing something was up, "Tina, please tell me what's wrong?"

"Oh, it is nothing. I am just still upset from the car crash and killing that man last night and the fact that Payne is still out there stalking me. I'm all right. Don't worry about me; just know that I love you. I have to run now, or I am going to be late for the meeting. See you around lunch time." I prayed that she would accept that and not follow.

I walked into the Tower entrance, biting my lip hard to hold back the tears. I barely made it to the elevator. My knees were shaking, my hand trembled as I pushed the elevator call button. I could feel Charlotte's eyes burning a hole in the back of my head.

Sure enough, when the elevator arrived and I had entered and turned around she was standing inside the lobby watching me. I forced a smile and then waved goodbye as the doors closed. Then the floodgates broke. I pressed the second-floor button and sobbed. Marianne and Charlotte were more than mere employees to me. They had become dear friends over the years; I hated having to abandon them like this without them knowing the truth.

The elevator doors opened on the second floor, and I fled down the hallway and into the Ladies room and sat in one of the stalls crying my eyes out for a good fifteen minutes. I walked over to the sink and ran some cold water, took one of the cloth hand towels and soaked my eyes thoroughly wiping away the tears, leaving behind only two bloodshot orbs in their place.

I straightened my skirt and returned to the elevator and chose floor seventy-five. The president and CEO had arranged to meet with me in their corporate suite. After walking into their sumptuous offices I was greeted by the receptionist who announced that I was expected; they were waiting for me in their conference room. She rose and escorted me to the large oak doors, opened one for me, and gestured for me to enter.

Both gentlemen rose to their feet. "Good Morning, Ms. McIntyre. It is so nice to see you again. Please have a seat here at the head of the desk. Would you like a cup of coffee or a glass of ice water?" Mr. Tomlinson, the CEO, asked.

I bit my tongue and forced my feet to propel me forward into the room. "Yes, please. A glass of ice water would be nice."

Mr. Tomlinson rose and walked to a small serving area that contained the coffee maker, an ice dispenser and a pitcher of fresh water.

"How many cubes of ice, Ms. McIntyre?"

"Three would be fine. Thank you."

After he had completed filling my glass, he brought it over and set it on a coaster on the desk in front of me.

"Now, how may we help you, today, Ms. McIntyre?"

"Gentlemen, this is probably a very unusual request, and I understand that it may take you a few days to complete. I wish to set up two new checking accounts, each to contain one million dollars apiece of my fortune. The names of the owners, their Social Security numbers, and Texas Drivers' License information are on this piece of paper along with their current addresses. They are to have full and total control of all of the monies in the accounts to do with as they please. Is that understood?"

"Yes, ma'am, we can have those two accounts created and ready for you within the hour. Anything else?" The president, David Wooten, asked.

"Yes, I need for you to deliver the checkbooks for those accounts to my driver, Charlotte Parker. She will come to the bank to pick me up around noon. I will not be here, but give the checkbooks and these two letters to her. One is addressed to Charlotte and the other to my housekeeper whose name you have there. Tell Charlotte to return to my apartment before she opens the envelope and share the other letter with my housekeeper."

"Now for the harder part of my request to you. I wish to liquidate the entire remainder of my fortune and transfer the monies into the name of my fiancé, Clifford Stinson. The entire amount should be transferred to him in an irrevocable process. He is to have total control of the monies, any future instructions that you receive regarding the money will come from him and only him. Is that understood and agreed?

"Yes, ma'am. And you are correct; much of the money is scattered in various accounts and will take several days if not a week or more to accomplish. But are you sure that you don't wish to retain some control yourself?

"This is very unusual and unprecedented in my memory. You are not being coerced or blackmailed in some manner into doing this are you Ms. McIntyre?" Mr. Tomlinson asked.

"No. I am doing this out of love for my future husband. And yes. I'm more certain of this than anything else in my life. This money means nothing to me, but Cliff means everything. I want him to be the leader in our marriage, the head of our home. I am doing this to remove an insurmountable barrier between us. I want to have no personal say so in what he does with it. I have his information on this form."

"You know, Ms. McIntyre, I have been in banking for over thirty-five years, and I have never known of anything like this before. You must have a deep love and trust of Mr. Stinson to do this for him." Mr. Worthington observed.

"I do love him; I love Cliff beyond trust. I do this not just for him; it is for the both of us. It will bond us together as nothing else would. He is everything to me; I would do more if I could. I trust him with my life; money means nothing to me without him. If, however, he should refuse to accept this gift, I wish the money to be given to charity. Please indicate that in the transfer. Under no circumstances is the money to be returned to my name."

Mr. Tomlinson replied, "Very well then, we can create an immediate checking/savings account and provide you with a checkbook for Mr. Stinson's initial use. He will need to come to the bank and sign some papers, of course, but more than likely he will have access to at least five million dollars by the end of banking today and more each day as your accounts close and his created."

Mr. Worthington added, "By the way, we both want to wish you every happiness in future. Am I to assume that you will be getting married sometime very soon?"

"Yes."

I crossed my fingers underneath the desk and uttered a silent prayer that it would be so.

"Then, let me call in my assistant to take some notes and prepare the papers for your signature. This won't take more than an hour or so. If you wish, you can wait here while the papers are finalized and we can have them all notarized."

"Thank you. That will be acceptable."

My body finally relaxed, and the tension in my stomach lessened. I sank back in my seat as a wave of relief washed over me. I could sense deep inside of me that this was the right thing to do. Cliff would understand me, accept my actions, and assume responsibility for our lives. He would keep me safe in his arms forever.

Mr. Tomlinson pressed a button hidden underneath his side of the desk and after several minutes, an efficient looking lady entered dressed in a very sharp looking business suit entered the room. Mr. Tomlinson spoke with her briefly, advised her what paperwork was needed, and she sat down at a computer, which was set into a wall niche, and entered several commands. After a time, she left the room but returned shortly with a stack of documents for my signature.

I provided her with a list of the outstanding checks which had not cleared yet, including the one closing out my lease. I provided her a copy of my driver license as she was also a notary. As I completed the signing of each document, she used her notary stamp to complete the process. The president and the CEO served as my two witnesses.

I glanced at the clock on the wall from time to time and genially chatted with both the president and CEO. I did not want them to think that under any circumstance I was under pressure or being blackmailed. I was happy to be doing this, Cliff was my life. I wanted him to have total control of myself, my money, and my future.

At exactly 11:15 the final papers were signed, notarized and the checkbooks for Charlotte, Marian, and Cliff had been delivered. I selected the one for Cliff, stuffed it into my clutch. Then placed the other two, along with the letters to my former staff in a large manila envelope. These would be delivered to Charlotte by the CEO when she arrived. I rose from my chair, took a long drink of the cold water. I extended my hand and thanked both men for their help over the years.

They shook my hand and wished me well. I turned and left the conference room and entered the hallway. There was a man waiting there dressed in workman's coveralls. He stood waiting by the door to the roof. As I appeared, he turned, unlocked the door and held it open for me.

I passed through the entry, thanked him, and ascended the stairway, nervously climbing upward into what I prayed would be my happy future. I heard the door close and lock behind me. There was no turning back.

I opened the door to the heliPad area. The wind was whipping wildly. I had to grab my skirt as the wind pulled it nearly to my waist. I found Joseph waiting expectantly on the other side of the door. The helicopter was standing not far away; its rotor blades were turning slowly.

"Hello, Tina," he greeted.

"Joe," I smiled back weakly.

I grabbed Joe's hand, and he helped me into the passenger seat. After he had climbed into the pilot's seat, he pointed to a pair of earphones for me to wear. These not only let me hear his conversations with flight traffic control but were also noise reduction devices. Joe then helped me with my seatbelt buckles and then strapped in himself.

The sound of the powerful blades spinning above me increased dramatically, but the headsets canceled out most of that noise. Joe flipped a couple of switches and grabbed the joystick. The helicopter lifted gently away and began the long journey north to Lake Conroe.

The tall skyscrapers of downtown Houston slipped past below my feet. The view below my feet was so exciting. It had been several years since I had been up in one of these majestic machines, but the thrill never left my memory. Joe pointed to a traffic jam on Houston's downtown freeway spider web as we passed above. There were cars packed together like sardines in a can. I loved this city, a dynamic powerhouse of six million people.

I had built a life here, found friends, and a great job, enjoyed personal success and finally found love. As I watched the city pass beneath my feet, I wondered if somewhere below Payne was lurking. Biding his time until he would find me and strike me in some horrible way that would destroy me and those whom I loved. I vowed never to let that happen, even at the cost of my life.

Soon Joe turned the helicopter and quickly we were on a path which took us northward, up along the I-45 corridor. I waited rather impatiently for the miles to slip by below. My heart was anxiously wanting them to rush me to my fate, sooner rather than later. The gently bump, bump, bump of the machine as it pressed forward in the air became a soothing balm to my heart. I knew that my plan would work because I knew how much that Cliff loved me. I trusted Cliff with everything. All that I was or would ever become was contained within his heart. I silently prayed that I was bringing the key that would open it for me.

Joe spoke happily of some of our shared memories, especially of his wife, who I had been friends with for years. She had been a fellow employee at a company I had worked for, and she had experienced a similar problem in her early life. Having been kidnapped and raped by a serial rapist. She had barely escaped with her life from his cabin. We shared a mutual misery from that kind of event and often shared tears of regret, until one day she had met Joe, and her life had changed for the better. Joe and I did not discuss that subject, it was too private between us.

CHAPTER 28

The helicopter arrived at the airfield at Lake Conroe after about forty-five minutes. After the helicopter had settled in place and the blades slowed, Joe turned to me.

"Tina, I'm praying for success for you and your fiancé. I know that you are going to be happy. If you ever need me in the future, please don't hesitate to call. I'll always be there for you." He leaned over, gave me a kiss on my cheek and waved goodbye as I stepped out into my unknown future.

Joes' assistant was waiting for me with a car to take me to my destination. I had specifically requested that it not be a stretch limo or other fancy car. I did not want to appear that I was some arriving movie starlet. I was arriving naked and exposed, no longer the rich playgirl, and mistress of all I surveyed. I was penniless, possessing little more in this world than the clothes on my back. No one to help or protect me, feed me, lay out my clothes in the morning. I was stripped bare of my life, completely exposed to the world's follies. Hopeful in my heart of hearts, yet trembling with fear of rejection and despair, driven to my destiny by desperation.

My fingers twitched nervously as we approached the address of the villa. The car pulled into the driveway; I spoke a little prayer to myself. I grabbed the door handle and stepped out of the passenger door. I thanked the driver, handed him my last ten-dollar bill as a tip and told him that it was unnecessary for him to wait.

At first, he refused to accept payment. Tears burst forth as I begged him to take pity on me and accept the money. Finally, he reached over; I placed the money in his hand. I stood watching as he drove away and then turned and approached the door. Through it led the path to my future, joy and fulfillment or desperation and oblivion. I wanted no life without Cliff.

My heart was in my throat as I rang the doorbell. I could hear the gentle chimes ringing inside and waited. At first, there was no answer, and so I rang again. Still no answer, all was quiet within the home. After a few more minutes, I decided to walk around to the back on the chance that Cliff was outside.

On rounding the corner of the house, I saw him. Cliff's face was turned away from me, on the deck of the boat tied to the small dock. He looked so peaceful and relaxed. Unaware of the explosive bundle of nerves so close behind him. He knelt quietly, and appeared to be scratching something on the deck of the boat.

I called out "Hello." My heartbeat pounded in my ears as I desperately fought to hold back my tears.

Immediately he turned, saw me and jumped to the dock and ran up the walkway towards me.

"Christina! How did you find me? Did you find my note? Why are you here?"

"Cliff, slow down a bit. I can only answer one question at a time. Let me answer your last question first. I am here because I love you, more than life itself. And yes, I did find your note. And your note gave me the information that I needed to find you. Your mother provided me the address.

"Now, it is my turn to ask you questions. But, before I ask those questions, do you have the keys to the boat? Perhaps we could take a tour of the lake, just the two of us? It will be quiet, and we can talk in peace, uninterrupted by the outside world."

"I would love that. And, yes, I do have the keys, the boat is fully fueled. This house is owned by my entire family. We share it for quiet times when we feel a need to get away from the world. I have been here scores of times, very often when I was searching to find a meaning and purpose to my life. I know the lake pretty well and would love to give you a tour. Let's climb on board and head out, shall we?"

Cliff then took my hand in his and led me as we walked down the ramp and assisted me as I stepped onto the deck and took a seat on the rear deck cushion while Cliff started up the motor. He brought me a life preserver, helped me tie the straps and then released the rope ties to the docking cleat. Soon we were slipping through the channel outlet and into the lake. Cliff steered out to the middle of the lake and then I asked him to stop the engine and drop anchor.

After he had done so, the boat bobbed gently back and forth in the gentle waves. I patted the boat cushion next to me in the hope that he would join me. I did not have to repeat my gesture as he was immediately by my side. He reached out and took both of my hands. I curled my fingers inside his palms, and smiled up at him, my heart relaxing with the familiar touch of his hands over mine.

"Cliff, I have some things to confess and tell you and this may be the last time that I have an opportunity to do this. I beg you to wait until I finish before you speak."

"All right, Christina, as you wish. But before you begin…" suddenly he grabbed me, pulled me into a passionate kiss, holding me tightly within his arms. I drew strength from his embrace for what was to follow.

We kissed long and deep, our tongues exploring each other, loving and taking comfort in each other. His arms reached around my body and pulled me to him. I pressed myself tightly against him feeling the strength of his arms and the taught muscles of his chest and stomach. I only wished that we could remain locked together like this for eternity. Tears ran down my cheeks. He gently pulled away from me and reached up and tenderly wiped my tears away with one finger.

"Don't cry, precious. Please don't cry," he begged.

I braced myself for what I was about to tell him. My future was going to be in his hands.

"Cliff, please. I need to tell you a story. First, here on this notepad, I have written down a list of the ways that I have wronged you on this paper. Part of the story you already know. Part is buried so deep inside me that I have kept it hidden for these past seventeen years. I could not tell you this in the past; it was too shameful to me. Something that I thought that I would die before revealing it to any person alive. I owe it to you to reveal a dark secret of my past. I feel that if I don't share it with someone, I will never be free. I have hidden it for far too long. I must let it out, purge my soul of this or die in the attempt."

"That night, the night when the boys raped me, I didn't confess everything to you."

"Christina, it is not necessary…"

I interrupted him, "Yes, Cliff, I need to remove all final barriers between us. I am ashamed of my actions toward you even now. The thought of telling you, even at this moment is almost more than I can bear. I have done you wrong since the first day we met. Because of what happened, I was terrified of men; I wanted to control everything around me. I feared that any place that I might go that would put me in a position where I might be alone with someone and something -- like what I am going to tell you might happen to me again.

"Every time that we have been together I have tried to control the situation. Like not allowing you to pay for your new clothes that the first night. Not allowing you to choose the restaurant, or the meal, forcing you to wear that silly red suit to the family get together; taking control of the food for the party. I was afraid, terrified and needed the control that being in charge of situations gave to me.

"I regret that I treated you more like a stranger than my fiancé. I can never forgive myself for that. I promise that if you can find it in your heart to forgive me and let me start over, I will let you be the man in our marriage."

"But, Ch…"

"No Cliff, I have not finished yet. I am trying to gather the courage to tell you my deepest darkest secret and it is very hard." I sobbed gently, forcing myself to continue."

"Christina, Please No. You don't need to continue," Cliff insisted.

"Yes, Cliff, I must get it all told. I must reveal my hidden secret. You must understand fully how evil and depraved the man is who is trying to kill me."

"Very well, I will hear you out."

"When the boys raped me I became pregnant. I don't know for sure which boy was the father, but my guess was James Payne because he was the one who had raped me three times that night. To hide my pregnancy, I changed high schools twice. Once during the pregnancy, and then after the birth. I gave the child up for adoption. I have never sought the child out because of fear that if the men escaped from prison or found me later after they were released they would demand custody and the child.

"That child would then know she was the result of rape. It is bad enough for me to have that knowledge, I truly did not want the child to be ashamed of their birth. I have no idea what happened to the child or even if she is alive today. I have always regretted abandoning that child, my child, to an unknown fate with unknown people. Things may have happened to her which I might have prevented."

I broke down in sobs, unable to continue. After a few moments, I searched Cliff's eyes for my future.

"Christina, precious. Please shut that memory away, it has no further place in our lives. You were too young. Had you kept the child you might have ended up poor and unable to protect her. The child, most likely, found a loving home and family. You might have struggled and been unable to give her the things in life she has found with her new parents. You had no way of knowing what the future held. The money awarded you by the courts came much later.

"Often in life, we are forced to make decisions because we have no other options at the time. It is something that happened a long time ago. One of the boys is now dead; another is back in jail. Payne will get what is coming to him when the police kill or capture him again. If you wish, at some point we can search out the child, possibly offer assistance if it is needed."

I sobbed violently into Cliff's chest for a long time until I had no more tears in my body. Had he said 'our' lives?" Had he just offered to find the child with me? Hope sprang in my heart. I sought and found forgiveness in his eyes.

"But I have another thing to share with you, and I beg of you, please let me say it all before you speak."

I paused and looked up into his eyes; they were filled with pain and tears. He nodded his head and motioned for me to continue.

"Cliff, today you see before you a woman who has arrived on your doorstep possessing little more than her name. I have taken actions today to divest myself of my past. I left instructions with the hotel owners that I was moving out of my apartment and canceling my lease. I left with only what you see before you, the clothes on my back and ten dollars in my purse which I gave to the driver who brought me here.

"All of my clothes, jewelry, furniture, and belongings are going to be given to Good Will or Salvation Army. This morning I went to my bank and spoke with the CEO and president and signed away all of my fortunes. I gave one million dollars each to Marianne and Charlotte and wrote a letter to each telling them of this, sending along a checkbook to each, with a note thanking them for their years of service.

"Christina ---"

"As for the remainder of my fortune, I have signed all of it over into your name. It is in an irrevocable trust which only you will have access. In my purse is a checkbook in your name which the bank assured me will have at least five million dollars immediately available to you, the remainder of the monies are being transferred to you as quickly as they can over the next several days.

"You will need to go to the bank and complete some minor paperwork, but for all intents and purposes, the transactions are a done deal. No further action on my part is needed or even allowed. If you refuse the money I have set the transfer so there will be no possibility of returning it to me. It is to be donated to charity. I will be penniless, and should you reject me; I will be alone.

"In short, I am here, surrendering my entire self and future to you. I don't even own a change of underwear or dress. I depend on you in the future for all that I require. If you will take me back and no longer wish me to work, then my life is yours to command. If you don't wish to take me back, then I no longer wish to live. My life, my future belongs only to you. You mean everything to me. I am nothing without you. You have given me the gift of your love and through that, I have found the strength to surrender myself to you. For many years, I have been trapped in a prison of others' creation. You have given me the key to open that door, but only within your own heart.

"One final thing. I need to contact the police to find the status of Payne. I was very careful when I left the bank. I have a friend who owns a helicopter service. He flew me away from the bank from a little-used heliPad atop the Chase Tower. I am positive that anyone waiting for me would not have thought anything about a helicopter lifting off of a bank tower in downtown Houston. So many buildings down there have these and this would have been just like any other and might just have been one of the bank officers or someone flying away on business. The pad is seventy-six stories above the street so no one could have seen me from street level.

"For all anyone knows, other than Marianne and Charlotte, I have vanished off the face of the earth. I am hoping beyond hope that we can take this time and use it to make my final escape from this criminal who is trying to kill me, but that is your choice and not mine. I will agree with whatever plan you have or can think of if you still want me in your life. I pray that you do, but will understand if you don't. I will not leave this place alive if you don't want me in your life, I want no other life without you.

"There, I have said it all. Thank you for your patience and the love that you gave me in the past. I will not hold you to anything that you may have felt that you committed yourself to me, should you wish to nullify that now. I set you free of any obligations and throw myself on your kind mercy to determine my future."

When I had finished I sat quietly, my heart hopeful, my mind resigned, patiently and desperately anxious. Waiting to hear my fate, a life of happiness, or oblivion.

CHAPTER 29

Cliff looked at me, astonished by all that I had revealed. He stood up, paced to the other side of the small boat, then turned and stood in front of me. He remained frozen in place for several seconds, then he kneeled to the deck before me and took my head in between his hands, lifting my eyes to his which I could see were filled with tears.

"Christina, I hardly know what to say. The things you have spoken of today are both depraved on the part of the boys who did that to you. Overwhelming and shocking to me, to whom you have given such a trust. Christina. You alone know that I want you, need you, treasure you, and want to take care of you and keep you safe. I love you more than anything in the world. I am bound to you, not by your money, but by our mutual love.

"When I left you that note last night I was depressed that I had so little to give to you. I was afraid that you would find me wanting in some way. It was not only that but these criminals who are pursuing you. And now Payne seems to be after me as well. I was afraid that perhaps my presence near to you was causing you to be more easily located by Payne and less able to be protected by police.

The bombs at our buildings, endangering so many other lives. I was praying that if I stayed at some other location, Payne might come after me. I could draw him away from you, and the police could more easily capture him. I would give my life for you, do anything to keep you safe. But I think that I begin to see now, Payne was never after me; it was always you. By blowing up the tower, he was hoping to strike at you through our love for each other. Had I been injured or killed he would have achieved part of his goal of torturing you.

Payne cannot have known that I had only just proposed, and you had not accepted. That is unless one of his friends was in the steakhouse restaurant that Friday night and reported our actions. We were not expecting anything like that, and it is likely that that is the case. The restaurant was packed, diners coming in and out, our attentions focused on each other. That is probably how they learned of our relationship and began their plans to strike at both of us at the same time.

Now, as to your money --I can hardly believe that you would do so much for me. No, those are not the right words. You have done this for us. You truly are the most wonderful woman in the world. I know that I could never deserve all that you have done. I was not insulted and did not feel degraded by your choosing of the restaurant or meal; I loved the clothes that you purchased.

"Maybe not that bright red coat so much, I felt like I was a bright neon sign while wearing it, but all the rest, yes. I loved them; I love you. I would give my life in place of yours at this moment if it were required. I never want you to leave my side. Please forgive me my foolish thoughts and actions. I did not want your fortune, but if by giving it to me you feel that will cement our lives together, then so be it. You have given me your trust in such a way that I am beyond any ability to express my feelings. I think that I understand why you have done this, and I can only pray every day that I can somehow live up to your example of selflessness."

"There is nothing to forgive, Cliff. It was all my doing."

"Christina, we are going to have to get one thing straight if we are to go on from here."

"Yes?"

"That one thing is that we love each other and each share in any blame for misunderstandings we have had in the past, and might have in the future. Do you understand this? We are both to blame. There will be no more secrets between us, and the decisions that are made in the future will be mutual. You will be a part of me and share in all that we do or have just as if you were one of my arms or legs.

"I will discuss everything with you completely. We will arrive at mutual decisions. There will be no me and no you. There will only be us, and decisions that we shall make will be made together. I want us to share everything. We are partners in life and love. Are we agreed?"

"Yes, Cliff. Now, can I kiss you again?"

Cliff's answer was immediate and without words. He took me in his arms, and we spent a long time holding and kissing and loving each other while the boat quietly bobbed in a circle held by its anchor chain.

Cliff then knelt down on the deck at my feet and began,

"I have little of my sins to confess to you. I dated in high school and kissed several girls. In college, I had a brief fling with a young lady whom I still consider a friend today. But through all of this, I remained and still was a virgin until our first night together. I had never had sex of any kind with any of the girls that I dated. Not because I did not want to, it was because I wanted to save myself for my future wife. Not out of some religious fanaticism. I just did not want to bring a lot of baggage to the wedding bed. To have to confess to past trysts that might have caused my wife pain to know of them.

"I do confess, I have looked at photos of girls in magazines and become sexually aroused and, I have even read the occasional dirty book. I was a bit of a rowdy child and was involved in several fights, but no one was injured, and later I became friends with the boys I had fought.

"As I have mentioned before, I have dated several women since I graduated from college, but for some reason, none of them had any qualities in which I was truly interested or attracted. I truly don't know exactly what it was that I recognized in you, but it was immediate and sudden and shook me to my core.

"I knew instantly that you were the woman of my dreams. I did not need to hear you speak, or delve into your past or go on dates with you. I saw love in your smile that day, and it awakened a need in my heart that I could not deny. I am humbled that you have taken actions that will bind us together, and I pledge to you my fidelity and love.

"Then that night in your apartment, if felt so right, I let myself go. I took pleasure in claiming you, in taking your body and joining it to mine. It felt as if we had become one. I was not afraid to touch you, to enjoy the pleasures that your body gave to me. My mind soared to new heights as we made love together. I felt -- I felt, I...

"Oh Christina! I felt as if my entire soul was swallowed up by you and I wanted to possess you, to make you mine. I wanted to have you belong to me and only me. It was like a drug. The more that we made love, the more that I wanted you.

"And then when you told me just how wealthy you were, I became concerned. As I said in my note, I thought when you told me that you were wealthy, I thought regarding hundreds of thousands of dollars, or even a million. But not in tens of millions. All that I could think of was how desolate that I would feel when you woke up one morning beside me, realized that I had given you so little if we were to be married. I could see other rich men pursuing you and winning your heart, stealing you away from me. And I thought back on how hard it had been, all those years denying myself, saving myself for marriage. Then what we had done that night, it became a travesty, just as if I were just another one of those three boys who had assaulted you.

"Cliff, ..."

"No, Christina, I need to get it out, just as you did for me. I was wrong to abandon you last night. I see that clearly now. I was being foolish and thinking only of myself. I was confused and for a time believed that I could distract Payne away from you.

"And then my foolish pride in thinking that I had made a mistake in giving myself..., No that's not right..., Letting ourselves be carried away in the moment. When two people, truly meant for each other, truly love each other, there is no right or wrong.

"I believe that when God created a woman he bestowed the gift of beauty, attractiveness, and the desire to share her body with her life's partner. I don't mean that only physically beautiful women have that gift. When a man loves a woman that woman is a perfect TEN in his eyes. No matter her outward appearance. It is the inner beauty to which I refer. When he created a man he bestowed the gift of desire for the woman, to look beyond her outward appearance and see her inner beauty, to possess her, to protect her from harm, to love her and cherish her. He gave to both of them the gift of love. The love for each other.

"When a couple that God has joined in love expresses themselves sexually there is no right or wrong; there is only love, nothing else. Had God intended otherwise he would not have given us sexual organs that give and take pleasure from the joining of the two. He might have given us something else, some uninteresting and bland means of procreating. Like, I don't know, maybe we would interlock our toes together, or simply join hands and that would suffice. Instead, he has provided the most sensual and overpowering joining of two people's bodies together in a manner that is truly wonderful.

"I had temporarily let your wealth hide that truth from my mind. I began to think that somehow all that I had was the lust for your body, and perhaps a temporary lust of me by you, which I feared could be torn asunder by someone else. How stupid and foolish I was. You have truly proven to me how wrong that I was, you stripped away the blindness from my eyes.

"What we have found, we have found together, not separately. We have mutually surrendered to each other and pledged our fidelity as surely as we have joined our bodies. No one and nothing will ever separate us again. I swear that to you today with my life."

Cliff paused and looked up at me with blazing eyes. All that I could see in them was love.

"Thank you, Cliff. Thank you for sharing that with me, Cliff. You are my love and my life. Together we will become as one. I adore you. I have given my entire life to you of my free will. I belong only to you, and you belong only to me."

"And I adore you as well." Cliff's expression suddenly changed from the one of deep contemplation of a moment before to one of playfulness. He looked at me, a small smile twisting his lips up at the corners.

"I just realized sweetheart; I need to take you someplace."

"Where's that, sweetheart?"

"Shopping, silly! You said that you didn't even have a change of underwear. I need to get you back to shore before the stores close. I believe that I have a checkbook in your purse which might contain just enough to get you an extra pair or two of undies. I am not sure what women's undies cost nowadays since I have never had the experience of purchasing any myself. -- I may have to take out a loan or something," he teased.

"You say the sweetest things," I giggled wildly, as Cliff started up the engine and steered back to shore. He had more trouble steering on the way in because I kept occupying his mouth with loving kisses, and we very often ended up with the boat circling round and round before we finally reached the shore. My future was assured. I would never be alone again. Cliff had cleared away the last cloud from my past as if it had never been. We were one, body and one soul.

"Oh, yes, Cliff?" I said, suddenly remembering something. "When I came around the back of the house earlier I saw you kneeling down and you seemed to be preoccupied with something. Please tell me what it was that you were doing at that moment."

"Sweetheart, look down by your foot."

I did as he suggested and there by my left shoe there was something scratched into the skin of the boat. I leaned closer to see; it became clear that something was written there. I leaned even closer and discovered that it was a heart with an arrow in it. Scratched inside the heart were our names and one more word.

Cliff

Christina

Forever.

"Yes, Cliff. Forever." I looked into his eyes and knew that I would forever be in his heart as he was already in mine.

"Cliff?"

"Yes, my love?"

"Can you go over the details about the interlocking toes part again? That sounded so sexy! Should we give that a try?"

Cliff reached over the side of the boat and splashed me with a handful of water!

I squealed and splashed him back.

CHAPTER 30

When our boat had pulled alongside the pier at the Stinson lake house, Cliff stepped ashore and quickly wrapped the boat tie to the metal cleat to secure it in place.

He then assisted me as I stepped off of the boat into his welcoming arms.

"Oh, Cliff, I live to be held in your arms. That first day, when I fell into your arms from Larry's truck sticks in my memory to this day. Our bodies, crushed together, just as they are now. I wanted to stay there all day instead of going in to eat. My appetite evaporated, and my senses were on fire. I wanted you desperately at that moment. I must have known, even then, that I belonged to you."

"The feeling was mutual," Cliff replied. "Your skin was so soft, and your eyes were hypnotic. I was entwined in your spell from the first moment. I was desperate to ask you a million questions but was afraid of the answers. Your gaze lit a fire in my heart. I wanted to kiss you, to taste your sweet lips, to hold you and keep you safe. The three days between that first meeting and our first date were agony to me. I spent that entire first night without sleep, building that tower vase for you.

"I did not want you to slip out of my hands just when I had discovered you. I could not sleep, and I rushed to find a special delivery person who would take my poor offering to you as soon as your building opened because I knew that you would be there. My heart despaired in agony waiting for the longed-for phone call from you telling me that you had received the flowers and vase. Each minute was torture and seemed to last an hour. I desperately needed to hear your sweet voice again. To know whether or not I had any chance to win your heart and hand."

"You have my heart," I said looking into his eyes. "You have my body, and you have my soul. Please treat then tenderly. They can be easily broken should you ever leave me. I cannot and will not ever live without you. You mean everything to me. I am lost to you completely. I love you with all my heart, Cliff. Here is my hand which now belongs to you, placed over your heart, which I know now is mine."

We stood, entwined in each other's arms for long moments relishing the joys and depth of our feelings for each other. Cliff finally broke the spell saying,

"Hey, Christina, guess what? I don't think that you have ever seen my ride, have you? I am so sorry that I wrecked your beautiful car, but I have my truck right over here in the garage. It is not as impressive as Larry's, perhaps, but it gets me from point A to point B quite nicely."

He produced a clicker from his pocket and shortly the garage door opened to reveal a beautiful Ford 350 pickup.

'Wow! A typical guy's ride. What is it with guys and pick-up trucks?' I thought. *'At least this one did not have elevated suspension, and the side step mounts were perfect for my high heels to master.'*

Cliff walked me to the passenger side, opened the door for me, picked me up in his arms and lifted me into a deliciously comfortable bucket seat.

After running around to his side, he easily climbed in and pulled out his truck keys and soon the engine roared to life.

"Sweetheart, this baby has more horsepower and torque than any other truck on the road. It has a 6.2 liter V8 engine that will leave the competition in the dust."

"Oh, Cliff, I love it when you talk dirty to me," I giggled.

Cliff roared in laughter.

"Sweetheart, we had better get out of here and into the shops before I do some other things to you and then you will not have any fresh undies to put on in the morning."

With that, he pressed on the accelerator and backed out to the roadway; we were off on our first of many shopping adventures.

I couldn't say for sure, but he did seem a bit embarrassed on this first shopping excursion. We wandered around the Ladies panty and bra aisles. When the customer assistant clerk asked him how she could help, I would swear that he turned as red as a sugar beet. He simply pointed to me and slinked away six aisles down to the automobile motor oil. He seemed quite intrigued looking at the cans, trying to decide whether he wanted a synthetic or a synthetic blend. Occasionally he looked in my direction and snickered.

I mouthed "I love you" silently to him. Then I decided to tease him a bit. I chose several particularly sexy looking bra and panty sets and took them over for his approval.

"Honey," I mewed in my sexiest voice. "Which one of these would you like to buy for me?"

I fluttered my eyelashes at him while I held them up for him to approve the pictures on the boxes.

"uhhhhh, ahhhhh, well, …Tell you what, why don't I give you my credit card and I will wait in the truck. Also, please pick out a couple of nice dresses while you are at it. Surprise me!"

He said over his shoulder as he skittered away.

"Do I have a credit limit, Cliff?" I shouted after him.

"As much as you like, Christina. There are no limits between us."

The sales clerk and I giggled as we watched him slip quietly out the side door.

"Oh! My man is going to get another reward," I giggled to the clerk.

I made a decision that from then on that whatever I wore underneath my outer clothes was going to be super sexy. I wanted Cliff to be happy with me and what better way than to show off my body to him in the sexiest underwear possible.

No more 'Pain Jane' white undies and bras. I was going to reward his senses with the most shocking and sensual lingerie possible. I wandered down the aisle with my shopping cart and dropped in a stack of boxes that would have blown my mind three months ago.

I felt like a wanton woman, imagining myself wearing them. Oh, Cliff, you are going to get rewarded tonight. I could hardly wait. Next, I needed a few dresses to wear, I wanted them to be enticing so that it would give him the desire to take them off of me in private, but modest enough to wear in public.

I was Cliff's, and I wanted him to be happy to show me off to his friends. I chose three from the ready-to-wear section and added them to my stack of 'Cliff's Rewards' as I now labeled my purchases. Two of them had so little material used I could not believe the price they were charging.

After reviewing my stack of flauntingly sexy purchases my cheeks were flushed and my heart pounded in my chest. I would have to be very brave to hand these things to the checkout clerk. I braced myself for the crisis that I knew that I would have at the register and proceeded to the checkout lane.

Gah! Wouldn't you know? The only register free at the moment was manned by a rather good-looking teenaged boy! As each item from my cart slid by his scanner, his eyes became larger and larger. Finally, he looked up at me and gave me the wickedest grin.

How embarrassing,

'Oh well, it is all for Cliff. I will do anything for him.'

I could now picture myself enduring this kind of torment many times in future. I resolved to make all such purchases in a Ladies lingerie store in the future where the clerks would all be female.

I presented Cliff's credit card and signed my name to the ticket. I was surprised when the sale was approved. The clerk bagged all of my 'unmentionables' and then said "Enjoy" with a wink. I turned red and fled from the store with my bags in tow.

After getting to the truck, I found that Cliff had phoned the credit card company and added me as an authorized user. This was so nice. I think that I could get used to using someone else's credit card. I was so used to spending my own money; it felt strangely different to spend someone else's.

I sank into the truck seat.

"Now, Cliff, I thought that we agreed that we would discuss and agree on any financial activities mutually. You did not give me much help in selecting these things." I teased.

"Christina, I think that I may have to revise that mutually agreed on part for some items. That was pure torture. I have never been so embarrassed in my life, shopping in the Ladies' underwear aisle! I was praying that I did not run into someone I knew in there. I am not sure my mom would have approved," he laughed.

"You know, I think that tomorrow we should run up to Dallas and find a nice clothing store for you. I would love to help you choose a new wardrobe. Especially someplace I don't have to worry about one of my friends seeing me pick out Ladies panties and bras. You have a wonderful figure, and I would love to help choose the clothes that would show you off to your best advantage. You could pose in the clothes, and I could oogle the model. What do you say?"

"I say, sounds like fun."

Cliff laughed, "I just don't want any of my friends from work or church seeing me handling underwear for you. I would be embarrassed beyond belief. Now, were you able to find anything to wear in there that looked nice?"

"Cliff, I think that you are going to be pleasantly surprised. I will model some of these for you tonight if you would like."

"Okay, but let me get you home. We have things to talk about that don't involve women's underwear or dresses. I want to nail down this marriage thing. I don't like having you living in sin like this. My wife is going to be the most respected, and most beautiful lady in town.

"That is if I have any say in it, and from what I have been told recently, I do. I want you to have the most beautiful clothes and jewels that money can buy. I seem to have recently come into a healthy supply of that stuff, and I want to make the best use of it that I can."

Needless to say, I was only able to model the first dress and lingerie set. And we never did get around to that discussion Cliff had mentioned. I was not the least disappointed, though. The remainder of the night was spent going over some of the lessons that Cliff had given me that first night in my apartment. He also introduced me to several new variations that I thought quite enjoyable.

The one that I liked the most, he called the pretzel position. It was performed..., I won't go into great detail here, but needless to say, he enjoyed it as much as I. I especially liked the one where he fed me strawberries and cream and put lots of whipped cream all over my body before licking me clean.

"Oh, Cliff! Ahhhhhh! Don't stop, I begged."

"Never," he whispered.

"Oh, Cliff, that is shocking!" I pretended that I was scandalized.

Cliff paused what he was doing to me.

"Ummm. Please don't---mmm stop." I begged.

He resumed.

Ummmmmmmm!"

"Cliff, I have an idea. Let's try….."

Sorry,-- that part had to be censored! (author)

CHAPTER 31

The days flew by rapidly as we made our plans for the wedding. Since Payne was still at large, and he knew where Cliff's parents lived, we realized that would not be the safest of places to hold the event. Anything was possible at that location, from driving into the house with a car bomb to swimming ashore from the lake and taking some violent action against the family. I could envision so many scenarios that it quickly became obvious the Stinson home was out of the question. I spoke with our wedding planner often and kept her up to date on our plans.

Furthermore, since a wedding announcement might be seen by Payne, we elected to hold the wedding at a distant location. The problem was settling on one that not only Cliff and I, as well as the entire family would enjoy. Cliff and I had decided to lease a corporate jet for the occasion and fly the entire family to whatever location we decided. We withheld the exact location from the newspaper announcement.

The wedding planner offered numerous suggestions; we went through numerous catalogs containing exotic places, hidden away places, locations with nearby entertainment for both adults and children. After days of daydreaming of different locales Cliff and I finally settled on Alberta, Canada as the perfect getaway.

The venue would be a spectacular remote mountain location and would take place in the early evening hours. It possessed exciting activities for everyone, young and old. Watching dog sledding and snowboarding for the kids, and skiing, mountain biking, hiking, and fishing for the adults. To top it off the Northern Lights would steal the show and create a spectacular display of colors to dazzle the eyes and senses of all ages.

Cliff agreed that we each would choose our wedding attire without the others' involvement. That way my gown and his tuxedo would remain a mystery until the actual event. Cliff arranged for a specially constructed outdoor wedding chapel be constructed on the edge of a beautiful mountain lake.

Ruth and I went over hundreds of catalogs for dresses, rejecting many, but saving three times that in the possible list. Finally, after days of agonizing deliberations, I found the one dress that would show off my figure to best effect, to dazzle Cliff's eyes when he would first see it as I came down the aisle.

The original design gown was the traditional color of white Oleg Cassini, inspired by the gown worn by Grace Kelley. It featured symmetrical scroll lace appliqués, an illusion neckline, a chapel train and those oh-so-desirable pockets. I wanted to look especially beautiful for my man. To reward his eyes with a stunning presentation at the altar and this was the one. I knew that he would love it the moment my eyes found it in the catalog.

The cost of the dress was very reasonable at nine thousand dollars. The corset, and undergarments, if you could call the tiny things that barely covered the intimate parts of me, ran another three thousand.

'What the heck, you only get married once,' I thought. 'This was all for Cliff. If it meant making Cliff happy, I would have been equally happy with an old potato sack. Just so long as the person opposite me at the altar was named Clifford William Stinson and he was happy with his selection of a bride.'

CHAPTER 32

I woke up early, my mind in a whirl. Today I was to be married to the man of my dreams. I wanted this day to be special. I wanted to create a memory for Cliff that he would treasure. I had scheduled a full spa treatment for the morning, hair, bathing in scented oils, a wax treatment for down there, legs and underarms as well. I wanted my skin to look and smell delicious and tempting for my husband. Oh, that sounded so wonderful, my husband. I repeated it over and over.

Ruth, Mary, Cynthia, Carol, Kristen, and Gail were to be my bridesmaids. We had invited and flown Larry, along with his wife and children, up to be the man who would give me away, as I had no close living relatives of my own.

We ladies all laughed and giggled as the spa staff painted our faces with oil and hot wax.

I had opted for the Brazilian wax for my unmentionable,' *Oh well here goes nothing – my genitalia. There, I said it, get over it!'*

I am talking one of the thorough Brazilian jobs, during which a beautician, or I came to know her as my professional torturer. Bella pushed my ankles up past my ears, paused before she began. I am sure she must have trained with the CIA guys who did waterboarding. She spent the afternoon punishing every pore below my naval.

"Breathe," she cried just before — with a loud '**UMPH**' — she pulled a six-inch strip of wax off of body parts that had not seen daylight since my last diaper change in 1984.

"**OWWWWWW!**" That hurt. I tried to console myself that it was all for Cliff. And he did deserve it. He had been so wonderful to me over the last weeks. I would suffer anything to make him happy. I had requested what was commonly known as a 'peach smoothie.' What came next almost made me change my mind.

"Do you normally use an exfoliate?" Bella asked my vulva as she performed a mild cleansing under the bright aesthetician's light.

I wondered, '*Vulva?*' *how do I respond to her, or perhaps she expected my vulva to start talking on their own?*' I blushed at the thought.

"Um, there?" I asked, looking toward a place on my body that had only been seen by Cliff and the same gynecologist during annual exams since the year 2005. "I would say, generally speaking, -- no."

After cleansing, Bella applied a triple-action organic scrub, and then she cleansed again. She looked closely for eruptions.

"Some women get terrible acne," she said. "You grab the hair, and once you get rid of it and all the pus and inflammation, you use a high-frequency wand to destroy the bacteria."

We had now arrived at the portion of the peach smoothie where ingrown hairs would be addressed.

"Thank God," I mumbled to the ceiling. "I don't have any ingrown hairs."

Oh, but Vulva had other plans.

"Look at all these ingrown hairs!" Bella cried with a giddy clap of her hands. She got to work plucking and picking and springing free the offending curled buds, then tweezing them away. She applied a dab of Queen Reigns, a serum that prevents ingrown hairs and razor bumps and that also helped with discoloration and hyperpigmentation.

At least, that's what she told me; I had no first-hand knowledge myself.

As an add-on, she offered the silken baby's bottom, which cleanses, exfoliates, and uses an acid peel to rid your buttocks of acne, scars, and bumps.

"I am just not going there, even for Cliff," I said.

'You have to draw the line somewhere,' I thought to myself.

Bella pouted her disappointment.

My treatments at the hotel spa had been simple massages and facial oils. It turned out they have now invented numerous ways to torture the female body into a state that acted as a magnet to the masculine subconscious. By the middle of the afternoon, I felt like my body had been transformed into a sex object. It seemed that I was prostrating it on a pedestal of almost erotic-like desire, creating a false kind of perfect woman whose beauty and polish could be attained only after weeks of personal grooming and high-end hygiene.

'Oh well, it was all for Cliff,' I tried to distract my aching pores as I lay there being prodded and poked in every possible location. My argument was beginning to lose the force that I had felt when this process started. I certainly hoped that he liked the results.

My bottom had its doubts; it was sore, and my legs were so tired from being held in positions no legs should have to suffer. I would find out for sure sometime tonight if this had been worth it. I secretly hoped that it would be sooner rather than later. I was missing Cliff so much right now.

After being released from Bella's torture chamber, as I had officially renamed the place, I valiantly tried to hobble back to the cottage, looking more like a bow-legged cowboy than a lady on her way to get married. I was somewhat comforted by the knowledge that my beautiful wedding dress would hide my awkward gait from the expected audience.

I had chosen a mid-calf, green chiffon dresses for my bridesmaids and soon to be family. They would look stunning at the altar amid the beautiful sylvan location.

Cliff had chosen a beautiful white tuxedo ensemble framed in black lapels for his brothers and brothers-in-law to wear. I had no idea of what Cliff had chosen for himself. By agreement, we had purchased our attire separately, but I did try to cheat a bit and snuck a look at his notes to the wedding planner.

All that I found was a cryptic note in big bold letters, from Cliff –

'Aha, caught you cheating!'

Shucks.

'Oh, well, he had yet to see my gown as well,' I consoled myself.

I waited nervously in the cottage where I could hear the announcement made.

"Everyone, please be seated now. The wedding will commence in two minutes." My stomach filled with butterflies; my heart must have skipped a dozen beats. *'This is it. This is the moment that I've been waiting for all of my life.'*

I had chosen Marianne to be my bridesmaid; she was resplendent. in her beautiful gown. I was so happy for her; She was the one who had always encouraged me and told me never to give up hope.

To the sounds of *Pachelbel's Canon in D,* my future nieces, Della, Abby, Arlene, Heather, and Rita, led the procession scattering rose petals in their wake.

One by one my bridesmaids sallied forth from the cottage door, led first by my future mother-in-law, Ruth, and then in order of birth, Mary, Cynthia, Carol, Kristen and finally Gail.

Each was greeted by their spouses; George took Ruth's arm, followed by Tom, Mike, Al, Michael, and Lee. I could see the entire procession advance toward the altar through the front window, but I kept care to hide behind the curtain.

At first, I had not noticed because I had been so excited watching my future family proceeding me. Then I looked up toward the altar and there he was.

'Oh! How magnificent he looked.'

There he stood. His tuxedo was a perfect fire engine red from head to toe. His beautiful ruffled shirt and bow tie looked resplendent in the evening sunlight. He knew that I would love what he had chosen, and I realized that he had selected this color just for me. My heart leaped nearly out of my chest. He looked so handsome standing there, waiting patiently for his bride to be to appear. If it had been possible, I would have loved him even more at that moment. He was the picture of true love.

Just then I heard the music begin the wedding march, and I pinched myself. I could hardly believe this day had arrived. I was the luckiest girl in the world, and my soon-to-be husband awaited me at the altar.

Charlotte had remained in the cottage to assist me with last minute issues and gave me a kiss as I prepared to step forth.

"You go out there and knock them dead, Tina, You are the most beautiful bride that I've ever known. Cliff is one very lucky man. Now, just smile and don't trip and everything will work out perfectly.'

"Thank you, Charlotte. Thank you for all that you do for me."

I stepped forth from the cottage and could hear the gasp of everyone's breath at the beauty of my gown. Susie and Mira served as my train bearers holding my dress carefully. I prayed that I would not trip.

Larry joined me at the door, wrapped my arm around his and escorted me down the aisle.

"You look stunning, Tina. Cliff is truly the luckiest man in the world."

"Thank you, Larry. But truth be told, I am the luckiest woman in the world. Cliff is everything that I have ever dreamed that I could want. He is truly my other half. Thank you for being my friend and rock every time I felt low, these past several years. I see only happiness and love in my future thanks to you."

After that, all that I could see was the altar before me, and the wonderful eyes and beautiful smile of the man who would soon be my husband.

You could hear the excitement in Larry's voice when the minister asked:

"Who gives this woman in marriage?"

"I do," Larry responded with pride in his voice and handed off my arm to Cliff.

When the minister called for the ring, little Clarence, Gail's 6-year-old son, had been chosen to present my ring, the same that Cliff and I had chosen what now seemed so long ago. He presented it to Cliff on a soft velvet cushion.

Upon taking the ring, Cliff pronounced his wedding oath.

"With this ring I, thee wed, Christina Laura McIntyre. I pledge my loyalty, honor, and fidelity for as long as I shall live to only you. I give you my life to share, my heart to belong only to you. My body to worship and honor yours, to protect and keep you safe from all harm. In sickness to be by your side, in health to drink in life's wonders from the same glass, and to provide you with all of the happiness that you deserve, now and forever."

Cliff placed the ring on my finger and kissed it.

'This was not the oath I had seen on his notepad,' I thought. *What a wonderful gift that this man was! He constantly surprised me with the things he did and said. But this was truly special.'*

Now, I had a surprise of my own, for my sweetheart. I reached into a carefully hidden tuck of my dress I extracted his ring of which he knew nothing.

"With this ring I, thee wed, Clifford William Stinson. You are my life and only future. I pledge my entire being to be faithful and true to only you. I give my life to you; my heart is yours to possess. You are the inspiration that I awaken to each day, the nourishment that my body craves. You are the fulfillment of my every dream. In sickness, I will never desert you, and in health, we will walk down all of the life's paths together. Now and forever, I am now and will forever be yours.

Yesterday is our past.

Today is the present we live in together.

Tomorrow is our future, filled with the promise of all of our dreams."

I placed the ring on Cliff's finger and kissed it.

I could barely hear the minister as he advised Cliff that he could kiss me, the bride, as the audience of our family stood and applauded. Cliff took me in his arms and gave me the most loving kiss of my life. I was truly the luckiest girl in the world.

The minister then turned to the audience and announced:

"Ladies and gentlemen: Mr. and Mrs. Clifford William Stinson."

There was wild applause as all of my new family stood while Cliff and I walked back up the aisle to the sounds of cheers and hoorays from all. Clifford announced that the wedding reception was being held at the local meeting hall, and everyone was invited to attend. We directed people to load into their cars and proceed the short distance to the hall. Cliff and I would change in the cottage into our traveling clothes because we planned to leave for the honeymoon early the next morning.

At the hall, I changed into my white spaghetti strap reception dress, and Cliff donned a super sharp looking Tux with lots of bling. During the reception, I was totally amazed to find out that Cliff was an excellent dancer. Evidently he had taken dance lessons for over three years and was quite the star of the party. He was such a good dancer that he was able to make even me look good despite my two left feet. His ability to take the lead and natural rhythm swept me off my feet more than one time.

He had hired a local band to do the honors, and I was whirled to and fro by his expert guidance to the sounds of the fox trot, mambo, and tango and finally we had the one dance he had promised me but because of the bombing we had missed – the *salsa*.

My especial favorite was a wonderful way that he taught me the waltz. While twisting and turning, spinning me around, he controlled my body as an extension of his own. I was mesmerized because he had not mentioned a single word that he knew how to dance so well, and then some. What other surprises lay in store for me from this wonderful, talented man?

"I am so happy that I married you," I whispered in his ear.

"I am the fortunate one, Christina. Of all the women in the world, you are truly a unique jewel. Your natural beauty and exquisite body dazzle my eyes and overwhelm my senses. Your compassion and love of life are truly unique. I plan to make those promises I made to you this evening come true every single day of our lives. I love you to the depth of my soul."

"And I plan on being a true partner to you, surrendering myself to your will, and loving you until the day that I die."

When it came time to cut the wedding cake everyone gathered around and we grasped the knife to cut the irresistible three-tiered lavender cake. After we made the first slice and smeared it over each other's faces, everyone shared with us as the Baker cut the remainder for each. Shortly after that we dug into the sumptuous reception feast, enjoying the food and fellowship of my new and gregarious family.

CHAPTER 33

It was around 3:00 a.m. when Cliff and me -- that is Mr. and Mrs. Clifford Stinson, boarded the private jet bound for a honeymoon where only Cliff knew the final destination. I had wanted him to surprise me with something bold and beautiful. After the plane had lifted away from International Airport in Alberta on our mystery journey I tried to tease the location from my obdurate husband.

"Tsk, tsk, Christina. You cannot trick it out of me. We might as well get some sleep because this is going to be a rather long trip. There is a bedroom in the rear for us, and I plan to take complete advantage of all of its many benefits. I sure had to pay enough to get one with a bedroom! Although, I consider every penny well spent, my dear."

"Oh! You can be so stubborn! I am dying to find out where we are going; you are just not helping. Perhaps I can tickle the pilot and finagle it out of him," I pouted.

"You will do no such thing. I have other plans for tickling and they certainly don't involve the pilot, Mrs. Stinson. Oh, that sounds so nice -- Mrs. Stinson. I love the sound of it in my ears. Mrs. Stinson. So beautiful, so perfect, almost as perfect as you, my wife."

"Now, Mr. Stinson, tell me about these plans that you have. Are they anything like the plans that you and Larry were discussing with each other that first day when I was so miserably trying to find something to eat?"

"I certainly didn't discuss those exact details with Larry, but he did give me some clues that helped me to win your hand."

"Cliff! He didn't do that. Did he? Please tell me." I tried pouty face one, and it seemed to work.

"To tell you the truth, I did tell him that I liked you very much. I asked him if you had a boyfriend and what were your interests. He was very co-operative; I think that he is just an old romantic at heart. He told me that to his knowledge you were not involved with anyone and dated rarely. He guessed that you enjoyed quiet walks, and that is why we strolled past the Koi Ponds.

"The next day, when I spoke with him on the phone, he also told me that he had never seen you hold any man's hand before. He was very surprised when he noticed us holding hands in the truck on the way to the restaurant. I knew that you felt something for me because of the way you curled your fingers up inside my palms. My heart was pounding when you never tried to retrieve them. And then the way that you were so flustered, you were simply charming."

"Charming? I don't think I would have described myself that way. More like totally freaked out; crazy in the head; out of my mind; completely flustered would be more accurate descriptions. You upset every nerve ending in my body. There were a couple of times that I simply wanted to crawl over the table to you and kiss you madly."

"You should have. I would not have objected in the slightest. But getting back to that lunch, I was desperate to speak to you alone. So I had asked Lary to come up with some excuse to stay behind in the restaurant and give me some private time with you so that I might ask you out on a date. He was very nice about that. Then, I was not sure what had happened in the tower when you would not come alone with me to your new office because I had asked Larry to stay behind. I had hoped to steal my first kiss from your sweet lips. I understand now completely and love you all the more for that because it meant that no other man had that chance before me. I was very honored."

"I have another secret that I have to tell you as well. I had totally forgotten this, but Larry was quick to remind me today of a time, a few years back, before he got married, we were in the singles class at the church one day. He had mentioned that he had a very beautiful new assistant working for him that he wanted me to meet. At the time, I was just too busy with my job to take any time out for dates. So I told him that I wasn't interested. I only wish now that I had listened to him and taken him up on his offer to introduce us. That was probably the very worst decision of my life."

"I think I even remember a very similar thing happening to me. Larry was dating his girlfriend, now his wife, and he mentioned something about this wonderful guy he knew at church. I simply blew him off; I just was not going to get involved with guys people knew from church. So, I'm not so sure that I was ready to meet you at the time. We may not have worked out as well then, as we have now. I'm much happier that we found each other when we did. Our attitudes had changed to the point where we were ready and accepting for that next step in our lives."

"I only know that now, I want you filling every minute of my life with your love. You are my present and my future. I just don't know what I am going to do with you, Mr. Stinson. Oh, hold that thought. I just remembered exactly what I am going to do to you and with you. But we need to retire to our private space. We don't want to embarrass the stewardess, now, do we?"

After closing the bedroom door and locking it behind him, Cliff began working on my dress.

"Christina, did you choose this dress on purpose? It must have fifty buttons on it!"

Cliff fought to extract me out of my dress. The buttons were very small, and the tiny threads that hold the seams together kept slipping from his large fingers, just as I had hoped.

I chose to give my new husband my surprise first. I twisted around after he had undone only three buttons from the top. I grabbed his chest and pushed him back onto the bed. He looked at me quizzically, but before he could object, I climbed on top of him, pinning his legs below my butt. I gazed into those exquisitely brown eyes as I loosened his belt, pulled down his zipper down and freed his beautifully stiff erection from the imprisoning boxer shorts.

Leaning down, I planted a row of kisses on his stomach, then slowly trailed down his abdomen. Kissing and moaning all the way which made him squirm eagerly underneath me.

"Christina..." he moaned.

When I reached my goal, it was already swollen and throbbing in anticipation. I held it tightly in one hand and looked up at his eyes which were now hooded and intense.

"God -- Christina......"

Swiftly I ran my tongue up and down his manhood.

Cliff grabbed the sheets tightly and fisted the bed coverings and moaned my name.

"Christina, ...God, Christina...," his body writhed below me, a prisoner to my passion.

I tasted the sweet essence a small drop of his seminal fluid from the tip of his cock with my tongue.

"Mighty fine, Mr. Stinson. You taste mighty fine."

I swallowed the entire length of his shaft, coating it with my saliva as he luxuriated in the sensations of my love making. Never letting my eyes drift from his, I drove him wild with lust as I pleasured him.

I lay on the bed between his legs with his powerful organ in my mouth. I tortured and teased it with my tongue and teeth. I nibbled gently up and down and then licking and swirling my tongue around him, coating his beautiful dick with my saliva. Cliff struggled to contain himself, his legs tensed and relaxed over and over as I could see his eyes grow larger as his body tensed. I paused, allowing his mouth to open and close slowly unable to speak, his lips trembled, before resuming my torture.

He moaned my name over and over, seemingly lost in a dream of sensual desire, twisting his fingers in my hair, grasping, pulling, and then releasing as the sweet pleasure of his arousal paralyzed his senses. When he finally released his seminal fluid inside the back of my throat, I smiled up and him and licked my lips in pleasure.

"Yes, Mr. Stinson, you taste mighty fine."

He immediately rolled me over onto my back and pulled my dress top open and released my breasts from their imprisoning brassier. Exposing my tender nipples, completely extended from my pleasuring of his cock, his tongue slavered my entire breast. His tongue, swirling and licking everywhere, his mouth sucking in large portions of my breast and finally capturing my tortured nipple, gently teasing it with his teeth. I never knew that such pleasure could be induced by his onslaught as he alternated between my breasts, licking, sucking, and teasing first one and then the other. My body quivered with each pleasurable touch of his tongue.

His hand reached beneath my panties to caress my mons. I was soaking from my own juices flowing and lubricating my folds, which were constantly being pleasured by his palm and fingers. His middle finger sank deep into my love canal, all the while his thumb circled and caressed my clitoris as I squirmed underneath him.

I lost count of the times that my body climaxed, only to be brought to the point of explosion over and over. Finally, he lifted my skirt, pulling it as far as he could above my waist. His hand pushed down into the flimsy thong I had on, and with a sudden and swift twist, it exploded in his hand.

His cock was again hardened by the force of his desire for my body, and splitting my legs between his knees he pushed into me forcefully. He sank so deep inside of me that I was sure that if I had been able to look, I could have seen his cock pushing outward on my stomach.

God! He was like a madman, taking me with such strength and so lovingly that I had experienced three orgasms before he achieved his final release. Afterward, we lay spent, our bodies exhausted from the experience.

"Christina?" he whispered.

"Yes, Cliff?" I moaned dreamily, my mind in a haze.

"I would like to do that again."

"Oh, my. That's surprising, and so soon? Mr. Stinson, but do you know what?"

"What, my love?"

"I certainly won't object. Please, Mr. Stinson, it is your turn to start."

"Oh! You should have warned me what a naughty woman that I was marrying, Mrs. Stinson."

"Cliff, would you mind very much?"

"What's that, Mrs. Stinson?"

"My dress. I am very sorry that I chose this particular one for this evening. These darn buttons are killing my back. Can you help me undo them?"

"My pleasure, Mrs. Stinson. It will give me better access to some other interesting parts of your body that I really would enjoy. That will also give me a few minutes to rest up from our last experience. I don't know about you, but this love making sure makes me hungry."

"Why, Mr. Stinson. You say the most shocking things."

"Turn over Mrs. Stinson. The sooner I get this task completed, the sooner I can get back to doing what I was doing before. Then I'm going to see if there are any chips or pretzels on this plane."

Most of the rest of the flight was spent moaning and mewing. Nothing much intelligible came out of either of our mouths. I prayed that the stewardess was either visiting the pilot in the flight cabin or possibly taking a nap. Several of my cries of pleasure were rather loud.

Many hours later I was awakened by the screech of the airplane tires as we touched down and slowed. We taxied for a bit and came to a stop. I sat up sleepily and looked out the cabin window. Outside I could just make out the terminal and airport sign. Fa'a'ā International Airport.

"Wow!" I squealed in delight. We were at Pape^ete, Tahiti, in the Polynesian Islands. I leaned over and woke Cliff up with a deep and loving kiss.

"Thank you, Cliff. This is so wonderful. I could never have asked for anything nicer. We're in Tahiti."

"Oh, I thought we were going to Detroit!" he teased with a huge smile.

"Mr. Stinson., are you going to lay about in the plane all day, or are we going to get dressed and have a good time?"

"If I can convince a certain lady friend to join me, I have some things planned that she might just find are pleasing to her. But on the other hand, if she wants to stay in bed. I have other things we might do right here," he yawned.

"Oh, yeah. And who is this lady friend? Surely you are not thinking of that cute looking stewardess out there are you?"

I did not exactly get a straight answer out of him before he began tickling me until I surrendered.

"I give up, please. Okay, all right. I will be the lady if you want me to, but you will have to stop tickling me first! You are such a brute."

"Mrs. Stinson, there is no other lady in the world that I would want to escort around this island. Let me get some pants and a shirt on and we will be on our way. See if you can find anything to wear in those ten suitcases you brought along."

"Mr. Stinson, I think that I brought along just the dress you might enjoy." I fished through my suitcase labeled Island Wear. I had packed ten suitcases because I didn't know whether we were going to the mountains, desert, or a tropical island. Cliff had taken me shopping on many occasions, and my wardrobe was now greatly expanded from the rather plain business suits and floppy dresses I normally wore. I was ready for just about anything.

I completed a quick shower in the small bathroom and finished applying my makeup. I squeezed into my strapless green and white floral dress which featured a split up the front almost to the mid-thigh. Cliff went forward and spoke with the stewardess and pilot, and gave each of them an envelope containing ten thousand dollars, an amount we had both agreed on. He told them to enjoy themselves. We were to remain on Tahiti for about two weeks.

I was completely surprised when they agreed happily. It seemed that Cliff had planned ahead, and this particular Captain and hostess were husband and wife. My darling husband, he always plans ahead.

Cliff advised them that they were free to leave and come back if they wished, but they needed to be available should we desire to return to Houston earlier than planned.

When I finally stepped out of the bedroom area, I felt young and sexy, happier than I had ever been and ready to begin life with my new husband.

"Wow, that is one sexy looking dress. And that certainly includes the beautiful lady inside it. Perhaps we should stay on the plane after all!" Cliff teased.

"No way, Mr. Stinson. Today is a play day, and I am getting off at this stop! You may stay here if you wish."

"Mrs. Stinson, as long as you are wearing that dress, I am not letting you out of my sight!"

"Very well, then. Shall we go, sweetheart?" I demurred.

"After you, Mrs. Stinson," he pointed, his fingers split, sure that no matter my choice he would be the happier man.

Cliff and I spent the first day walking on the beach, having lunch sitting in the ocean on beach chairs. Our days passed quickly, as we wandered the streets and stores, and I let my husband show me off to the tourists. Our afternoons were spent lazing on hammocks or basking in the sun-soaked beaches. We talked and spoke of both our past and future. Developing thoughts and plans of where our lives might be in five, ten or twenty years.

"Christina," Cliff questioned after we had been there a full week. "Are you happy? Are you really where you want to be? I mean in your work? Do you think that you are ready to manage a large group? I know that you've spent most of your working career in more or less administrative assistance roles. What if you suddenly had to manage a large group, say fifty, or even a hundred people? Could you handle that task?"

"Yes. I'm certain that I could. I worked toward that goal for the last number of years. Larry has shown me through example how he leads. How he manages the flow of work between staff. Teaching me that some people are less experienced and work well on things at the start of a workflow.

"Others, who have been working in the field for a year or two can easily not only take the work from the lesser experienced, but also assist in training them when they receive work from them where things or either missing or incompletely done.

"Finally, the ones who are the most experienced help all of the other workers in knowing all of the ins and outs of getting things done. Knowing who to call for guidance, knowing exactly what to do in critical situations. Yes, Cliff. I am ready for that kind of role. I just need the opportunity. Why do you ask?"

"Oh, I was just wondering. When you go back, have you decided if you will go back to your old job?" he asked.

I could almost sense some underlying reason for that question. No matter how I probed, though, I received the same answer. Finally, I gave up. Perhaps it had been just an innocent thought.

"So what do you have planned for tonight, Cliff?"

"Just some more lazing on the beach in the moonlight. Your skin looks so perfect when the moon is shining brightly. I also heard that clams are in season. Perhaps we could use one of the resort small buckets and shovels and find a few fresh ones on the beach. The hotel restaurant has a sign saying they will prepare and cook them for guests who bring them."

"That sounds exciting. Fresh clams. I haven't ever had those. The only ones I've had the fortune to eat were picked up at a grocery store. Let's go, before the sun goes down."

****

And sunsets and the nights were…exquisite. Sigh!

The days blended in a sequence of joyful sharing of the ocean and the town of Pape^ete and the nights, what else can I report? They were unforgettable. Some of them were exceptionally memorable, but I shouldn't talk about those details either.

CHAPTER 34

Our blissful two weeks in the fun and sun finally came to an end. I had learned more about Cliff's life before he met me and I filled him in on my past which I had not previously revealed. Leaving the island was a sorrowful occasion. We had experienced our first real joy of togetherness. Life was peaceful here; there was no one to interrupt our hours of happiness together. We'd truly bonded and became one person; all of our dreams for the future merged into one.

Cliff had decided that because I enjoyed my work at Tilden Industries, and I did not feel my life fulfilled by lying lazily in the apartment, he did not object to my returning to work, as long as precautions were taken to protect me should Payne appear again.

Cliff had taken leave from the tower construction, but when he had contacted his office after we had been in Tahiti for a week, he was advised that the building inspectors had given final clearance to commence repairs and completion of the tower. He spoke with Edward Hale, the young man he had hired to help organize materials and supply deliveries. Edward assured Cliff that future deliveries would be on time and complete, or else the company would lose the contract.

Cliff was excited to hear that because of the delays he had previously experienced in the preceding months. Edward had even lined up a company which was prepared to step in immediately should the first supplier fail in their on-time delivery promises. From the sounds of the conversations that I overheard, it seemed that some areas of the building were ahead of schedule now, and some staff might be moving soon. I couldn't overhear who, but I knew that whichever group it turned out to be they would be overjoyed in their new surroundings.

The flight back to Houston was pleasant, lasting about ten hours, about an hour less than from Alberta to Tahiti. We lounged comfortably in the cabin, and dozed from time to time, lost in our pleasant daydreams of island life.

"Christina, I will let you choose where you want to go for our first anniversary," Cliff told me at one point. "You will have a whole year to think and plan. I cannot remember ever being as happy in my life as we were in Tahiti. I only hope that all of our anniversaries can be as rewarding."

I replied, "That is going to be a real challenge, Cliff. However, because you have warned me ahead of time and I have an entire year to plan, you can bet that it is going to be very special."

The next time I awoke the wheels were touching down at Houston Intercontinental. I stretched my arms, yawned and looked over at Cliff. He was still sleeping peacefully. I leaned over and awakened him with a wet kiss, which brought him awake with a start.

"Hey, you," he said.

"Hey," I jostled him again. "We're here, back to the old rat race. Time to wake up sleepyhead."

"If I can get another one of those kisses to awaken me, I am going back to sleep right now."

"Silly -- you don't need to be asleep to get one of those. Come on over here; I'll give you another right now."

When we deplaned and entered the terminal, we were met by George & Ruth Stinson. "Welcome home, you guys," George shouted. "We have a welcome home celebration all planned out and ready for you. We hired a limo for you two that should be enough to contain that mountain of suitcases that you have, Christina."

I blushed, realizing he was right. I had packed clothes for both tropical and winter climates since I had not known our destination and Cliff had suggested that I pack for both, just in case.

"Yeah, well, Cliff refused to reveal where we were going, so I have everything from sun dresses to winter parkas in there."

We loaded up the suitcases, climbed in and soon were on our way. "By the way, exactly where are we going?" I asked.

"It is a surprise," Cliff said with a smile.

"You and your surprises. But I have loved all of them so far. I'm sure this will be just as exciting." I smiled up at him and then sank dreamily onto his shoulder.

The limo picked up speed as it exited the airport and took the freeway ramp. We had traveled for about twenty-five minutes when the limo changed over to the south loop. When we exited on Broadway, my suspicions were raised quickly. They were satisfied when the driver turned in at Brady's Landing. Oh, what fond memories I had of this place.

"Cliff, you set this up didn't you?" I asked.

"Who, me?" He smiled. "Whatever would give you that idea?"

It appeared that Cliff had hired out the entire restaurant, and we were their only customers. We walked to the entry and were met inside by the entire family and several of my friends from the office. The restaurant was decorated with streamers and a huge '**Welcome Home, Cliff and Tina**' banner. The kids had small signs and balloons welcoming us back, and they tossed streamers into our hair.

I had never believed that I could have possibly become part of a family so willing to accept me. They all hugged and kissed me warmly. Who would have thought that I could have such a welcoming family? Six months ago, I was alone except for a housekeeper and bodyguard. Now I had a husband, ten brothers, and sisters, and twelve nieces and nephews, -- and from the looks of Cynthia, there was another addition on the way.

Cliff escorted me over to the same table that we had sat at on that first day. Larry was waiting for us there and as we approached he stood and took me in his arms and gave me a welcome home kiss on my cheek.

"Larry, it is so good to see you again. And at my favorite table in my now favorite restaurant."

"All that I have to say is, wow! That is some dress you have got on there, Tina. I hardly recognize you. And your tan, you look positively gorgeous. It sure looks like that construction manager husband of yours has been treating you well. Welcome back, both of you. Welcome Home."

I leaned over to Larry and whispered in his ear.

"If you think this is something, you should see what's underneath it. It is a surprise for Cliff for later tonight."

"Hey, what are you two whispering about?" Cliff asked.

"Tina was just telling me about a special surprise that she has for you." Larry demurred.

"Oh? What's that?" Cliff queried.

"No dice, fella. It is all on a notepad right up here," Larry tapped his head with his finger.

The three of us had a private laugh at that, recalling how Cliff had pulled the same thing on me that first lunch.

Just then a tugboat that was passing by gave a giant blast on its fog horn -- evidently a pre-arranged signal by the family. My eyes welled with tears. Never had I felt so loved and treasured. I turned to the family gathered around me and said aloud,

"You have welcomed me into your family in so many wonderful ways. I treasure each and every one of you. I am honored by the love you all have shown me. Cliff and I thank you for everything. Now, what do you say we order something to eat?"

I sat down just as the first time. My husband directly across, his leg touching mine, and Larry next to the window. I looked over at Larry,

"Larry, the last time that I was here I had trouble holding down a salad. This time, I am ordering one of those delicious looking steak and lobster combos. That may have been why I fell in love with this wonderful man. He had the most intriguing way of sopping his meat in the sauce."

We all laughed and sat down to enjoy a meal with family and friends.

"Cliff, memories that's what it all about. Happy memories that family and good friends provide. They are the true spice of life." I squeezed Cliff's hand, lifted it to my lips and gave it a tender kiss.

"Thank you for being the wonderful man that you are."

"Now what's that surprise you have?" Cliff begged.

"Un-uh, big fella. You don't tell me your surprises, and I am not telling mine. So there," I stuck my tongue out at him.

After the long plane ride, and the wonderful dinner with family and friends, we finally arrived back at Cliff's apartment. Stacking the suitcases and wraps in a corner, he said that he was tired and was going to lie down for a bit and left for the bedroom. I waited a few minutes until I could hear him sink onto the bed. I peeled off my dress and entered the room. He was laying on the bed, stretched out, having removed his shoes, his arm slung up over his eyes.

"Cliff." No response.

"Cliff, are you awake?"

He lazily let his arm fall away and then suddenly sat straight up on the bed. "Uh, Oh," he smiled. "It sure doesn't look like I will be getting much sleep tonight."

"C'mon over here, you sexy thing, you," he begged excitedly.

He was right. We didn't get much sleep at all that night. But I was not complaining! What an outstanding way to end the honeymoon of a lifetime. I could not have asked for more. After making love, we talked and joked with each other until the wee hours.

Cliff shared with me that the tower had been progressing well. His boss had called and congratulated him on the hiring Edward Hale. Evidently supply deliveries had greatly improved, and several areas were now actually ahead of schedule. Workers were able to complete work which in the past had been delayed due to missing supplies or wrong parts being delivered.

I was excited to learn about the inside story on how a big tower gets built. Cliff asked me probing questions about my job. He was genuinely interested in what and how I did my job.

What the company's plans for the future when the new staff would start to handle the new contact we had just won? Would there be a new manager hired to lead them? Perhaps a promotion from within. Again, there was that nagging feeling in the back of my mind. Something I couldn't quite put to rest.

He knows something, but what?

CHAPTER 35

I awoke the next morning to the sound of purring. I thought that perhaps there was water running somewhere, or it could have been an electric shaver. I opened my eyes slowly and immediately let out a scream. There was an animal laying across my chest. Cliff jumped up out of bed and looked around, probably thinking that Payne had found us.

Cliff looked all around and was ready to defend me to the death. After not finding any violent invaders inside our bedroom he turned back to me, "where is he at?"

"Cliff, what is this thing on my chest?" I shouted.

"Thing? -- Oh, you mean Cardo? Why, sweetheart, that is my cat. He's the most loving thing I'd ever known, or at least until I met you, that is.

"Cardo, meet Mrs. Stinson. Mrs. Christina Stinson that is. Christina, meet Cardo."

Cardo, being a cat, did what cats do. He totally ignored me. He had found a soft place to lay on and did not much care whether it was on top of a human or a pillow. But he did have the most calming purr. I tentatively reached and stroked his fur. He lifted his head slightly, seemed to consider my hand for a moment, and then decided to allow me to continue stroking him. After all, that was what cats do. They possessed all that surrounded them, and only permit humans to stroke them if they so desired. At the moment, he seemed agreeable to my hand.

'He is rather cute,' I thought.

"Cliff, you never told me that you had a cat. How old is he?"

"He's four years old. I rescued him from the pound about a year after my last date. He's a full blooded Siamese. I was getting lonely, he seemed the perfect companion, that is until I recently found a better one."

"But Cliff, we have been gone from home for two weeks now. How has he been cared for? Did you leave out a bunch of food and water for him, I assume that he is a male?"

"Yes, Christina, Cardo is very much a male. He has been neutered, had his front paws declawed so that he does not scratch up the furniture. And yes, he has been fed while we were away. My parents were keeping him for the past month, since the bombing. Then when I decided to add a permanent new member of my household, I realized that we might need some help. You know, to cook, do the laundry, run to the grocery. Stuff like that.

"I arranged to hire some extra help to help us keep the place neat and tidy as well as another assistant for you. I had told them that we had needed privacy for our first night home, but I believe they should have arrived by now. I think that I even smell breakfast on the stove. So let's go out and meet our new staff."

"Cliff, I thought that we were going to make decisions mutually -- and here you go and hire people that I have never met. I only wish that you had consulted with me. I am so disappointed -- our first big decision and I did not even get to offer an opinion."

Cliff looked at me sorrowfully, then apologized, and yet there seemed to be a hidden smile behind his frown.

"I am so sorry, Christina. It was just that I was in a rush, the wedding, arranging the honeymoon and all. But I did try to find ladies that you might like. Just give them a chance. They come very highly recommended by a lady that I know.

"You will come to like them; I just know it. They were extremely nice on the interview and begged me for the jobs. I could hardly turn them down. I even got them both at a bargain rate."

"I'll try," I pouted. "But next time, I'd at least like to meet with private staff before you make the offer, okay?" I pouted. However, the smell of fresh, smoky bacon and coffee cooking sure was tempting my taste buds. My stomach was winning out over my mind at this point.

"Give me a few minutes to get cleaned up and find some PJs and a robe. I will be out shortly."

Secretly, I was terribly disappointed with Cliff. How could he have done this after saying that we would share in everything? Oh, well. I guess that it is a done deal. I'll try to be civil. Perhaps I'll get to like them after I get to know them.

I dug around in my 'nightwear' suitcase and found a pair of PJ's and my favorite cozy short robe.

'Here goes nothing.' I thought. 'Now be nice, Tina. Cliff probably went through a lot of interviews and the ladies are probably very experienced.'

I crossed through the bedroom and opened the door. At first, all that I could see was some dark brunette hair leaning over the stove. The woman's back was to me, but she looked oddly familiar. When she straightened up and turned around, I let out a happy shout.

"Marianne, what are you doing here? Oh, I am so happy to see you. I thought that I would never see you again. But how? What?"

I looked over at Cliff, who had a huge grin on his face. Then it dawned on me. Cliff had hired Marianne to be our housekeeper.

"Cliff, you didn't! Oh, thank you, thank you, thank you!"

"But Marianne, I gave you a million dollars so that you could live your own life. Go wherever you chose, not have to worry about working."

"Ms. Tin -- I'm sorry, Mrs. Stinson, I guess that I am kind of just like you, even with all that money I found that I only enjoy working, and keeping care of you. It is what I have gotten used to, and when Mr. Stinson called me, I begged him to let me come back. I want to make my home with you for now. The two of you, and evidently we also have a cat. But he seems nice and is no trouble at all. If you don't wish me to stay that would be all right. Mr. Stinson said that you would have final say."

"Oh, Marianne, how could you even think that I would not want you here? I love you! And besides, no one knows as well as you how to make that delicious cup of coffee that I crave every morning. Yes, I would love to have you here, if you want to stay."

Just then the outside door opened, and a very familiar blond entered.

"Charlotte!, "I cried, "Don't tell me that Cliff finagled you into coming as well?"

"Yes, ma'am. When I received Mr. Stinson's call, my heart leaped for joy. To be able to continue in my old job was just what I wanted. I don't care much for living alone, and so far I have not met Mr. Wonderful, as you have. If you will have me, I would love to be your bodyguard and driver again."

"Charlotte, you know that you can have that job as long as you want. Now come on over here, you two. I want to give you both a hug. Welcome. Welcome to our new home."

"Cliff, that includes you, as well. These two ladies have been my rock and life's support for the past four years. I cannot thank you enough for what you have done." I hugged my two friends and gave Cliff a very wet kiss.

"But you said that you got them at a bargain rate. Marianne? Charlotte? He's not cheating you is he? How much did he offer you to get you to come?"

"Mrs. Stinson," both responded.

"You go ahead, Charlotte," Marianne suggested.

"We wouldn't accept any money for this, Mrs. Stinson. You have already rewarded us far more than we deserve. Mr. Stinson did offer to pay us a big salary, but we both declined. Other than household expenses, we will be serving you for the money that you already gifted to us. It will be an honor for us to stay with you, and we will not allow you to pay us. That is out of the question."

Both Charlotte and Marianne nodded their heads.

"Cliff, you're forgiven. I should have known that you would do something like this. You seem to know my wants and needs even before I do. I'll never doubt you again."

'Cliff, you just earned another big reward, fella,' I thought to myself. *'What had I ever done in life to deserve this wonderful man? He was always thinking of me, doing things that made my life complete. I would have to come up with something so mind blowing that he would treasure it for a very long time.'*

I checked my purse and found my wallet. In it was the new debit card** that Cliff had the bank issue in my name. There was no spending limit attached, so I would have the funds if I could find the right gift. But he already had many nice suits and shoes. He didn't seem to care about wearing a lot of jewelry. He already owned a Rolex watch.

'Hmmm. This is not going to be easy. I would have to think very hard.'

The four of us sat around, talking and bringing the ladies up to date on all the details of our honeymoon, well, perhaps not ALL of the details. After everyone had eaten their breakfast, Cliff suggested he wanted to take me on a drive.

"Where to, Cliff?"

"You know me, Christina. What do I normally say?"

"Now, Cliff, this is just getting too frustrating. Don't tell me it is another surprise."

"Yes, Charlotte you can follow us. We will be heading out Highway 290 about ten miles or so."

"Oh! Someday I am going to surprise you with something. I love your surprises, but my curiosity drives me wild trying to guess what you have found for me."

"Do you remember what you told me one time? That you were rich, and you said that I would have to get used to you buying things for me. Now it's time for some major payback. I am going to pamper and spoil you silly. I told you, from now on, you are going to be the most coddled lady in town."

"Cliff?"

"Yes, sweetheart?"

"I love you."

"Now you know that will only get you more things to spoil you. But today is something different. I have suddenly realized that we are going to be desperately in need of this particular item. So let's get dressed. I have somewhere special I want you to see."

True to his word, Cliff had been too embarrassed to go into a Ladies lingerie shop with me. I think that it had something to do with him having been raised with three very pretty sisters. Perhaps he had seen them, at various times, in a state of undress and been shocked by their near nakedness.

No matter, I stocked up on a large supply of items that he had never seen, and I tried to wear something new underneath each day to surprise and entice him every evening. So far, it had worked very well. Since I did not know exactly where we were going today, so I searched my lingerie drawers to have something unusual to wear underneath. I thanked heaven that I had spent so much time in the workout center taking care of my body. I would have never believed that all of that hard work and sweat would pay off like so well.

My new motto was "be prepared," and I wanted to be available and enticing should Cliff ever present the opportunity. I finally found the perfect item for Cliff's eyes only tonight, or sooner -- A girl could hope, couldn't she? It was a naughty French maid fantasy costume with an apron, cut babydoll fashion, and trimmed in white lace and bows and ruffled lace panties.

Cliff was a very vigorous, and sensual man. How he had been able to restrain himself, all of those years was truly incredible. Once awakened his sexual proclivity was potent. I was very grateful that he had chosen me to be his life's partner. I intended to reward him in every way for his devotion to me.

On several of the shopping trips, I had turned the tables on him. One time we were passing by a huge Western Wear store and I demanded that we go inside. After about two hours I had him all Duded up in the most beautiful cowboy jeans and shirts, boots and string ties, and a beautiful western style belt buckle. I even made him get a ten-gallon hat on top of everything else. He looked so handsome; I wanted to eat him up right there. I told Cliff that today was the perfect day to wear his new duds, so he put them on while I went in search of something for myself.

I rummaged through my closet full of expensive outer clothes and dresses that Cliff had helped me select. I found a cute little outfit to wear over top of my surprise. Then slipped into it and pulled my dress down, being sure to tuck in the apron. Then I straightened my hair and came out of the bathroom just as Cliff was putting on his left shoe.

"How's this? Will it be appropriate for wherever we are going?" I had found a faux leather panel dress with a deep V-neck, exposing just enough décolletage to be enticing, but still modest enough for public display. Made of rayon, nylon with a spandex trim that hugged all of my curves in just the right places. I added a pair of elegant sandals with gold hardware at the back of the heel and a buckle closure at the ankle strap which featured a four-and-a-half-inch heel. It went very well with his cowboy duds.

"Holy cow! Christina. I don't know how you do it. If you keep finding all of these wonderful dresses to put on that, I may never leave this apartment! You make me want to stay here and take them all off of you again."

"Oh, Cliff, you say the nicest things. But no hanky-panky right now. You have got my curiosity on high alert, and I am itching to find out what you have up your sleeve today. Besides, if you saw what I have on underneath, I know that we would never get out of here for a week."

"At least can I have a sample? Perhaps one of your extra special wet kisses?" he suggested.

"That I can do," I smiled sweetly and fluttered my eyelashes at him.

After several minutes, I felt a hand roaming where it shouldn't be,

"All right buster, no more samples for you today. I'm sure Charlotte is getting impatient, and remember, she does carry a six-shooter to protect me from sex fiends," I teased.

"Oh, does she now? Well then, I guess that we should be on our way then."

He broke off the kiss, gave me a rather disappointed smile, then grabbed my hand, and we passed through the den while my fingers curled into my favorite position.

CHAPTER 36

As we traveled down Highway 290, Cliff lets me in on his surprise.

"Christina, I don't know if you have had time to think about this because I did surprise you this morning with the staff additions to our home. I have lived there for the past six years as a bachelor. Cardo joined me four years ago and then you two weeks ago while we stayed on the lake in Conroe, although last evening was your first night in my actual apartment. With the addition of Charlotte and Marianne my bachelor pad has outgrown its usefulness. I only have the three bedrooms, while that technically is sufficient for now, it really isn't designed for a married couple and two unrelated adults.

"I was watching you lying on the bed this morning with Cardo on your chest; I thought perhaps you would feel more comfortable having a real home. So I called a realtor, she suggested that we might take a look at one of the subdivisions out in the Fairfield area. But if you think that some other area might be better, I am not set on that one in particular; I just wanted us to have a look. We don't have to finalize anything yet. We're just browsing today."

"Thank you, Cliff. You always surprise me with your thoughtfulness. I don't have any specific preference and had not considered it before. Living at the Grecian Condominium was not a home. But, yes, you are correct, your apartment probably isn't quite the right fit for us now.

"When I lived with Charlotte and Marianne there were just the three of us. All girls that is. Now that I have a man around the house so to speak, I am sure that they would like a bit more privacy than your apartment provides. This was an excellent idea, and it's just one more reason that I love you so much. You always think of others before you think of yourself."

We exited the freeway at the entrance for Fairfield Colony. We stopped at the entrance and picked up a handsome full-color brochure from the sales office. This was the first time that I have ever looked at an actual home and considered it as a place where I might enjoy living.

Charlotte joined us as we toured the area. The layout of the subdivision was incredible and boasted all of the latest amenities, such as a fifteen-thousand square foot athletic club, full-size basketball court, a fitness center, a competition-sized swimming pool, tennis courts, a twenty-acre sports park for baseball, and a soccer field. Also, it featured eight lakes and six neighborhood parks, six neighborhood pools plus numerous pocket parks and greenbelts.

"Cliff, I think this subdivision is incredible. This may be exactly the type of area we need, but I'm not sure yet. Before we make a final decision we might consider some of the individual homes around Houston."

Cliff suggested some of the obvious benefits.

"The freeway offers easy access to downtown, and any other part of Houston we could wish. There's the community pool. Just look at the size and beauty of it. And the brochure points out that Fairfield has six more neighborhood pools to laze around in, as well as many of the homes have private pools in their back yards."

Cliff and I spent the rest of the day looking at models and homes for sale with Charlotte in tow. We fell in love with three of the houses located on Caramel Apple Trail. The homes were all priced starting at around $560,000, had five bedrooms and plenty of areas where Charlotte and Marianne could have alone time, or sit and chat with each other.

We ended up by speaking with the sales agent and then taking more brochures on those specific homes. We were excited about the opportunities but decided we needed to explore more options and to think about making a decision for several days. The brochures all contained full photographic displays of the interiors and exteriors of the homes. So we had plenty of material on which to base a decision.

Charlotte was impressed with several of gated parts of the subdivision with security guards on duty twenty-four-seven.

"Cliff, I hardly believe it. Was it only a three months ago when I was content in my apartment near downtown? Now I am considering moving into an actual home of my very own?"

I daydreamed happily as Cliff drove us back to our apartment. There we sat around the dining table with the brochures spread out in front of us discussing our future, and sharing them with Marianne, and Charlotte.

Later when we were alone, I brought up another subject that I hoped would happen sometime in the future.

"Cliff, please tell me how it was growing up in such a large family. Six children and your parents all in one house. What if we were to have that many children ourselves? My brother died when I was small, so I don't have any concept of how I would deal with so many little kids in one place."

"Christina, you wouldn't be trying to tell me something, would you?"

"No, I did not mean that. But then, we have been going at it like bunny rabbits for a while now. I hadn't given too much thought to that because so many things have been happening lately.

My point was that the homes that we are considering all have five bedrooms. If you count us, and Charlotte and Marianne, that only adds to three. We haven't talked about children before. Do you want children, and if so how many were you considering?"

"I haven't given it any thought to that either. But now that I am, my pastor currently has seven children with another on the way."

"Surely not, you are not thinking of eight are you?"

"How about a bakers' dozen then?" he winked mischievously.

I prayed that he was kidding. *'Thirteen kids? Holy cow!'*

"I was just teasing, Christina," he relieved my anxiety. "I don't have a number in mind. But to answer your first question, I would love to have children with you. Growing up with my two brothers and three sisters was very rewarding. We were always doing things and going places together. I was able to play many games with my brothers like baseball and soccer, and some touch football.

"My sisters were very much into music and athletics. Mary plays the piano quite well, Cynthia plays the French horn, and Gail likes to sing and is very good. She has even sung several times with the local opera company. Cynthia also played varsity soccer in school. Al played the 'cello for years. I do think that he may have slowed down on that lately becoming very involved with his three children's activities. So yes, I would love to have children, watch them grow up, and help them in any way that I could. How about you? Would you like to have children, and how many?"

"I'm very much like you, Cliff. Not having even considered it before, I do want to have children, but as to how many? I would like to have as many as you want me to have. One is not a good number; it leaves the child with no sibling playmates and lonely, much like I was when I was young. Two, five, ten, whatever my husband and lover is pleased with -- that would suit me perfectly. What are your thoughts?"

"It was just the surprise of the thought of children. I've been on my own for so long. Kids never entered into my thoughts until now. The more I do consider the thought, the more that I am excited by the challenges they would provide. Yes, I want lots of children. They would make our house a home, and their laughter would fill my life up with happiness." Cliff mused.

"I know that any children that we are going to have will inherit their father's gentle ways," I added. "The way that you approach making love with me as if it is still a wonder and new experience each time. You are so tender and gentle with me, treating me with reverence and awe that inspires me to love you even more. You have no idea how much that means to me. The one thing that a woman needs to feel in a relationship is to know that she is 'treasured.' You show me that every day in every way."

"I do hold you in reverence, Christina. What you have done for us, for me, I don't need to go over it again. You know how I feel. I can never repay the honor you have given to me in giving me your entire trust. I was a stranger to you, and yet you stepped out on faith, taking a chance that very few would have done."

CHAPTER 37

On the following Friday afternoon, I received a phone call from Larry.

"Hi, Tina. Larry here. I am just calling to let you know that the police and fire inspectors have cleared our office building for occupancy and repairs have been completed to all of the damaged areas. I have been notified that we can return to work next Monday.

"I know that your situation has changed dramatically since the bombings, so I am letting you know that should you choose, you will be welcomed back. However, I would completely understand if more recent events have caused you to decide not to return. I would miss you dearly because you have been an outstanding employee and have helped me over many a rough spot."

"Thank you, Larry. I appreciate the confidence you have had in me. Cliff knows that we don't need the money from my working, but told me that he will support my decision whichever way that I decide. He's already back at work now at the Tower. If you don't mind, I had like to have an opportunity to speak with him again. We've been looking at houses, he might have different thoughts now that we are considering moving. I can call you back after that and give you a definite answer."

"Sure, Tina. Not a problem. I'll wait for your call."

I immediately phoned Cliff,

"Hello, Christina. What's up?"

"Hi, Cliff. I just received a call from Larry. They have cleared our building for occupancy and repairs have been completed. Larry has given me the option to return if I should choose. He would understand if I chose otherwise. I wasn't sure after our discussion a few days ago. You might just want me to stay at home. You know, 'barefoot and pregnant.' I told Larry that I wanted to confirm it with you before I make the decision."

"Christina, you know that you have my full support in whatever you want to do. But I do want you to consider a few things before you make your final decision. One of those is to remember that Payne is still out there. He knows where you work, as well as myself. He knows where my parents live. He probably knows that you have moved out of your suite at the hotel, but may not know where my apartment is located. And we are considering the purchase of a new home.

"I checked with HPD, and they advised me that they haven't found him yet. But they are certain he is somewhere in the ship channel area. For the past month or so there have been many reports of office workers being beaten and robbed in that area. It's a run down area, and there are a lot of street people who hang out over there. Most of the descriptions of the culprit are identical. He wears the same tattered shirt and pants. The shirt has dark blood stains, and he smells as if he hasn't bathed in a long time.

"We have avoided him so far, but he is a real danger to you. I think that you are his main target and now that he is on his own, will focus all of his energies on you and not me. If you return to work, you may be placing other people in danger who might be injured or killed, based on actions he has taken in the past. All of that aside this decision is yours. I will support your decision whichever way you choose.

"But just think, he may try to kidnap you while you are on your way to work. I can think of a hundred scenarios that would make you vulnerable to him. Even a trip to the grocery store may present an opportunity. The company that I work for, as well as Tilden Industries, has already increased security at the tower as well as your current building. But we can't let thoughts of him take over our lives and live in fear.

"They have his photo, so everyone knows who to look for. Even with that information there is always the fact that a determined person can avoid detection and strike out at the least expected time and place as he has proven already. Charlotte may be an excellent bodyguard, but she can only be in one place at a time."

"Thank you, Cliff. You have given me a lot to consider. I will wait until I have thought it through completely before I make my decision. I will consider it over the weekend and give my decision to Larry by Sunday evening. I love you. Please take care and come home to me safely when you can."

I phoned Larry and explained some of what Cliff had given me to think about, and told him that I would call Sunday evening again with my decision.

Throughout the Saturday I struggled with the problems that Payne might cause me should I return to my old job. I awoke about 2:00 a.m. that night the issue still whirling through my thoughts. But a new realization struck me. I knew what I had to do. I agreed with Cliff. I could not live my life continually burdened by the memories of my rape and let it continue to rule my life. I had suffered through seventeen years of turmoil and separation from people because of him. Let Payne try his worst. No matter what, I would win out over him in the end.

I reached over and wrapped my arm around Cliff. He stirred in his sleep but did not wake. I whispered in his ear, tomorrow I will join with you in every respect and together we will grab our future and walk forward with pride and happiness and without fear. I love you, more than life itself."

"uh. Did you say something, sweetheart?"

"No, precious. Go back to sleep. All is well."

CHAPTER 38

I awoke early Sunday morning; my mind resolved to give Cliff the reward that I had resolved on would be the one thing that would seal our love more than anything I had done before. He was sleeping peacefully so I nudged him gently, "Wake up, sleepyhead."

"Um." He moaned. "What time is it, anyway?"

"It is 6:45, silly Time to rise and shine."

"Omm. How about letting me have another fifteen minutes? I was up rather late last night, as you might remember. If I recall correctly, you were right there with me."

"No dice, sweetheart. We have places to go and things to do. This is a big day for me!"

"Mmmmm. Big day? What's up? Is someone coming that I don't know about? What do you have planned in that pretty little noggin of yours?"

"No way! This is my big surprise, and I am not telling. First, it's Sunday. I want to go to church. Services are at 9:00 a.m. and I don't want to be late. Come on big boy. Hop to it. You get shaved and showered, and I will lay out one of your nice suits and join you in a minute."

Cliff and I had settled into a morning routine that involved showering together. He scrubbed my back and all of the rest of me including my hair, my breasts, legs and even my privates, and then I, in turn, had the pleasure of doing the same for him. It was a routine that bonded us together not only physically but spiritually. It was an intimate activity that allowed us to demonstrate that our bodies were one as we washed and loved each other.

After Cliff was cleaned to my satisfaction, he stepped from the shower and dried himself. Still completely nude he proceeded to finish by shaving, combing his hair, and applying deodorant. I stood in the warm water of the shower watching him, enjoying the view. His body was in excellent shape, and his muscles toned. The long cut on his leg from the bombing was now completely healed with no scar. His left arm was now fully functioning; the injured nerve had healed completely.

The only evidence left from the bombing was a small, almost invisible scar on his cheek. He looked into the mirror and saw that I was watching, mesmerized by the view.

"Enjoying the show, sweetheart?"

"Very much, Mr. Stinson. Had I known that you put this kind of show on daily, I might have said yes that first night." I teased.

"Oh, I understand now completely. You married me for my body. Naughty girl!"

"The body and other things. But you do a have certain part that I especially enjoy," I giggled.

"Shame on you, Mrs. Stinson. You are a true libertine. What am I going to do with you? Oh, wait, I have an idea."

"Oh, no you don't, Mr. Stinson. No hanky-panky this morning. I have something else planned, and if I don't get out and get dressed, we are going to be late."

"What is this that you are so much in a rush to do?"

"I told you. It's a big surprise. This is payback for you not telling me that we were going to visit your parents until we were a block away. So there," I stuck my tongue out and relished the sour look he had on his face.

'Oh, this was going to be really good. I had been desperately searching for a reward for Cliff's love and thoughtfulness since he had brought Marianne and Charlotte back into my life.'

262

I stepped out of the shower and towel dried. Then I pulled out the blow dryer and had the pleasure of Cliff trying to tease my secret from me. He sat on the bathroom stool, watching me as I had watched him. Oh, he was getting very frustrated. He tried to guess several things but never came close to the truth.

After my hair had dried, I applied some deodorant and several squirts of perfume, some mascara, lipstick, and blush. Studying my face and hair in the mirror for a few minutes, I was satisfied with the result. Then we both returned to the bedroom and began putting on our underwear and clothes.

Searching through my lingerie drawer, I suddenly realized that I didn't have anything that was a normal modest ladies underwear.

'Oh, well! The minister will not be inspecting my lingerie today,' I thought, *'only my soul.'*

I'm going to have to go shopping again. Sigh! Now what to cover all this up with? Ah! Yes. This is just the thing. A reward for Cliff underneath if he wanted to get frisky later, which he often did, but outside demure and presentable. It was a rather sexy looking low hung thong that only just covered up my privates. I felt positively sinful.'

Cliff had already finished polishing his shoes and had his suit and tie on; he looked delicious. He was going to enjoy my surprise. I knew deep down that it would be a joy to his heart.

"Ready, honey?"

"Let me finish my shoelaces and I will be ready," as he tied the last lace with a flourish and stood, holding out his hand for mine.

I swept up my purse, draped it over my shoulder, took his hand, gave him a kiss and a little tug.

"All ready, sweetheart, let's be on our way."

CHAPTER 39

The minister was completing a sermon on salvation, I knew that not only did Cliff want this, but more importantly, I wanted it.

> *The sermon was taken from Romans 10 : 9 That if you confess with your mouth, "Jesus is Lord," and believe in your heart that God raised him from the dead, you will be saved.*
>
> *10 For it is with your heart that you believe and are justified, and it is with your mouth that you confess and are saved.*
> *New International Version (NIV)*

As the pastor finished his message, he made a call to the congregation for any among us to come forward and confess our belief in him and accept *Jesus* as our *personal Savior.*

The invitation hymn was sung as a solo by the music leader, and his beautiful tenor voice rang out throughout the auditorium.

> *I will sing of my Redeemer,*
> *And His wondrous love to me;*

On the cruel cross He suffered,
From the curse to set me free.
  Refrain
  Sing, oh sing, of my Redeemer,
  With His blood, He purchased me.
  On the cross, He sealed my pardon,
  Paid the debt, and made me free.

I immediately rose and stepped out from my chair and went forward. Cliff had shown me his faith multiple times over the past months; now I wished to join with him and share in the joy of that belief. The agony and misery of that night long ago was in my past, not future.

  I will tell the wondrous story,
  How my lost estate to save,
  In His boundless love and mercy,
  He the ransom freely gave.
    Refrain

Cliff was on his feet immediately and followed me down the aisle. As I approached the pastor I felt Cliffs' hand clasp mine as he whispered, "whither thou go, I will follow."

  I will praise my dear Redeemer,
  His triumphant power I will tell,
  How the victory He giveth
  Over sin, and death, and hell.
    Refrain

I felt joy and peace that I had not known before. Today was to be the first day of the rest of our lives. The pastor welcomed me into the fellowship of the church along with fifteen other people who were either professing their faith or had come down the aisle to join the church.

I will sing of my Redeemer,
And His heav'nly love to me;
He from death to life hath brought me,
Son of God with Him to be.
Refrain Phillip B. Bliss, 1876 *

After the congregation had welcomed us, we were led off to a small room outside the sanctuary. One of the staff pastors interviewed me.

"Are you coming forward as a new convert or are you wishing to join by a letter from a prior church?" he asked.

"I was previously a member of a church in the Washington State," I explained. "Although I do have a prior membership, I wish to come by profession and be baptized,"

Cliff explained that he was there in support of my decision.

"That is excellent. We are proud to welcome you to our church," the pastor continued. "You will need a change of clothes for the baptism service since anything you will be wearing would be soaked. We also offer a special set of clothes if you don't have any yourself."

"That won't be necessary. I will be able to bring an extra outfit next week and be baptized in front of the church."

I was ecstatic; I truly felt that Cliff and I were now on the same page and could travel life's path together with nothing to separate us.

After filling out several forms providing my information, including the previous church where I had been a member, Cliff and I thanked him for his time, shook hands and exited from the conference area. Outside I was very surprised to find many members of the classes we had attended there to congratulate me on my decision and offer their support in any way that I might need. Tears flowed liberally down my cheeks at the outpouring of support that the church was offering me.

I knew that this was the right decision and was glad that I now had many new friends as well as Cliff's family members to call on to support me in my marriage and life. My life now felt complete. I had been so alone for so many years; counting Larry, Charlotte, and Marianne among my only close friends. As we left the church, I knew that the promise of hope and future were now mine to claim. Just as the lesson of Jeremiah had promised me that first Sunday.

After the service, Cliff decided to have lunch at Fish King Restaurant where he and I shared a seafood platter for two in a private room off of the main dining area.

The platter consisted of fried catfish, oysters, shrimp, stuff crab, hush puppies on a bed of French fries, with plenty of red cocktail and a creamy tartar sauce and was far too much food for one.

Cliff spoke our Grace:

> *Dear Lord Jesus, thank you for this food, bless it to serve as nourishment for our bodies. Thank you for the wonderful woman that you have brought into my life. Keep and protect her from harm. Help affirm her decision to follow you today, may it strengthen our marriage and life together. We praise and worship your holy name. Amen.*

"Amen," I added, overjoyed that I could share my life with such a tender, loving man.

"Christina, you have no idea how much your decision today means to me. I had prayed that our attending church last Sunday would be the beginning or your pathway back. I know that you have had a rough life and had fallen away.

"But today was a big step for you, and I will be glad to help you in any way that I can. Perhaps we can start a home Bible study to go through the books of the Bible, and I can help with any questions that you might have."

The room that we were in was private, the external door closed. We could see the other patrons at their tables, but they would be unable to hear our discussion.

"Yes. Cliff that would be a great way for us to spend some quality time together doing something other than what we have spent most of our time on lately. Now, this may not be the time and place for this discussion, but I desperately need to understand a bit better your position, more specifically the church's position on sex. We have been doing a lot of different things since our first night, and I am pretty new to this, as you know. I don't want to be doing anything that would be contrary to the church's rules."

"I don't know that I am a true expert on this," Cliff responded. "nor can I speak for the church, but my understanding is that the church affirms God's plan for marriage and sexual intimacy – one man, and one woman, within the bond of marriage for life. Pre-marital sex is not a valid alternative lifestyle." The Bible condemns it as sin. It is not, however, an unforgivable sin. The same redemption is available to all sinners.

"Concerning human sexuality," he continued "the church has held to what can be referred to as traditional and conservative views. Thus, with other Christian traditions, our church believes that intimate sexual relations are a gift from God to be enjoyed between a man and a woman in the context of the covenant of marriage."

Delving deeper into his understanding, Cliff offered me his thoughts.

"I am not clear about our first relations myself, and the Bible is rather ambiguous on the subject. Consider King David, who is referred to as a man after God's heart. He seduced another man's wife, and then had her husband killed in battle to satisfy his sexual lust for the man's wife. He then married Bathsheba and had children, who are listed in the lineage of Christ. There are others who are prostitutes and thieves in that lineage on both Mary and Joseph sides.

To be clear, I need to add that Joseph was not the father of Christ. He, having been born of the Virgin Mary and God's gift. It is noted in the Bible that Joseph accepted this fact and abstained from intimate relations with Mary until after Christ's birth. Joseph is recorded in the Bible as being a Righteous Man, meaning he was without sin. So the lineage of David to Christ on Joseph's side was broken by that fact of King David's sin.

So to say a particular thing is a sin and unforgivable can be disputed by searching the Old Testament and finding other examples of men and women who committed acts that might be considered sinful by some, but are not regarded by religions of all faiths, as irredeemable in the Bible. Think of Samson and Delilah.

"There are also many contradictions and strange beliefs fostered by ignorance. Abraham, considered the father of several religions, including the Muslims and Jews is another example. Isaac was the child of Abraham and his wife, Sarah. But Sarah was also his half-sister since they shared the same father. How is one to resolve a question like that in modern terms? A brother and sister married and having children? Scandalous in many peoples' minds. And to add more confusion Isaac, their son, married his first cousin Rebekah, granddaughter of his father's brother."

"Christina, we are married now. Whatever we do together sexually within the confines of marriage is considered sacred and not condemned by the church. I don't know if I have answered your question, and we would need to speak with one of the church pastors to delve further into the subject. Personally, I don't believe there is any exact answer to some of these questions. I have searched and found there is nothing in the Bible that says sex in only to be allowed in this manner between these two categories of people. Very often the messages are confusing and conflicting."

"I am perfectly happy and satisfied with your answer, Cliff," I touched his arm in reassurance. I just did not want us to go down roads that might cause friction between us in later life. I enjoy everything that we do together and consider it a part of the bond of matrimony. I was only afraid that you might look back on it at some future point and feel regret. I, myself, will not. I gave myself totally to you because I love you. I have no barriers or hesitation in making love to you in any way that makes both of us happy."

By the end of our meal, the sun was out; the temperature had cooled down to a pleasant seventy-five-degrees. It was a pleasant day in early autumn.

"Christina, I have an idea. Would you like to go for a drive?" he offered.

"Oh, do you have someplace special in mind?" *I knew the answer Cliff would respond with before the question was even asked. I was learning to recognize when Cliff had a surprise in store for me, and my heartbeat quickened at the thought.*

"Yes, come to think of it. Let's head over to Katy. There is a grand opening today, and I think that I would like to take you."

"Oh, and where's that, sweetheart?" I teased.

"Mmmmmmm." He mumbled.

"Where?" I persisted.

"Mmmmmmmmmmm" he repeated.

"Darn it. Don't tell me this is another of those Clifford Stinson specials."

"Yep," he grinned.

"Grrrrrrrrrrr. You are going to drive me crazy with those things. But that is just another reason that I love you so much. All right Mr. Stinson. Let's see what that devious mind of yours has planned for me today."

Cliff's Ford F-350 ate the miles up smoothly as we headed down the Katy Freeway out to Barker. Cliff turned off on South Mason and soon we were pulling up in front of the Packard Shopping Center. I gave a quizzical look at Cliff as we pulled into a parking spot.

"Honey, Charlotte was telling me the other day that you have missed several of your target practice sessions over the last few weeks, and I don't want you losing your edge. There was an ad on TV last evening, and I've asked Charlotte to wait inside for us. I am a little rusty since I have not done any target shooting in several years.

Charlotte brought your weapon along. She retrieved it the other day when HPD called and said it had been released and was no longer needed for the case against the man who was killed and the other who has now been sent back to prison. I understand that the shooting range has several firearms for sale inside today. They also advertised some vintage and historical weapons that I could look over. I might find myself in a situation where a gun might come in handy; I thought that we could all enjoy a little change of pace."

"Cliff, you sure know how to 'target' a girl's heart," I joked.

""Christina, I only 'aim' to please," he smirked. "Let's go on in and loosen up that trigger finger of yours. I seem to recall you are pretty good at this stuff, and I will never know when I might need to call on your skills again."

"I am at your service, kind sir, whenever you need a bodyguard, I will be there. As you know, I have developed quite an attachment to your body, and would be quite upset if something were to happen to it."

As we entered the building where the shooting range was located, we had to check in and show our Texas driver license. Charlotte was waiting for us on a bench in the corner. She smiled happily as she jumped up and came over. She handed me my .38 Special which she had picked up from the property room at the police station after it had been released. We registered for an hour's use of two of the ranges. Cliff and I would share one and Charlotte would have another rnearby. Before entering, we were provided eyewear to protect our eyes and noise reduction earphones. There was an array of guns available for purchase as well as ammunition and other things, such as tee shirts, caps, and holsters.

Cliff wandered around the displays of pistols, automatics, and rifles and finally settled on a .357 Magnum pistol. It was a beautiful weapon with simulated wood grip. Also, he purchased enough practice ammunition for all three of us to use for the afternoon. Upon entering the range area, we donned our glasses and ear protection. All of us then had a fun time, firing away at the paper targets. I, on the other hand, paused, and a tear slipped down my cheek. A memory of a not-so-distant time when I had fired this gun in fear and anger had crept into my thoughts.

Cliff noticed and asked, "What's wrong, Christina?"

"Cliff, I'm sorry," I replied. "It's just that every once in a while as I fire at the paper target the image of the dead man hanging out of that car seat comes into my mind. I pray that I will never have to fire my weapon again in anger. I know now that he was one of the boys who raped me, but still…." my voice trailed off.

"Christina. Had you not fired when you did, neither one of us would probably be alive today. I've never crashed into a car deliberately before, either. But if that situation were to happen again, I can tell you truthfully; I would not hesitate at all like I did that night. You were correct to ask me to do that, and I should have understood the gravity of the situation without you needing to explain it to me.

"I am so proud of you and your ability to remain calm and deliberate and take things under control. You are probably just as good at doing those things as I am sure that you are in your job. You are a natural leader and others will always look to you for guidance. Never doubt yourself. Be strong in the face of adversity as I know that you are now, and will always be in the future."

"Thank you, Cliff. I love you. Now, where's that next target? I think my trigger finger is getting itchy again." I chuckled. I felt encouraged and strengthened in my resolve. No matter what happens in the future, I would face it with strength and dignity.

The next target was posted on my range, and I put my ear buds back on and fired away happily. I even tried Charlotte's trick of creating a smiley face and to my amazement, it worked.

Even so, when we were finished, Charlotte was still the best shot, hitting nearly all bulls-eyes. I had an okay day, with over 89 percent bulls-eyes, and Cliff surprised me by hitting several bulls-eyes and most of his other shots hitting close to the center ring. On our way out, Cliff purchased ten boxes each of critical defense hollow point ammunition handing Charlotte her share.

I had to admit that after the shooting practice I felt safer. I had my favorite weapon back. Payne was armed and dangerous, and each of us needed to be able to defend ourselves should the occasion arise. Both Charlotte and I already possessed concealed carry permits, but Cliff did not. He filled out the forms to submit to the DPS and signed up for class with a CHL instructor.

After spending an hour or so shooting we had worked up an appetite, so we three decided to stop by the County BBQ restaurant where the choices were mouth watering.

"Cliff, with all of this fancy eating, I am going to have to add some extra time in the fitness center. You don't want a fat old lady for a wife, do you?"

"You're right about that unless that fat old lady is you. I'll keep you no matter what shape you have. And I've noticed that my tummy is gaining a little paunch. But the pleasure of the meal will be worth the pain in the gym. In fact, why don't you and I sign up for membership in one of the nearby fitness centers when we settle on a place to live? We can work out together."

Afterward, Charlotte and I stopped by the local Target to pick up some 'normal' female underwear. I found a selection of lingerie that was fairly modest and proper underwear for my baptism the following Sunday. I certainly didn't want my outer dress to be soaked in water and give a stripper performance for the church audience! I found a nice day dress, that was modest, and opaque enough to hide what I had on underneath, even when wet.

I had agreed to meet with Cliff at the Saab dealership afterward to select a new car, my old one having been totaled. We browsed the lot, and I eventually fell in love with the Saab Aero. It featured high performance and the ability to outpace most other cars on the road. Cliff had it modified for bullet proof glass all around and bulletproof shielding on the driver and passenger door walls. That upgrade would cause the delay of delivery for about five days.

Later that afternoon I telephoned Larry.

"Larry, it's Tina. I have discussed my decision with Cliff. I have also done a lot of soul searching and have come to a firm decision. If the company will have me back, I would love to come. For the past seventeen years, this man has ruled every part of my life. I no longer want that. I am giving his fate over to the Lord. The HPD should be able to capture him. My future does not depend on Payne or his evil plans. I want to live free. I want to move on with my life and job and plan an exciting future for Cliff and myself."

Larry's voice has an excited tone in it as he replied,

"I'm so excited. I've worked with you for a long time now, and you are a valuable asset to Tilden Industries. We would hate to lose you, and I was prepared to do just about anything to get you to come back. We have a surprise for you when you come in tomorrow, so I will be expecting you bright and early and eager to get to work. You will have some new responsibilities and duties. I cannot tell you more than that on this call. But be prepared for anything."

"Awggg," you and Cliff and your surprises. "It seems a girl cannot get a break around you two. Okay then, nine a.m. it is. Someday I am going to have an opportunity to pay you guys back big time. So you'd better watch your back," I teased.

CHAPTER 40

Cliff drove me into work the next morning because my new car would not be ready until the end of the week at the earliest. He pulled his truck into the valet lane outside the building and stopped.

"Now you go on in there and do your best. I know that Larry's missed you handling everything for him, and probably has a ton of paperwork for you to go over." He smiled mischievously.

I began to suspect that he knew more than he was willing to tell me about Larry's surprise. Memories of some of the questions and things Cliff had said over the past weeks came back to my mind.

"What have these two guys got in mind for me?" I gave him a look that told him that I was on to him. "Cliff, now if you know all about this and aren't telling me, I am going to be very upset. You know how I hate surprises."

"Who, me? Why -- sweetheart, whatever would give you that idea?" His snicker told me otherwise.

"**Grr**!" I growled. "You are going to get it, buster. You'd better hope this is a nice surprise, you two guys are up to something, I just know it." I tried to make a really serious face but failed, because I knew that if Cliff was in on it, it would be wonderful.

"Just kiss me and go on inside, sweetheart. You don't want to be late for your surprise." He leaned over and kissed me good-bye. "I will pick you up around five p.m. honey. Now you behave today."

I stuck my tongue out at him and jumped down, waved and turned to enter the building. I displayed my badge and passed through the new metal detectors and increased security, which included a bomb-sniffing dog from HPD bomb squad. I noticed detective Connor standing by the elevator. I gave her a wave as I passed by and she nodded her head in acknowledgment.

I entered the elevator and pressed the button for floor three as several other employees' crowded in after me, pressing buttons for various floors. When the last person had entered, and the elevator doors closed, I say hello to several of my co-workers. The elevator climbed to floor three, and the doors opened. Outside I found a large group of faces, some that I didn't recognize. Larry was standing in front of them with a big smile.

"Welcome back, Tina. I would like you to meet your new staff. The company has selected you to be the Vice President in charge of the new support staff for T & J Industries."

The gathered group broke out in applause. I was totally flabbergasted. Promotion? Vice President? It was one of my most cherished dreams since I'd started working. I could hardly believe it. In the past three months I had gone from single and alone; now married to the man of my dreams; inherited a huge family; gained back a staff that I had thought lost to me forever, and now this -- The job of my dreams and responsibility for so many lives.

Tears welled in my eyes, "Thanks, all of you. I'm going to work doubly hard to ensure that we will be successful."

"Thank you, Larry. I could not have done this without your help." I smiled happily at everyone.

"You need to meet with me in my office," Larry stated. "I have all of the paperwork ready, including your new base salary, performance bonus information, and a roster of your new staff. These employees are all assigned to you, and you need to set up their work assignments and begin to make plans to move all of them, including yourself to Floor eight in Tilden Tower. I will be your mentor in assisting you in your new responsibilities.

"You may check with the Construction Manager as to a move in date," he said with a wink. "I believe that your floor will be the first one in the new tower that will be ready for use since the bomb destroyed and damaged so much of the first three floors. Floor seating charts will be high on your list of assignments. It seems someone has some pull with the construction manager."

I thought '*Ohhh! You are so going to get it tonight, my devious husband, How awesome it is to have two such men in my life.*'

"All right guys," I addressed the group. "Let me meet with Larry for a few minutes. Then I will get back with all of you and begin working on getting things set up for our move. Why don't you wait for me in the conference room, down this hallway on the left? I should be there in about fifteen minutes."

The crowd milled off in the direction of the conference room while Larry took me in tow to his office.

"Larry, what a wonderful surprise, but how, when?"

"It has been in the works for some time now," Larry responded. "You've worked harder on this account than anyone else, including myself. You know more of the details and inner workings of what we plan to do than anyone. So who better than you? When I suggested it to upper management, they jumped at the opportunity, having seen firsthand how involved you were and how meticulous you have been in preparing the details.

"Then, that day at lunch, you blew me away, having only had a few minutes to work out a location for this staff you came up with a near-perfect floor plan. That settled it, and when I spoke with the President, he was highly complimentary, having seen much of the work that you submitted. When I told him how very often you had great insights into things and were a quick problem solver, he immediately agreed that you were our new VP.

"Thank you so much, Larry. I appreciate everything that you have done for me. But evidently my staff is waiting for me in the conference room. I don't want to hold them up for too long."

"Over here is your org chart, which lists people's names and how they rank within the organization. You already know most of their names. Here is a roster of staff, and basic outline of what you need to set up, but otherwise it is a blank form. Also, here is a company credit card for you to use as you need. Everything is yours to run as you see fit. You will make all of the decisions, hiring, firing, who sits where, what jobs are a priority.

"Your new salary will be five-hundred thousand annually, with performance bonuses attached based on goal achievements. You will now be reporting directly to our President, Eric Johnson. After you get your staff set up, please set up a meeting with him and go over your plans. I am here if you need me, but from our past working together, my guess is that you are going to hit the pavement running and never look back. I am going to miss your support here, and I wish you the best in everything. You are by far the best assistant that I've ever had, and I always had a hard time staying ahead of you. You're brilliant, insightful and caring. Everything this staff will need to succeed. Again, I am just a phone call away if you need anything at all."

"Thank you, Larry. I will try not to disappoint you." I gave him a kiss on the cheek, "You are the best. I hate to kiss and run, but it seems I have a whole room full of people waiting on me to tell them what to do."

"You go, girl. Grab that tiger by the tail and run." Larry had a tear in his eye as we hugged good-bye.

As I walked toward the conference room, my emotions were running high. I was a bit frightened that I would fall flat on my face. By the time that I reached the conference room door that feeling was completely gone, I was ready for this. I have the knowledge and skills. Yes, I would succeed. I pushed open the door.

"Good morning, staff. My name is Christina Stinson. As you all know, I have just been appointed to this position. However, I have been working on setting up your jobs, your daily duties, and even created the floor plan for our new location at Tilden Tower. As you already know, we had some trouble there a few weeks ago, the bottom floors were damaged by a car bomb. Building inspectors and safety engineers have been going over the entire area for the past two months. They have given us the go-ahead to begin occupying the building as soon as the floor setups have been completed.

"I will be getting with the construction manager later this afternoon to get an exact move in date. In the meantime, I would like to take a few minutes to meet all of you as a group. Then later over the coming days, I will meet with each of you individually. I would like to meet you personally so that we can all start out on the best foot possible. You will learn what I expect of you, and what support you can expect from Tilden Industries and me."

"Since this is the first time that you have met me, and probably all of these other staff, why don't we take some time to find out who is who and what are their responsibilities. I would like you to begin by giving everyone your name, your job position and tell a little bit about yourself and what you expect to do for Tilden Industries, and what we can do for you.

"That said, who would like to go first?"

"Yes, you in the brown suit on the second row... Your name and position first."

"Hi, my name is ...."

****

The staff not only met me but introduced themselves to each other, learning how they fit together and where to go when they needed something. Once I had identified who my new personal assistant was, Linda Williams, I met with her for a few minutes on the side and gave her some instructions on what I needed for her to do for the group this morning. After that, I let the meeting run on until lunch time. Everyone was excited to begin their new assignments. Several of the new staff give humorous stories of their past jobs at which everyone laughed and began to relax amid each other's company.

I watched as bonds of companionship formed and new friends were made acquainted with each other. At 11:30, after the last employee has introduced themselves and various ones had asked questions of me, and what I expected of them, I requested everyone's attention,

"Attention, please! I have a special announcement; it's lunch time. I have asked Linda to arrange a special lunch for us all. If you don't mind, we are all going to take a small trip over to the Houston Ship Channel and meet at a restaurant named *Brady's Landing* where Tilden Industries will treat you to a special welcome aboard lunch.

"You will have the rest of the day off after that while I set up your instructions for tomorrow. So -- welcome to Tilden Industries. I will meet with you at the restaurant, and then you should make plans to be here on time at nine tomorrow morning. Be ready to dig in and make this division the best in the company. Remember, lunch is on Tilden.

"Linda, my new assistant, has a handout for each of you with a map and instructions for how to get to *Brady's Landing*."

As everyone was leaving, I rang Cliff's cell phone.

"Hi, Cliff, I need a favor. It seems that I have been appointed a VP here and now have my own staff."

"No way! When did that happen?" He pretended to be surprised -- unsuccessfully.

"All right, Mr. Construction Manager. It is my understanding that you have been in on this from the get-go. We will discuss that later tonight. In the meantime, I am going to need a ride over to Brady's Landing. Do you have anyone free that you could send to pick me up?"

"Why it just so happens, I do. I believe that he's waiting downstairs now. You will find him in the valet lane. Just look for a Ford 350 pickup. I believe that it is silver in color. I am told that there is a rather good looking man, who you might have met before, waiting for you. Now, remember, no hanky-panky with the driver. He has very strict instructions that it is just a ride to lunch, or so I understand."

"I love you, you big galoot. See you in a few minutes."

Cliff and I had an uneventful ride over to *Brady's Landing* where the restaurant had cordoned off a large section of tables, and my new staff has started to filter inside. After everyone was there, I stood and called for their attention.

"You may order whatever they wish from the house menu. Or, if you choose, there is a wonderful buffet line available with lots of wonderful selections. There is no limit on how much you can spend. Just have a good time and get to know your new fellow employees."

Cliff looked at me, surprised by my generosity.

"I want to have a happy team," I said. "I don't want them to feel limited in any way. Starting off this way, I believe, will inspire them to reach for the stars in their work. If they know the company would go all out for them, I am certain they would go the extra mile for Tilden in return. Besides, I'm going to be working them very hard in the future; this should start us off on the right foot."

Cliff smiled at me and patted my thigh under the table.

"Now that's the woman I saw in the truck that morning. Bright, ambitious and caring. Everything I could wish for in a wife. I'm very glad that I found her before some other guy did."

Cliff and I sat near the center of the tables, so that if any of the staff wished to speak to me I was accessible. I wanted them to feel relaxed and friendly with each other and myself. As many of them passed by, they shook my hand and told me how happy they were to have me as their new director.

Also, some expressed an opinion that they enjoyed having the chance to work for a dynamic leader like me. I was hopeful that I would prove to be one of those, but only time would tell. I smiled and shook hands with each one, proud that I would have a chance to prove myself in such an important position. This was a tough business, and there was a lot of competition. It was going to take some shrewd planning and a lot of hard work.

Cliff and I chatted among ourselves, as I looked out over my team. My heart swelled with pride, as I observed so many young people, eager to prove themselves and to be part of a winning team. I began to put names to faces and tried to remember where everyone fit on the org chart. Some, I knew from the start, would not be successful. Perhaps some of those that I might have gotten a wrong impression of during their introductory spiel might turn out to be my brightest stars. I am anxious to begin working with them.

"Cliff, now about our new offices on floor eight. Larry said that you would have an estimated move-in date for my team."

"It just so happens that I have your updated floor layout in my pocket," he said as he reached into his pocket and pulled out the floor plan. If you will notice this office already has a name on it. Oh, I see now, that is your name. Imagine that! I wonder who told the draftsman?"

"Silly, get serious now, I am so excited, and you are just teasing" I pouted.

"Not at all. Christina. Every slot on here has space for you to enter a name. I believe that you designed this floor plan yourself and the company has left it blank for you to fill in however you wish. Also, as you may remember, floor fourteen is also designated for the T & J Industries contract. Your permanent office is located there, but it has not been framed in as of yet. Your team for that floor, as I understand it, has yet to be hired. It will be your responsibility to fill in the blanks on that floor layout as well since you will be over the entire division.

"I concentrated all of my workers to complete floor eight first so that you would have somewhere to begin. I reviewed the status of the floor this morning before I came to get you. I would like to report that the area is completely ready for you to move in as early as the day after tomorrow. There is some paint in the area that needs to dry completely before people show up in business suits and dresses. All of the cubicles, desks and chairs are ready. Telephone connections are done, as well as lighting and shelving have now been completed.

"A parking area has also been cleared for your staff, in the underground parking area. I have directions to the tower and parking instructions being prepared as we speak. They will be delivered to your office the first thing in the morning. Now that this floor has been completed, I have sent my workers up to floor fourteen, and when they have completed your official office there, I will let you know. As soon as it is ready, I have staff who will assist you with your relocation."

"It sure is nice to have an inside connection to the Construction Manager," I tapped him on his shoulder lovingly. "It seems to be very helpful indeed." I fluttered my eyelashes at him. "And we are going to go over some of this tonight, Mr. Smarty Pants. Exactly how long have you known about this?"

"Larry told me to have things ready for you even before we had met. He had always wanted it to be a surprise, and I was anxious to see if you had any special thoughts for the area. When Larry invited you to go to lunch with us, I had no idea what was going to happen. I had thought that I was going to meet this stuffy office lady, full of herself and pushing for a big promotion. Then, that moment when I saw you in the truck with Larry, my entire world came into focus. As time went by and we became involved with each other, I almost let it slip a few times. I could tell that you were suspicious every time the subject of you going back to work came up. I had a hard time in not saying anything to you.

"You are usually pretty good at figuring things out for yourself. I had to do all of the contacts when you were either asleep or by e-mail. It got very frustrating at times because, you know, we were doing a lot of other things during that same time if you remember. I would have to wait until you drifted off to sleep and then work quietly in order not to wake you."

"I'm going to forgive you, this time, Cliff. Gosh, probably all the other times too. I don't know what I ever did to deserve such a loving husband. How about a kiss?"

"None of that now. It is my understanding that the construction manager has a crush on the new vice president. I don't wish to get him in trouble with upper management with a public display of affection," Cliff winked at me.

"You are so cute; you know what? I am going to do something that I desperately wanted to do the very first time that I came to this restaurant with you."

"What's that, sweetheart?" Cliff flashed his trademark smile.

I rose from my seat and walked around the table and gave him a movie star kiss, placing my arm behind his neck and leaning him back in his chair as my tongue searched his mouth. His cheeks turned red as everyone cheered and banged their silverware on their tables like a drum roll.

"There, that's payback for the way you drove me wild my first lunch date with you, Mr. Stinson."

"Can I have seconds?" he begged

"You are going to get lots of seconds tonight, Mr. Stinson, but for right now I need to speak with my employees."

Turning to the audience, I cried, "Ladies and Gentlemen, I would like you all to meet my husband, Mr. Clifford Stinson. He is the construction manager for Tilden Tower, and he has just informed me that, as of the day after tomorrow, you are scheduled to move in as the first occupants of the tower. I will have a seating plan ready for you before you leave work tomorrow with directions to the tower as well as information about the underground parking which has been assigned.

"Now as I mentioned before, there was an incident there about two months ago and as a result, HPD will have extra security in place. Please expect delays as there will be checkpoints for explosives, with dogs and armed police. There is no reason for any of you to be alarmed. These will be normal procedures to make sure that everyone is safe, works in a safe environment and goes home to their loved ones safely at the end of the day."

Everyone applauded again, and all seemed eager for the move and being the first occupants. Cliff looked at me from his seat as if he were seeing someone new in the dress that his wife had worn to the office this morning. I felt different. I felt alive and happy. I was in love with the most wonderful man in the world. I had a new job that would utilize all of the skills and training that I had worked so hard to attain. Life truly was full of hope and the future.

******

Five blocks away in a seedy motel on the ship channel, James Payne turned over in his bed.

"Shit. My arm still burns from the bullet where that bitch shot me. I had no idea she had a weapon and could shoot so well. And what's more, this whole town has been on lockdown as far as doctors. I can't find a doctor anywhere who will treat me on the sly. Joe is dead and Bill is in jail. No matter, I'm going to get that bitch yet. I'm going to have sex with her for old times' sake, and then dump her body in the Buffalo Bayou.

"Now let me look at that map again. Her office is here. Hmmm. I wonder if she ever gets dropped off in front. I think there's a bench there. Yeah! I'd bet anything that sometimes she sits right there waiting for her husband to drive over from the tower.

"But I'd need some disguise to wear that wouldn't scare her. Every cop in town must have my photo by now. What could I wear that would be a good disguise? Oh, yeah! That's it. I know exactly what I need." he marked several large Xs on the map. "Yep, that's going to be the spot."

"Shit! No sex, but at least she will finally be out of my life. The time, the place, the actions to take. Everything was coming together just like I wanted. Now I just had to find the right opportunity. That bitch is going to pay really for my seventeen years in prison. Now, what did I do with that bottle of alcohol? Oh yeah, there it is under the bed."

"Ow! That crap stings, but it's all that I can find to pour on this wound. Damn that bitch."

CHAPTER 41

Tuesday was a very hectic day as I reviewed the various staff members' qualifications and assigned them to their new positions. I selected the two most senior staff to be managers. However, there was only going to be one office for them until my office on floor fourteen was ready. After studying the plans, I had made a decision that the new directors office would be on floor fourteen, little realizing, but secretly hoping, that person was to be myself. Since that area was not yet ready, the new managers would have to share. I called them into my office, which until tomorrow was still my old area across from Larry until tomorrow.

The two employees, Helen Martinez, and Dennis Black arrived, and I went over some of my thoughts with them for the next few days. The new staff would be reporting to them, rather than directly to me. I explained the need for them to share an office until mine was ready, which I had been told would be less than two weeks. I went over the divided duties with them and provided them listings of which staff would fit well into their separate groups.

Once that was settled, I provided each with a copy of the seating chart and explained that they needed to determine where each of their employees would be seated. That was an important part of my plans for the most efficient functioning of our operations. That done, I gave them three hours to have their layouts ready and to report back to me so that copies could be made for distribution.

Then I sat back in my chair and relaxed for a time. This was going to be exciting. My new managers would execute the overall plans, and I would get to direct them in what goals I wanted the groups to achieve. This would allow me to function freely, without having to work with fifty or eventually one hundred different employees.

I realized that as soon as Cliff had floor fourteen completed, I would need to go through some of this same process. There would be one more manager to hire and another fifty staff members. Many of those would be support staff to the ones already working directly with T & J personnel. Perhaps one of the new employees already on board might be that manager. I would need to review their resumes, and if unsuccessful in identifying a talent within, I would need to notify HR to begin a search for qualified candidates.

This management stuff was not going to be as easy, and I had believed. I was going to have to work as hard as my new staff to make sure that my goals were being achieved on time without seeming to become a slave driver. Hmmm. I think that I might call Larry from time to time after all. He always got things done and treated everyone fairly. He had made it all look so easy. I'm going to have to pick his brain for some of his secrets.

I called my new assistant, Linda, to go over her responsibilities and what I expected of her in the future.

"Linda, you are not going to be a slave for my every whim; hired to fetch me coffee. I want to encourage and train you so that you, too, can advance within the company. I expect you to take responsibility for making sure my day calendar is up to date with appointments."

"Yes, ma'am," she replied with a look of surprise.

"Also, I need to meet with the president next week. I will need you to check with his assistant to block out a three-hour period with him to go over my plans for the division. I expect you to attend, take notes and offer any ideas that you might have. You will be my right hand. I want you to be able to answer questions in my place in case of my absence. Familiar with all that I do, my alternate ego."

"Mrs. Stinson," Linda replied, astonished. "When they hired me for this slot I thought that I would be locked into a dead-end job with no future. I worked hard in college and majored in business administration. You are doing me an honor that I am humbled to accept. I will work doubly hard for you to make sure that our division is the best in the company's eyes. I would like to accept the challenge that you are giving me and hope that I never fail you. Thank you for your faith in me."

"It is not going to be easy, Linda. There will be many hurdles ahead. Right now, I have a doctor's appointment this afternoon that I simply cannot miss. I had made it before I was aware of all of these changes and my promotion. I am going to meet with Helen and Dennis at 1:00 p.m. and then I will be out for the afternoon. They will have some floor seating charts that will need to be photocopied and distributed to staff, so they have directions for tomorrow.

"You will need to make name labels for all of the new cubicles and be at the new tower early tomorrow morning to get them placed. That should help the staff find their desks faster. If you need help with that, check with Helen and Dennis, they will provide you whatever support you require. You will need to field my calls while I am away. Here is my cell number should any real emergency arise and I need to be involved."

I left the office at 1:30 p.m. after meeting with Dennis and Helen and approving their seating arrangements. Linda offered to make the copies and Dennis, and Helen designated two of their staff to assist and get them distributed and help post name signs for the morning. I took a taxi over to Doctor Nguyen's office because that would save time by not having to search for parking. I had been to see her in the past few years, but always for routine checkups. This was special, and I was hopeful there might be good news. It could never be said that we failed for lack of trying. Even so, when she came back into her office with a sly smile on her lips I knew that something was up, but I was not as well prepared for the news as I expected.

"Triplets? Did you say Triplets? As in three?" I cried.

"Yes, Mrs. Stinson. There is no mistake. You will have three babies."

"But Doctor, no one in my family, or Cliff's family, to my knowledge, has triplets in their history that I'm aware. How is that even possible?"

The good doctor explained the birds and the bees to me.

I smirked. Even the medical profession seems to have its humorous side now.

'Oh, no! What is Cliff going to say? How will I ever explain this to him?' We agreed that we wanted children, but I thought we were thinking to start with one, and then, if that worked out well, then maybe a second. But three in one bundle, holy cow!

'Then I remembered the houses that we looked all had only five bedrooms. 'Looks like we are going to need a major upgrade. What if we have more children? What if I have another set of triplets? Good Grief! We may need to have a barn or something to keep all of them inside. I chuckled.

'A nice pretty red barn like Dad used to have in Washington,' I laughed at my thought, *'you don't keep kids in a barn. Perhaps something as large a barn. What if we continue to have children in future, and I have twins, more triplets?'* My mind was going crazy with possibilities.

'All right, calm down, Tina. Other women have had triplets before. It is not like I am the first one is history. I will need to do some research. Do women keep having more children or close off that option? I am going to need to check with Cliff on this. It is too important a decision to make by myself. He does not even know about this set, so I shouldn't start worrying about having many more, at least not yet.'

'Let's take this one thing at a time, correction, three at a time. I guess that I am going to have to start thinking of things in a three at a time mode. Let's see, three baby carriages, three baby beds, three mountains of diapers. -- I am going to need to hire someone to help me with this,' I realized.

I decided to meet with Cliff back at the office so that it will seem like a normal day. The cab driver dropped me off in front of the building, and I wandered over to the bench outside to wait for Cliff to arrive from a meeting he had with Tilden management at the tower.

After a few minutes, I looked around and noticed a policeman standing on the corner, not far away. He looked rather unkempt, and his right arm was in what looked like a homemade sling. His cap was pulled down, hiding most of his face from me.

'That's very odd. I cannot ever remember seeing a police officer on duty with his arm in a sling. I thought HPD had plenty of sick leave available for injured officers.'

As he began to walk in my direction and I became very uneasy. There was something that was not right here. Just then one of the security guards from inside the building strolled out and asked me if everything was okay. I motioned for him to come closer. He walked over to my bench. The police officer who had been approaching suddenly turned and walked to the other side of the street.

"Is there a problem, Mrs. Stinson?" The security guard inquired.

"How did you know my name?" I inquired.

"I'm one of the extra security your husband hired to protect you. All of the guards have been alerted to who you are ma'am. Since you seem to be the target of this criminal. We have been given your photo and instructions to take extra care that no one approaches you that might endanger you. We also have James Payne's photo and are on the lookout for him as well."

"Oh, good. I feel much safer then. By the way, did you see that officer who was standing down there at the end of the block?"

"Police officer? No ma'am. I don't think that I noticed him, at any rate, he seems to have moved on. There is no one there now."

"Thank you for your concern, I feel better now. May I ask you to stay here with me for a little while, at least until my husband arrives?" I asked hopefully.

"That wouldn't be a problem, Mrs. Stinson. We are here to protect you. I'm glad to be of help at any time."

Cliff pulled up in the valet lane just then, so I thanked the officer again, waved at Cliff and rose from the bench to begin walking toward the truck. Suddenly a shot rang out and dust flew up from where I had been sitting only a split-second before. The guard dropped to his knee, grabbed his gun and began searching for the shooter. I dropped flat to the ground and struggled to get my weapon from my purse. My eyes began searching every corner for a muzzle flash. Other guards begin to rush from the building, their weapons drawn. It was mass confusion as Cliff jumped from the truck and rushed toward me.

Then I saw a muzzle flash from the corner of the building across from me; a bullet struck the dirt right beside me. That was answered by two shots from my area. One from the guard, and then I looked over my shoulder and saw Charlotte, who had been hiding out of my sight behind me. All of the guards then begin running toward the garage where the shots had been fired from. Cliff finally made it to my position and lay down on top of me, protecting me from any further injury. The guards called out to each other in their effort to locate the shooter. Charlotte ran over to me to make sure that I was uninjured.

"Tina. Are you okay?" she asked, concern heavy in her voice.

"Yes, he missed me by only an inch or two," I replied. "I must have moved just as he fired. Did you see anyone?"

"I saw that policeman earlier walking in that direction," Charlotte responded. "I thought it strange that he had one arm in a sling, so I tried to keep track of him until he disappeared into that parking garage over there."

"Yes," I answered. "He was standing down there when I first noticed him. His uniform looked rather unkempt and that arm sling. I felt very strange when he started to approach me. But then the security guard came out, and he must have changed directions then. I did not see where he went."

Just about this time, several of the security guards came out of the entrance to the garage and shouted that the area was vacant, but there was a small streak of blood by the entrance. They were unable to find anyone, but would continue the search. At the same time, two police cars pulled up, and four officers jumped out with guns drawn. They spoke with the guards for a few minutes and then appeared to radio in messages to other police that were in the area. One of the officers came over towards me, so Cliff rolled over and helped me to stand.

"Mrs. Stinson. Just to let you know, we just found one of our officers murdered not far from here; his body stripped of his uniform. It is very probable that it was this guy James Payne who did that. Evidently he then stole the officers' uniform, and he was lying in wait for you here. Detective Connor is on her way over now. She will have a few questions for you, and then I think that for your safety, we will have these two patrol cars escort you to wherever you had planned to go next."

"Thank you, Officer. We very much appreciate your assistance. This man Payne is deranged. He seems to stop at nothing in his efforts to harm my wife." Cliff responded. "I think that we need to move from this area as quickly as possible after speaking with the detective."

Detective Connor rolled up at this moment and came over to speak with the officer first, then approached Cliff and me. "Mrs. Stinson, Mr. Stinson."

"Good afternoon, detective," I responded.

"This guy is certainly good at giving us the slip. The two bombings, the attack on you in the car, the murder of one of our officers and now this. We have increased security details for you and your family. There is a BOLO out for him to the entire department. But now that we are positive that he is somewhere in this area we will increase our patrols. Maybe we will get lucky. But he may have fled the area entirely now. After he had killed the officer, he stole his patrol car. That makes him a bit more visible to us, but he will probably abandon that, knowing that we are certainly going to be searching for it. We have the car ID on police alert and should find it very soon. Our guess is that he will abandon it in a shopping center and then steal another car from there."

Charlotte joined us now, having given her statement to the other officers and provided her information if they needed to follow up with her.

"I only caught a glimpse of his face, but I am positive that it was Payne," Charlotte began. "His injured arm may have saved you. I think that the other day when you were shooting into the car at the end of the chase, you probably winged him in his right arm. That may have been his shooting arm, and he does not seem to be quite as good shot with his left. I think that I may have struck him as well. It was hard to tell because he was hiding beside the garage entrance and I did not have that good of a shot. But I think that I saw him stumble away."

"Thank God for small miracles," I replied. This brought back to mind that I desperately needed some time alone with my husband to reveal my news.

"Detective Connor, will you need anything further from my husband or me?

"Not at this time. I have assigned these two patrol cars to follow you for the rest of the evening until you return home, and your apartment building will be under constant surveillance until this man is captured or killed."

"Thank you, Detective."

"Cliff, I need to speak with you somewhere quiet, where we will not be disturbed."

"All right, let's see, Oh, I have an idea. Climb in and I will take you to a place that I know Payne certainly will not be able to follow us."

We both climbed into the truck, and Cliff started the engine and pulled away. The two patrol cars fell in behind us. We circled for a few blocks and then Cliff turned up San Felipe and headed toward the medical center. Before reaching all of the hospital complexes he turned off on Montrose and circled down into Hermann Park.

It was fairly busy this time of day with people going in and out of the Hermann Park Zoo. There were thousands of cars, with people walking this way and that. We turned into one of the larger lots and circled for a moment until Cliff located a space large enough for the truck. He then pulled in and turned off the engine. The patrol cars circled the lot while we sat and talked.

"Cliff, that was a very brave thing that you did back there, placing your body over mine. I know that you mean well, but I would be devastated if something were to happen to you. Please don't do that again."

Cliff looked at me for a moment thoughtfully. "Christina that is a request that I would never be able to honor. Your life means more to me than anything. I would suffer anything than to see you injured in any way.

Truly, I don't think that I could go on if something were to happen to you. I have told you before; I would give my life in place of yours at any time. Please don't ask me that again. You have given up everything in your life for me. You surrendered everything to show me how very much that you love me. How could I do any less for you?"

"Thank you, Cliff" I realized there was no point in arguing any further on that subject. "Now, on to a different subject. You know those houses that we looked at the other day?"

"Yes, have you decided which one that you would like?"

"Not exactly."

"Oh? What then?"

"I don't exactly know how to say this. But all of them had only five bedrooms."

"Yes?"

"What if we were to need more than that?"

"I don't understand."

"What if we were to have a need to have rooms for say 'four more'?"

"Four? Why so many, are there people who might be coming to stay with us?"

"For one, let's say we would need a nanny."

"A nanny? Whatever for? Why would we need a nanny?"

"Umm, I was beginning to wonder if all guys met news like this with such lack of understanding. It must be something in the male makeup.'

"Let's say we were to have a nanny and three little ones."

"Little ones? You mean puppies or kittens?"

"No, silly. Three little people?"

"Little people? What little people?" Cliff was finally beginning to get the drift and looked at me askance.

"Let's say these little people showed up at the hospital one day. Do you think that you could take them in and love them, as you do me?"

"Christina! You are not saying what I think you are saying, are you?"

"Yes, Cliff. There are three little people who will be coming to live with us in a few months, and they are going to need a lot of attention and love."

"Christina, you're pregnant? And triplets? Wow! Get over here and let me kiss you now. Three little ones, three little people. How? When? Oh, I love you so much. I am going to be a father! Wow!"

"As to the how the Doctor explained it this way," I relayed the doctor's story about the birds and the bees, which had Cliff nearly rolling on the floor of the truck laughing."

"No way. The doctor did not say that, did she?" Cliff's expression was priceless.

"Yep. I asked her the same question that you just asked and got the same lecture. She is a young Vietnamese lady, and when I asked her that same question, I think that she may have misunderstood, her English has never been that great. She took my question literally. Then thinking that I did not understand the basics of sex she gave me the full spiel, she even had illustrations. I was very embarrassed by the time she was finished. You know how some of these foreigners can be. Often they take the literal meaning of our words rather than the figurative.

I thought that Cliff was going to have a stroke from laughing so hard.

"So, Mr. Construction Manager, I thought that we could build a barn out back and house a dozen or so of these little people. What do you say?"

Cliff started to tickle me.

"Stop tickling me, Cliff; you know that I get upset when you do that. Fine, all right, I give up, we will just have to buy a bigger house. Does that make you happy?"

"Everything you do makes me happy," he laughed. "You know that already. I believe this calls for a celebration."

"Cliff, I received a strict set of instructions on what I have to eat and drink while the three little ones are percolating inside me, and liquor is not on the menu."

"All right then. How about a Diet Coke? Surely the new additions might enjoy one of those."

"Let's head on home. I am a bit tired after such an eventful day. Promotion, new staff, new office location, triplets, being shot at again. I think that I have had about as much activity as my nerves will take today. I just want to go home, stretch out on the couch with a nice soft pillow and my husband in my arms."

"Normally, your wish would be my command, sweet lady. However, I have a surprise for you tonight."

"Cliff..."

"Shush, pretty lady of mine. I think that you will love this one. Instead of watching old TV reruns tonight I have here a special treat. Something that I think you need to take your mind off of things and relax. I stopped by the Alley Theatre box office and picked up two tickets, front row center for their production of Charles Dickens' *A Christmas Carol*. It starts at 7:30 so we will just have time to get changed and have a bite to eat. It's an excellent production in their newly remodeled theater."

"Cliff!"

"Yes, sweetheart?"

"That sounds like a perfect evening. I haven't been to a play in a long time. And this sounds like the perfect change of pace. It's a great story from old England. I can enjoy the sets, costumes and actors without having to suffer through a thousand commercials. What are you waiting for? I think that I have the perfect dress to wear, and you can wear one of the new suits we picked up in Dallas."

*****

Several miles away James Payne staggered back into his motel room. He was bleeding from a superficial wound in his side.

"Damn that woman. I didn't see that damn bodyguard of hers hiding around the side of the building. Next time I will not miss. I need some more target practice with my left hand. I never was too good of a shot with it, and now it is all that I have left.

"I am going to get that woman no matter what it takes. And little piss ant bodyguard. I don't care how good a shot she is. Next time she will get it as well. The police are going to be too observant around her office building, so I am going to have to find a better location. I wish Bill and Joe were still with me. It is going to take me some time to scout her out again. Damn, my side sure hurts like hell. Let me see if I have got some more alcohol to pour on this wound."

CHAPTER 42

The play had been excellent. Cliff and I had enjoyed the story, even though we had seen and read so many other TV and movie versions before. The ghosts, the frightening scene with the actor playing Death, were very exciting. The little boy playing Tiny Tim stole the show. I was able to take my mind off of the prior days' events for an entertaining two hours.

"Cliff," I asked on the drive back to the apartment. "Do you think we could attend more events like this one? Perhaps even get season tickets?"

"Sure," he smiled. "I truly enjoyed myself tonight. I think that I'd even enjoy some shows over at Jones Hall with the Houston Symphony. I think they are giving a Christmas Concert next week. Would you like to go?"

"As long as it is with you, my dear husband, I will be there with you anytime." I was happy and at peace for at least this evening.

I awoke around two a.m. that night. My mind filled with images of the strange happenings of the prior day. Some were so rewarding, thinking of my promotion and new responsibilities, the play at the Alley Theatre. Others were frightening; of being shot at; of Payne's mysterious escape again. Then the wonderful news of new lives growing in my womb filled my mind with hope.

'I must protect them above all else.'

Turning over to face my husband I watched him resting quietly, lost to the world. His actions in protecting me swelled my love for him even more. This man, this wonderful man who was my husband. I loved him beyond words. How God had blessed me in finding him.

I reached over and stroked the stubble of his beard, loving him in his sleep. My hand slipped down to his chest where my fingers twisted in the thick mat of hair covering his chest. Slowly I tripped my fingers down across his stomach, down his happy trail leading to his manhood. Silently I unbuttoned his PJ bottom and lowered my head to his waist. His erection gradually became swollen in my hand as I gently stroked it, not wanting to awaken him. This was my time, my reward that I wanted to give to him. No other woman had loved him in this way and no other woman besides myself ever would.

I lowered my mouth around the top of his cock and gently licked the bulbous tip. Slowly, gently my mouth sank deeper and deeper down his shaft until my lips touched the surface of his ball sack. I let my saliva soak and wet his organ in a frenzy of love. Sliding my lips up and down, twisting and twirling my tongue around the entire shaft, and gently nibbling with the tips of my teeth.

Cliff stirred in his sleep, and I paused. Soon his breathing relaxed and slowed. I resumed making love to him, gently sucking and licking, teasing the end with the tip of my tongue, tasting the pre-cum which leaked slowly from the opening. My mouth delivered a message of love to his core. I gently increased the strength of my sucking motions, gradually bringing him to ejaculation. He moaned in his sleep, "Ummm," mumbling my name incoherently in his sleep.

"…stina."

I quieted my movements, relaxed my tongue. Gently and slowly letting his now flaccid cock slip from my mouth. Pursing my lips, I kissed the end gently.

"Good night my love."

I stretched my legs and arms, slid up to my pillow and drifted off to sleep.

CHAPTER 43

When my eyes opened again, it was still dark. Cliff had awakened before me. He lay quietly, waiting for me to join him. His hands lovingly stroked my hair, and his eyes were hooded, brilliant with desire. Upon finding that I had awakened, he lifted my head lovingly and brought my lips to his. He captured my lips with his and kissed me, his tongue delving deeply into my mouth. Our tongues kissed each other, each absorbing the essence of the other's taste.

"Christina, I love you so much," he cried as he broke our kiss. "Your kisses are so luscious; you taste as sweet as nectar. I'm going to turn you over now and take you as I never have before," he whispered, lifting my hips and twisting my face onto the pillow.

My breasts hung down freely, my buttocks were in the air. Using his knees between mine he spread my sex open so that it was fully ready to receive him. As his cock touched my vagina I experienced a spasm of desire.

'Please, Cliff," I begged.

He pushed his cock into my vagina. The sensation was mind-blowing. He had never penetrated me this deeply. My juices flowed liberally, easing his entry and lubricating his way into my most intimate parts. His hips pounded against my cheeks again and again. His lips trailed a row of kisses down my throat to my back causing my loins to beg for release. My body seemed to crash apart on a bed of rocks splitting me in two.

"I am going to reward you as never before for the priceless gift of the love you have given me. I think of you constantly, wanting to make love to you until you and I become one completely."

My clit begged for his attentions. I ached to have him deep inside me. He withdrew his cock and his fingers slipped between my folds and began to thrust in and out with extraordinary speed. I was being finger-fucked and thought that I was going to combust and explode.

Just when I was on the point of the most explosive orgasm of my life, he thrust his cock into me again and again. When he had filled me with his semen, he turned me over and began to suck and laver my left breast. His teeth nibbled gently on my nipple all the while his hand palming my mons and twisting my clitoris gently between his thumb and finger. The sensation of the dual stimulation of my breast and mons at the same time brought me a second paroxysm of splendor. His mouth switched to my right breast; I moaned in ecstasy as his left hand fondled my breast while his tongue swirled and teased my right breast, his thumb and index finger teased and squeezed my nipples in alternating motions.

"GOD. Cliff, mmmm!"

I was lost in a pool of sensation, my mind swimming against the tide as the waves of pleasure sweeping through me. I couldn't remember the exact moment because my body was totally under his control. I crashed again on the shores of bliss; my mind shattered into a thousand pieces. Somehow he regained his strength and his newly engorged cock rammed into me and spurted his warm seminal fluid and filled my vagina cavity and I sank into a world of oblivion, my body sated, my mind overwhelmed. My love fulfilled.

"Cliff, the doctor told me that we are going to have to slow down on the love making sometime soon. I don't mean to say that she said stop now. Just that, there are three of them, they are going to need a lot of the 'hotel space' that I've got inside of me."

"Okay," he sighed. "I guess that's the price that I have to pay to be a father. After a few more minutes, I could hear his soft breathing, I drifted off to sleep again.

I awoke some time later, Cliff's arms around me, holding me tightly.

"Sweetheart, we are going to need to get up and take a shower and get moving, or they will be hiring a new VP of T & J Industry's Division, and a new Construction Manager to get their building built."

"Maybe they should. It is only a job," I pouted.

My body yearned to experience the joys of the night again.

"I could care less about that old job. I want you again."

"Christina, up and at 'em. You know that you don't mean that. You have worked too hard to achieve this promotion. And I've worked too hard to get your offices ready for you. I don't want you to throw this away. We could certainly afford to, but this is not about money. It is about your happiness. You know it, and I know it. So?"

"Cliff."

"Yes?"

"I thought that it was your' turn to turn on the shower. You know that I hate to step in when the water is cold. -- Stop that tickling," I giggled in response to his fingers. "You know how much I dislike that.... I giggled.

When he didn't let up I finally cried out:

"All right I'm going. I'm going. The last one in the shower is a silly goose," I laughed and dashed for the shower door.

Cliff, being on the opposite side of the bed -- closer to the bathroom door, jumped up and raced into the shower ahead of me. Even though the water was cold when he turned it on, he climbed in and stuck out his tongue.

CHAPTER 44

Oh, this wonderful man, who could drive me wild in the night, and awaken me to life in the morning. I wanted nothing more than to forget the world outside. This was where I wanted to be all of the time. Held in his arms, lost in his passionate love making.

But he was correct. We both had lives to live. People depended on both of us. I stepped over to the shower where he was waiting. I could see the love in his eyes as he waited for me.

I reached in and filled my palms full of the cold water and splashed it onto his stomach.

Cliff grabbed my arm and pulled me in with him and placed me directly under the shower stream. Thank goodness it was beginning to warm, but it was still very cool.

"Come here, you big galoot. I grabbed his neck and pulled his lips down to mine." My profession of love was smothered by his lips as he kissed me deeply.

I grabbed his tube of shower gel and squirted some over his chest and begin lathering him, under his arms, and down his stomach. My hands were now covered with soap, I reached behind him and swiped my hands up and down his back. He reached over, grabbed more shower gel and lathered my neck and chest, paying special attention to my breasts, then down to my legs, between my legs and then my back. Oh, I love it so much when we shower together each morning.

'Who knew that bathing with your husband could be such fun?'

We began to giggle together at our foolishness. But we were happy again; our playing had accomplished his goal of waking me up. I stood under the shower head, the spray sweeping away the last of the lather and I was clean. We exchanged places while I stepped out onto the rug and grabbed his towel and stood, dripping on the rug, waiting patiently for him to complete his shower. As he stepped out onto the rug, he took the towel from my hands. Together we dried each other, wiping the last traces of the water drops from our bodies. I lifted my left leg and rested it on the tub edge, and he reached under my leg, toweling me up and down and then repeated for my right leg.

I repeated this process for him, first his left leg, then his right. I turned away, and he made sure that my back was completely dry, then I performed the same duty for him.

After we had performed our other toiletries, we returned to the bedroom and gathered our clothes for the day. Underwear, outerwear, shoes, watches, and jewelry were applied in a sequence similar to a ballet maneuver. At last, we were ready to present ourselves to the world. Breakfast was already on the table, and we continued the ballet, eating the food; drinking the coffee; thanking our staff for their attentiveness; placing our soiled dishes in the sink; and rising in unison. We smiled and kissed. Since we have the same destination this morning, Cliff, his duties in completing the tower, mine in meeting my staff on floor eight, Cliff was to drive me into work.

I could get used to this, I thought. But then, I remembered that often we had different duties in our work, and he may have to make an emergency run to a supplier while I may have a business luncheon or meetings at a different location.

I wished that my car was ready.

We descended to the main floor of the apartment building and approached the valet lane. Cliff's truck sat there, motor running, driver's door open. Just ahead of his truck, there it sat. My new car. How?

"What happened, Cliff?"

Cliff smiled and handed me the electronic car bud.

"I had several special installment technicians and equipment flown in early last evening. They worked overnight to install the car windshield and side glass installed, and get the bulletproof shielding fitted so that you could have it immediately, sweetheart. I know how much you like surprises," he smiled happily.

"I couldn't stand the thought of you being either in my truck or any other vehicle that was not as safe as I could make it, Christina. Payne has proven over and over that he will stop at nothing to get at you. I intend to foil him at every turn that I can. There are two squad cars waiting outside that will escort us to the tower, so even if he is lying in wait somewhere along the way, he will not be able to penetrate the protective barrier I have surrounded you within your beautiful car.

"The company security guards are already in place in the tower waiting for you. They will escort you to your new offices. There are other guards who are already in place on floor eight and have swept the area to ensure that he is not hiding somewhere on that floor. They will remain on that floor all day. Please take it easy on the way there, and enjoy your day in your new job. Now kiss me and we will be on our way."

"Mr. Stinson."

"Yes, sweetheart?"

"Do you know why I love you so much?"

"Why's that, sweetheart?"

"Not only because I love the dickens out of you, but because your first concern is always my safety over yours. What do you say that we get into our vehicles and make our way over to the tower?"

"I'll lead the way, honey. You follow behind, as I need to get there first to show you your new offices and Charlotte will probably shadow us along the way."

I slid into my car, relishing the new car smell and trying to memorize all of the new switches, dials, and buttons. I touched the start button the engine purred to life. Cliff leaned in, gave me a kiss, and told me to drive safely and then closed the door. My excitement grew as my foot touched the accelerator, I shifted into drive, and the car lurched forward as I pushed down a little too hard on the gas.

I flushed, looking into the rearview mirror at my now laughing husband, I lifted my arms indicating 'sorry'. This time, I pressed a little less forcefully, and the car began to drift forward and then picked up speed as it exited the garage area.

'Wow! What a car! I love it. It is simply the most powerful car I have ever owned. I felt safe and protected. I could feel Cliff's love for me, wrapping around me like a glove. It gave me a warm glow inside.'

I reached up and pushed the FM radio button, and the sound of Beethoven filled the car. One of the install guys must like classical music, I thought. From the sounds of this piece, I recognized that it was his Seventh Symphony, I knew that I loved this music as well. This was a powerful piece of orchestra music. Pounding bass, silken strings, thundering tympani. I left the radio on that station all the way to work. The powerful sounds of the strings and tympani continued to cast a hypnotic spell. Oh, my! The stereo system in this car made me almost believe that I was sitting on stage, in the middle of the orchestra 'cello section.

The first squad car slid in place ahead of me; Cliff was just ahead and the second squad car fell into place behind him. I thought that I could see Charlotte's car sitting about a block away. I lost track of it as I concentrated on steering and taking in the joy of the feel of the powerful engine. The luxurious sound of the orchestra, pounding out chord after chord, driving the orchestra onward to its mighty finale gave me thrills.

Our parade of vehicles slipped quietly up the on-ramp to I-59 as we began the circle downtown Houston to our destination at Tilden Tower. Exiting on Clay Street, we quickly reached the safety of the tower and pulled into the underground parking garage. The HPD bomb squad was there to scan our vehicles. As we slowly cleared through the inspection area, I followed the signs down to the parking area designated for my team. There I found a specifically marked parking spot designated with a sign having my name, and my title '**VP Christina Stinson**.'

My beautiful new car slipped into my space just as the last chord of the symphony sounded. I pulled to a stop and looked around before I exited the car. There were already a few cars here from my staff. At first, I didn't notice, but then as I looked around, I saw one of the Tilden Company guards waiting for me by the elevator. The elevator opened and two more guards exited and motioned to me that the area was secure, and I could exit and proceed to my work location.

I felt much more comfortable; my company has taken extra steps to protect not only myself but other staff as they arrived. I swelled with a bit of pride. My company did care about its employees and property. It gave me the confidence that we would get through this no matter what.

I proceeded to the elevator where the three guards smiled and greeted me by name and motioned toward the elevator. Two of the guards joined me as I ascended to floor eight. Exiting from the elevator, I looked around the floor. My husband stood not far away awaiting my arrival.

"Welcome, Mrs. Stinson. Would you like a tour of the floor, or would you like to proceed directly to your office?" Cliff asked.

I appreciated that he was addressing me by my proper name rather than by our familial titles or nicknames. I wanted to be recognized for my accomplishments here, rather than just the wife of so and so. My name would give me that liberty.

I smiled up at him, "Thank you, Mr. Stinson. I believe that I would like the complete tour. Even though I more or less designed the floor layout, it would be exciting to see it brought to reality. So, please show me everything."

Cliff smiled back and motioned for me to follow along behind him, as another concession to my position. Rather than taking my hand inside his which he would normally do in other circumstances.

I whispered a quiet "Thank you."

As we walked among the new cubicles and offices, I suddenly realized that during all of the time that I had spent following Cliff around he had carefully not let me see this particular floor. He must have known at the time about my promotion and didn't want to give away any hints that the floor was being made ready on a rush basis.

The first area near us was the large conference room. Opening the door, Cliff pointed to the expansive conference table equipped with overhead projectors. There was a drop down screen for presentations during office meetings; numerous computer connections, as well as telephone conferencing capabilities.

"All very impressive, Mr. Stinson."

Cliff pointed out the white boards and other equipment ready for use. Lighting was subdued but sufficient for complete illumination of the area. There were several remote controls placed on the table for the equipment, each control labeled for its' specific device. The chairs were arranged neatly around the table with plenty of room for additional seating as needed.

We turned and exited the room and proceeded down the line of half-height cubicles. I noticed several of the staff were already at their new desks. Each very excited and seemingly pleased with their new work locations.

I walked into the area and asked if they were satisfied with their locations or had discovered anything that was missing or they thought might improve their work area. No one had any ideas yet as it was all so new. I advised them that at any time they did find some hindrance or improvement that needed to be resolved, my door would be open.

I turned to Cliff, who was patiently standing outside the cubicles.

"Cliff, I think that I'm ready to see my temporary office now. I will return here after I speak with you privately for a few minutes."

I wanted to return to the area and be available as the staff arrived, to greet them and assist them in acclimation in any way that I could. But right now I had an entirely different mission in mind.

"Yes, ma'am. Your office is just down this way. And if anyone should have issues today or in the coming weeks, I have staff ready for assignment of resolve those issues, whether physical, electrical or other. I have assigned one of my staff, Bob Roberts, to be here with you to take notes and make sure those issues are resolved quickly."

Cliff motioned to Mr. Roberts, who had been standing off to the side, gave him instructions to stay close to me during the day and make note of issues and get them resolved.

"If you have any issue that you cannot handle," Roberts confirmed, "notify me immediately and I will take care of it," Roberts explained. Yours is the first team in the new building, as you are aware, Mrs. Stinson, so we always expect little things to pop up here and there. We are going to be here to help. Don't hesitate to call for assistance on anything that you find. I will remain here to assist the new arrivals as they come in." he smiled and walked back to the cubicles.

Cliff looked around, "I need to get back to floor fourteen after I show you your temporary office. I have put a crash effort to prepare the one on fourteen for you, possibly as early as next week. Floor four is also expected to be released for occupancy next week, and the Executive offices the week after that.

"The rest of the tower still has a long way to go before it is completely ready. There is still a lot of work to be accomplished. So I am going to be pretty busy today. I don't expect that either of us will have time to go out to lunch today, so I had asked Marianne to prepare us a meal; you will find it on your desk."

We continued down the hallway towards my temporary office; my eyes were now focused on the strong muscular back of my husband. My thoughts drifted back to our wonderful evening and morning together.

"I hope that we have some time today to meet," Cliff continued speaking as we walked. "I don't expect there to be a lot. Things are backed up around here, what with all of the repairs that are happening on floors one, two and three, my days are pretty booked. Oh, just in case, I forgot to show you the restrooms. They are just down past the elevator and on opposite sides of the short hallway on the left." He ended as we stepped inside my new office.

"Will there be anything else, Mrs. Stinson?"

"Cliff, please close and lock the door," I asked.

Cliff looked at me curiously for a moment and then did as I had asked.

"Please sit here on the top of my new desk, Cliff. I need to reward you for being the love and treasure that you are to me. I want to love you anytime, anyplace."

Before he could open his mouth to protest I had grabbed and captured his cock through the outside of his pants and squeezed gently. I could feel it expanding and extending inside my palm.

"Cliff, I love your penis. I love what we did together last night. I love the feel of you inside me, inside my vagina, filling me completely.

"I love the feel of your cock inside my mouth; the taste of it, and the delicious essence that you deliver to my mouth. I want you. I need you inside my mouth now. I need to taste your' cum on my tongue, feel it as it drifts lazily into my throat and down into my stomach. I need you to understand that I am yours completely. I hold nothing back, not my mind, or my body. You have freed me from my past. I was ashamed of myself, of my body, of my life. I want to give you all that I am and will be."

"God, Christina…" his eyes were ablaze with passion.

Cliff's eyes hooded and surrendered to my passion as I slowly undid his belt and lowered his zipper, my hand never released its firm grip on his manhood. Pulling his trousers open I reached into his boxers, pulling his swollen cock free. I lifted my mouth to him, capturing his tongue, sucking the juices from him, and then watched his eyes, themselves frozen in a state of lust, growing round and feverish. I knelt in front of him and took him inside my mouth. I deposited our mixed saliva, coating his cock completely. Strands of my lovemaking stretched from his cock to my mouth as I looked up at his eyes, which were tortured with desire.

His hands grabbed the sides of my face as my tongue drove him wild, his hands twisting wildly in my hair. He moaned in sexual agony as I nibbled at his shaft, then I unsheathed my teeth and slid up and down his shaft, swirling my tongue around the tip until he could stand it no longer and released his cum onto my tongue in three enormous spurts that nearly filled my oral cavity completely.

"Chris...., Ohh Ohh!" his eyes closed for a moment of ecstasy, then opened and looked deep within my own."

I opened my mouth to display his juices to him while I struggled to keep it all in, then swallowing once, twice and then a third time. I relished the warm and salty taste of his precious gift on my tongue. I smiled up at him in contentment. I wanted him to know that I was his, all of me, and he was mine to possess and pleasure beyond his wildest dreams.

I looked up into his eyes.

"Thank you, Cliff. I needed you at that moment. I wanted to make you satisfied and need you to remember me like this, kneeling between your legs with your cock inside my mouth. Loving you, my tongue worshiping you, my mouth swallowing all that you give me. Think of me while you are working today, I am yours completely to do with what you need. Whether we are apart or together, I am yours whenever you wish.

"Just call me and I will be there for you. I have surrendered everything that I was or ever will be to you. My body is yours to do with whenever, wherever and as often as you desire me. If you need me to suck on you, or you wish to taste my juices, all you have to do is ask. I will strip myself naked in front of you for you to gaze at any time and place. I have no shame where you are concerned. I want to fulfill every pent up desire that you have. No other woman will ever satisfy your needs as I will."

I smiled up at him, his eyes, shocked with the surprise and unrestrained passion of my love making.

"God, Christina. You are so wonderful, such a sensual woman. I only wish that we were home so that I could repay you in kind." He rose from the desk, his knees weak from his spent passion. He tucked his flaccid, totally spent organ inside, out of sight again, pulled his zipper closed and buckled his belt. As he straightened his shirt and pants, his face was flushed with the remnants of my love making and words of loving trust awash in his mind.

I pulled the compact and mirror from my purse and straightened my hair and adjusted my lipstick.

"My reward comes from knowing how much that you love and think of me. Your tenderness and consideration. I love you more than life itself. These are my surprises for you. I hope they make you as happy as the ones that you do for me. And, besides -- Mr. Stinson, I wanted to christen my office in a very special way today.

"Now, I think that about covers everything. Didn't you say that you had somewhere important you had to be?"

I fluttered my eyelids at him in a sinful bit of teasing.

"Oh, -- one second please." I walked around my desk, picked up a notepad and pen and scribbled a short note, folded it in half and placed it in his shirt pocket. "Now please don't open that note until you are back in your office.**"

"You leave me breathless, Christina. I cannot wait to get you home tonight." He swept me into his arms and held me tightly while kissing me. His tongue, reaching deep into my mouth, his eyes never leaving mine. With a final gaze at me, making sure that I was presentable, he turned and unlocked and opened the office door and with a grand gesture, beckoning me to proceed him.

As I swept through the door, he whispered in my ear, "You know, I been rethinking my schedule for the day, there might be some time for me to fit in another inspection of your office, should you wish."

"Cliff, you say such shocking things." I giggled as we walked together toward the elevator to return to his work day. Thoughts of what had just happened to him, swirling in his mind.

I returned to the cubicle area and was joined by Mr. Roberts. We continued to wander through the area, chatting with staff as they arrived. I prayed that he had not noticed how flushed I was from our mysterious tryst in my new office. Ms. Martinez and Mr. Black joined me a few minutes later and not long after the remaining staff was all in place. My breathing began to calm, and my heart returned to its normal pace.

'What an enchanting day this was turning out to be.'

I inquired of my managers what their plans were for their teams for the day. Both advised me that they had already set up two meetings with their separate staffs. One, scheduled for 9:30 and the other followed at 10:30. In those meetings the plans that I had worked on for individual work projects would be discussed and team leaders and specific assignments were assigned. They both expressed hope they would have developed targets for initial accomplishments and team goals by the end of the week. I asked them to stay on top of that and report their results to me no later than Friday. I would need their input when I met with the company president next week. My thoughts were only of Cliff, his touch, his love and how much that I wanted him to take me to new heights. To set my heart on fire.

******

**Cliff's note

I truly enjoyed myself last night. I have called it "Love's Dream."

> *Should you wish it again, simply whisper "love's dream" in my ear.*
>> *Any night, or every night.*
>> *Your wish is my desire.*
>> *I am completely yours to command*
>> *Anytime, anyplace, anything*
>> *You are my life and love*

Christina

CHAPTER 45

Over the next several days I noticed several strange activities on Cliff's part during the evenings. Whenever I would question him, he was very reticent and secretive. He would spend time searching for things on the internet and then go driving off someplace by himself. By Thursday morning, I was about ready to have it out with him. I was afraid that it was something that I had done, and I was having a tough time dealing with the mystery.

"Christina, do we have anything scheduled for Saturday? I have someplace that I would like to take you, and it will probably be nearly an all-day event."

"Does any of this have to do with this mystery that you have been keeping from me all week? This isn't another of the Cliff Stinson secret specials is it?" I questioned.

"Whatever do you mean by that? Haven't every one of my 'specials' been nice?" he pouted.

"You know, Cliff, I used to hate the idea of surprises, but I am very much enjoying the ones that you have for me. They never disappoint and what with all of the excitement this week, I would like a little bit of quiet time with my husband. So, yeah, go for it. Schedule whatever you have in mind and I will tag along happily."

When Saturday morning arrived, he rose excitedly early that morning and teased me to join him.

"Christina, I have a surprise for you for this morning. You are going on a treasure hunt," he announced, his voice full of eagerness.

"A treasure hunt? What's that about?" I asked. "Am I going to looking for a pirates' treasure?"

"To tell you the truth, you are going on a treasure hunt to find the pot-of-gold at the end of the rainbow," his voice was full of mirth.

"Cliff, now I know that you have lost your mind. Haven't you heard? Pots-of-Gold is just an old fairy-tale."

"Not exactly, my love. At the end of this treasure hunt, you are going to find a real pot-of-gold and bring it to me."

"Sure I am," I replied as if he were out of his mind. "So what's the catch?" I asked him, my curiosity aroused.

"The first thing this morning you are going to be starting on the hunt for the missing treasure. Each place that you find will be a clue as to what you might find at the end of the rainbow. The location itself will be the clue representing something that will exist at the end of this magical rainbow. You will find an envelope at each location giving the location of the next clue."

"Are you up for some fun?" he smiled mischievously, looking as anxious as a schoolboy on a secret mission.

I could hear the excitement in his voice which was infectious, and I suddenly became excited to join. "I have never, ever been on a treasure hunt. It sounds rather exciting. So what exactly do we do?"

"There will not exactly be a 'we.' I will be at the rainbows' end anxiously awaiting your arrival. I don't want to prematurely give anything away. I have your first clue inside this envelope. You will need to read the clue inside, figure out what the clue means. Then go to that location and there find the hint for the next location. There will be seven clues, and I will be waiting for you to go to the address you will find inside the pot-of-gold. Your job is to follow the clues, reason out what they mean and meet me at the end, bringing me the results of your journey."

"Oh, Cliff, this is the greatest tease that I have ever had. I am so excited now that I can hardly wait."

"Yes, sweetheart. Everything is set and ready for you to begin. I am just as excited as you are because there is a very special surprise at the end of the rainbow waiting just for you. Now I will help you with the first clue but after that, you are going to be on your own. Are you ready?"

I was completely mesmerized by this new adventure.

"Cliff, all that I know is that if you are waiting for me at the end of the trail, I will be certain to find it. Now let me see the first clue."

Cliff handed me an envelope. Inside I found a fountain pen and a note.

"Find the 'first' of these at Zsa Zsa" there find an envelope taped behind the name of the first."

"All right Cliff. Is this referring to Zsa Zsa Gabor or something?" The clue makes no sense to me."

"Very funny, Christina. No, it does not mean Zsa Zsa Gabor. Each clue will be similar to this; you need to use the information in the clue to go to the location, and there you will find an envelope with the next clue. So if you will study the clue a bit, it all should become clear.

"The envelope contains a 'fountain pen' and the word Zsa Zsa. The first of these would be the word 'Fountain' and the 'Zsa Zsa' would be a location in and around Houston with that name. So, using your iPad, perform a Google search and find something with 'Zsa Zsa' in its name."

I dug out my iPad and searched and found a location named Hotel Zsa Zsa. In the photo of the hotel, I noticed that there was a fountain located directly in front.

"Cliff, this is going to be so much fun. But what if someone steals the envelope before I arrive to find it?"

"I have taken a few precautions to keep that from happening. Charlotte has the seven locations already and will be there before you, watching. Some of the envelopes might be inside a place with the clerk or owner instead of outside. So, now you have your first clue."

"I expect to see you at the end of the rainbow by noon today. So don't delay, these places are not exactly side by side; you are going to have some fun breaking in your new car. Remember I have my cocoon of love surrounding you so that you will be safe and well protected."

"I would like Marianne to go along with you for companionship and possibly help when you need her? She is waiting in the den. I've explained the rules to her; she is quite anxious to go with you. I know that you two will have a great time together. So, run along now, and don't be late!"

"Does she know the end destination? If so, I will trick it out of her and beat you to the gold." I smiled hopefully.

"Sorry, she does not have a 'clue,' no pun intended sweetheart. She will be as surprised as you will be when you reach the end of the rainbow."

Cliff gave me a good-luck kiss and watched as I collected Marianne at the door and headed down to the valet lane to find my car. Marianne and I were both giggling with excitement as we rode down in the elevator. Anxious to be on our way and excited to discover this 'pot-of-gold' that Cliff had for us. After we had both seated ourselves inside my car, I brought up the hotel information on the IPad again and plugged it into the Saab's GPS, and we were off to the first destination.

When we arrived at the hotel, we saw the fountain directly across the street. I parked in the temporary parking lane, and Marianne ran over and found an envelope taped to the edge of the fountain just behind the fountain name plaque. Returning to the car Marianne opened and read:

"Closely associated with Pearl Harbor, and cherry trees in the capital, not far from elephants and giraffes."

"I know, I know!" Marianne giggled. "Pearl Harbor – the first thing you think of is the Japanese attack. And the Japanese donated hundreds of Cherry trees to Washington, D.C. Where else would you find elephants and giraffes than the Hermann Park Zoo? Obviously, it must be referring to the Japanese Gardens there, in Hermann Park. And if I remember correctly, there is a small cove of Cherry trees located inside."

"Great work, Marianne. Hermann Park is close by; we should be there in just a few minutes."

As we arrived at the Japanese Garden inside Hermann Park, I told Marianne that it was my turn to retrieve the envelope. I climbed out of the car and strolled into the garden. After a brief walk, I noticed a solitary cherry tree with a small envelope taped to the trunk. I grabbed it and returned to the car. About one half block away I saw Charlotte's car parked and she was watching. I waved at her and returned to my vehicle. Opening the envelope, I found a small marble and another cryptic note.

One of these and what happens to water at thirty-two degrees.

"One of these? The marble? And what happens to water at thirty-two degrees. Oh, I think that I understand, Marian. Water 'freezes' at thirty-two degrees. So he must mean a 'Marble Frieze.'" I giggled in excitement and then pulled out my iPad to do a search on Google. After a few minutes, I found a company named Architectural Supply, which specialized in marble friezes and their address. As we are on the way there, Marianne and I discussed the first clues to see if they could be put together and suggest anything. I listed them out for Marian;

1. Fountains
2. Gardens
3. Marble frieze

So far, there was not enough information for us to discern the meaning of the clues. Where could you possibly find these things in one place? Perhaps the next location will reveal something important. I headed over to the Architectural Supply Company, which was only three miles away. Upon arrival, I did not see anything special where an envelope could be attached. I told Marianne that Cliff had said the envelope might be inside a location. So Marianne scooted out of the car, went inside and returned a few minutes later with an envelope.

"A gift of these was my first to you and a failed presidential candidate's name the clue."

"Marian, Cliff sent me a box of two dozen roses. Let me do a Google search on Public Gardens near here. A list of various Public Gardens came up, and I spotted the name, McGovern. Yes, that's it. Oh,..., I have it! He must mean the Rose Garden over at McGovern Centennial Gardens. That is not far from here. Let's head over there," I squealed in excitement, I felt like a little school girl about to sneak her first kiss.

Marianne and I were both getting more excited now. There were seven clues, and we had now solved over half of them. It was almost 10:30 a.m. so we seemed to be making good time toward the goal. I pulled up in the parking area at McGovern Gardens; it was my turn to go into the office.

Sure enough, when I identified myself to the young secretary inside she handed me an envelope. My stomach was full of butterflies as I returned to the car and handed the envelope to Marianne. She opened it and read the message.

"You have now been to several of these, but this has an ancient Iranian name.

Marianne and I put our heads together on this one. "We have been to several of these, easy enough, we have been to several 'gardens' already. But the 'ancient Iranian' theme is confusing. I pulled out my iPad and Googled 'old name for Iran.' Immediately the answer popped up on my screen. Why sure, Iran used to be known as the country of Persia, so we are looking for 'Persian Gardens.'

A Google search listed the Persian Garden Center. It was just off of Loop 610, not far from our current location, so I headed in that direction while Marianne tried to make sense of the clues so far:

1. Fountains
2. Gardens
3. Marble Frieze
4. Persian Gardens

Neither of us could put it together yet. Maybe this next one will be the turning point. *'What the heck has all of these things in one place?'* I wondered.

I pulled into the parking area of the Persian Garden Center.

I was beginning to get very frustrated with my husband. He is such a tease, pulling off the most wonderful surprises for me. The tension in my stomach was building. I was so anxious to solve the puzzle -- and even more excited to find Cliff at the end. He would always be the real treasure that I was seeking.

This is so different than anything anyone has done for me before. I never played a lot of games as a child. This was exciting. I know that there has to be something very special. All these hints are about to blow my mind. Spectacular gardens, marble friezes, beautiful fountains.

'What can it be that we are going to find?'

Marianne returned from the cashier with our next envelope.

> *I was thirsty in the desert of life, and then you appeared*
> *Like a magical Oasis from the mists of time.*
> *Use the last clue to put it all together*
> *Go to the only other city in Harris County besides Houston*
> *for the last message.*

There were only two cities within Harris County: Houston and Tomball. All other locations are just suburbs or small villages. A Google search revealed an Oasis Pools of Tomball.

We were on our way immediately, excitement building for this last clue. Obviously, it was a lake or swimming pool of some sort.

Marianne and I discussed all of the possibilities and came to the conclusion that it must be one of Houston's many fancy garden centers, or perhaps a large public park. But what could that mean, what relationship can those have to a 'pot-of-gold'?

At the Oasis Pools, the manager handed me a note that I would find the 'Pot-of-Gold' at the Home Depot on Highway 249, not far from our current location.

At the Home Depot, after I identified myself to the manager he reached under his desk and pulled out a small pot wrapped with cellophane tape. Inside the pot was full of golden coins with an envelope on top.

I retrieved the envelope with a message printed on the outside and asked him to have the pot loaded into the trunk of my car.

Please return to Clifford Stinson at 16750 Memorial Drive.
Use gate code to 5123 for entry.

After typing the address into my GPS, we were quickly on our way. So what could all of the clues mean? All of the gardens, fountain, marble, and a swimming pool, and the last location being a Home Depot. What could be the meaning of that?

Then it dawned on me. 'The Home Depot contains all of the various things that are used to build a home. The 'pot-of-gold' we are bringing to the end of a rainbow. "It must be a home. Cliff has found a home for us!' I nearly shouted out to Marianne.

Oh, I hope so, this wonderful husband of mine, gathering us all into the place of our dreams. But none of the houses in Fairfield had gardens, marble friezes, or an Oasis. This must be a very special place.

I exited off of Loop 610 to Memorial Drive and searched for the address. The GPS said it was two and a half miles away. Marianne and I chatted, wondering what this place would look like as we drove along. Finally, there it was. The address was posted on a large iron gateway. I entered the gate code into the driveway entry gate box.

The gates slowly swung wide revealing a long driveway which passed through a beautiful Japanese Garden along the way to the main home. There were hundreds of rose bushes on both sides of the drive; fresh petals carpeted the road.

"Oh!" we both exclaimed. "It's so beautiful!"

Rounding the last curve in the driveway the home came into our view.

My heart was pounding in my chest. I loved it. It was a home found only in a dream. Charlotte had arrived shortly before us and was standing in the entryway waiting. Marianne and I joined her at the doorway where a large sign announced

WELCOME TO OUR NEW HOME, LADIES.
PLEASE COME INSIDE.

I opened the huge custom oak doors, and they swung open as if balanced on a feather. We extracted the pot-of-gold coins from the trunk and Charlotte, and Marianne carried it into the house.

Inside we found a second sign:

Please proceed to the back patio directly ahead.

We walked through a huge foyer and into a sumptuous living room that was so large it might easily convert into a ballroom, if needed. There were two sets of French doors opening onto the back yard area where I saw Cliff waiting for us, sitting by a beautiful oasis swimming pool and fire pit which was ablaze with a beautiful log fire. There was a table set for the four of us, with lunch being served by the head chef from B & B's, whom I recognized from my many visits to his restaurant.

Charlotte and Marianne set the pot-of-gold coins down on the edge of the fire pit. But before I even began to think about food, I grabbed Cliff and hugged him to me tightly.

"Cliff, you are truly the most wonderful husband. Marianne and I had a wonderful morning gathering your clues which have only made the surprise of this place even greater. But how? When? Do we actually own this wonderful place?"

"The 'how' was easy, sweetie. I had notified our realtor that we were looking for something special, no price was to be excluded. The 'when' was on Tuesday, she called and told me that this was a private listing, and it only came on the market that day. No one else has toured the place as of yet. I spent the whole week finding locations and setting up the clues.

"Ms. Walker will be here in about one hour to show us the home in its entirety. The moment I heard her description I knew that this was the home we all wanted. It's a place to be secure in, to protect us and allow us to grow over the years. Your final question was 'do we own it'? Not quite yet. I put down two million dollars in refundable earnest money to prevent anyone else from seeing it before we make a decision. It awaits your final approval.

"Together, after we tour the home, we can make our final decision, and if and only if you like it will we complete the paperwork required. You know that I would never make a decision like this without your agreement. The chef has been here for several hours preparing our lunch. I have developed quite an appetite from all of the delicious smells coming from the kitchen. So, what do you say? Are you ladies ready for a feast?"

"After running all over town, I know I, for one, am famished. Marianne, Charlotte, are you ladies ready to eat?" After receiving a positive response, we ladies were directed to enter the home and proceeded to half bath just off the patio where we could wash up for lunch."

Returning to the backyard oasis, we found that Cliff has arranged for a dry aged porterhouse steak with vegetables was for lunch, along with a sparkling champagne, and a specially prepared strawberry shortcake for desert. It all smelled and tasted delicious. Wouldn't you know? My husband was such a big steak fan.

And to end the meal, a delicious cup of my favorite hot coffee was set before us.

Marianne, ever the inquisitive one suddenly asked Cliff, "So, Mr. Cliff, do you have any brothers or cousins that are looking for a lady? You know, someone interested in a long-term relationship, as you and Ms. Tina?"

Charlotte also chimed in, "I'll second that request. If they are anything like you are, Mr. Stinson, we would be delighted to meet them."

Cliff laughed, "Both of my brothers are already married with children, but I do know some single men, both at my work, and at church. In fact, I know of a couple of them who mentioned that they were hoping to find the woman of their dreams like I have. Perhaps you two could attend church with us, and I might be able to introduce you around.

"I can assure you that all of the men were clean cut and honest. Several of the guys are seeking long term arrangements and might be good candidates for you ladies, who knows?"

I smiled inwardly. '*My husband, the matchmaker. Who would have guessed?*' I reached over and kissed his hand.

"Cliff, would you say the grace for our first meal in our new home?

"Certainly, my love. May we each hold hands?"
The four of us joined hands around the table and bowed our heads.

"Dearest Lord Jesus. We come before you at this time seeking your blessing on this meal. Bless it to the nourishment of our bodies. We also ask that you bless this house that it will provide the home for our family, present company and future children included. May it possess those things that will keep us safe, allow our family to flourish and give all who dwell within a happiness and years of pleasure and comfort.

Amen"

All three of us joined in the Amen.

CHAPTER 46

Ms. Wilmadean Walker from Tulane Real Estate Co. arrived and introduced herself to all. She was prepared to take us on a tour of the estate. When she inquired as to whether it would be just Cliff and me,

"No, certainly not," I responded. "These ladies are my private staff and will be living here as well. They will be just as interested in knowing more about the entire grounds as they will have to participate in the upkeep and protection of our home. This is Charlotte Parker and Marianne Williams."

"Very good, then. Are you all ready to begin?" she inquired. "And if so, do you have a particular area that you wish to see first, the grounds or the home itself?"

I looked to Cliff for guidance, I wanted to see everything at once and was so excited that I couldn't make a choice. Cliff had already seen the house and grounds; I knew that he would want to show off the best things first, and his surprises were always the best. Besides, from the smile on his face I could tell how anxious he was to show me something exciting. How could I not want the love of my life to lead me down new paths?

"Since it is such a pleasant day outdoors, let's start by touring some of the gardens and vistas," Cliff offered.

I grabbed Cliff's hand and prepared myself for a tour of this wonderland come true.

"If you all would follow me," Ms. Walker said, gesturing at the area where we stood. "First, since we are already here at the pool area, I need to note that the pool is custom built in-ground Gunite pool and features a six-foot high diving board at the one end, as you see, where the depth is about fifteen feet. Of course, at the opposite end there you see the heated spa and a child's wading pool. I believe the pool holds a total of approximately fifty thousand gallons of water and features a self-cleaning pool sweep and filters.

A pool servicing company is under contract that maintains the water quality of the pool bi-weekly with chlorine bombs and other standard chemicals to keep the pool free of germs and mold. They also clean and replace your pool filters at the time of service. The only condition you should be aware of is that you must wait for one hour after the chlorine treatments before entering the pool to allow the chlorine to be absorbed. Otherwise, the pool is available 24/7 every day and has custom lighting in and around the pool for nighttime dips."

"This fire pit has a specially built Barbeque spit for cooking large selections of meats. The rotisserie spit for the barbecue is located here, disguised inside this storage unit. Now, if we may, let us proceed to the Japanese gardens. The entire estate encompasses fourteen acres with several gardens and terraces.

As we stepped away from the backyard oasis and pool area, we entered into the gardens, comprised of a heterogeneous mesh of various flowers, plants and trees. There was a hedgerow maze, including a pagoda, various sized obelisks and a gazebo covered with climbing roses and honeysuckle. The gardens also encompassed a small Koi fish stream fed by a tumbling waterfall.

"Oh, Cliff, this brings back so many memories to me of our first walk together. I am totally entranced by everything," I sighed.

Charlotte and Marianne are equally enthusiastic, admiring the charming waterfall and beautiful moss covered stones and rocks around the stream. Beautiful golden and white Koi swam peacefully here and there, as well some small turtles. The crushed stone pathway, with circular foot pads, led us further on through the Zen garden. Eventually, the path opened up on a stunning Persian garden just off of the Master bedroom.

"Surrounding the home are Grecian friezes along the walkways and entrances," Ms. Walker pointed out as we continued, "The home is Renaissance inspired with statues at various points throughout the meticulously manicured landscape. Maintenance is performed by a private firm contracted exclusively for this estate.

"All in all, the entire estate is breathtakingly beautiful and the only one like it in the Houston area. Are you ready to tour some of the homes' unique features or should we continue our leisurely stroll through the remaining gardens?"

Although we are all in awe of the landscapes, our desire is to see if the interior of the home lived up to the outside vistas was boiling over in all of our minds.

Cliff looked around at the faces of the three ladies beside him and then suggested, "Please, let's have a look inside now," Cliff pointing us the way back to the main entrance.

Ms. Walker led us back into the main entry foyer Entering through the main doorway, facing us was an elegant grand staircase.

"With the help of Houston designer Jim Johnston," Ms. Walker continued the tour explanation, "the owner, Tom Brewer, built this showcase home in three years. A champion of Houston craftsmen, Mr.Brewer, commissioned several local artisans to craft much of the furniture, chandeliers, and furniture that you will see inside as well as the outside statuary you've seen already. Two different gardening firms worked on creating the gardens and surrounding landscaping. Now, inside the home, from the ornate dining room furnishings, to the many chandeliers and cabinets, as well as the marble statues in the gardens you will see the work of some of Houston's finest artists and craftsmen."

"The twenty-one thousand square foot home has ten bedrooms, with ten full baths and three half-baths. Five-hundred rosebushes edge the circular driveway and a seemingly endless list of unique extras. The master wing has a private courtyard modeled after a famous Iranian Persian garden and a stunning master bath, larger than some homes at 1200 square feet. Each bedroom has oversized closet space and unique features to each area. Paintings and statuary, several on the lower floor have marble fountains outside their French doors.

"The elaborately tiled floors, one of a kind light fixtures and even the door pulls are also unique, each looking like a jeweled pin. The Brewers traveled to France and Italy, visiting palaces and chateaux for inspiration. Like Versailles itself, many of the walls and ceilings are hand painted. A wonderful local artist, Clara Jones, did the work you see here. She spent about ninety days in this room alone, for example, creating this original wall art," Ms. Walker explained as she pointed out the formal living room's spectacular paintings on the ceiling and walls.

"Of course, the three-year-old house has all the modern conveniences," she continued. "An iPad or iPhone can control all the heating, A/C, audio and video elements of the house. The home theater boasts a 105-inch curved screen, ultra-high definition surround-sound speaker system, and custom built movie theater seating."

As we continued, I asked Ms. Walker, "So, you said the home was only three years old. And it is so very beautiful. Why, then, is Mr. Brewer selling the home? Is there something wrong with it?"

"Certainly not. In fact, everything about the home is in pristine shape. Full warranties exist for all of the appliances and equipment. No. The fact is, Mr. and Mrs. Brewer decided that the home was not large enough for them. They host some very large events here and have found, even as large and expansive as this location is, it is too small for what they need.

They are currently building a new home for themselves which will be some forty-thousand-square-feet. To accomplish that here would have meant destroying much of the gardens and terraces. They found they didn't have the heart to do that.

"Their new home will have a large outdoor theater for plays and musicals. Currently, they are touring not only Europe but some of the huge royal palaces in Russia to get some fresh ideas for their new home. The Brewers are avid music lovers and have even hosted the Houston

Symphony for small concerts for their friends and family. Often they invite famous musicians and actors to stay with them, so they have a large staff to assist the many guests."

Ms. Walker continued our tour as we climbed the staircase and entered the second floor. As she pointed out other bedrooms, our mouths continually fell open in delight as they each fell into two categories: 'wow' and 'to die for'! Even the half-bathrooms were larger and more luxurious than most homes full baths. On the ground floor, there were other rooms, scattered throughout both floors of the home.

A fully stocked library, an extraordinarily plush piano room with a huge Steinway Grand Piano, a playroom with billiard table, and so much more. "The piano is the one that Van Cliburn played on when he won the International Tchaikovsky Competition in Moscow." Ms. Walker noted. "Mr. Cliburn visited the home several times before his death, as well as other famous pianists, and performed recitals for visiting guests."

"I almost totally forgot," Ms. Walker turned back to us. "Mr. Brewer was an avid newshound. In recent times, he had noticed the increase and rise in gang violence in and around Houston, especially areas close to Memorial. He became concerned that this home might be the target of such gangs in the future. Hidden away behind the external fence and not visible from the streets what with all of the trees and landscaping it might offer a tempting target for hooligans. He strongly believed that the home might present a target for kidnappers or gangs to invade and hold the inhabitant's hostage or worse. Especially since once inside the perimeter, they would have free reign to create havoc without being seen.

"During the construction of the home, Mr. Brewer added some unusual security features that are totally invisible to the casual viewer but are meant to be available to protect the homeowners in case of such an attack. For example: here in the entry foyer these columns on either side of the doorway are not only ornate and beautiful but by pressing on this hidden button…"

She pressed a button hidden inside an ornate flower. Suddenly a panel opened up the back side of the column. Hidden inside the panel was revealed a sawed-off shotgun and boxes of ammunition. Also, there was a large hunting knife and two automatic pistols with ammunition, as well as a kevlar vest hanging inside the column.

'The other column is an exact duplicate with similar weapons,' she continued pointed to a similar flower on the opposite column. Now just below the upper flower with the panel button is a similar flower containing another button. She reached up and pushed the button as she spoke. Instantly three steel bars sprang from the floor at the base of the entry door locking it in place.

"This door, which, as you may have noticed when we came in is counterbalanced and swings open at the slightest touch. However, looks can be deceiving. The door, constructed of solid steel with a faux wood covering disguises it principal use. When those bars come up on this side of the door, they transform the door into an almost impregnable wall. It would take a small tank to bust through that entry at that point.

"In the master bedroom, here on the ground floor, there are similar protections. The glass windows, for example, are reinforced and bulletproof. Additionally, for example, if someone were to try and invade the property, there is a hidden motion detector underneath the balcony above. Let's say a biker were to try to ram his cycle through this window. There is a hidden barrier, which is spring mounted just outside the window when activated by objects approaching the windows at moderate speed. The bike would trigger the motion detector, which instantly springs up with a steel mesh barrier, causing the biker to ram into this barrier at the last second, and the rider would probably be thrown forward against the brick wall. The bike would probably be ruined and the biker, himself, would more than likely be seriously injured or worse in the attempt."

"Ms. Walker, I'm sure that we would never have occasion ever to utilize such devices. But I'm certainly glad that they are available just in case." Memories of James Payne flooded my mind along with his lunatic idea to kill me and those whom I loved.

'One other security feature I also need to explain. This feature is located on the second-floor. The balcony surrounds the entire home. Just beside the balcony door of each room, there is a control button, hidden inside a similar flower as these. By pressing this button, a person standing on the balcony would be shielded by a one-way bulletproof glass. This shield drops down from the exterior ceiling attic area. Thus, the observer on that floor would be able to overlook the area, but would be invisible to those outside.

"Located at equal distances along that shield are small openings which can be used to overlook the gardens, driveway, and terraces all around the home. The openings are large enough for a person to position a rifle or handgun and fire at hooligans in the grounds and driveway below without being endangered themselves. The holes are too small for someone firing from below to target easily. So a person could stand on the balcony and have a commanding control of nearly the entire property."

'That is simply incredible,' Cliff observed. "This is exactly the kind of home that I was looking for and now am more certain than ever that it will be perfect for our needs. Can you give us a few minutes alone so that we can speak with my wife?"

'Certainly, Mr. and Mrs. Stinson. I will wait outside by the pool."

Cliff and I stood off to the side and discussed the possibilities of this wonderful home between ourselves. The first thing that we agreed on was that in no way could one single person maintain this vast estate. Marianne would have to have some help. The home was worth every penny of the asking price of eleven point four million dollars.

The question was staffing. We began to calculate in our heads our possible needs. Certainly a groundskeeper or two seemed to be already contracted; at least one more housekeeper; and possibly others. The housekeepers most certainly would live in various of the bedrooms. And this last bit of information about the hidden security features was astounding. The size of the property even brought visions of things such as horses and a riding path to mind."

"Well?" Cliff looked at me, a huge smile on his face.

We stepped outside to the pool area to speak with Ms. Walker.

"Ms. Walker, -- have the papers prepared and drawn up. This house is SOLD," I exclaimed, grabbing Cliff and kissing him firmly. "Marianne, Charlotte, it seems that we will be moving to a slightly larger place than Cliff's apartment very soon."

"Mr. Stinson, Tina, this place is so very incredible. I know that you two will be very happy here" Charlotte replied. "As for Marianne and myself – WOW! This place is a homeowner's dream come true. Congratulations."

"Well, Mr. Stinson," I whispered in his ear. "You are now not only an expectant father but a proud homeowner. I have some idea that you might want to celebrate the occasion in some manner tonight?"

"I can't imagine what you are referring to, Mrs. Stinson. Did you have something in mind? Possibly a game of checkers?"

"Oh! Silly. I was thinking more in the line of a game of Strip Poker!"

"Shame on you, Mrs. Stinson," he laughed as I blushed, realizing that I had spoken the last out loud, and all three ladies could hear us quite clearly.

CHAPTER 47

The following day I was working with Ms. Martinez and Mr. Black in my office on the presentation for the president of the company which was scheduled for the following morning when the phone on my desk rang.

"Hello, Tina Stinson, how may I help you?"

"Oh, good, Mrs. Stinson, just the person that I need. This is Bill Webber, one of the contractors here on level nine. We need to have Mr. Stinson look at an issue we have found. Do you know where I can find him? We have been looking for him for over an hour now, no one knows where he is? We thought at first he was somewhere in the tower, but we have looked in all of the active construction areas, and no one has seen him this morning."

The hair stood up on the back of my neck.

"No, Mr. Webber, we came into the building together at just before 9:00 a.m. today as we do every day. He got off on floor two to get some things from his office, I continued up to my office on eight. I don't recall if he told me that he had to make any outside runs for anything today. Here, let me give him a call on his cell."

I pushed the speed dial on my cell for Cliff. It rang, and then rolled to voice mail. There was no answer. That was very strange. Cliff never turned his cell off during the daytime.

"Yes, ma'am. We also tried calling his cell now many times, and there was never anyone there." Webber told me.

"Has security been alerted?" I asked, my heart tensing in terror.

"Yes, ma'am. About thirty minutes ago we asked for help in locating him. His truck is still parked below in the garage and does not look disturbed. His office is in a state of disarray, but I thought that might be left from the bombing, and he had not cleaned up the area yet."

"No, Mr. Webber. Cliff is a very neat person and well organized. He does not allow lots of things to be out of place. He had his office put back in good order two weeks ago. I am going to be coming down right away. Can you meet me at his office?"

"Sure thing, ma'am I will be there."

"Ms. Martinez, Mr. Black. You will need to excuse me. There seems to be a problem, and I think that I need to investigate."

"You go ahead. We'll handle things up here." Mr. Black replied.

I grabbed my purse and proceeded to the elevator and punched the button for floor two. When the elevator door opened, I was met by a burly looking man who identified himself as Mr. Webber. The floor was still pretty messy from the bomb blast, but most of the debris has already been cleared. There were still a few ceiling tiles hanging strangely askew, and much of the sheetrock was still missing. Cliff's temporary office was just down the corridor.

When I opened his door, I was horrified. The place was a total mess. It appeared that a struggle might have taken place. A chair was turned over, and his desk was slightly out of place. Papers and blueprints lay scattered over the floor. There were drag marks across the floor tiles. Immediately I realized that something must have happened to Cliff -- Something violent --, and he may be in great danger.

My first thought was to contact Detective Connor with HPD and Passmore of Metropolitan Security; perhaps they could help. My second thought was of Charlotte. I phoned all of them and told them what I had found; that Cliff was missing. Connor and Passmore advised me that they would be in the building within the next ten minutes. Charlotte would arrive in about twenty minutes, having taken Marianne to the store.

"Mr. Webber, has anyone searched level two to see if he might be injured and crawled somewhere nearby?"

"No ma'am. There was no construction scheduled on this level today and after checking his office, I returned to level nine. I would be happy to walk with you around this area to see if we can locate him."

"Agreed, but we can't go too far. I have help on the way in just a few minutes; I told them to meet me on this floor."

"Very well, let's start in those rooms which are close by here," Webber replied.

Webber and I carefully searched room after room on the floor. Most were in total disrepair from the bombing, most of the broken and ruined materials had been removed, but there was still a lot of dust and dirt on the floors. We didn't discover any additional footprints or drag marks in the dust that looked out of place. But we did notice a set of wheel marks in the dust leading down to the service elevator.

"Mrs. Stinson...,?"

I heard a call from down near the elevator.

Webber and I returned and found both Connor and Passmore had arrived at the same time.

"Good Morning, Mrs. Stinson," both greeted me.

Detective Connor then asked, "Can you tell us as briefly as possible what has happened?"

"Cliff and I both arrived here at the tower around ten minutes to nine as we normally do. We took the elevator; Cliff got off on this floor while I proceeded to level eight where my offices are located. I have been there the entire morning meeting with my staff until I received a call from Mr. Webber. That was about thirty minutes ago, at which time I decided to come down and see if I could find anything. If you follow me, you will see the condition of his office. Cliff is a very organized person, and even though this area received a lot of the bomb blast, he had already cleaned up his temporary office.

"Now, you can see, it looks as if a struggle happened in there. Neither I nor Mr. Webber entered inside; we just looked through from the open door here. We did notice those drag marks on the floor, and there are some strange wheel tracks in the hall leading down to the service elevator."

"Ma'am," Webber spoke up, addressing Detective Connor. "We have been searching for Mr. Stinson since about 9:30 when I needed him to resolve an issue on level nine. We notified security, they say they are searching as well. You will need to contact them for what they may have found. I believe their temporary office is on level six while their original offices are being repaired from the bombing."

"All right," Connor replied. "Let me handle that from here. I will get with security and call for some additional assistance if they don't have anything. Why don't you return to your office and I will get back with you as soon as I can give you an update."

"Very well, Detective. Mr. Passmore, please come with me back to my office where we can discuss this." I asked.

*****

Back in the safety of my office I closed the door and turned to Passmore. "If something has happened to Cliff it will have been my fault. For bringing him into my life and having brought my problems to his doorstep. I will never forgive myself."

"No, Mrs. Stinson. This is not your fault. This is the doings of a crazy, deranged man who is taking out his years of imprisonment on you and your husband. Payne did something evil to you when you were a teenager, and has built up a rage and anger within himself which is beyond reason. It is not your fault that he went to prison. It was his fault for doing the things that he did which put him in that place. Not you."

Charlotte arrived after having dropped Marianne off at the grocery. I brought her up to date on what I had discovered.

"Charlotte. What am I going to do? I have got to find Cliff, to bring him back safely. Where could he be? What has happened to him?" I turned and paced the floor.

"Right now, we can only wait for an update from detective Connor and building security. She may have good news and everything will be back to normal." Charlotte replied, trying to calm my fears.

I paced back and forth around the room, stopping in front of the windows many times, seeing my face in the reflection. The minutes went by very slowly. Each one seemed to last an hour. The second hand on my wall clock seemed to move in slow motion. Ten thousand scenarios fill my mind with terror.

Has he been captured by Payne? If so, is he still in the building, or has he been taken somewhere else? If not Payne, then what, who? Who else would want to harm him? Perhaps someone has found out about the money that I gave to him and wanted to ransom him for that money. But the money can only be released to Cliff, no one else. I would give it all to Payne to get Cliff back safely in my arms., But I gave specific instructions that I would have no say so over the use of the money.

"Charlotte, do you have any ideas?"

"No ma'am. Not yet. Connor should be calling soon with an update."

Just at that moment Detective Connor entered the office. She looked at me and immediately shook her head indicating there was no positive word yet.

"I spoke with the head of security here," she reported. "He indicated that they have instituted a floor by floor search. They started with the ground floor. As they have moved upward, they have been leaving a guard by each elevator and stair exit. If your husband is being held somewhere in the tower, Payne will not be able to escape past them without being seen.

"The parking garage was checked already," Passmore reported. Your husband's truck was still there, so he did not leave in that. The security cameras are being reviewed now for all vehicles which left the premises between 9:00 a.m. and 11:00 a.m. If he is still in the tower, I am sure that we will find him soon.

Connor then said, "However, there was an unusual event around 9:45 a.m. An ambulance picked up a patient. We are checking now, but so far, no area ambulance company has a record of one of their vehicles having been dispatched to this location and security has no notes related to someone being injured here this morning. We are checking with the local ambulance companies to have them verify the status of each of their vehicles. Perhaps one has been stolen."

At that moment my office desk phone rang and the caller ID registered as unknown. I lifted the receiver.

"Tina Stinson, how may I help you?"

CHAPTER 48

"Hello there, Tina," a man's voice said gruffly in my ear. If there are any police in the room with you now, you had better act natural, or you will never see your husband again."

My heart sank, and I nearly collapsed into my chair. I looked over at Connor and shook my head indicating that it was Payne on the phone. She raised her fingers to her lips to tell me that she didn't want Payne to know that anyone else was in the room.

I pressed the button to change to speakerphone so that everyone could listen, holding my fingers over my lips to make sure that Charlotte understood to make no sounds.

"No. There is no one else here. They are all out searching the building right now. You S.O.B. What have you done to my husband? You had better not harm Cliff, or I will never give up the search for you."

"Not so easy, bitch. I have your husband here with me. He's a little worse for wear, but otherwise, he's okay."

"What is it that you want, you monster? Haven't you done enough to ruin my life already? Please tell me where my husband is and I will give you whatever you want. Please."

"Now, that is a lot better, bitch. But you are going to owe me an awful lot. You killed one of my friends and put the other in jail. You shot me in the arm, and your bitch guard has given me a crease on my side. So I am pretty fucking pissed at you right now. I am going to want money for sure, and that is not all. I am going to want to take up where we left off seventeen years ago. You remember the promise that I gave you in the courtroom? Well, I'm here today to collect on that debt you owe me."

I blushed at his ridiculous insult "You bastard. I am not going to have sex with you under any circumstance. You can go to hell as far as I am concerned."

"It sounds as though you don't want this good looking guy back that I have tied up on the bed here, do you?"

"God! Please let me talk to him. Please."

"Sorry lady, he's not awake right now. Maybe later, while we are having sex he can watch as I told you that day, then you can tell him how much better I fuck than he does. What do you say, sweetheart?"

My anger boiled over inside me. I could hardly control my voice.

"I'm not going to have sex with you, you fool. What is it that you want, you S.O.B?

"Lady, I already told you, I want another chance at the fine piece of pussy that you have, and lots of money."

"The first I will never give you and the second I cannot give to you. Cliff controls all of the money that we have. I have no say so in its use and cannot even write a check on the money," that wasn't exactly true, but Payne didn't need to know any more than he already did.

"Then there is not much more to talk about, is there? Say good-bye to your husband, bitch."

"No, -- Wait. – Maybe there may be a way, but I would have to have a little time to find out what I can access. I might be able to get some amount of cash, but I have to contact the bank."

"Now you are talking. I am going to hang up now. I'll call you back in thirty minutes. At that time, you'll let me know exactly what you can do. I'll give you instructions on where and when to meet me with the money. Remember, no police or your husband gets it." He hung up.

"Hello, Hello?" There was only a dial tone. I sank back into my chair, worn out from the ordeal, frightened by his threats, and in my head struggling to come up with some plan, something, anything to save Cliff from this monster.

Connor looked at me, a concerned expression on her face. "This guy is some piece of work. What we know for sure is that he has already killed one police officer and probably wouldn't hesitate to hurt your husband. You need to do something that will make him believe that he is going to get what he wants."

Charlotte asked, "I don't understand. You told him that you were unable to access any of your money. Why is that?"

"Before Cliff and I married," I explained. "I signed over my entire fortune to Cliff in such a manner that I no longer have any control or say-so in how the money is used. I did that out of love and didn't regret that decision whatsoever. But that also presents me with the problem of how to get any money for Payne in a short period."

Detective Connor then contacted her office to see if she could get a trace on the phone number but was told she would need a court order, but said that would take several hours. She left to obtain the warrant.

After Connor had left, Charlotte looked at me, pained and angry. "This guy is so hung up on having sex with you that I may have thought of something, but it will involve placing you in a bit of danger. I hate to suggest it, but it may be our only hope of tricking him into letting his guard down long enough for someone to intervene.

"First, Tina, this man is pure evil. There is no way that you can agree to his demands. I will do everything in my power to prevent that from happening. Does Payne have any way of knowing how much money you have?" Charlotte questioned.

"I don't have any idea what his resources might be. But he does seem to have gathered at least some information about me while in prison, such as where I lived and worked. Why do you ask?"

"Because, Tina, first of all, he may not be aware that you received money after your parents' death. Second he might believe that during the seventeen years since you won the award of twenty million, much of that may have been spent.

"If you were to present an offer of some smaller number and make it seem believable, such as you gave the rest to charity, gambled it away, paid for your new home in cash, or some excuse, he might be more accepting if you were to offer some smaller amount. What if Marianne and I were to return the two million dollars to you for purposes of tricking him into the open so that he can be captured?"

"Charlotte, I cannot simply ask you and Marianne to make such a sacrifice."

"Nonsense, Tina. It is the only logical solution that we can devise on such short notice. We now have less than fifteen minutes remaining before he calls again. If Payne is captured or killed, then nothing is lost, everything is gained."

"Very well, Charlotte. But you would need to obtain an agreement from Marianne for any such deal. I cannot ask her myself. And should Payne escape with the money and Cliff be set free, then that money would be replaced by Cliff. I know that he would agree to such an arrangement."

While waiting, Passmore and I discussed what options his company could offer. He suggested that he had tracking devices in his car that could be hidden in the money bags so that they would not be discovered. Finding the money would be a bullseye of where Payne would be located. Passmore would assign his best men to follow and capture or kill him, whichever opportunity presented itself. But he suggested that they would need something that would distract Payne, make him less alert to his surroundings so his men could sneak up on him easily.

Passmore further stated that "involving the police in this plan might cause them to make a mistake and reveal themselves at an inopportune time which would ruin any plans we might devise to catch him. Many times when police are involved in these situations, they cause more harm than good."

"I think I have an idea and exactly what will distract this guy," Charlotte added. "Let me contact Marianne and make sure the first part of my idea is in place. If that part is agreed to, then I will explain my idea to both of you."

Charlotte called and spoke to Marianne for a few moments and then shook her head yes, Marianne has agreed. The second part was now up to Chase Bank. Charlotte contacted them, and they agreed that there would not be a problem in either or both ladies closing their checking accounts. But it would take at least two hours for that much cash to be made available."

The phone on my desk rang. I noted that the caller ID was the same anonymous phone number as before. I hesitated and let it ring a second time before I lifted the receiver.

"Hello, Tina Stinson…"

"Hello again, Tina. Why did it take so long to answer the call?"

"I'm sorry, I have been pacing the room since you called. I was at the window when it rang," I lied.

"All right. So do you have any news for me, or should I just hang up?"

"No, please don't do that. I have some news for you. I spoke with the bank, and I can obtain two million dollars in cash today. It will take about two hours or so, but I was assured that I can obtain that amount easily."

"Why so little? If I remember correctly, you received a total of twenty million from my parents and the school?"

"Payne, it has been seventeen years. I never really wanted the money in the first place. Much of it was spent on doctors and psychiatrists. I gave away millions to charity, and I have had lots of expensive living arrangements since then. There is very little left of the original amount."

I silently prayed that Payne would accept my lies as truth. I kept my fingers crossed, and tried to control my breathing so that it appeared normal and not overly nervous.

"Now you promised that I might speak to my husband. Is he there? Can I please talk with him?"

"I need to know more about the money. You say that you gave away millions to charity? How can I possibly believe that?"

"I never wanted the money in the first place. My parents instituted those lawsuits. I always considered the money as coming from an evil thing that happened to me; I did not want to touch it. But then I realized that perhaps by giving it away to places like the Red Cross, and Salvation Army and other charities it might do more good for others whereas it would always be tainted and useless to me. – Now -- you promised that I could speak to my husband. Is he there? Please let me speak to him."

"I don't know if I believe you, but if I find out that you have been lying to me your husband is a dead man. I am going to let him speak with you for just one minute. Here he is."

"Hello, Christina," I heard Cliff's voice, and I could not contain myself. He was alive! Tears of joy streamed down my face.

"Cliff, I love you. Are you all right? Has he harmed you in any way?"

"We had a struggle in my office, at least until he hit me over the head with his gun a second time. I'm okay, just a big bump on my head. I love you. Don't agree----"

I heard a tussle and then Payne was back on the line.

"That's enough, bitch. You heard. He's alive and anxious to watch as we have some fun together, like old times."

I could hear some muffled sounds in the background.

"Listen, you bastard, I told you before, I will not have sex with you, I will only go so far as giving you money."

"We'll see about that won't we, honey? Like I said, no sex means no husband; you got that now?" he threatened. "I'm going to call you back in two hours and then we will make arrangements for me to receive the money."

"I want to see Cliff before I hand it over," I demanded.

"You will baby You will see him watching in awe as we make love."

"You bast…..", I yelled, but the line went dead again.

CHAPTER 49

I hung up the dead receiver and looked over at Charlotte and Passmore, who had both been listening.

"We bought ourselves about two hours, so let's see what we can come up with to derail this bastard," Charlotte smirked.

"I would prefer to give him the money in a public place. I'm afraid to be caught alone in a dark alleyway with him where he can attack me again, and I need to rescue Cliff at the same time."

"That may not be possible," Passmore observed. "This guy seems to be overly cautious."

"Let me explain my idea that might derail him," Charlotte continued. "Especially since he is so hung up on having sex with you. Then I need to be on my way to pick up Marianne and the money. While I get the money, you and Passmore can discuss locations and timings.

"You may not like this thought much, but I think this will distract him just enough so that this entire mess will be over faster than Payne could ever believe. Mrs. Stinson. I have been on some shopping trips with you. Lately, the lingerie you have obtained is, let me see if I can say this correctly, downright sexy."

I blushed a bright red. "Charlotte!"

"Please wait, don't be angry. I want you to use some of that underwear to distract Payne when Passmore's men show up. The way that I figure it, Payne has not seen a live woman scantily clad outside of a Playboy magazine in nearly eighteen years. If I know men's habits, he will be so busy looking at your underwear that you could drive a bulldozer past, and he wouldn't notice. The trick is that he has to believe that he's going to get something out of your display. It will focus his entire mind on that and nothing else. If I can be there, hidden until the last second, he won't have a chance. Now if I get Marianne to bring one of your least revealing outfits and a small coat to cover you up that may just do the trick.

"You would wear only the lingerie underneath, slowly slip the coat off, his eyes will then focus on your body before he knows what's happening, he will either be captured or dead. Please consider my idea and we can discuss further when we have the cash in hand. I need to leave now to get Marianne and the money."

As the door closed behind Charlotte, I turned to Passmore and shrugged.

"Do you have anything else that might preclude my having to do that?" I asked hopefully.

"I must say it highly irregular and exotic, but it may just work." He nodded in agreement but had a slight blush at the thought to what he has just agreed.

I was shocked, but after consideration and unable to think of anything else quickly, I finally shook my head in agreement. It did sound like an idea by which a crazed sex fiend could be easily tricked.

"Mr. Passmore," I finally resolved, "I believe that this is an idea of merit. It involves a lot of risk on my part, but we need that moment of surprise to keep Payne from doing any further harm. Don't you agree?

"I think we have both parts of the solution," Passmore concluded. "The tracking devices will allow us to know his location within a few feet at all times. I will have one of our drones follow whatever vehicle he is in at all times, and he will not see it. It is one of the smaller versions on the market and is almost impossible to be noticed in a traveling car versus a large helicopter which is too large and noisy. Charlotte's idea might just be the key to resolving this thing."

"Charlotte is going to pick up my housekeeper and proceed to Chase Bank to cash in those accounts. Payne said that he would call back in two hours to tell me where to meet him, so we have about a little less than that remaining. All that we can do now is wait. One further thing, I need to explain some of this to my assistant, Linda. She will have to cover my office in my absence."

I called Linda in and explained that my husband was currently being held captive by a maniac. I was working with Mr. Passmore; we had devised a plan to recover my husband and resolve the issue with Payne. I couldn't reveal the entire crazy scheme or causes of all of this turmoil. Only that she needed to remain calm during the remainder of the day and cover whatever might come up regarding my division.

"Yes, ma'am. I will handle things here. Please don't be concerned about that. You go and take care of things with your husband. That's the most important thing for you at this time. I wish you best of luck and will pray for you and Mr. Stinson."

Linda returned to her desk while Passmore and I went over the details of what actions I needed to do.

"When Payne calls again," Passmore suggested, "whatever you do, don't agree to meet him in a non-public location. We can have the drone stationed close by wherever he wants to meet and then track him from there. When your staff arrives with the money, I have a very small GPS device ready to place in the case containing the money. Once either Payne or you are on your way to his hideout, my men will follow about a mile or so behind. That way he won't be able to see their car.

"The GPS locator in their car will keep them well within range so that no matter what tricks he pulls they will stay on his trail. He's been in prison so long he probably is not all that familiar with the electronic tracking devices which we have available today. Now I need to alert my office and explain this plan to my two best men."

Passmore then phoned his office and went over the plan in detail, while I paced the room waiting for either Payne's call, Charlotte's return with the money or news from Connor on the progress of obtaining the warrant.

"I've covered in detail," Passmore said as he hung up his cell, "with my two best men what you are going to do when you see them. It's going to be tricky, and there's no guarantee that you won't be injured or worse during this. Do you understand the risk? You need to wait until the last possible second before you fall to the ground. That will give my men time to get into position."

Just over an hour and a half later Charlotte returned along with Marianne.

"The money is in my car trunk," Charlotte said. 'Is everything else set?" she questioned.

"I have discussed the plan thoroughly with Passmore. I think he has devised a method of not letting Payne escape this time. Payne is too smart for the two of us. He has evaded every trap so far and even murdered a police officer. Metropolitan Security is offering their drone to shadow the money from a distance that he won't be able to notice them. No matter what happens, Payne will probably stick close by the money and be easier to capture or kill as the situation merits."

"Has Payne called back yet?" Charlotte asked.

"Not yet, we have about another ten minutes," I replied.

Passmore received a call from his company. "Yes. I'll pass that along," he replied.

"The police just found an abandoned ambulance in a shopping center down by the ship channel. The driver had been clubbed over the head and left for dead. His uniform had been stolen. That's very likely how Payne was able to enter the tower unnoticed. Luckily, the driver was still alive and has been taken to the hospital."

"Charlotte, I have made a decision. Payne is just too dangerous a criminal, and I will not risk your life any longer in trying to protect me. I want you to remain here. I will call you after Payne has met his fate. When that is over, why don't you and Marianne meet us back at our home?"

"But, Tina…"

"No, Charlotte that is my final decision. I treasure you too much to let something happen to you. Please accept my decision."

We were interrupted by the phone on my desk ringing. Again I waited for it to ring the second time before lifting the receiver.

"Hello, Tina Stinson. How may I help you?"

"Hello Tina, this is your old boyfriend again. What was the hold up this time?"

"You are not and have never been my boyfriend. There was no delay. My bodyguard just returned to my office with the money; I was helping her bring it in the door." I lied again.

"Ah! That's perfect. I'm anxious to get this over with and be on my way. But before that, I'll be especially excited to see you again. You and I have some unfinished business. And your husband is very anxious to be entertained. We need to set up a place where I can pick you up and bring you to him."

"No dice, Payne. I am not about to get into a car with you alone. Would it be okay to bring along my bodyguard?"

"No. That bitch already gave me a crease on my side; I am not about to let her get into a car behind my back."

"Then do you have any alternate suggestions? I would prefer a public place where there are lots of people."

"I have just the place. There is a McDonalds at 1101 Gray St. It's very public and has a pretty good flow of customers. Do you know where that is?"

I looked to Mr. Passmore.

Passmore nodded in agreement.

"Yes, that will be perfect, I'll meet you there." I agreed.

"I'll meet you there in thirty minutes, bitch. Again, no cops, and leave your bodyguard behind or that'll be the end of your jerk husband. If I see cops anywhere near that place, I won't call again. You got that?" Payne's threats sounded very real to me.

"Yes, you S.O.B. I got it. I'll be there in thirty minutes. And I want my husband back first..." The phone had already gone dead before I completed my statement.

"Marianne," I asked after hanging the phone up. "Please, let me have the package that you brought."

"Yes, ma'am. I hope this will be sufficient. I tried to find something that wouldn't' embarrass you. Please be careful. I'm so afraid for you," she cried.

"Mr. Parsons, I need to change in the restroom before I leave. I will be right back."

In the restroom, I removed my dress and changed into the items inside the package and then returned to my office. Included in the package was a special surprise that Charlotte had slipped inside. I pushed it into the back of my lingerie.

"I'm ready," I said on returning to my office.

I looked over to Charlotte, "Thank you." She took my meaning and smiled.

"Now, if you and Mr. Passmore can help me transfer the money to my car I would appreciate it. Marianne, you remain here, Charlotte will return as soon as the money has been loaded into my car. I will contact you both as soon as I am able. I believe that Passmore will be in contact with his men, so you both will be kept up to date. Please don't worry. All will be well. Charlotte has arranged a special surprise for Payne."

After the suitcases had been loaded into my car trunk, Mr. Passmore retrieved the tracker from his car, turned the small GPS on and then slipped it into a side pocket of one of the bags carrying the money. We waited while Passmore contacted his firm. He gave them the code number from the tracking device, and they confirmed the electronic connection. The drone was launched and settled in position on a building overlooking the restaurant.

I pushed the button to start my engine and waited. After several minutes, Passmore gave me the signal that the drone was reporting that it was locked onto the GPS at the tower, and the drone was just then settling into a spot on the roof of the McDonalds.

"Now, Mrs. Stinson, please remember, the drone is small, but it still might be noticed if Payne has any idea something like this might be tracking him. If you end up in the same vehicle with him, please, under no circumstances, look out the window and try to spot it yourself. You don't want to give him any reason to be searching the sky.

"My men are already close by the McDonalds since it was not very far from our main office. They are in an unmarked car and have the drone on their car tracking device. My company has performed several tests involving scenarios similar to this. The men understand what you have planned. They are going to do everything in their power to protect you and Mr. Stinson. They will follow the GPS to his hideout, but will be far enough behind him that he won't notice. If you are with him when he returns to where your husband is being held, please stall until the last minute and you have seen my guards before you distract him. Good luck to you and may God help us to stop this lunatic before he kills someone else."

"Thank you for everything, Mr. Passmore. I hope to see you very soon with my husband on my arm."

"We will do everything in our power to make that happen, Mrs. Stinson. Now you had better be off. Everything is in place, and I am going back to your office to monitor, along with your staff, and I will say a prayer that all goes as planned."

"Yes, all is in the Lord's hand now. He has promised me that all will be well, and I am trusting in Him."

After taking a deep breath and exhaling, I was quickly on my way to what fate held for me. Charlotte's surprise rested comfortably against my back.

CHAPTER 50

Ten minutes later I arrived at the McDonald's and parked in the center of the parking area and waited. I looked around, but I didn't see anything out of the ordinary. Several cars pulled in and went through the drive-thru lane, purchased some hamburgers and were soon gone.

Then, I saw what I was certain must be Payne arriving in an older model car which had the front drivers' window broken out. Most likely he had stolen this car when he abandoned the ambulance.

The car circled the parking lot three times before settling into a space next to my car. Payne leered at me as he got out of his vehicle and walked around to my car door. His arm was bandaged, there was dried blood spots showing on the torn sheet that he was using as a sling. His shirt was torn on his right side. I assumed that was due to the bullet that Charlotte had creased him with the previous day.

All in all, he was a sorry sight. His face looked much aged and hardened since that night he had raped me. He had a scar, possibly a knife cut, on the left side of his face from some old injury. I thought that I also recognized my nail scrapes across his face. The ones that I had given him that night long ago. Also, there was a more recent scrape, possibly of the car wreck or a struggle with Cliff. I rolled down my window half way and listened as he demanded to see the money before he agreed to take me to Cliff.

"The money is in the car trunk, you S.O.B." I shouted angrily, and released the trunk latch, opening up the trunk so that he could inspect his ransom.

I watched in the mirror as Payne walked to the rear of the car and unzipped the money bag. He thumbed through the bundles of cash for several minutes.

"All right, bitch, the money appears to be there. Now, for the other part of our bargain, we are going to have to drive over to my room. You can have your husband back after we have sex while he watches."

"I never agreed to that, you bastard. I demand to see my husband," I said forcefully.

"I told you before, that is the bargain, and I mean to have you. You're going to have sex with me and then suck me off in front of your husband and then I am going to take off with the money. Are you going to follow me there? Or should I just take the money from your car and we forget about the rest? Suddenly he reached into his belt and retrieved his gun.

Pointing it directly at me through the driver's side window, "Move over, bitch, I'll drive since I know where we are going."

Having no other choice, I pushed myself to the other side of the car as he opened the door and slipped in behind the steering wheel.

"All right, bitch, let's pick up where you left off that night at the game." He unzipped his pants and pulled out his dick. "I been waiting for this for years. Now get your damn mouth over here and show me what you can do."

"I refuse to do that," I screamed. "You might as well stick it back in your pants because the only thing that I would do to you at this moment is to bite your fucking dick off. I demand to see my husband, to know that his is alive and well."

Payne looked at me for a few moments and then, realizing that I probably meant what I had said, pushed his smelly dick back inside his pants and pulled the zipper up to the top.

"All right, bitch, but I am not releasing your husband until I get some pussy from you. You got that, whore?"

"I am not a whore, you coward" I shouted back at him. "But yes, I understand. We will discuss that when I see my husband, you bastard."

"I'm going to drive us to my room," Payne leered at me as if he knew what I would do for him before the day was over. "Then we can finish our business together, sweetheart."

He gave me a disgusted look and then, confused because there was no ignition to insert a key into, "How the hell do you start the engine on this thing?"

I smiled to myself, "What a jerk," and pointed to the Start button. Payne angrily jammed his finger against the button and the engine came alive.

"You and your goddam fancy machines. Nothing is like the old days when you just stuck a key in a slot, and cars started. It is going to take me a long time to get used to all of the fancy things they have invented lately. But with your money, and my smarts, I'm going to have one hell of a time enjoying myself."

I fought my temptation to laugh out loud. *'Payne, you haven't seen anything yet,'* I thought. *'You are about to find out that things are nothing like they used to be, and if I don't kill you, I am sure my husband will.'*

Payne pulled out of the parking spot and onto the street. After two blocks he made a right turn and headed for the freeway entrance. His driving was a bit erratic due to his injuries. His right arm appeared to be badly damaged; there was fresh blood which dripped from his torn shirt sleeve, possibly a fresh injury from a struggle with Cliff. He favored his right side where Charlotte had creased him with her bullet.

His left hand held the steering wheel, but he often seemed in extreme pain and twisted his fingers tightly around the wheel, as if trying to fight off the pain of his wounds. He took the entrance for Highway 59, and we proceeded to travel north until the split off for I-45, which he took at the last second, swerving across three lanes of traffic. Car and truck horns blasted at us as he narrowly missed a truck and two cars, and just barely made the cutoff lane.

I pulled my seat belt tighter around me as I began to realize that he was trying to evade anyone who might be following us by trapping them in the wrong lane until it would be too late for them to take our same exits. He continued this process for several miles, taking several exits, performing U-turns and then flowing back onto I-45 in different directions. I smiled to myself at his arrogance and realized what a fool the man was.

After another ten minutes of this confusion, he moved over to the far lane and took the Loop 610 south, and we ended up exiting close to the ship channel. He pulled onto a small side street, where he stopped the car at an abandoned gas station. We waited for a time while he watched the traffic to determine if there was anyone who might have been able to keep up with his crazy effort at concealing his trail.

Finally, satisfied that he had evaded pursuit, he started the engine again, we proceeded further into the neighborhood. It was populated mostly with old wooden buildings. Many of them had collapsed roofs and vacant holes where doorways used to exist. Few, if any, had any intact windows left, mostly just broken shards of glass in their place.

Eventually, he pulled up in front of a rundown motel system that still seemed to be still in business, probably used by homeless men and women. Or even more likely, by people from the nearby office buildings. Possibly only needing the use of a room for thirty minutes while they did their sordid business and then moved on, not wanting to be discovered by one of their co-workers, who very often used the same motel for their sleazy noontime trysts.

Payne stopped the car and got out in front of a small unit at the very back of the complex. He stood outside for a few seconds and kept watching the street. Eventually, he leaned over and told me that we were at the motel. He ordered me to get out and come inside. I was a bit hesitant and stalled for time.

After a minute, I slowly reached over and grabbed the door handle, opened the door and stepped out cautiously. Payne walked over to the cabin door and paused, waiting for me to approach. I looked around at the mostly broken down cabins, most with doors sagging open, others with windows busted. The unit he stood in front of was probably one of the better units, having both a door and a boarded up window frame.

I stepped a bit closer, "Please open the door. I am not coming any closer until I can see my husband inside."

Payne pushed the door open with his foot. I peered inside, but it was too dark to see much as there was no light. As I got a bit more acclimated to the darkened room, I finally was able to see Cliff. He was stretched out on the filthy bed, his arms handcuffed to the bedstead and he was blindfolded with a pillowcase.

"Cliff," I cried out, and he stirred.

"Christina, what are you doing here?" he shouted.

Payne broke in between us. "Your pretty little bitch of a wife has agreed to have sex with me while you watch, that is what she's doing."

"NO! CHRISTINA. YOU MUSTN'T. PAYNE, YOU BASTARD. LEAVE MY WIFE ALONE," Cliff shouted.

Not wanting to reveal my surprise, "Cliff, it's all right. He has promised to release you if I give him what he wants." I looked at Payne to see if he had believed my lie.

"NO! CHRISTINA. GOD NO!" Cliff shouted again.

I saw two shadows emerge from behind the building. Slowly I released the belt on the coat that I was wearing. It fell to the ground around my feet.

As my undergarments were revealed, Payne let out a long whistle.

"Wow! What a beautiful cunt you have got there, Tina. SO much prettier than when you were just sixteen."

Cliff screamed, **"NOOOOO, CHRISTINA!"**

Payne's left hand fell to his side in amazement. He was totally distracted by the sight of my partially exposed body as I watched the two Metropolitan security guards emerge from behind the building.

"Look at this, Payne. I slowly lowered my body to the ground in a provocative move. I let my legs spread slightly open, revealing my inner thighs. This also had the effect of revealing the two security guards from Metropolitan Security standing about eight feet away.

"Drop your weapon, Payne" both of the guards suddenly shouted at him.

Payne was startled by the sudden appearance of the men. "You damn bitch. You tricked me."

Payne's gun hand started to rise in confusion, but it was too late. He fired as I rolled out of the way, reaching behind my back. I felt the sting of the bullet as it grazed my left thigh.

I grasped the handle of Charlottes' Glock. Yanking the gun free from my underwear I whipped it around and emptied the entire cartridge into Payne's body. The pent up hate of the seventeen years of anger and shame locked my finger around the trigger. Even after the magazine inside the weapon was emptied, the continued click of the hammer inside the weapon went on and on. I couldn't seem to release my finger. Finally, after what seemed like an eternity, I felt the hand of one of the guards touch my shoulder.

"He's dead, Mrs. Stinson."

"The guards' hand then slowly drifted down my arm and touched my weapon as the constant 'clap, clap, clap' of the gun's hammer sounded. He gently took hold of the weapon.

"Please, Mrs. Stinson. I'll take the weapon. You need to attend to your husband. He is crying inside, ma'am. He needs you."

His words finally broke the spell, and I released my finger, and the weapon slipped from my hand. I grabbed up my coat and ran into the room. I began ripping the pillowcase from around Cliff's head and kissed him repeatedly.

In the excitement of the moment, our questions overlapped each other as we both were desperate to find out if the other was hurt in any way.

"Cliff, please tell me that you are okay. Are you hurt anywhere? What did Payne do to you?"

"Christina, how did you find me, did Payne do anything to you? Where is he? I heard a series of shots, are you hurt?

"It's only a scratch on my leg, Cliff. I'll be all right." That was true, but it still hurt like hell.

Finally, after several moments, we began to sense that the other has survived the nightmare that was James Payne. Our breathing slowed, my arm around his neck gave him the peace that I was okay. One of the security men entered and produced a key for the handcuffs and freed Cliff from the bed.

The guard bent down and observed the wound to my thigh.

"I've called for a paramedic, Mrs. Stinson. The wound doesn't look bad, Just a crease. They will be here in a few minutes and will check the both of you over."

"Christina, **GOD**. I thought that he was going to... Are you all right? What happened? Tell me where is Payne? And what in God's name are you wearing?" Cliff's tears streamed down his cheeks.

"It's over now Cliff. Payne is no more. The men from Metropolitan Security helped me to distract him. Charlotte loaned me her Glock; I'm afraid that I used up all of her bullets on that S.O.B. It is a long story and as usual, I don't want to go into it here. I just want to get you back home and get you rested; I will explain everything."

I retrieved my cell phone from the coat pocket. I clicked the speed dial for Charlotte.

"Charlotte, it's Tina. It is over. It is finally all over, thank God. The guards were here, and I distracted him, Payne has been killed. Your plan worked just as you hoped. You have saved my life once again. I will never be able to repay you for all that you have done for me. Oh. Please tell Linda that we're both okay and will be in tomorrow.'

"Have her call and reschedule my appointment with the Mr. Johnson. I'll give him a call when Cliff and I get home and explain. I'm very tired, and I know Cliff is as well. I think that he has a big bump on the back of his head, and I have a small scratch on my leg."

Three police cars and an ambulance screamed into the motel lot and screeched to a stop. Detective Connor was among the first officers to run up to the cabin.

"Mrs. Stinson, are you all right?" She looked outside at the lifeless body that was James Payne. "It looks like Payne is taken care of for good this time," she sighed. She noticed my leg bleeding and directed the medics to hurry and attend me.

While they cleaned and bound the wound, she looked at Cliff and me. After a moment, she turned back away from us and spoke over her shoulder while watching as the officer's searched Payne's body for other weapons. After binding my wound, the EMT inspected Cliff's head then suggested that a few days rest and lots of aspirin would be the best cure.

"On behalf of the HPD we want to thank you for ridding the planet of this piece of trash. You and your bodyguards will have to give statements downtown, but you may complete yours at your convenience, Mrs. Stinson. I know that right now you and your husband will need some alone time. So why don't you run along and we will clean up the trash. We already have your gun licensing information, so if you will leave your weapon where you dropped it, I will log it in and have it returned to you after all of the paperwork has been completed. Give me a call when you are ready to stop by my office."

"Thank you, detective. I'm sorry that we kept you out of the loop on this, but there was so little time after Payne called. You have no idea how much that we appreciate your help."

"I understand, Mrs. Stinson. Sometimes police activity takes more time to get things accomplished than it should. I'm still waiting on approval for that wiretap. But I don't guess that I'll be needing it any longer."

One of Passmore's guards assisted Cliff as we walked back to my car.

"Cliff -- Marianne, and Charlotte are waiting in my office. I've asked them to head back home. What do you say about taking the rest of the day off?"

"I say, I haven't heard a better suggestion today. Besides, I have a terrific headache."

On the way back to our home, I had to explain the outfit that I was wearing to Cliff.

"Cliff, look at me, look into my eyes. The clothing that I have on now was meant to distract Payne from all other things. Charlotte came up with the idea because Payne kept insisting that he wanted to have sex with me. She felt that if I were to show up in this skimpy outfit, which reveals nothing of my actual body, but is simply suggestive, covered only with a thin overcoat, it would distract him those few seconds that the security men needed to get into position.

"Payne had demanded numerous times that I agree to have sex with him. I refused each time, but he would not listen. He was obsessed with taking his revenge on me for sending him to prison, and that poisoned his mind and made him vulnerable to making mistakes. When I saw that he was still in pain from the wound that I had given him after the car chase, I knew that he must be weak, and his mind clouded.

"Passmore helped greatly by the use of a tracking device he had placed inside one of the bags with the money. His company used a small drone to track us as Payne drove wildly around the freeways thinking he was evading cars following him. He's been in prison so long he was not aware of all of the advances in technology that have been made.

"In truth, there was only the drone and the GPS inside the money bag. The security guards followed us far enough behind so that he never saw them. When I saw the guards emerge from behind the room where you were held, I simply dropped the coat on the ground. Charlotte had loaned me her Glock as the lingerie was too flimsy to hold my heavy .38 Special."

"I am probably the first woman Payne had seen in a state of undress in many years and his obsession with me proved his downfall. When I dropped the coat to the ground, his hand that was holding his gun fell to his side. On seeing his hand by his leg, I fell on top of the coat which was the signal for the men to take him. He did not have time to lift his gun back up to firing position. When he fired, I was rolling out of the way, and his bullet only grazed my leg. I was able to empty my gun into him before he knew what was happening."

'But, Cliff, how did he end up capturing you?" I asked while stroking his head, feeling the large bump very gently.

"The bastard surprised me when I went to my office. He was hiding behind the door. He struck me hard the first time, and I was dazed. We had struggled for a minute or two before he hit me again with that damn gun handle. I don't remember anything after that until I woke up in that building. My head is still throbbing, and you can see this huge swelling on my head. But no more about me. Your leg..."

"The dressing the EMT put on the wound will be sufficient for now, sweetheart. I will see a doctor tomorrow to have it looked at properly. But right now I feel underdressed and very tired. I just want to get you home and put on some proper clothes."

"Oh, there was a Mr. Webber looking for you earlier. Said something about a problem on level nine you needed to resolve."

"Don't worry, Christina. I'm sure that by now he has checked with my assistant, Henry Slate. I'm sure the two of them can work it out. If not, I'll take care of it in the morning. Besides, I'm sure this is going to be front page news in the Chronicle tomorrow. We are both going to have to prepare to be bombarded by the media to explain all of this. I need some rest before that happens, and several large aspirins."

"Christina, before this night is over and we have to face the press and police again, I have other plans that are much more exciting," he grinned mischievously at me.

"Why, Clifford Stinson. You are turning into a dirty old man," I smirked.

"Only with you, sweetheart, only with you."

As we left, I had to step around the gruesome remains of my bitter enemy James Payne. As I looked down at his bullet-riddled body; I felt no remorse. In fact, what I felt was pity. The man, now lying there dead by my hand had wasted his life. I'm sure that his parents had raised him better, in hopes that he would turn out to be a decent man. I guess that no one would ever know what went wrong. How had his life become what it had? He might still be alive and living a happy and rewarding life, except for the poor choices he had made. What a terrible shame.

I slipped in behind the steering wheel of my beautiful car and thought no more of Payne. He could never hurt me or anyone that I loved ever again. My last thought was: Good Riddance.

I switched the car stereo system on, suddenly everything became happy again. The music was an old favorite and served to remind me that life was sweet, and happiness would always be there for me in this season as in any other. The dark clouds of my past were washed away in the pure white beauty of my future.

Neil Diamond and Sleigh Bells Ringing

Just hear those sleigh bells
ringing and jing ting tingaling too
Come on its lovely weather for
a sleigh ride together with you

Outside the Snow is falling and
friends are calling yoo hoo.....
Come on its lovely weather for
a sleigh ride together with you

Giddy Up, Giddy Up,
Giddy Up, Let's Go!
Just look at the show,
were riding in a wonderland of snow

Giddy Up, Giddy Up, Giddy Up
Its Grand, just holdin' your hand
were riding along with the song
of a wintery wonder land.

Our cheeks are nice and rosy
and comfy cozy are we,
Were snuggled
up together like birds of
a feather would be

Lets take that road before us
and sing a chorus or two,
Come on its
lovely weather for a sleigh
ride together with you

There's a birthday party at the home of
farmer grey
it'll be the perfect ending of a perfect day
we'll be singing the song we love to sing without a single stop
by the fireplace while we watch the chesnuts pop.

There's a happy feeling nothing in the
world can buy,
when they pass around the
coffee and the pumpkin pie
It'll be like a picture print, by Currier and Ives
these wonderful things are the things we remember
through our lives!

Just hear those sleigh bells
ringing and jing ting tingaling too
Come on its lovely weather for
a sleigh ride together with you
Come on its lovely weather for
a sleigh ride together with you

Oh yeah its lovely weather for
a sleigh ride
with you
with you
with you
me and you

What a wonderful Christmas it was going to be. I already had the greatest Christmas present in the world, my darling husband. Very soon now three little Cliffs would join in making my happiness complete.

"Cliff, I think that I'm going to drop the name 'Tina.' It sounds so childish to me now. I don't think that I want my new staff to address me that way. In fact, I don't think I want anyone to call me that ever again. I'm a grown woman, not a child. Yes, Christina is what I want to be called by everyone, especially you. You have such a wonderful way that you pronounce my name. It may be just because I love you, but there is no other sound in the world that I love better than when you speak my name. It sets off a chime in my heart and a bell in my head."

CHAPTER 51

The minister held me behind my head, as he dipped me below the surface of the baptismal waters.

"I baptize you in the name of the Father and of the Son and the Holy Spirit."

As he raised my head from the water, the church congregation applauded.

I looked out to the front row where Cliff, Charlotte, and Marianne, as well as the members of our Sunday School Class, have stood in support of my profession of faith. My face broke out in a huge smile. I had never been so happy in my entire life. Cliff and I are now truly one person, joined in faith, love and hope for the future. My life is just now beginning. All of the evil from the past has been washed away. Payne no longer exists to torture my sleep. Our new family is growing happily within my womb. My career has exploded with new opportunities; I have the best friends in the world.

The pastor's message for today: Church: A Hospital for Recovering Sinners, not a Country Club for the Elite. The message struck home with Cliff and I. We decided to devote time to the churches' missions including counseling for young girls who have suffered sexual abuse. Cliff volunteered to help repair or rebuild homes for the homeless and train others seeking job training in construction skills.

****

Two years had now passed since that terrible day when my tormentor met his fate and released me from my shame and secrets. Cliff and I are the proud parents of two little girls, Marianne, and Charlotte, and our son, Cliff junior. Life is now all that I could ever hope. Cliff is a doting father who loves his children without end. Charlotte Parker has now married a gentleman that Cliff introduced her to at church. She has a new assignment with a woman who is being stalked by a crazed ex-lover. We hired a second housekeeper to help Marianne with the large home and a nanny for the small children.

My work is going so well that my division now leads the company in income, and I am being considered for promotion to Senior Vice President, second in line to our CEO, Mr. Johnson, who is set to retire at the end of the year. At work, I have been training Linda Williams, my assistant to be ready to take my place if I do make that promotion. Cliff has started his own construction company, Stinson Construction, and already has a signed contract for the building of a fifty-story tower in downtown Houston.

My life has risen from the ashes of that terrible night so many years ago and has blossomed and flowered. My future is full of hope and happiness. After the death of James Payne, we had realized that we would now never have cause to use any of the hidden security features of the home. We now slept peacefully and contented each night. Safe from the terrors of the world.

Or so we thought.

As I lay in the bed that evening beside my beautiful husband, the news from my visit to the Doctors office is causing me some worry.

"Cliff?"

"Yes, sweetheart?"

"I was just thinking about our home. The Doctor was explaining the birds and bees to me again. It seems that are to be visited by the stork, and we are going to be having twins."

"So in addition to the big birthday celebration for our children and the upcoming family reunion with Cliff's ever expanding siblings' families you need to be checking on the extra bedrooms."

"Christina, I love you, and no matter how many you have, I will love them all. We can always build a separate home for the housekeepers and nannies. You know, that barn you mentioned one time begins to sound better and better, my dad and I do build things, you know!"

"Cliff, I knew there was a reason I chose a construction manager for a husband."

--Cliff, stop tickling me like that. *OHHHHH!* You are so incorrigible, which must be another reason I married you."

"Christina, there are so many reasons that I married you, that it would take at least another one-hundred years to give all of them to you.

"So let me start today with reason no. one:

"You have the cutest smile that I've ever seen. You'll just have to wait until tomorrow to find out reason number two."

"Cliff?"

"Yes, sweetheart?"

"I love you, too."

EPILOGUE

My name is Christina Laura Stinson. I used to be called Tina. But that was before my husband gave me back my name and life after seventeen years of torment. A name that had been torn from my life the night Christina died and Tina was born. Tina, a name that died the day I emptied my gun into the body of the man who I believed had ruined my life forever.

It was a very busy day that Wednesday. Getting the three oldest kids ready for kindergarten, even with the help of the two nannies, was often a chore. Cliff junior was a handful. He would escape from his nanny and run around the house screaming without a stitch of clothes. It took Cliff senior's assistance to capture him and address the pants issue.

"Cliff, were you like this when you were little?" I asked.

"Christina, you remember that the first day you met my parents, my mom was going to tell you a secret about me?"

"Yeah. I do remember something vaguely, is that what it was? You running around the house with no clothes?"

"Not exactly, sweetheart. I was at school in the first grade and for some reason I must have thought that I was still at home, and I ran out of the boy's restroom with no pants. All of the girls were in the hallway including one young lady substitute teacher. They ran screaming in all directions. I did not think that I would ever live that down," Cliff blushed bright red.

"And you are not allowed to tell that to a soul. My siblings still tease me about that to this day, and that is bad enough."

"That is a hoot. You should have warned me on our first date. I might have run out of the restaurant screaming myself," I giggled and winked at him. "And keep those tickling fingers to yourself, Mr. Stinson if you don't mind."

Hours later while sitting at my desk I was still laughing at the thought of little Cliff running around the schoolhouse with the girls running away. '*Oh, Cliff, you are a treasure.*'

I was sitting in my chair, looking at the office tower vase which Cliff had made for me and, that had miraculously survived the bomb blast without any damage. I was about to run down to the company cafeteria and grab a sandwich when the phone on my office desk rang. I lifted the handset to my ear. "Tina Stinson, Tilson Industries. May I help you?"

"Hello? Is this Christina Stinson?" a young ladies voice asked.

"Yes. Who is this?" I questioned.

"Were you Christina McIntyre before you got married?" The girl's voice continued.

The hair on the back of my neck rose in suspicion of who might be the other end of the phone line.

"And just exactly who am I speaking to, young lady?" My hand began trembling; I feared the answer that would come.

"I believe that you are my mother. I am your' daughter; my name is Lidia."

The handset slipped from my hand and fell onto the desk.

To be continued: *My Daughter in Ashes* – coming soon.

*** *I Know That My Redeemer Lives* (The words were written by Phillip P Bliss in 1876. They were found in his luggage after he died in a train wreck. He survived the initial crash but was killed when he went back and tried to save his wife.)

****

*author's note: I get so many questions and observations about 'Tina's' money I would like to clarify my objectives on that subject below:

****

Tina refused to spend the money when it was hers alone. Her subconscious belief was the money was tainted: ($20 million for the rape was like trick money for a whore; $30 million for her parents' death was blood money for their death). She also would not touch the increases from investments as that was money gained from those tainted sources.

The only way that Tina could deal with the money was to give it away. She repeatedly says throughout the early chapters that the money means nothing to her. The possessions, beautiful clothes and jewelry obtained with it were meaningless, and of little value in her life. She yearned for more: Love, family, happiness. Cliff brings those things to her. In exchange, she gives him the money. The only bargain between the two is the love they share. Nothing is spoken or signed. It is simply the understanding of two people who are deeply in love with each other.

Cliff recognizes Tina's subconscious abhorrence for the money and accepts her bequest, because he understands this feeling that Tina has about spending that money on herself.

The debit card represents a 'money laundering,' so to speak, allowing Tina to use it as she wishes because she has given 'her' money away. This is now 'his' money, washed clean by the transfer of her love to him.

Throughout the novel, whenever any of that money is used by Cliff, (the wedding; the honeymoon; the home) it is ONLY with the agreement of Tina. She says when and how it is to be spent. Example: it is not Cliff who says "This house is sold," it is Tina. Cliff always discusses those expenses with her beforehand, or in the case of the rehiring of Marianne and Charlotte, allows her the final decision. Cliff uses his personal credit card and monies to purchase things such as jewelry and clothing for Tina, not her debit card.

Note this sentence: *'I was so used to spending my own money, it felt strangely different to spend someone else's.'* Even though her wealth was now part of Cliff's money, she no longer regards it as having anything to do with herself. It is 'his' money, washed clean by his love for her. All of her past views have been swept away. In fact, throughout their long marriage, money is something that she will always regard as belonging to her husband. Even if it is money gained from her employment. It is his to share with her, even though, deep down, she realizes where it originally came from, it is like a life blood that she receives not from her employer, but directly from her husband's heart. Christina is not insane; she is in love.

In fact, the debit card she has is the only one on the account. Cliff does not spend any of the money on himself. He spends his own money that he earns from his work. Eventually, Cliff's business takes off; his company constructs scores of office towers around Texas. Christina ultimately joins him to manage the business. The marriage last for some fifty-two years when the couple passes on to glory within an hour of each other. They leave a family of eight children between them, Lidia, whose story will be told in the novel *Born from the Ashes*, Christina's daughter from the rape, and an adopted daughter (who you will learn about in the sequel to this story *My Daughter in Ashes)*; forty-six grandchildren, and seven great-grandchildren.

So, gentle people, please give my tender lover Cliff the credit he so richly deserves. Christina certainly does. Cliff is not a money hound. He truly is Christina's Prince Charming in every sense of the fairy tale that I have constructed.

Made in the USA
Coppell, TX
09 March 2021

51528404R00229